Plantagenet Tales
(Volume 1: 1377-1388)

A collection of notable accounts concerning the decline and demise of England's greatest ruling dynasty.

First Edition
Published by Archington

Cover design and illustrations: Zac Loftus

British Library Cataloguing-in Publication Data
A catalogue record for this book is available from the British Library.

ISBN 978-1-3999-3747-4

Plantagenet Tales
(Volume 1: 1377-1388)

by

Mark Wilson

To Jenn

Table of Contents

-- Prologue --

A.D. 1485

-- THE EXTRAORDINARY TALE OF THOMAS SWYKE --

The streets of Leicester, 25th August 1485.

It's night-time, he's breathless, and there are unknown menaces in every shadow, but nothing distracts **Thomas Swyke** from the jittery boy that flits ahead of him like some urgent sparrow guide.

Having shuffled with great purpose from the cool comfort of his sumptuous chamber in the grounds of Leicester's otherwise ruined castle, Swyke waddles out past the small stone gatehouse and down St Mary's Church Lane. Then across the deserted hard-packed gravel and flint of the wide north-south thoroughfare which, from its south gate a stone's throw at his right, sweeps off to his left for half a mile between countless indistinct rickety dwellings towards the town's north gate.

On into the dark shit-strewn thoroughfare of Friars Lane; shambling house frontages now flank his left side and the dilapidated twelve-foot high Roman wall overlooks him from the other. In the gloom he silently curses the richness of the interrupted beef and ale that now pulls and pummels his belly. He's a man of age and means, and both are factors that account for his large size and loud wheezing.

The walk from the castle to the chapel of Friars Minor is in truth but a few hundred paces, but the night-time's heavy summer air - and thoughts of what may lurk in passageways and darknesses - makes a few hundred seem like a few thousand. All men fear God in the sobriety of daylight, but cheap tavern ale and night-time bravado combined can encourage malice in this oft-evil realm. Not for nothing does Leicester, like many English towns, still ring the curfew bell of an evening; and that loud clang had rung hours ago. Now a pleasing tradition rather than solid law, Swyke is all too aware of how perilous it can be for a rich man to be out alone in the night.

Even if that rich man is well known to all as mayor of this old town.

The boy, sent by the warden of the much-respected grey friars, is insistent on greater speed although still irritatingly vague in his urgent appeals to hurry. Swyke again offers thanks to God that the friary is not far away as his laboured gait takes him ever deeper up Friars Lane, until presently he is gladdened to pass under the overhang of a large dwelling, and which is followed by a reassuringly familiar low wall...

The priory, at last!

The wall becomes a gateway, whereupon a left turn onto a pathway leads to an oaken door of the friary's south range building. Beyond that, out of sight to all but the birds and the monks, it is known of a pretty cloister, flanked to its east by the austere chapterhouse and then, at the north of that, the friary chapel; a long, straight-edged high-roofed stone-walled building that bears a central tower and spire.

Swyke's belly rolls its contents with this evening's unexpected exertion. It would seem that this week is going to continue with its extraordinariness.

-- THE TWO KINGS --

*Seven days ago, **Mayor Thomas Swyke** of Leicester had received King Richard III (and his army) upon approaching the town's north gate peaceably enough on his way to do battle with the popular pretender Henry Tudor. Welcoming King Richard of the House of York graciously was politically unpleasant for this particular mayor as Leicester had always been a town that was favoured by those with leanings to the rival house of Lancaster. But the Yorks had killed all the Lancasters, and in any case the King is the King, so attending to him was still an honour that he'd well performed. Even if he'd wanted to keep the odd little Yorkist crown-bearer out, Leicester's thick and ancient Roman walls had enough well-worn breaches to leak an army in anyway.*

All have said that Richard died bravely in battle but, even so, far fairer is the new king that returned to Leicester than the predecessor that left. For Henry Tudor, having won victory and England's crown in the fields of Bosworth, is strong and good and fit to lead a kingdom, and in all ways Swyke contemplates the new to be far better appointed than the former.

Especially so in light of certain grim rumours that will now always cling to Richard.

After the Bosworth battle, the violated body of that twisted wretch (now proven to be untrue in the eyes of God on account of his defeat in battle) had been laid out at the Newarke church and hospital, within the shadow of Leicester's castle defences. Swyke, as Mayor of Leicester, had dutifully shown a genial interest in the Yorkist's remains when shown them by his new king. But in truth, he is better versed in business and money than in battles and blood, and his principal desire now is for a profitable peaceful reign under Henry the Seventh.

Finally, after a hundred years of family war over England's throne the foundations of which were laid during King Richard the Second's reign, God in His wisdom had chosen; and in the end He had chosen neither the House of Lancaster nor the House of York. Royal blood had instead emerged where none had thought it remained, and King Henry's House of Tudor had come forward as one final dynastic option; an option entertained by England's beleaguered aristocracy perhaps only because both the Lancasters and Yorks had in the end simply proven themselves unworthy. May God in His divine glory be thanked for Henry Tudor.

King Henry had eventually this morning left Leicester for Coventry on his way to London. Having attended to the king until he'd departed, Swyke's intent was to remain awhile at the Great Chamber in the grounds of old Leicester Castle to indulge in as many rich royal leftovers as possible before presenting the scraps to the poor. Well-earned vices after two days of high level mayoral duties, Swyke supposed, but now alas interrupted for this mysterious pressing request of an audience at the friary; a benevolent organisation led by John of Leicester and well known to Swyke and the citizens of this borough.

-- THE GREYFRIARS, LEICESTER --

The boy leads a sweat-drenched **Thomas Swyke** through the gate in the wall and onto a freshly-raked cinder path that treads through immaculate lawns and gardens of roses, lavender and herbs which form this side of the grounds of the friary. In spite of these encouragingly peaceful tended surroundings, his stomach maintains a discomfiting swell and surge.

With a whomping in the head and a tightening in the calves Leicester's mayor wipes his stinging eyes and allows himself a slower walk in the darkness along the garden path. His blubber-tight body isn't built for flight, and fine living oozes through every part of his stinking summer skin. Even though the boy had run ahead to rap on the door of the friary, and in spite of all the apparent urgency, Swyke has a lesser want for speed now he's on holy ground and away from the unseen dangers of the public street behind him.

As the thick wooden door opens, the boy awaits a coin, still as fresh in his little sack boots as he was when he came to interrupt Swyke. But in his swiftness Swyke has neglected to bring his purse and so presumes the Franciscan brothers will no doubt press a clipped farthing or some such trifle into that grubby little hand for his trouble.

Looking now for someone of importance to apprise him of his summons, he there acknowledges in the gloomy silence beyond the doorway John of Leicester, the most senior friar and known as the Warden. As a great solemnity hangs here, Swyke elects mute curiosity for now and shuffles into the tiled hallway with reverence.

The grey-robed elder leads the puffing mayor through the priory, along the dark and silent cloister walk, past the two-storey chapterhouse then, at the imposingly-dimensioned church's south transept, steps up into the dark of God's House, makes a right turn and, from the floor in front of that area usually occupied by the choir by his right hand, stops to bow his head towards the presbytery and whispers brief prayers to God. Then, peace made, he turns to face the mayor three feet behind him.

In doing so he holds out an open hand, thus inviting Swyke to look beyond, and the mayor, still roughly drawing his breath, stretches his vision into the black space.

He knows he has been led into an inner sanctum of this holy building that does not usually welcome ordinary men; not until they're both rich and dead, at least. Shady shapes, unmoving and indistinct at first, slowly solidify. A sharp and persistent low-level stench is permeating up through the usual faecal pungency that one quickly accustoms to when visiting on or living in any town. He blinks, and wipes his eyes, to better clarify what he is supposed to comprehend. The large bejewelled cross, of course, stands tall on the stone altar beyond at the east end of this room. Before it, the area designated for the choir is empty and silent.

Swyke seeks explanation from the inscrutable warden, but with none forthcoming he looks again. Now his eyesight is adjusting itself to the church dark, he notices a miserable black lump on the floor laid directly before the altar. A baggage. A sack of wheat, perhaps; though much bigger, so not wheat.

But certainly sack. It is bulky indeed.

Maybe man sized.

He gasps.

King sized!

=====

SCENE. THE CHOIR AND PRESBYTERY OF THE GREYFRIARS, LEICESTER – NIGHT TIME

***THOMAS SWYKE**, Mayor of Leicester, stands in a dark silent church with **JOHN OF LEICESTER**, Warden of the Greyfriars. They both contemplate the bulky sack on the floor in front of them; though Swyke has the fear of God in him.*

**THOMAS SWYKE,
MAYOR OF LEICESTER**
Richard...?

**JOHN OF LEICESTER,
WARDEN OF THE GREYFRIARS**
(with great gravitas)
Before departing, King Henry himself requested we bury the remains in holy ground to rest in everlasting peace.

**THOMAS SWYKE,
MAYOR OF LEICESTER**
After leaving them untended for three days at the Newarke? In naked view of all men and women?

**JOHN OF LEICESTER,
WARDEN OF THE GREYFRIARS**
He was a casualty of war, sir. However our right and proper King Henry is humble, and understands that even Richard played his part in God's divine will.

THOMAS SWYKE,
MAYOR OF LEICESTER

I accept with joy that Henry Tudor is our true king, but this ill-stamped atrocity was an affront to God.

JOHN OF LEICESTER,
WARDEN OF THE GREYFRIARS

Richard was once our anointed sovereign lord, and therefore God-chosen of his time.

THOMAS SWYKE,
MAYOR OF LEICESTER

Even so, we honour the Yorkist with a holy grave?

JOHN OF LEICESTER,
WARDEN OF THE GREYFRIARS

It is the King's wish, and therefore God's wish, that the remains are respectfully interred within our sacred grounds.

THOMAS SWYKE,
MAYOR OF LEICESTER

May God bless King Henry the Seventh for such reverence! But, Sir, he dishonours Leicester and its citizens. For a grave provides a rallying point for York sympathisers.

JOHN OF LEICESTER,
WARDEN OF THE GREYFRIARS

Though we are bidden to dig a grave and do so gladly in the name of our Lord, King Henry insists upon no stone or mark.

Swyke turns his attention to the sack. He approaches it slowly. He begins to understand.

THOMAS SWYKE,
MAYOR OF LEICESTER

You wish to hide a body.

JOHN OF LEICESTER,
WARDEN OF THE GREYFRIARS

We do. And we wish to do so legally, and secretly.

Swyke, standing over the sack, nods in the darkness. Grunts.

JOHN OF LEICESTER,
WARDEN OF THE GREYFRIARS (cont'd)
As senior magistrate of this town...

...will Leicester's mayor ratify our surreptitious act?

Swyke tentatively prods the sack with the ball of his foot. What he touches through the sack-cloth, and the way it squashes, causes him great revulsion.

THOMAS SWYKE,
MAYOR OF LEICESTER
Make a grave...

...here.

We tell no-one. Then the King's wishes and God's Will are both fulfilled, and rebels of York - wherever they are - may be forevermore distracted.

JOHN OF LEICESTER,
WARDEN OF THE GREYFRIARS
And this is legal?

THOMAS SWYKE,
MAYOR OF LEICESTER
It is extraordinary. But I declare it so.

JOHN OF LEICESTER,
WARDEN OF THE GREYFRIARS
Then hurry away, sir, that we may arrange our subterfuge for good of God, King, England, and man.

THOMAS SWYKE,
MAYOR OF LEICESTER
May God be with us.

=====

=====

108 years earlier...

=====

1: The Boy King

A.D. 1377

=====

-- THE SHORT TALE OF ALICE PERRERS --

Sheen Manor, 21st June 1377.

The silk has a cool softness against her eyes, and moistens gently at the touch.

In this summer heat, her standing as most beloved consort of the old king means she is closest to the rasping warlord to swat at the flies that care little for the demise of England's noblest.

Alice Perrers sits on the large comfortable bed and, in full view of a small gathering of respectful royal court attendees, unskilfully tends to a king who elevated her and kept her. She knows the high regard he always held for her is not shared by anyone else in this bedchamber, but still employs her diminishing advantage to be the one to hold his hand as he gradually fades.

King Edward III will lose his last battle today. So sad, that he is finally laid out, despite his celebrated strength and bravery as recognised by all in England (and, in truth, beyond).

To the surprise of no-one, it was only after a combination of violations that finally rendered what was presumed endless to be mortal. Long had this vicious general terrorised the French as a younger man, fighting for and earning thousands of acres of foreign land that he truly believed was his by right of succession. And long had he defied physicians as an old man, even when the festering abscess had leaked agony and rot into his glorious royal body.

But, though ravaged by time's decay and pestilence, it was the heart that finally broke. Just over a year ago King Edward's energetic virile heir, the much-respected Prince of Wales, had died while on campaign in France from that unmerciful leveller; dysentery. And Alice knows that in spite of all Edward's recent physical challenges, his grief at losing his eldest son is really what did for him.

Alice dares to gaze at a diminutive blue-eyed boy standing dutifully across the room. **Richard** obediently holds his palms together - *God love the golden-haired flea* - and most likely does not understand that soon he is to be declared England's next king. For the late Prince of Wales was his father, and this little royal heir has been brought here, all dressed in his finest, to bear respectful witness to the passing of his grandfather and thereafter the unavoidable immediate ascension of his little self to England's mighty throne.

Likewise, she seeks out old Edward's remaining sons. These battle-bashed brothers, and next in line after young Richard, would wish the death of the decrepit king just to get her off his bed and out of this royal palace. **John of Gaunt** is a tall hawkish middle-aged man, and Duke of Lancaster. **Edmund of Langley** is a stocky dull but otherwise inoffensive chap, and Earl of Cambridge. And **Thomas of Woodstock** is an ambitious young fellow who has been promised the title Earl of Buckingham by his dying father and still intends on keeping him to it.

Alice likes none of them; an opinion that she knows well is reciprocated. It's a state of affairs that has never troubled her overly, although she understands this room's tolerance for her will last precisely as long as King Edward does.

Her king coughs long and splutters on the sputum that rattles up within. He seems to weakly swallow it all eventually, but the effort leaves him struggling with dangerously shallow breaths.

She grips his hand. A wrinkled thumb responds briefly.

She sadly notes his cloudy eyes, and he is looking at her but he is too tired to move. She yearns for a smile from the lop-sided mouth, or some other final acknowledgment. Are his cracked old lips moving at all in silent prayer? They are not.

She grips his hand again.

And just as she hopes for a return in kind, she realises that he is not now breathing.

His eyelids remain half-open.

She glances at the muttering priest.

The priest alerts the physician and the latter leans in to the old mouth. That kindly learned man, who is clothed and capped in black velvet, then places a hand on the revered chest and, after a few moments, gently presses the eyelids so that old Edward's remains may begin their eternal peace.

The men in this bedchamber bow their heads, and womanly gasps and sobs are heard.

But there are no sounds from Alice Perrers, whose gaze again lands upon the little boy. **King Richard the Second** remains standing with his palms together, a yellow-haired poppet, his big sapphire-blue eyes steadfastly staring at the beautiful raven-haired woman on the bed who sits by his lifeless grandfather.

Alice hopes young King Richard will be guided wisely by his uncles John of Gaunt, Edmund of Langley and Thomas of Woodstock. But such politics aren't hers to worry about any more.

It is time.

Her final act of privilege is to use her last moments with him to methodically ease off the thick gold rings from the dead fingers of her benefactor.

The attendants ripple. Women in the room sob a little more while the men bow their heads a little more, deliberately ignoring her disgraceful indecency out of respect for the outgoing king; just in case this appalling atrocity is what their esteemed monarch had charitably intended for his favourite whore.

Alice, her fists full of king's gold as a final *post mortem* payment for consort services, still effects a respectful, submissive and loyal walk backwards to the door, before slowly spinning round, and out.

Her footsteps on the corridor tiles, loud and slow, belie the fear she feels. She presumes that at any time John of Gaunt will burst from the royal sanctum, knock her down, slap her face, and retrieve her gold.

But neither he, nor anyone else, emerges.

=====

To the Ryght Reverend John of Ashby,
Abbote of Croyland,
30 day of June 1377

My Lord Abbote I wryte with gretest melancholie.

It is with utmoste weight and import that I sheyre my concerne for the weal of oure glorios realme. To witte,

Item one, oure beloved Kynge Edward is lately dead, Godde rest hys soule.

Item two, oure beloved Kynge Edward's eldest sonne is long dead, Godde rest hys soule.

Item three, thus remains singulerly Richard, the infant heir, grand chylde of Edward, and now undoubted ryghte and soverein Lord of Englond.

Suche dread we have, inasmuch as yong Richard has but ten yeres to hym.

Here is a boy kynge of Englond who woldst not reign by hymself, or rule men by hymself, or fight in warre or produce an heir for many a long yere. But in the absense of his princely long departed fader, he now woldest inherit oure beloved crown meyny yeres afor we might have presumed he wolde.

Oure fortunes do stande or falle dependyng on the worthinesse of oure kynge. Oure barons often prove a lustye lot and neede to be mayntayned by a kynge of trewe and strong demeanour. And kynges sholde holde wyse counseill whereby some grete grevaunces between Erles and Lordes shall arise. And how sholde a young kynge know hys owne ryghtes in law, so that he knows hys counseillors giveth gude counseill.

Be it also had in mynde that all thys while, Fraunce, those malcontentes across the sea, do espy and covet oure grete lande and fortunes. Thus with a boy kynge on the throne, we do depend alle the more on the excellent dysposicion of those in committee around hym.

I pray that the lordes, byshoppes and knyghts in parlement may togeder guide oure soverein Lord wysely in materes of governaunce bothe high and low. I truste to Goddes grace that alle oure daily workes in pursuying both right and reson shulde take the better spede and conclusion.

May Godde in hys mercye bless and seyve us alle.

Youres respectfullye in Christe,
William of Clowne, Abbote, Leycestre Abbey

=====

SCENE. THE PAINTED CHAMBER AT WESTMINSTER PALACE – EVENING

16th July 1377.

A well-furnished room. Colourful paintings, with biblical figures and religious themes such as 'vice' and 'virtue' adorn the walls.

A ten-year old boy, the new **KING RICHARD II**, *is being dressed by a middle-aged man, his uncle* **JOHN OF GAUNT, THE DUKE OF LANCASTER**, *who has just fitted a heavy full-length crimson robe with ermine lining to the boy.*

The most exclusive apparel in England.

The younger shrugs his shoulders with concentration until the robe sits straight and comfortable. He is deeply distracted by his thoughts.

The elder is a rugged-looking craggy-faced man who wears his own heavy expensive attire with ease and effortless style.

KING RICHARD II

Must I really dine in all these fineries?

JOHN OF GAUNT,
DUKE OF LANCASTER

A king must always be seen as such, my young Lord.

The young king's clothes are heavy and cumbersome, and he'd rather be playing leapfrog with his cousin Henry, John of Gaunt's son.

KING RICHARD II

(yawns)

I am surely now the king, then.

JOHN OF GAUNT,
DUKE OF LANCASTER

Why, yes! Did we not, recently, place a crown on your head?

KING RICHARD II

(pulls a face)

It's heavy.

JOHN OF GAUNT,
DUKE OF LANCASTER

We also anointed you with holy oil, to set you above all other men.

Richard looks puzzled for a few moments.

KING RICHARD II

How might a boy rule over men?

You're my uncle, and you are old. Should not the crown have passed to you when my grandfather died?

JOHN OF GAUNT,
DUKE OF LANCASTER

I'm thirty-seven!

And the crown had to pass down your late father's precious pure noble bloodline to his son, rather than <u>across</u> to a brother.

KING RICHARD II
Why?

**JOHN OF GAUNT,
DUKE OF LANCASTER**
Because those are the God-given laws of our mighty kingdom.

KING RICHARD II
Hmmm.

John of Gaunt patiently stops adjusting his nephew's clothing to explain further. He indicates diminishing heights – high, middling, low – with a flat right hand, palm facing down, as he explains:

**JOHN OF GAUNT,
DUKE OF LANCASTER**
King Edward the Third: your grandfather.

Your father: the Prince of Wales.

You.

Young King Richard nods his understanding of the basic concept of a family hierarchy, so John of Gaunt continues, still illustrating his lesson with his hand.

**JOHN OF GAUNT,
DUKE OF LANCASTER (cont'd)**
King Edward the Third.

His eldest son was your father.

Your father's <u>only</u> son is you.

Richard nods again. The hand thing is working, so Gaunt uses it again.

**JOHN OF GAUNT,
DUKE OF LANCASTER (cont'd)**
When your grandfather died...

...your father was already dead, so his crown...

...passed directly down to you. Therefore you are now king.

KING RICHARD II
Even though I am but ten years of age?

I do not know where I would begin, but I shall rule wisely and justly.

John of Gaunt laughs, to Richard's annoyance.

JOHN OF GAUNT, DUKE OF LANCASTER

You won't need to bear a king's burden for a few years, yet. Parliament will elect a regency council to serve you, advise you, and help you rule.

Richard is puzzled.

KING RICHARD II

Then am I king or not?

JOHN OF GAUNT, DUKE OF LANCASTER

You are England's undoubted king. But until you're twenty-one, you shall benefit from the greatest advisers in the land, who shall rule in your name.

KING RICHARD II

Then why not wait to crown me until my head is big enough to bear it?

JOHN OF GAUNT, DUKE OF LANCASTER

Because a kingdom needs a king.

KING RICHARD II

And a king needs a regency council?

JOHN OF GAUNT, DUKE OF LANCASTER

A boy king needs a regency council.

Richard is clearly disappointed with this revelation.

KING RICHARD II

I thought I would be a real king.

JOHN OF GAUNT, DUKE OF LANCASTER

You are.

A real king who is a boy, and who needs a council to help with the burden of rule.

Richard is pondering again.

Eventually...

KING RICHARD II
So I am a boy king.

JOHN OF GAUNT, DUKE OF LANCASTER
You are.

KING RICHARD II
And I do not have any sons.

JOHN OF GAUNT, DUKE OF LANCASTER
Not yet.

John of Gaunt helps fit a white-with-speckles ermine cape to his nephew's shoulders.

KING RICHARD II
So, if I were to die this day-

JOHN OF GAUNT, DUKE OF LANCASTER
-Your Grace!

KING RICHARD II
Hush, Uncle! If I were to die this day, who would then be king?

JOHN OF GAUNT, DUKE OF LANCASTER
Your Grace, I find a great distaste to this-

KING RICHARD II
-Indulge me, Uncle of Lancaster. If I die this day, then I do not have a son to pass my crown to.

JOHN OF GAUNT, DUKE OF LANCASTER
Indeed.

KING RICHARD II
So if my line is ended now, the crown would seek... my eldest living uncle?

JOHN OF GAUNT, DUKE OF LANCASTER
Those were the wishes of old Edward the Third, as set out in his will.

KING RICHARD II
A crown can be bequeathed, thus?

JOHN OF GAUNT, DUKE OF LANCASTER
If there is some ambiguity regarding succession of said crown.

KING RICHARD II
The ambiguity being: where would the crown settle if I were to die without a son?

JOHN OF GAUNT, DUKE OF LANCASTER
And there you have it.

Richard is frowning, lost in thought.

JOHN OF GAUNT, DUKE OF LANCASTER (cont'd)
Something troubles you, my lord King?

Richard is uncertain of his thoughts.

KING RICHARD II
Old King Edward had five sons who reached maturity.

My father, then <u>Lionel</u>, and then you. Then Edmund and Thomas.

JOHN OF GAUNT, DUKE OF LANCASTER
Correct.

KING RICHARD II

Therefore my father was the first son, Lionel the second son, and you are the third son.

JOHN OF GAUNT, DUKE OF LANCASTER

Also correct.

KING RICHARD II

Then upon my death should not the crown pass to the second son, Lionel, before the third son, you?

JOHN OF GAUNT, DUKE OF LANCASTER

As you know, Lionel died some years ago.

KING RICHARD II

Yes, I mean should the crown pass to Lionel's heir after my demise, instead of you?

Gaunt takes a moment. Then pours a small amount of red wine into an ornately enamelled gilt-silver cup, and drinks the lot.

JOHN OF GAUNT, DUKE OF LANCASTER

Poor Lionel had but one child. A daughter, Philippa.

It is England's tradition that our crown seeks and favours the male.

KING RICHARD II

Very well. Then might the crown pass through Philippa across to her husband?

JOHN OF GAUNT, DUKE OF LANCASTER

A crown never passes through a woman to her husband.

KING RICHARD II

Then should the crown pass down to Philippa's son, Roger?

Roger has old King Edward's blood.

(uses his hands like Gaunt did)
It runs through his grandfather Uncle Lionel...

...and then his mother Philippa...

...and thence to him.

JOHN OF GAUNT,
DUKE OF LANCASTER
That may be, but young Master Roger Mortimer is but three years old.

The crown prefers our kings to be men.

The ten year old Richard frowns very deeply and with much annoyance.

John of Gaunt huffs to cover his embarrassment, and pats down the boy's ermine-covered shoulders.

KING RICHARD II
So women cannot inherit crowns? Or estate?

JOHN OF GAUNT,
DUKE OF LANCASTER
They may inherit estate, so they can pass it on to their husband. At that point, a principle known as *jure uxoris* may be applied.

KING RICHARD II
Latin is the language of our laws.

JOHN OF GAUNT,
DUKE OF LANCASTER
(smiles)
Veritas! It means, "by right of the wife."

A man might, with the gracious consent of his king of course, assume his wife's estate, when she inherits that estate from her father.

And if the estate comes with a title, she may pass that on too.

KING RICHARD II

Is that why you are also known as Lord of Spain?

**JOHN OF GAUNT,
DUKE OF LANCASTER**

My dear wife is a princess of Spain, therefore I am a lord of Spain *jure uxoris*.

However, in England...

...a crown <u>may</u> conceivably pass down <u>through</u> the blood of a woman to a son, but <u>never</u> across a marriage bed to a husband.

KING RICHARD II

And thus, a man might assume his wife's inherited title, but a man cannot marry a lady heir to a crown and thereby assume the crown.

**JOHN OF GAUNT,
DUKE OF LANCASTER**

<u>*Veritas*</u>!

Our king already has all the makings of a great and wise lawmaker.

KING RICHARD II

A man must have our royal Plantagenet blood to be King of England.

**JOHN OF GAUNT,
DUKE OF LANCASTER**

Oh aye. He must, that.

Our family's royal Plantagenet blood, and the continuance of our precious bloodline, is God-given and therefore more important as a whole than any of us individual men.

KING RICHARD II

So if, this evening, I ate a poisonous toadstool...

**JOHN OF GAUNT,
DUKE OF LANCASTER**

Saints preserve us! Come, we must go to dinner. Please summarise this fantasy of yours.

KING RICHARD II

Very well.

When a king dies, the crown seeks a legitimate male, and our own English traditions discourage it from passing down through a female to reach that male, although there is nothing legally to prevent that from happening if another obvious legitimate male is not alive.

**JOHN OF GAUNT,
DUKE OF LANCASTER**

Veritas.

KING RICHARD II

I am the only son of old Edward III's first son.

The late Lionel was old Edward's second son, but upon my own death the crown would ignore his line. That is because his only child was female and her son and heir is but three years old.

And so the crown would instead seek the third of old Edward's sons.
A certain John of Gaunt, Duke of Lancaster.

**JOHN OF GAUNT,
DUKE OF LANCASTER**

Well I wouldn't thank you for it, I can assure you that. I have enough work to do without being king of England as well, as if you hadn't noticed.

KING RICHARD II
(ignores his uncle)
And if then you died, your beloved son who is my beloved cousin Henry of Bolingbroke would inherit the crown.

JOHN OF GAUNT, DUKE OF LANCASTER
There's more dying than usual going on, here. Are we returned to war with France while I was in the privy?

KING RICHARD II
Haha, this is fair. I like Henry Bolingbroke.

JOHN OF GAUNT, DUKE OF LANCASTER
Rest assured young sir, it is truly God's Will that you are king, and let's leave the matter there.

The young boy is insistent.

KING RICHARD II
But then if you and cousin Henry died, then Uncle Edmund as old Edward's fourth son would-

JOHN OF GAUNT, DUKE OF LANCASTER
Begging your pardon, young Master King, but I will not be inheriting no crown, nor will your Uncle Edmund. And nor would your Uncle Thomas's second squire's sister's goat.

The boy chuckles at his uncle's combined seriousness and frivolity. But then he frowns again, in thought.

KING RICHARD II
And this is God's Will?

JOHN OF GAUNT, DUKE OF LANCASTER
It is, young Sire.

KING RICHARD II

Oh, Uncle! Has there ever been a king as young as I?

JOHN OF GAUNT, DUKE OF LANCASTER

Perhaps not, young master.

KING RICHARD II

Then, Uncle of Lancaster, do you not think that God must have quite the plan for me?

John of Gaunt, Duke of Lancaster and uncle to King Richard II, stands back to admire his nephew, likes what he sees, and nods in agreement with genuine pride.

=====

-- A KYNGDOMMES CURIOSITIE --

Sir, thys mattere is moste uncerteyn accordyng to the juste lawes of oure noble lande.

Sholde Richard, kynge of englonde, be decessed, woldst trewe ryghte of sauvereunty be thereafter dytermined by kynge Edwards seconde sonnes blood through the Lady Philippa and to her sonne Lord Roger Mortimer, or by kynge Edwards thirde sonnes blood direct to John Duc of Lancastre.

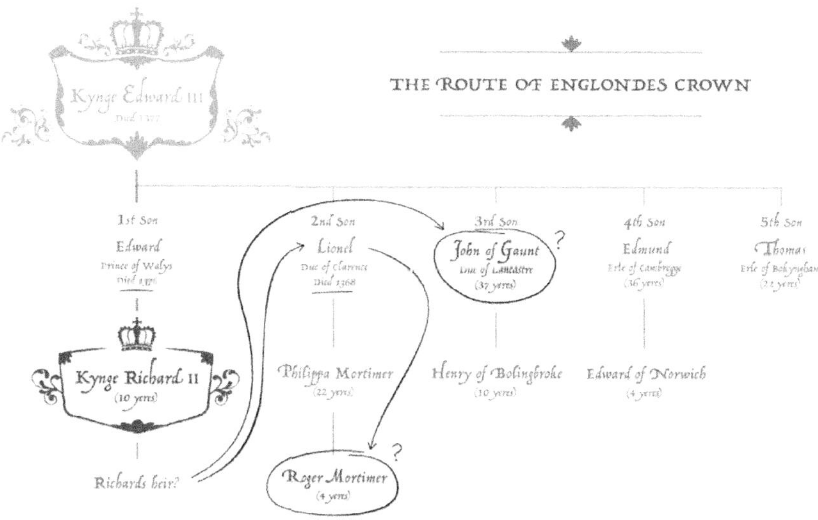

Olde kynge Edward willed englondes crowne to the ryghte trusted and honourable Lancastre sholde mishappe befalle younge Richard.

Howevre some sayeth, sholde some suche unfavourable circumstaunce prevaile, then by rule of primogeniture sholde Lord Roger Mortimer be heir apparent.

In trewthe, such customes in englonde are not committed to lawe, and we pray that kynge Richard does marry and prevail, as he sholde with Goddes good grace.

=====

-- A COMMONER'S TALE --

Dorsetshire, 13th August 1377.

She turns her back on a bleary-eyed priest too emptied of faith to acknowledge her with anything but shame, and walks barefoot from the rough-cut edge of today's pit; each footstep carefully pondered, for while grass is soft and damp, stones and nettles are sharp reminders of her destitution.

God had in his divine wisdom visited her small homestead once again, though why it had not been possible for Him to shoo the melancholic daemons that clung to her rags instead of taking from her the kindest and gentlest husband, she does not know. All she knows is; everything is God's will.

Margery of Holworth recalls Ralph with pain in her heart and hopes he is warm and happy in Heaven and returned to their children. She sees his and their faces in a vision, all around them sweet golden Heaven in all its glory, and then, appalled at her momentary lapse of irreverence, stops and says a little silent prayer of forgiveness to God and Jesus both.

Temptations in this world are real, and any weak-willed visions in contemplation of anything but the life that God serves you will damn you to hell. For hell is every bit as real as Heaven, and to live a life in the name of God means to serve Him, praise Him, and accept that all that happens is His Will. To do the otherwise, and bemoan one's lot, is a severe sin punishable by a fiery eternity in the hell as truly shown by the terrifying frescoes in church that even in her thirtieth year she still hardly dares glance towards.

Like everyone around them, they are churchgoing God-fearing simple folk who have travelled more miles than their own parents and grandparents did between them. The Great Plague had seen off most of those previous generations, giving the workers of the ground the opportunity to seek better remuneration. As Ralph said, those lords that wanted their land farmed best, would have to pay something called a wage to cover that assurance. And, convinced by her husband and his complex ideologies, she'd supported him and followed him like the good wife she was.

And it had been as Ralph said it would be. A better way of living. The work was every bit as hard as it ever had been, but soon Ralph told her they'd be able to afford stonework foundations instead of their sticks and mud-built home. And they'd laughed and dreamed and held each other. And loved. A baby girl had come, and then a baby boy and then another.

But as if the earthly fortunes of the meek had somehow displeased God, then came tax collectors to relieve them of their coins and leave them with less food and chattels than they had when they were tied to their first lord.

The pestilence had come again, and again, each time leaving dead friends in its silent breath. The infant girl was called to God. The boys, too. And, no considerer of rank or greatness, the local lord and master did also fall to the pestilence in the wind.

And yet still they endured. With more deaths, said Ralph, would come more coin, and her wily fox did indeed look their betters in the eye and declare his wage to be ever higher. He understood the masters needed our farming and husbandry skills more than ever before, and if you wanted a workforce to meet production promises, then you had to pay for the hardest working or else the hardest working would move on to the next manor, leaving the tight-fisted lord to explain any wastage to his earl or duke while his more generous neighbour rejoiced in the praise of the King. It was even heard of lords being called to the King himself to account for shortfalls, such are these infamous days and years.

And yet as their income increased, so did their taxation. But not in some fair-handed way, instead in some greed-inspired way that somehow twisted in nature to assure they paid amounts in tax unfair and inappropriate, and thus the more they earned, the less they earned.

And those damned poll taxes taxed them further still. A whole fivepence paid to the bailiff twice in one year was enough to send many begging to the church, and many went back to old masters and begged to be tied to their land once again and live as beasts; working for food without the need to fret about how the barons did their money magic.

We work, and we starve. But we endure until we die.

It was seven days ago, when her beautiful strong man had been carried back from the field, too exhausted to walk of himself. And she sobbed within for she knew straightaway her infant, then her two boys, and now her husband, had this great pestilence chosen.

Her beautiful, hardworking Ralph, a man who once told of seeing old King Edward himself from the field, during one hot summer, when the king and all his retinue rode past on some such royal duty. Oh how her own beloved ruddy-faced husband filled with joy when he recalled the day he saw our great warrior king! Astride a white horse as big as a cottage, he was, and all bedecked in dazzling armour from toe to top that shone across the barley with light from God himself! Her husband told of how this right anointed king was truly sent from God, and how he could not breathe in such proximity to this heaven on earth, and how like all the other men in the field he dropped to his knees in sheer joy and fear before this majesty! And how behind the king another rider held aloft a flag of such colours that have surely never been seen before, cut from cloth of gold with ruby- and sapphire-stained reds and blues, and lions too! And, as quickly as he'd emerged, he disappeared, leaving the men in the field to stare wild-eyed and wide-mouthed at each other and hold their hats to their heads in disbelief that their own king had just ridden past! Some bolder fellows ventured to propose on where he was going, and what royal business had taken him within an old man's whiskers' length of their own field. And other fellows told how their knees were now shaking! A wonderful day that was. And how Ralph wept with pride and joy as he often told her about the day he saw the King, as she now weeps with grief. A wonderful day that was, indeed.

Ah, the joy and ache of remembrance is too much, and she kneels down by a hefty oak tree using its ancient trunk to ease herself lower.

So tired. How odd.

She closes her eyes.

Lifts a hand to scratch the back of her head.

And winces at the sudden pain in the armpit.

She gasps. And with the other hand, explores, and finds, the tender pus-filled lump she knows is there.

Tears form, and run down her cheeks to drip off her pretty chin.

Margery smiles. And then chuckles. And looks to the sky and closes her eyes with salt water on her face and bliss in her heart.

Because, finally, after everything.

God has now chosen her too.

=====

SCENE. THE GREAT HALL AT WARWICK CASTLE – NIGHT

19th September 1377.

A very large sumptuous hall with a huge fireplace that provides healthy heat-giving flames from big crackling logs. A large long oak table is the centrepiece, and the only two men here, who sit at the table close to one another, are dwarfed by their surroundings.

***John of Gaunt, Duke of Lancaster**, is enjoying a late evening drink with an old friend. **Thomas Beauchamp, Earl of Warwick**, is nonchalantly rubbing a painful knee.*

**JOHN OF GAUNT,
DUKE OF LANCASTER**

How often do you have this room to yourself?

**THOMAS BEAUCHAMP,
EARL OF WARWICK**

(smiles)

Isn't it odd how when you're young, you surround yourself with as many people as possible, and yet, as you get old, the more you yearn for some peace and quiet.

**JOHN OF GAUNT,
DUKE OF LANCASTER**

People keep saying I'm old! You can't be forty, yet, either.

**THOMAS BEAUCHAMP,
EARL OF WARWICK**

(smiles)

Am I still so young?

**JOHN OF GAUNT,
DUKE OF LANCASTER**

We've seen much of life.

**THOMAS BEAUCHAMP,
EARL OF WARWICK**

And death.

**JOHN OF GAUNT,
DUKE OF LANCASTER**

You still think about those days?

THOMAS BEAUCHAMP,
EARL OF WARWICK
France? And Castile? In truth, more and more frequently.

JOHN OF GAUNT,
DUKE OF LANCASTER
You wish to fight again?

THOMAS BEAUCHAMP,
EARL OF WARWICK
(chuckles)
Not with this knee.

JOHN OF GAUNT,
DUKE OF LANCASTER
Then why do you recall the past so fondly?

THOMAS BEAUCHAMP,
EARL OF WARWICK
We were in some melees, you and me.

Who was that young lad? So scared, he was, that he pissed his armour before every single battle.

JOHN OF GAUNT,
DUKE OF LANCASTER
(laughs and nods)
What was his name? Aumerle?

THOMAS BEAUCHAMP,
EARL OF WARWICK
(shakes head slowly)
We all pissed in our armour!

JOHN OF GAUNT,
DUKE OF LANCASTER
But he was the only man of us foolish enough to confess it.

They laugh softly, and drink wine from goblets.

THOMAS BEAUCHAMP,
EARL OF WARWICK

I've begun to remember things about those times. If I sit quietly I can recall certain events.

JOHN OF GAUNT,
DUKE OF LANCASTER

Why would you do that?

THOMAS BEAUCHAMP,
EARL OF WARWICK

(reminiscing)

I recall a battle. Of cutting some peasant in... Gascony... somewhere.

I swung my sword with a hard backhand into his midriff, straight through his gambeson just above his hip, and in toward his backbone. Then pulled my blade from out of his belly. He responded as if I'd winded him with nothing more than a cudgel.

In the instant, he seemed to recover his wits. And raised his mace, hammer, whatever it was.

But in doing so the stretching of his arm fully opened up the wound I'd just made, and his blood and guts slopped out at his feet.

Gaunt chuckles, and drinks wine.

THOMAS BEAUCHAMP,
EARL OF WARWICK (cont'd)

More surprise on a man's face have I never seen, before or since. I thought it amusing at the time.

But as he went, his eyes pleaded with me, for, what, I don't know. It was too late for mercy.

He was frightened, John. These were his last seconds. He was going in the moments to come, and by my hand, and he was terrified of it.

Terrified!

Why was he terrified? What did he see that I could not?

Did I send a man's soul to hell that afternoon?

JOHN OF GAUNT,
DUKE OF LANCASTER

(sniffs)

What if you did? He was French, and about to kill you.

THOMAS BEAUCHAMP,
EARL OF WARWICK

And then what if, by killing him, and all the dozens of others in my time, I have damned myself to hell? *Ne occidatis*, John!

JOHN OF GAUNT,
DUKE OF LANCASTER

God blesses us in battle when we kill in his name. You know this.

And God knows the church extorts enough money out of us forevermore to assure our eternal souls are still welcomed in Heaven.

THOMAS BEAUCHAMP,
EARL OF WARWICK

I suppose. Do you know, I've lately taken to laying awake at night, wondering what his name was.

JOHN OF GAUNT,
DUKE OF LANCASTER

I often lay awake at night wondering if Katherine is recovered enough from the time before to go again.

The sombre mood is broken. They laugh heartily, and clank their goblets together.

THOMAS BEAUCHAMP,
EARL OF WARWICK
Is Katherine well? It has been so long since I saw her, last.

JOHN OF GAUNT,
DUKE OF LANCASTER
Oh, the same as ever. Very beautiful, very loyal.

THOMAS BEAUCHAMP,
EARL OF WARWICK
And what of the...

(grandly)
...heir of Lancaster, Master Henry Bolingbroke?

JOHN OF GAUNT,
DUKE OF LANCASTER
In fine fettle, my good lord.

THOMAS BEAUCHAMP,
EARL OF WARWICK
He has, what? Ten years?

JOHN OF GAUNT,
DUKE OF LANCASTER
(nodding)
Ten years.

He shows great aptitude with weapons already. Takes after his mother! May God rest her soul.

They laugh with fondness for Gaunt's late first wife.

THOMAS BEAUCHAMP,
EARL OF WARWICK
How old are young Katherine's sons, now?

JOHN OF GAUNT,
DUKE OF LANCASTER
(pulls a face)
Six years? And two years? And I suppose the infant is a few months.

THOMAS BEAUCHAMP,
EARL OF WARWICK
They are all healthy?

JOHN OF GAUNT,
DUKE OF LANCASTER
As far as I know.

THOMAS BEAUCHAMP,
EARL OF WARWICK
A fine brood, indeed! You are surely the most fortunate baron in all of England. I make a toast!

(grandly, again)
To John of Gaunt, Duke of Lancaster, Lord of Spain, and father to many strong sons!

JOHN OF GAUNT,
DUKE OF LANCASTER
Well said, Warwick.

THOMAS BEAUCHAMP,
EARL OF WARWICK
And so...

...speaking of Spain...

...how is your wife?

=====

-- THE OPENING TALE OF CONSTANZA, DUCHESS OF LANCASTER --

A Spanish princess, born in old Castile.

Happy days in the sun had little **Princess Constanza**, the eldest and most beloved child of King Pedro of Castile.

A creamy stone palace she remembers, with floors and walls of marble, and open doorways everywhere so that she could run and dance and laugh without care. Everyone she met - nurses, and tutors, and games masters and mistresses - would smile at her, whatever she said or did, and all would agree that she was quite the most delightful and beautiful princess in the whole world, and how she would marry a handsome duke, and how she would rule as Queen of Castile after her father, with wisdom, justice and strength with some handsome consort.

With no brothers, and only one younger sister, she cannot remember a time when she did not know she was born to be queen.

One summer evening long ago, as she walked in the warm golden glowing sun with her father during a rare and valuable moment together, she had asked him *where is Castile?*, and he had squeezed her hand, taken out his jewelled dagger, knelt under the shade of the twisted old olive tree, and drawn a large square on the floor in the soft baked dirt with the blade. Then drew lines across to divide the square into nine smaller squares.

Starting at the top left square, the squares are numbered; 1, 2, 3... then 4, 5 in the centre, and 6... and then 7, 8, and 9.

The big square is Spain and Portugal together, he said, *but disregard squares four and seven for they are Portugal*, he said, and placed his foot on them before swiping them left and away. *Castile comprises squares two and five.*

And you are King of Castile? she asked her padre, and he had smiled.

You are the king of squares two and five! she said. *The king of squares! Two and five!*, and then hopped away in distracted delight towards the sudden sound of cicadas in the scorched brush.

Their palace was on a well-travelled route of a great pilgrimage, and while this attracted a great many good Christians all eager to alleviate themselves of the burdens of their sins, this also attracted a great many bad sorts all eager to relieve the good Christians of their material possessions. As a result, King Pedro of Castile was a strong king who ruled with a well-balanced, inclusive, though at times hardened justice which was every bit as tough as it needed to be to keep the peace in their home land.

And her good padre endured and succeeded, and had the love, the respect, and the fear of almost all of his subjects. But as with so many kings before him, Pedro suffered from a most feared predicament. His queen died when Constanza had only seven years of age, and as Constanza only had a younger sister (Isabella), this meant her father was without a male heir, and without the prospect of one either. And though unlike France who had prohibited female succession of any kind, Castile, like England was a kingdom who would tolerate the passing of a crown through a woman... but not if it could be helped.

The whole kingdom of Castile bristled with uncertainty, which was antagonised greatly when King Pedro was eventually particularly irritated by an illegitimate half-brother named Henry of Trastámara, who did have a son and heir, and who gathered an army when Constanza had only twelve years, and endeavoured to take Pedro's crown for his own Trastámara family dynasty in a great civil war.

Fortunately Pedro had a great and mighty ally; old King Edward III of England and his daring vigorous son the Prince of Wales. Those great men and more (including another son of King Edward, John of Gaunt the Duke of Lancaster, no less) assisted Pedro and for a while deterred the filthy troublemakers.

Her home was then a dangerous place to be, and so Constanza and her younger sister Isabella were secreted under guard and in disguise, eastwards across Spanish Navarre and into Aquitaine, an otherwise French *province* long-occupied by England and well administered by that tall, handsome and commanding Duke of Lancaster. They trundled north until they came to Bordeaux, in which a little English court had been established under Joan, the royal consort of the Prince of Wales. This stunning princess, the most beautiful maid in all England, took the two young exiles in as if they were her own flesh and blood, and in spite of the unfamiliarity of her surroundings, and the frustration and worry of not seeing her father, this was a relatively peaceful time for Constanza.

In fact, with so many of those pale and rugged Englishmen in this court, Constanza began to dream of being matched with one of the wild northern men, and taken to live in his castle, where the wind and rain would smash against the thick stone walls while she and her nobleman would spend long cosy nights by their crackling chamber fire, all wrapped up in wolves' furs, drinking wine, and listening to all the daring tales he tells of the adventures he had before her.

But as those Spanish civil wars endured, England's interest waned. It became too expensive for the white lions to stay in Spain, and the food, water, and heat ultimately did not agree with their delicate constitutions. Dysentery, that great and grievous sickness that rots the inner and then flushes itself out with violence, killed hundreds of brave Englishmen. It also disabled countless more, including Princess Joan's revered husband the Prince of Wales, who became riddled with that undignified malady and thereafter struggled to walk without his servants after using up almost all his mortal strength to avoid the death of him.

Slowly, and then noticeably, the English diminished in number.

And in 1369, after three long years of destructive resentful greed, Henry of Trastámara saw his opportunity and persuaded her father King Pedro into a peace talk. But he was so much more malicious than anyone could ever know, and when her wonderful trusting father settled down in the tent in which they had chosen to *parlai*, the revolting pretender distracted her beautiful unsuspecting father and viciously schlucked a dagger into his darling face, again and again, until he bled his honourable royal blood over the steel and the hand of the bastard usurper.

The English army, by now without the heart or the means of punishing the Trastámaran, returned more quickly across the sea, and the Spanish princesses shared their heartbroken farewells with the beautiful Princess Joan. But John of Gaunt remained in Aquitaine, and presently supplied Constanza with exciting news. She was to be his wife, and together they became the Duke and Duchess of Lancaster after marrying in Bordeaux. At about the same time, Gaunt's younger brother, Edmund of Langley selected young Isabella for his wife and together they became the Earl and Countess of Cambridge.

Two Spanish princesses for two English noblemen; these were fine matches indeed. It was a tragedy that her father couldn't have seen her do so well.

Even upon the demise of her father at the hands of Henry of Trastámara, and in spite of that murderer's claim to the Castilian crown, there is no doubt that Constanza is still the rightful heiress. But now she is half a world away from her rightful home land.

Constanza finds living in England challenging due to the unsophisticated language, the blandness of the food, and the consistently heavy damp weather. All these things have at least brought her closer to God, because her one true pleasure is in having plenty of time to read and study the scriptures. There are many learned men from which to discuss such matters. The Duke of Lancaster seemed happy to allow Constanza such freedoms but, as Constanza discovered fairly quickly upon arrival in England, this may be because her husband has a well-established mistress that by many accounts needed much attention.

Katherine Swynford had been the nurse to her husband's son by his first marriage - Henry of Bolingbroke - and was no doubt fondly available upon the death of Henry's mother. Katherine, for her part, has played her game well, giving the duke three strong sons whereas Constanza could only manage for him a beautiful daughter, Catarina, and a son who lived long enough only to be named John before they buried him.

As for the duke, he may be unfaithful, and selfish in the bedroom when he does make an appearance, but he is courteous and generous beyond it.

Gaunt is mindful of her inheritance, and he has always maintained that they must live in England and wait for the right time to return and take their place in the kingdom of Castile. He has, after all, had the Castilian royal coat of arms incorporated into his own well-established Lancaster sigil, and even more dramatically has re-styled himself John of Gaunt, Duke of Lancaster and Lord of Spain.

And so she lives every day by God's good teachings, and if she thinks of Castile often, it is briefly in between her prayers. Above all, she shall be loyal and respectful of her husband. For he is powerful. And he is ambitious.

And if her deference means that someday the Castilian Princess Constanza might reclaim her throne from the Trastámaran bastard and claim her place as Queen of Castile, then John of Gaunt can do, and call himself, whatever he damn well pleases.

=====

A.D. 1378

=====

SCENE. THE KING'S CHAMBERS AT ELTHAM PALACE, KENT – DAY

August 1378.

A well-furnished room, colourful tapestries adorn the walls. The eleven-year old ***King Richard II*** *sits at a table with several rolls of parchment in front of him. He is signing them. This is official business of the kingdom.*

His eldest uncle, ***John of Gaunt the Duke of Lancaster****, and also* ***Simon Sudbury the Archbishop of Canterbury and Lord Chancellor*** *of the kingdom of England are in attendance, watching the young king.*

Presently the King places his quill down into its inkpot on the table, an action which causes the two men who are supervising to concentrate their attention on their sovereign lord.

KING RICHARD II

Are we King of France as well as of England?

The two men exchange an uncertain look.

SIMON SUDBURY,
LORD CHANCELLOR AND
THE ARCHBISHOP OF CANTERBURY

My, what a question for a young king to ask!

King Richard II frowns at the Archbishop.

JOHN OF GAUNT,
DUKE OF LANCASTER

Why should this matter trouble His Highness?

Richard considers this.

KING RICHARD II

It is our royal styling. Have we not taken, as did our predecessor, the royal style; "King of England and of <u>France</u> and Lord of Ireland"?

The two men begin to try and find the explanation, but they are too slow and Richard picks up the parliamentary roll he was supposed to sign, and tosses it away from him beyond the table.

KING RICHARD II (cont'd)

But if I am King of France, why do our worthy spies report to us that the kingdom of France is thought to be embarking upon a strategy of ship-building in order to sail upon our shores in grave acts of war against us?

And furthermore, the French already have a king; Charles the Wise.

Sudbury looks shocked at the King's precociousness, however Gaunt is smirking. Perhaps more at Sudbury's reaction.

SIMON SUDBURY
LORD CHANCELLOR AND
THE ARCHBISHOP OF CANTERBURY

Pfff, these are matters for your council, Your Grace.

King Richard II regards the ageing Archbishop silently. Only eleven years old, he already knows that the men around him are obliged by law to tell him the full truth or risk charges of treason.

KING RICHARD II

Matters for the King's Council...

...but not the King?

JOHN OF GAUNT,
DUKE OF LANCASTER

What the Archbishop means, Richard, if I may, is that the answer to this matter is one of complexity.

KING RICHARD II

We are not fearful of 'complexity', my Uncle of Lancaster.

We are at war with France, are we not? How am I King of France and be at war with France all at the same time?

**JOHN OF GAUNT,
DUKE OF LANCASTER**

These are all most worthy questions, Your Highness.

KING RICHARD II

Then answer, please.

**JOHN OF GAUNT,
DUKE OF LANCASTER**

Why are you styled King of England and of France. And are we at war with France.

KING RICHARD II

Those are the issues.

Gaunt and Sudbury share a look. There is no reason to avoid this conversation.

**JOHN OF GAUNT,
DUKE OF LANCASTER**

I might answer both issues with a story of history.

KING RICHARD II

Oh.

**JOHN OF GAUNT,
DUKE OF LANCASTER**

Ah now, young prince, this is a story that is fascinating in its detail.

Richard isn't convinced, but raises a regal hand to acknowledge Gaunt may speak.

**JOHN OF GAUNT,
DUKE OF LANCASTER**

Very well, the story begins thus.

A Plantagenet ancestor of ours, King Henry the Second, did two hundred years ago marry a beautiful French princess named Eleanor of Aquitaine.

KING RICHARD II

We were born there! Bordeaux.

(then, to Sudbury)

Aquitaine is the great and fertile sea-facing land to the west of France, and England's realm long since.

JOHN OF GAUNT,
DUKE OF LANCASTER
Indeed.

Aquitaine became part of England's realm when Henry the Second married Eleanor, for she brought with her this truly wondrous province as part of the marriage contract.

KING RICHARD II
Such a dowry is in keeping with a royal marriage.

SIMON SUDBURY
LORD CHANCELLOR AND
THE ARCHBISHOP OF CANTERBURY
Yes it is, Sir! This was a right and legal transaction of estate.

JOHN OF GAUNT,
DUKE OF LANCASTER
And so Aquitaine, once a duchy administered by the kingdom of France, became a duchy administered by the kingdom of England. The fruits of Aquitaine have been freely loaded onto ships bound for England ever since.

KING RICHARD II
We do not like the wine.

JOHN OF GAUNT,
DUKE OF LANCASTER
(smiling)
You will.

KING RICHARD II
And so then we are King of Aquitaine. What of the rest of France?

JOHN OF GAUNT,
DUKE OF LANCASTER
Ah, well, patience, my young king.

First you must understand about the importance of royal blood.

KING RICHARD II

(slams palm on desk)

IDIOT! Of course I understand the importance of royal blood!

SIMON SUDBURY, LORD CHANCELLOR AND THE ARCHBISHOP OF CANTERBURY

Of course you do, Your Highness.

KING RICHARD II

(swipes parchments off the table)

PRIESTS DO NOT CONDESCEND KINGS!

JOHN OF GAUNT, DUKE OF LANCASTER

(carefully)

Sire.

The remaining story is quite enthralling.

Richard, glaring at Sudbury, turns to John of Gaunt and slowly the King's fierce eyes... eventually... soften.

=====

-- THE TALE OF THE FOUR FRENCH KINGS --

(as told by John of Gaunt, Duke of Lancaster)

*Over 60 years ago in 1314 a French King, **Philip the Fourth**, died. He did, as fine kings may, leave three sons; **Louis, Philip** and **Charles**. And also a daughter, **Isabella**. All of good age.*

*But even after such diligent preparation, God looked unkindly upon that foreign royal family, for after King Philip the Fourth died, his eldest son - now **Louis the Tenth** of France - lived only long enough to reign two years before he died without an heir.*

*You'll recall the old king had a second son to whom the crown could pass. This second son was Philip, who thereafter became **King Philip the Fifth** of France.*

But alas, this unfortunate Philip died in the sixth year of his reign. And also, without an heir.

And thus the third and final son was crowned. ***Charles the Fourth*** *was France's fourth king in fourteen years.*

A happy end to a grievous tale, you might think?

Not so.

For Charles the Fourth, like his predecessor, died after but six years on the throne. And once again without an heir.

Which left Isabella as the last remaining living issue of old King Philip the Fourth.

And she was already Queen of England, as she had married our own King Edward the Second.

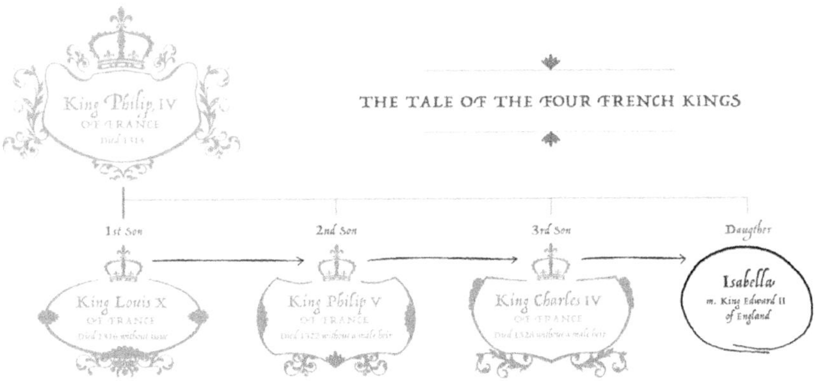

KING RICHARD II

Aha!

As the only remaining child of the old king, Isabella inherited the French crown!

Which then passed to good old King Edward the Second, jure uxoris... by right of his wife!

But even as he says it, Richard checks himself, and frowns in thought.

KING RICHARD II (cont'd)

But... it didn't, did it?

JOHN OF GAUNT,
DUKE OF LANCASTER

I did say this was a matter of certain complexity.

By this time - 1328 - Isabella was alive, but Edward the Second had died. The English crown had by now passed to their eldest son and heir; a very young Edward the Third.

KING RICHARD II

(nodding)

Our own royal predecessor and beloved grandfather. And now, through his mother Isabella, the rightful living heir to the French crown!

JOHN OF GAUNT,
DUKE OF LANCASTER

This was as Edward supposed, but there was a constitutional problem.

The French crown, by their own written Salic law, may not ever pass to a woman or through a woman to her husband, or even through a woman to her son.

KING RICHARD II

Not ever? Even if it is willed thus?

Gaunt is shaking his head solemnly.

JOHN OF GAUNT,
DUKE OF LANCASTER

Not by French law.

KING RICHARD II

But there wasn't any other man to pass it on to.

That first French king you spoke of, Philip the Fourth, had only three sons and one daughter, and the three sons had all died without issue.

JOHN OF GAUNT,
DUKE OF LANCASTER
Do you recall a conversation we had just after your own glorious coronation?

KING RICHARD II
Ah!

Where there is no heir, the succession passes back up the line to the next legitimate male. So if we were to die...

SIMON SUDBURY,
LORD CHANCELLOR AND
THE ARCHBISHOP OF CANTERBURY
Oh, Highness!

KING RICHARD II
Oh, *fie*! Canterbu*RYE*!

If I were to die, I have no heir, and so the crown would pass back up my own family line and across to my uncle of Lancaster, here.

Did that that last deceased French king have such an uncle?

JOHN OF GAUNT,
DUKE OF LANCASTER
There was an uncle. Charles, brother to old King Philip the Fourth. But he had, by now, also died.

KING RICHARD II
And so the crown would then pass down that family line, where it would seek a son to find a place to rest.

Did this late uncle have a son?

John of Gaunt, smiles. Young Richard is starting to apply his knowledge.

JOHN OF GAUNT,
DUKE OF LANCASTER
He did. Philip. Crowned King Philip the Sixth of France.

King Richard claps joyfully at his own grasp of this history, but soon ceases, and frowns in thought once again.

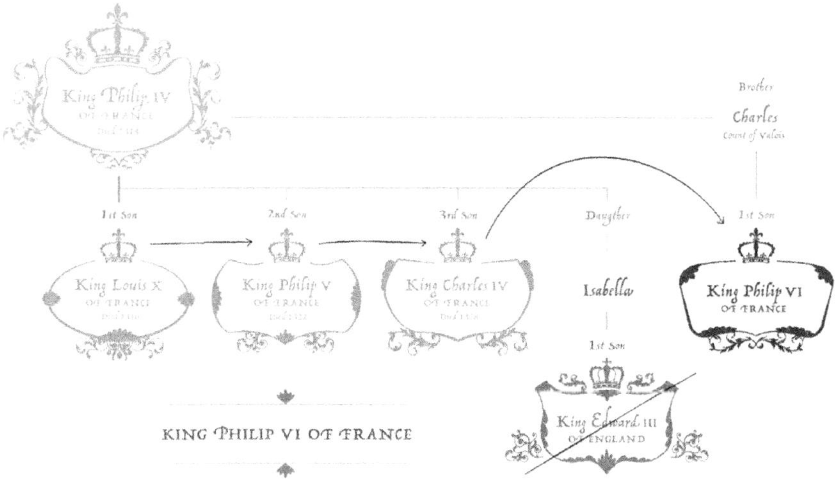

KING RICHARD II

(frowning)

But...

...how did my grandfather feel about this?

JOHN OF GAUNT, DUKE OF LANCASTER

King Edward the Third of England was furious.

He was nephew to Charles the Fourth the last deceased king of France, and yet the crown went to a cousin.

King Richard ponders this situation.

KING RICHARD II

Our grandfather was well known for war. Edward the Third spent most of his life in arms against France.

He fought, seized, and occupied Flanders, Normandy, and Brittany.

He won for us the port of Calais...

SIMON SUDBURY,
LORD CHANCELLOR AND
THE ARCHBISHOP OF CANTERBURY

Through which we now have unencumbered freedom to export so much of our profitable wool to Burgundy and the Holy Roman Empire beyond.

Richard rolls his eyes, to Gaunt's private amusement.

KING RICHARD II

He established the western duchies we still hold in Guyenne, Gascony, and Aquitaine.

SIMON SUDBURY,
LORD CHANCELLOR AND
THE ARCHBISHOP OF CANTERBURY

Our treasury still benefits greatly from wealth appropriated from administering these territories.

JOHN OF GAUNT,
DUKE OF LANCASTER

All quite correct.

KING RICHARD II

But old Edward's aggression was in response to the crowning of Philip the Sixth as King of France... instead of him?

JOHN OF GAUNT,
DUKE OF LANCASTER

Old Edward truly felt the French crown was his by divine right. And as God chooses the winning side in any legal duel or battle, he concluded that the right to the French crown must be won by force.

KING RICHARD II

But...

...the French were in this case following their <u>own laws</u>. If <u>their</u> law states that the crown cannot pass through a woman - in this case through Isabella, and on to my grandfather...

King Richard is grappling with the implications.

JOHN OF GAUNT, DUKE OF LANCASTER

Yes?

KING RICHARD II

It is their right to follow their own laws, is it not?

And the only way that our own late King Edward the Third can be also King of France...

...is by applying English tradition to a French constitutional issue?

The Duke of Lancaster is impressed with his nephew.

JOHN OF GAUNT, DUKE OF LANCASTER

That is undoubtedly the dim view that the French take of our own current claim.

KING RICHARD II

My grandfather went to war over this, many years ago.

JOHN OF GAUNT, DUKE OF LANCASTER

He did.

KING RICHARD II

And we are still at war, today?

JOHN OF GAUNT, DUKE OF LANCASTER

In a sense.

Over forty years ago old King Edward declared war on France, and the French declared war on England.

Neither side has since sued for peace.

KING RICHARD II

Where is this war at this time?

**JOHN OF GAUNT,
DUKE OF LANCASTER**

The war, such that it is, and to the best of my knowledge, is under a period of cessation at this time.

But such cessation is best thought of as being merely an interval between aggressions.

KING RICHARD II

An example of aggression?

**JOHN OF GAUNT,
DUKE OF LANCASTER**

Up until a few years ago, old King Edward used to lead his noblemen and their armed followers into France, to battle with the French.

This is how your father died.

KING RICHARD II

(greatly agitated)

My father. Yes. I knew this. But the King also goes to the battlefield?

**JOHN OF GAUNT,
DUKE OF LANCASTER**

Of course. The King leads his men into all battles.

KING RICHARD II

(very nervous)

Would I?

**JOHN OF GAUNT,
DUKE OF LANCASTER**

(nodding)

You are king.

KING RICHARD II

(terrified)

Did you follow old Edward into battle?

JOHN OF GAUNT,
DUKE OF LANCASTER
I did.

KING RICHARD II
And you never died in battle.

JOHN OF GAUNT,
DUKE OF LANCASTER
(smiling)
No. It was God's will that I would live to guide my royal nephew into maturity.

KING RICHARD II
What does an army benefit from battle?

JOHN OF GAUNT,
DUKE OF LANCASTER
If it wins the battle, many things. A battle fought in the name of God is decided my God, so for the winner there is great honour first and foremost.

It also wins the land on which it fought, and the towns and farms and people who are tied to the land.

KING RICHARD II
People? What is the benefit of this?

JOHN OF GAUNT,
DUKE OF LANCASTER
Money!

If a nobleman owns land, he owns the people who work upon it. They produce valuable crops and cattle which provide produce that is sold locally or exported by that landowner.

Every landowner who earns money pays a tenth to the church, and a tribute to their king. So the more land you own, the more silver the landowner earns, and you accumulate wealth for your exchequer.

KING RICHARD II

And so, one supposes, we already own all of England's land and thus acquiring foreign land is a way to increase our barons' worth, which increases the royal worth.

JOHN OF GAUNT,
DUKE OF LANCASTER

In essence, yes, that is how a kingdom is managed.

KING RICHARD II

Then where is our army currently?

JOHN OF GAUNT,
DUKE OF LANCASTER

You have many hundreds of men-at-arms based in those foreign territories, to defend the land you own.

KING RICHARD II

But we are not actually at war now?

JOHN OF GAUNT,
DUKE OF LANCASTER

It costs additional money to actually go to war. So if you were to decide to have an invasion into France, you must call a parliament, and declare a tax on your subjects. Your noblemen would then take the men they own, arm them, and join your army. The money thus raised by tax would pay for those extra fighting men's running expenses.

KING RICHARD II

(very nervous, again)

We are not calling a parliament soon, are we?

JOHN OF GAUNT,
DUKE OF LANCASTER

(laughs)

No, why?

KING RICHARD II
To lead an army into war...

**SIMON SUDBURY,
LORD CHANCELLOR AND
THE ARCHBISHOP OF CANTERBURY**
Oh my Lord, we cannot expect a boy to lead an army!

KING RICHARD II
But some day...

...you will expect your King to...

**JOHN OF GAUNT,
DUKE OF LANCASTER**
(carefully)
Someday, Richard, yes.

Richard is visibly agitated, his face ruddy, as he plays out several unknown but clearly terrifying scenarios in his imagination.

KING RICHARD II
This war.

It began because my grandfather desired the French crown, applied our English law to a French constitutional matter, and thus measured himself next in line to their throne, in conflict with their own French laws that they may well reasonably expect to apply for themselves.

**JOHN OF GAUNT,
DUKE OF LANCASTER**
Ah... essentially, yes.

KING RICHARD II
But do you think this was fair, uncle?

**JOHN OF GAUNT,
DUKE OF LANCASTER**
We have made lots of silver from our wars with France.

KING RICHARD II

But thousands of Christian French and English men have died for this, no?

We now occupy a quarter of what would otherwise be France. Over this old quarrel!

I call myself King of France for my grandfather's desire of a crown he had no right to?

**JOHN OF GAUNT,
DUKE OF LANCASTER**

As I said, Your Highness, it is a matter of complexity.

KING RICHARD II

But...

There's a long pause while young Richard processes all the information he now has.

KING RICHARD II (cont'd)

...we pursue our claim of France's crown, nevertheless?

John of Gaunt, the Duke of Lancaster, frowns heavy, leans back in his chair and seeks the gaze of Sudbury. The Archbishop of Canterbury fingers the golden crucifix that hangs at his belly, and looks to the floor.

=====

2: The Pawns of Politics

A.D. 1379

=====

-- THE DARK STILL OF THE NIGHT --

2nd April 1379.

A gasp, with arms out wide in black silence.

It is the same waking nightmare as occurs each night, to the point at which **King Richard** does not ever look forward to his bed with the same keenness, he notes, as those who keep the King's company.

With big eyes he surveys his surroundings and the king's private bedchamber is full of ugly hairy smelly men, all angry, with black teeth bad breath and murderous scowls. But only for a moment. And then they are not there at all.

But his fear remains. The sweat is real. And the breathlessness persists.

He tries to fantasise about all the knights and armed men in England who would stand before him to stop his enemies from breathing upon him, but this fantasy is weak, for it does not matter how many men stand for him, an overwhelming illumination remains; the conclusion at which he is murdered by enemies unknown.

He sobs at the violent injustice that his terror burns incessantly within him. For he is only a boy, even if he is a king.

And such injustice! There exists, not far away across the sea, a whole country who would wish him dead! A whole Christian country full of Christian men who would have him dead so he would not pursue a claim for their throne. A claim he doesn't have and a claim therefore he doesn't want to have.

So can he not let the French have their crown and let he have his, and be done? Or would his uncles and the barons call him a coward for such thoughts?

In truth he feels a little foolish, for he has watched the jousting contests that had been held in his name with much enjoyment, while seated in the middle of the tilt-field under a glorious white canopy. Where great and good English knights, and some most welcome foreign sorts too, did ride and bash at each other with great respect for one another's bravery, and he has come to love the colours, the spectacle, the heroes.

But how he'd been horrified to learn that these demonstrations were not just displays for him. It's fakery to impress ladies - and how it did! - but oh Lord the reality was so ugly and disappointing. The reality that these men exist, not really to provide entertainment for a king as he had first supposed, but really to mass and war and kill other good Christian men.

And furthermore, and far the worse, as it so happens the king does not exist to be entertained by these steel-wrapped soldiers, as he had first supposed. He exists to lead these same murderous men into battle. *Lead.* That means from the front. The King leads, and *they follow*!

He sees the blackened burning smoking battlefield so clearly. Look at the horde of savage dirty enemies, all hunched below sooty clouds with deadly swords, daggers and clubs: every one of them praying to God for a blessing on their own personal murderous intent for the little golden-haired cherub on a white charger.

He kneels on his bed, places his hands together, and looks upward to the God who listens to him before all other men.

He will devote his life to his kingdom, of course, because he was crowned and anointed with holy oil before God. And he will stand with strength among his barons to defend his kingdom as he knows that God and Jesus and Mary would want.

But he cannot believe that God would approve of acts of aggression on foreign soil against other Christian men.

And why would they want to hurt him anyway?

I haven't hurt anyone. I'm just a boy, he says to God.

God, in His serene wisdom, maintains (as He always does) a resolute silence on the matter.

=====

A.D. 1380

=====

-- OBSERVATIONS ON THE DUKE OF BRITTANY --

January 1380.

The Frenchie who isn't really a Frenchie, is known to God and men as John IV, the Duke of Brittany, and he reacts with well-practised obedience to each of the twelve men on the King's Privy Council with an irritating pigeon-like quality.

Every time someone in this chamber speaks, Duke John seems to twitch his face toward them and bob his neck in a curious foreign manner that is probably meant to look subservient. It's the sort of tic that you don't really notice on a man at first, but once you do it makes them look utterly ludicrous.

French is the language of nobility, of course, but **John of Gaunt, Duke of Lancaster**, listens to the Breton accent with displeasure. It's more resonant than that of central France, and it causes Duke John to sometimes almost sing when he speaks. It sounds soft compared with the no-nonsense procedural French of the English court and reminds him a little of every Welshman he has met. He liked none of them, neither.

His disliking of this foreigner isn't exactly mitigated by their history. Gaunt's father, old King Edward, appropriated the earldom of Richmond from his son nearly ten years ago and gave it to Brittany as part of some misplaced political accord of the day. Even more annoyingly, the Breton duke has always been a particularly honoured guest in England's court, for he is married to King Richard's half-sister -England's king and Brittany's fair duchess share a mother. And if all that wasn't enough, old Edward incredibly invested Duke John IV into that most exclusive of chivalric orders, the Order of the Garter; an unrivalled invitational honour comprising the 24 noblemen recognised by the King of England as being most beloved above all other lords.

So, a particularly highly privileged foreign visitor, is Duke John IV of Brittany.

But on this occasion he is visiting young Richard's court to petition for English support for a pressing Breton crisis.

While the region of Brittany is due south of Cornwall and Devon - countrysides separated by over one hundred miles of Celtic Sea although eminently similar in look and productivity - and while it has enjoyed especial amicable trade relations with England since before the time of the Romans, the Bretons had always pledged a regional loyalty to the neighbouring kingdom of France. Brittany traditionally enjoyed a self-declared self-defined regional independence from France, however recently it seems that the French king and his council have undertaken a much more formal policy of consolidation towards all their immediate neighbour provinces, and were exerting great pressure on Duke John to pledge the oath of fealty known as 'liege homage' that would render him legally subservient to the French crown with effectively the loss of the independence of his duchy.

The existing long-standing (and far more informal) 'simple homage' arrangement was more to Brittany's convenience, for dukes of Brittany had a tendency to say yes to England, France, or whomsoever last promised them some honour, title, land, wife, or trinket. But liege homage oaths made over the bones of saints were too binding a step for the Breton leader, and so when the latest French communications had become excessively aggressive and threatening, Duke John turned to the family over the water for support, and the twitching duke has now come to court to beg for the arrangement and conveyance of English feet onto French soil to remind the French that Brittany may be small but could call upon a northern sting to defend themselves when overly startled. Gaunt had expressed his sudden anger with an unrestrained laugh when Duke John IV claimed a mere ten thousand men would suffice, as if the English shires could spare ten thousand pitchforked peasants to fight someone else's battles.

Gaunt has disinterest. Breton John is here today because he is pressured by discord from France, just like he no doubt goes begging to the French court when he feels slighted by England upon occasion. And King Richard isn't interested, either. Every time anyone says the word 'battle' in his presence he turns white and then grey like he has done today.

In any case, for an English lord to jump to Brittany's aid would require the raising of an army, and before that the calling of a parliament and the raising of a tax to fund the whole expedition. Gaunt wouldn't waste a farthing on such folly. In his experienced view, the Frenchies are just grumbling rather than being aggressive, bullying one of the many duchies, provinces and palatinates that litter their continent to see if they crack; let them grumble awhile and see if they run out of grumbling. And then observe them as they move attentions to that other great independent duchy, Burgundy, nestling at the middle of their eastern border. Or the mighty independent county of Flanders to their immediate north-east.

"My Lords, I should be honoured to lead such a worthy chevauchée."

Gaunt starts at the most familiar voice with incredulity. For it is his youngest brother, all puffed up in his best court fineries and ready to solve the problems of the world like only young men are. All look now to Thomas of

Woodstock, 1st Earl of Buckingham, youngest son of old King Edward and therefore youngest uncle to King Richard II.

The twelve lords on the King's Council exchange approvals and nod favourably at one another, grateful for the volunteered solution that has presented itself, and overeager to sanction the diplomatic aid without considering whether or not they actually should. But most happy of all is young Richard, who looks fit to sob now a brave uncle has taken on the burden of leading Englishmen onto foreign soil for himself in the King's name.

John IV, Duke of Brittany, overjoyed now that he has what he came for, approaches the earl with uncomfortably over-familiar arms held wide and slickly embraces his young Buck as he would a saviour.

=====

SCENE. WESTMINSTER PALACE – DAY

21st May 1380.

***Thomas of Woodstock, the Earl of Buckingham**, is walking along one of the light and airy tiled corridors of Westminster Palace.*

*A door opens, and his elder brother, **John of Gaunt** the Duke of Lancaster emerges.*

**THOMAS OF WOODSTOCK,
EARL OF BUCKINGHAM**
Ah! Just the man.

Gaunt casually acknowledges the younger.

**JOHN OF GAUNT,
DUKE OF LANCASTER**
Really?

**THOMAS OF WOODSTOCK,
EARL OF BUCKINGHAM**
I set for France next week, and I would beg your assistance on some business in my absence.

**JOHN OF GAUNT,
DUKE OF LANCASTER**
Ah. I regret that my accounts are-

**THOMAS OF WOODSTOCK,
EARL OF BUCKINGHAM**
-No, not money, a legal matter.

I was hoping to conclude the minutiae before I leave, but neither the King nor his council have yet ratified the full settlement of my wife's inheritance, and I would beseech you to remind my lawyers in my absence that I am expecting settlement while on expedition.

**JOHN OF GAUNT,
DUKE OF LANCASTER**
The Bohun inheritance?

Old Humphrey has been gone seven years.

**THOMAS OF WOODSTOCK,
EARL OF BUCKINGHAM**
And I married Eleanor four years back, just before old Edward died. I suppose the administration was forgot when our nephew ascended.

And, of course, I've been waiting for her to turn fourteen.

**JOHN OF GAUNT,
DUKE OF LANCASTER**
Glory be.

And Eleanor's sister...?

**THOMAS OF WOODSTOCK,
EARL OF BUCKINGHAM**
Mary. I've been having her instructed in Christian ways on the one hand, while discouraging suitors with my sword hand.

Thereafter, a convent beckons.

**JOHN OF GAUNT,
DUKE OF LANCASTER**
She'd be well placed there.

For then she couldn't marry, and thus you wouldn't have to share that inheritance when it is finally released.

THOMAS OF WOODSTOCK,
EARL OF BUCKINGHAM

(nods)

Mary already has twelve years, so we need to act quickly. But legal processes...

...do you think lawyers would work faster if I set their robes alight?

JOHN OF GAUNT,
DUKE OF LANCASTER

None of the lawyers I've ever tortured have worked any quicker.

Gaunt slaps Buckingham's back and they laugh and walk together.

=====

-- GUTS AND GORE --

6th June 1380.

At last, a lesson worth his attention.

King Richard II and his cousin Henry Bolingbroke are pleasingly intrigued by their master **Sir Simon Burley**'s promise that, in today's tutorial, he is about to share details of the most bloody and frightening method of execution that has yet been devised.

It is known by its tripartite name; 'hanged, drawn and quartered'. It is a punishment reserved for the most heinous of traitors, and not only does it cause a protracted painful death it is also, most horrifyingly, designed to prevent the recipient's soul from entering heaven.

How men could conceive of such a dreadful penalty makes one shiver in fear of it. The thought that a king might order mortal earthly events that cause immortal heavenly consequences is another reminder of the closeness between King and God. Another explanation of why men tremble in the presence of their sovereign lord.

Tell us now, pleads Henry Bolingbroke, while King Richard quietly attempts to comprehend the power he undoubtedly has and yet cannot feel.

-- THE WORST OF ALL DEATHS --

(as told by Sir Simon Burley, tutor to the King)

If a man is accused of committing treason, then he is tried by a jury. If that man is found guilty, then he is sentenced to death by hanging, drawing and quartering.

This execution is delivered in three parts. Any of the parts may kill a man with shock of the delivery, but a good executioner will study a man's countenance and then tailor the punishment to ensure that all three constituents are administered so that he so convicted would die at length during the third of those.

Before the punishment takes place, the traitor is stripped to the waist and transported from his cell to the place of execution. His wrists are bound, and a short rope is affixed between those wrists and a horseman. The horseman then guides the traitor, who walks behind or beside the horse. But this is no easy walk. All know that if the traitor falls, the horseman would not stop and would instead continue, now dragging the prisoner behind across the cobbles to the great pain of he so bound. And thus many in the crowd will attempt to trip and punch the unfortunate, while many others would throw foodstuff at him to add to his shame. Upon reaching the scaffold erected for the execution, a great crowd such as would make any man tremble would be gathered. And so, after prayers for the condemned man, the punishment would commence.

First, the hanging. Unlike when a man is executed by hanging alone which involves said felon being first raised, then fitted with a noose and then caused to drop a yard so suddenly the noose tightens and his neck breaks, this other more pertinent hanging is designed to cause much discomfort over a longer time period. In our case, a man is bound by his wrists and ankles, then the noose is fitted around the neck, and then he is raised up slowly so that his feet dangle above the scaffold flooring and so the neck does carry the full weight of the man. This is extremely painful, and even more so in that the rope tightens around the neck to prevent the traitor from breathing properly. Did you know that when so restrained a man's face and hands do change colour to dark pink, then to a lustrous purple! The traitor, who does twitch and wriggle in breathless terror as soon as he is raised above the scaffold, becomes more spirited the darker he turns. I have even seen men so eager to end their discomfort that they raise their knees to their chest and pull down their feet with speed in the effort to somehow break their own neck as it is gripped by the noose. While this is an entertaining spectacle indeed, it would not reflect well for the executioner if the traitor, by lack of air or a breakage in the neck, died at this juncture. And so as I intimated earlier, the skilled executioner can assess the traitor's condition to prolong the hanging while keeping him alive for what is to come.

Second, the drawing. You must consider that when a man so hanged is returned to the scaffold floor and relieved of the tightness of his noose he is these things; terrified to the point of wanting to escape but, more than anything else, concerned with gasping air into his chest. This renders him helpless as he pants, yet the execution party know that some men are extraordinarily strong with fear. It is why at least two big men now stand the traitor up against the scaffold structure and bind him tightly to it. Mark my words, boys, for traitors at this point, their principal desire being to breathe air again, seem to not recall that the drawing is about to commence. Which makes it all the funnier when the executioner reveals his blade and introduces it with care into the traitor's midriff. The steel puncture does always cause an even more urgent malaise in the prisoner than that desperate need for air, and it is always amusing to watch the countenance change. This is the point at which many a man dies of shock, and so the skill of the executioner is to be applauded if he can complete the opening in full; which comprises a slice from below the rib cage to the lower front bone, then amid all the blood that spills he reaches into the wound to draw out the entrails. Once begun they slop out eagerly to the floor and remain there, hanging like deadly sausages from the inside to the out. No man would wish to see his own guts, so this causes much distress to even the most resolute of ruffians, and a quick death to those less sturdy.

Many men live long enough to see the executioner pick up those wet bowels and place them on the hot coals that burn in the adjacent brazier. Any watching man or woman curious as to how much pain this causes is in no such doubt after witnessing this, and most traitors faint or die with such ferocious violation. Those that live through the drawing will not live long, now. For this is where the final part of this dread punishment begins.

So thirdly, quartering. The traitor is unbound and laid down facing God. To much fanfare if the traitor is alive, and still enough even if he is by now dead, the axe is brought to the scaffold. The executioner may taunt the condemned with what is to come, before raising the blade and thudding it into the body or to hack off a limb. Or oftentimes removal of the, er, privy member. None last long under the axe. To continue their punishment into God's realm, the head is removed and the torso is separated from the bottom half, and the two remaining halves are chopped again to produce the four pieces. These pieces are disposed of separately and privately so that the traitor's soul does not know where the remains are rested, and thus is prevented from entering heaven's glory.

Do my young lords have any questions about this?

The two young lords sit silent, mouths and eyes agape.

Sir Simon Burley wonders if King Richard, more pale-skinned than ever seen before, is about to puke forth this morning's breakfast.

=====

-- THE ORIGIN OF A DUCAL PLAN --

13th June 1380.

The arrival of the boy is bracing.

The **Duke of Lancaster** offers a farthing to the messenger, a boy, who snatches it, nods a bow as if butting a gatepost, and runs away in such haste that he leaves the door open.

John of Gaunt calmly walks to the iron loop, pushes the door home to resume his privacy, and hooks a finger under the wax seal of the private letter to ease its security away.

The information revealed on the document was expensive to curate, but he can see that it is certainly worth what he paid for it: apparently the Bohun inheritance is every bit as considerable, and unsettled, as he'd hoped.

Humphrey de Bohun died seven years ago, but he is still a man of great interest.

Firstly, his great-grandfather was the great and mighty King Edward I, a mighty English king known by two impressive soubriquets; the *Hammer of the Scots* earned from ruthlessness shown to those heathens north of the border, and *Longshanks* because in his prime he stood well over two yards high. Old Humphrey most definitely had royal Plantagenet blood. And so, therefore, do his two daughters.

Secondly, he had through a series of prosperous family deaths and inheritances accumulated not one earldom, nor two, but three; those of Hereford, Essex and Northampton. And none of the titles had been re-assigned and were therefore waiting to be inherited *jure uxoris.*

Humphrey's family comprised a wife, the Lady Joan (herself of the well-heeled FitzAlan family who currently hold the earldom of Arundel), and two legitimate children who were both daughters neither of whom were married at the time of Humphrey's death chiefly because Eleanor had been six years old and Mary was still a two-year old infant.

Upon Humphrey's demise his vast estate, writes Gaunt's covert scrivener, has ostensibly passed to his widow in the first instance, but in escrow; in which the widow would hold the estate for the time being while the Crown decided what would happen next. That would usually depend much upon the King of England. It may be that the King might demand a political marriage for the widow and the Bohun estate would thereby pass to the new husband, or it may be that the three earldoms that comprise the Bohun estate be taken away from the remaining females, separated out, and awarded to other worthy noblemen, or it may be that the King would decide how much of the estate the Lady Joan should live off (a third was typical), and how much of the estate should then be passed on to the daughters Eleanor and Mary who would thereafter be wealthy and highly eligible heiresses.

What had happened since Humphrey's death had happened slowly. In the first instance, while Humphrey had died in 1373, old King Edward III had moved the widowed Lady Joan into Langham Manor. Thomas of Woodcock, King Edward's youngest son had then been married to Eleanor, the eldest heiress, in 1376. Gaunt knows this happened upon old Edward's insistence, because no such senior coupling as this would be valid without the consent of the king.

But old Edward had died in 1377, and - this is the knowledge shortfall that Gaunt has paid for - what happened to the Bohun estate after that was... nothing; a victim of the confusion in administrative organisation that one might expect when the new king that succeeds the old king is but ten years old.

Was Old Edward planning on awarding the whole inheritance to his youngest son? Nobody knows.

And so Lady Joan was still widowed and not remarried. The earldoms of Hereford, Essex and Northampton were still unawarded, and the young maids Eleanor and Mary remained without their inheritance.

As Gaunt's youngest brother had implied, having already married the eldest Bohun daughter, if he could then place the remaining Bohun daughter into a religious order, he stands to inherit all of old Humphrey's pile. (Mary having renounced all her worldly goods by becoming a nun, of course).

One would expect the King to make the final ruling to release the inheritance, but there was nothing extraordinary here to suggest that young Thomas of Woodstock would not at some juncture become a very rich nobleman.

Gaunt's intelligence is well worth the money he paid for it. Thomas had foolishly neglected to secure a place in a convent for the other daughter Mary and at twelve years now, she is of marriageable age. Particularly considering that Gaunt's own son and heir Henry of Bolingbroke is only one year older than her.

Gaunt reads the parchment again and catches his breath at the potentials.

In a world where a skilled labourer might earn £2 in a year, the Bohun inheritance is valued at £30,000. And indeed held in escrow until at least both daughters come of age and are married or resettled in religion.

If Gaunt moves quickly, and plays this game well, he might well turn a chance conversation in a corridor into the most profitable opportunistic business of his life.

=====

-- BUCKINGHAM DEPARTS --

30th June 1380.

This is life; when seas make rich promises!

A warm and sunny morning, tents as far as the rolling Kentish meadows can roll, and a lazy north wind to blow them all straight to Calais; what else could make a man's heart pound so vigorously as this?

The King, the King's Council, and his own lieutenants and accountants have agreed on the resources and the money. Five thousand fighting fit men and several chests of boxed silver to support them seems to be the accordant armed might of his first overseas expedition.

Finally has he reaped the privilege of being uncle to a king. As Earl of Buckingham, it has taken **Thomas of Woodstock** three years to manage the affairs of his lands so that, while he redeems only a small annual profit from them, they are at least now run with a predictable efficiency and - barely - profitability.

And, as with all twenty-five year old noblemen who have worked well with diligence to get their affairs in order, the next stage of life lures him away from them; military adventure. For why else do dukes, earls and other barons invest in retained knights to provide protection for their lords and vassals who then manage the villeins, peasants and serfs who work their land into money, if one cannot then petition the King's Council and parliament to raise more money to then travel over the sea and bash a few French bonces?

It's a wonderful system that has worked well for hundreds of years, since 1066, in England, and before that in Normandy and beyond, and it's extremely profitable and glorious... so long as you win your battles as England tends to on the field. Success is due predominantly to numbers. With a large army, a great many battles diminish into merely skirmishes, for if a grand show of strength and an aggressive willingness to fight is apparent, a good number of enemies yield well before the rivers and soil turns red.

Five thousand men is an enormous number to take abroad, and for this reason Buckingham has great expectations.

His preceding three years of hard toil were well invested. As a fifth (and youngest) son of King Edward III, he had always known that he would have to marry well in order to live as a wealthy man. When he married Eleanor his father granted him land from the Bohun estate that would yield around £600 per year, but all aristocrats know that to live well as an earl (what with all the accoutrements required to be seen as an earl) one needs income from their land to be over £1,000 per annum. When he was raised an earl at the coronation of Richard, he was awarded £1,000 per annum from the exchequer (to be paid from customs income from several of England's ports), but such an annuity is unreliable and this young Buck is routinely lucky to receive half of that. It is sadly true that Thomas of Woodstock, Earl of Buckingham, uncle to the king of England, and (by right of his wife) sole heir to the Bohun inheritance of £30,000 is currently, from year to year, struggling financially.

But he is careful. And he is just about solvent. And it is time he took the next step towards dukedom; this *chevauchée* to France. And during this expedition he would liaise with the disgruntled Duke of Brittany and together cause mayhem in Normandy, anarchy in Anjou, or any other havoc just so long as it causes France's old King Charles a merry pain in the arse.

Perhaps he will capture a port town. Boulogne, perhaps, or Honfleur. Or instead perhaps Rouen, that great inland citadel on the deep meandering Seine with its fifty-foot stone walls! Such gold and silver awaits those who are brave and honourable and God-fearing enough to go and claim it!

Whatever the spoils of war, he is obliged to declare them to his king upon his return. And in return, his king - the King's Council - will no doubt grant him more English land and with it perhaps another earldom. Or maybe an elevation to dukedom.

Or if his victory is total, and he routs his enemy thereby earning the right to settle on foreign soil, then he shall declare himself the duke of that location, and arrange for all the money made on that land to be collected into his own vaults. Of course he would send a few chests of gold and silver to England to maintain good family grace between an uncle and his nephew, and good political grace between an earl and his king.

May God bless me in my glorious hour!

Going to war, with 5,000 loyal foot soldiers and longbowmen, and several dozen knights on horse and in armour. Fighting with honour and pageantry and chivalry, knowing God is guiding you to earthly riches or everlasting heavenly glory.

There can be no other existence as honourable as this!

=====

SCENE. THE LESSER CHAMBER, WESTMINSTER PALACE – DAY

28th July 1380.

***King Richard**'s court is full of respectful men and women, who stand in clusters, and all of whom would petition Richard for some matter or other, if given the chance by the steward.*

*To Richard's right stands his second uncle, **Edmund, Earl of Cambridge**, a meek man but favoured by Richard as being wise in the ways of the kingdom and therefore worthy of consultation in a political arena where the King's incautious words could break the kingdom.*

***John of Gaunt** is Richard's eldest uncle, and stands with his head respectfully bowed before his king. Richard II is leaning forward on his throne, his elbow taking his weight on an* *armrest, his hand cupping half his jawline; a result of both intrigue and to relieve the discomfort and boredom of having heard many men speak to him today.*

KING RICHARD II
De Bohun. Remind us, Lancaster?

JOHN OF GAUNT,
DUKE OF LANCASTER
Mary de Bohun's living mother is of the FitzAlan family, and her maternal uncle is your esteemed Earl of Arundel.

KING RICHARD II
Yes! Arundel.

JOHN OF GAUNT,
DUKE OF LANCASTER
Mary's long-departed father, Humphrey, was descended from the mighty Longshanks himself.

KING RICHARD II
Worthy Plantagenet stock, indeed.

JOHN OF GAUNT,
DUKE OF LANCASTER
And therefore a perfect match for my own son and heir.

Edmund, Earl of Cambridge, leans in to whisper into Richard's ear.

Richard nods. Frowns. And sighs.

KING RICHARD II
We are told that the crown still has custody of much of the Bohun inheritance.

Gaunt glances without emotion at his younger brother, for just a little longer than he wished to.

JOHN OF GAUNT,
DUKE OF LANCASTER
That is correct, Sire.

KING RICHARD II
And we presume you are acknowledged of the value of said inheritance.

JOHN OF GAUNT,
DUKE OF LANCASTER
I am.

Richard turns to Edmund, Earl of Cambridge, who leans in for another whispered discussion. Richard's eyebrows raise.

KING RICHARD II
£30,000 is a great inheritance, my Lord.

Gaunt tightens his lips, and with much restraint remains elects a distinguished silence, in order to see where Richard is going with this.

KING RICHARD II (cont'd)
And is the Earl of Buckingham happy to share this fortune while he is bravely and gloriously representing his King abroad, we presume to wonder?

Ah, there it is. Edmund has ensured Richard has the most pertinent irritating fact. That his younger brother is already married to the eldest Bohun girl.

JOHN OF GAUNT,
DUKE OF LANCASTER
I would of course expect only a half share of the inheritance as dowry.

A union between young Henry and young Mary would prove strategically advantageous for our great kingdom, in that it would legitimately keep the Bohun inheritance exclusively within our own royal family.

KING RICHARD II
And yet we understand that in any case Buckingham would plan to deliver the child to a religious order, thus rendering her ineligible to marry, within or without our family.

And furthermore assuring Buckingham as the sole beneficiary.

(to Edmund)
Is this true?

Richard turns his head to his right shoulder, and Edmund the Earl of Cambridge bows his head with complicity and whispers in agreement.

JOHN OF GAUNT,
DUKE OF LANCASTER

My eldest son Henry of Bolingbroke is the heir of Lancaster, my Lords. He deserves a bride with all the stock and dowry that young Mary would bring.

My solution is just as legally secure as sending the girl to God's service, while at the same time wisely spreading the inheritance across two trusted uncles.

KING RICHARD II

As opposed to just one trusted uncle who isn't you?

JOHN OF GAUNT,
DUKE OF LANCASTER

(shakes head)

Eleanor is indeed married to our beloved and trusted lord of Buckingham.

But aligning Mary with my Henry would no doubt produce twice as many healthy boys, all with legitimate Plantagenet blood, to strengthen your own royal pedigree even all across Christendom.

Richard and Edmund consult one another again.

Gaunt suspects that Edmund harbours some ill-advised feelings of filial outrage towards the forthcoming halving of their absent brother's future inheritance.

Richard is nodding, and looks like he is being persuaded by today's favourite.

Eventually...

KING RICHARD II

I think not, Lancaster.

Buckingham secured the first daughter some years ago. He would quite reasonably expect to take receipt of the full amount, when the inheritance is released.

And especially since he has already taken steps to place Mary with a convent.

JOHN OF GAUNT, DUKE OF LANCASTER

But...

My lords...!

KING RICHARD II

Good day, my lord. This business is spent.

Gaunt glances around the court.

Those present are regarding him with subtle amusement.

If he stands here any longer, he will begin humiliating himself even more.

Finally...

JOHN OF GAUNT, DUKE OF LANCASTER

King Richard!

A fine word, that: business.

For I propose one more item, with the court's permission.

KING RICHARD II

Very well.

JOHN OF GAUNT, DUKE OF LANCASTER

I am... *ahhhem*... owed a not inconsiderable sum of three and one third thousand pounds, by the crown.

Richard tries to imagine what more than three thousand pounds of silver must physically look like.

KING RICHARD II

A debt unpaid that would be the ruin of most men. And yet you raise it as an afterthought?

JOHN OF GAUNT,
DUKE OF LANCASTER
I raise it as business.

This long-standing debt, Sire, was for long-past military services to the crown.

The Chancellor will find this noted in the Exchequer rolls. I forget the years.

KING RICHARD II
And you never requested payment, during these years.

JOHN OF GAUNT,
DUKE OF LANCASTER
As a loyal subject...

...and a man of means...

...I never troubled the exchequer for payment, no.

KING RICHARD II
But you now wish the debt settled.

JOHN OF GAUNT,
DUKE OF LANCASTER
(deep breath, then boldly)
My sovereign lord...

...I wish the debt struck off.

The court ripples with shocked murmurs.

KING RICHARD II
Struck off...?

(quickly works it out)
...In return for royal approval of the marriage of your Lancaster heir and the Bohun heiress.

JOHN OF GAUNT,
DUKE OF LANCASTER
A fair and worthy trade, Your Grace.

Richard is in whispered discussions again with Edmund, the Earl of Cambridge.

KING RICHARD II
Even though the Bohun inheritance is still held by the crown, and may not be released by the crown for many years, especially if this is contested by my uncle of Buckingham?

**JOHN OF GAUNT,
DUKE OF LANCASTER**
Yes, Your Grace.

The court bristles with the excitement of such a large sum being discussed, and the possibility of it being written off.

Suddenly, a new voice echoes out.

**EDMUND,
EARL OF CAMBRIDGE**
My Lord of Lancaster. There are some in this court who fancy you for a usurper.

**JOHN OF GAUNT,
DUKE OF LANCASTER**
(laughs)
Ahhh, the wisdom of brother Edmund, who has known me all his life, and yet still does not know me.

**EDMUND,
EARL OF CAMBRIDGE**
Then you deny in public that you covet the crown?

**JOHN OF GAUNT,
DUKE OF LANCASTER**
Dear brother, I already have one.

As is known by all, I acquired, by marriage, title to the crown of Castile which was taken illegally from the late father of my dear wife.

Richard is nodding almost imperceptibly. He knows this to be true.

**JOHN OF GAUNT,
DUKE OF LANCASTER (cont'd)**
(to King Richard)
Sire.

Before I begin any plans to claim the crown of Castile, I wish to ensure my son and heir is well placed as the representative of the House of Lancaster in my absence.

A well-arranged marriage at this juncture would encourage me to focus on faraway lands, and allow your favoured counsellors more freedom to continue their encouragement and guidance with regard to our Sovereign Lord's great and long continuing reign.

Another whispered discussion between Richard and Edmund. The two discuss this new matter at length. Edmund is becoming more frantic.

KING RICHARD II

This marriage is a key point in your efforts to strengthen our great family's roots, for the good of the kingdom of England that you leave behind.

**JOHN OF GAUNT,
DUKE OF LANCASTER**

You are most wise, King Richard.

Richard turns to Edmund again. Gaunt notes with a little pleasure that Edmund is definitely becoming agitated as the discussion continues, occasionally waving a hand to make his point, and turning a darker shade of crimson as he gradually allows a thirteen-year old king to have his way.

Richard is ready to make his proclamation.

KING RICHARD II

Then I do approve this marriage, and will authorise written confirmation forthwith.

**JOHN OF GAUNT,
DUKE OF LANCASTER**

(bows low)

My sovereign lord.

KING RICHARD II

But my dear cousin of Bolingbroke's good fortune in this matter, does significantly diminish my dear uncle's expectations in regard to the Bohun affair.

What thoughts have you toward the Earl of Buckingham becoming your son's brother-in-law?

JOHN OF GAUNT,
DUKE OF LANCASTER
(briefly searches for an answer)
With the grace of God, we each of us are responsible for the fortunes of our own glorious houses.

Thomas seeks his in France with Brittany. While I seek mine in places that are less reliant on France, or Brittany.

=====

-- INCREASINGLY SOURING FAMILIARITY --

29th August 1380.

Oh quiet, man, for the dear love of God!

Thomas of Woodstock, Earl of Buckingham, would frankly rather his twitchy little companion would rest for prayer, or for sleep, or even just for silent contemplation.

What turgid slop does pour from this little man's spout, and so incessant it is to the exclusion of all other more favourable sounds.

Yes it is raining, and yes the rain is warm, and yes when collected correctly it constitutes fresh safe water for his men and that's all very well and good. But, as so many thousands of Englishmen abroad have discovered for themselves, if it's raining, they'd really rather be at home and so they can be quiet in more familiar misery.

It wouldn't be quite so bad if there were battles to fight, but in six weeks this experience had become so unexciting that he'd tired of running his blade through whimpering French peasants for lack of the sport.

He might as well bash caged hens with a mace for all the fight these farmers could offer. His men liked to raid for food and women, of course, and that was good for morale. But it isn't what he came here for. He came here for adventure, fortune, and most of all to meet the army of the King of France on the field.

But the French king and his army are not engaging. Having landed and amassed in Calais and joined with Duke John IV of Brittany and his few hundred men in mid-July, they have together since meandered south and east by Arras, Clery, Rheims and Troyes with barely a few angry pitchforks to irritate them. Apparently the Duke of Burgundy, Philip the Bold, had massed when they'd strayed close to that great duchy which separates France to the east from the Holy Roman Empire beyond it, but Buckingham's heart wasn't in that direction. He'd travelled to fight France, not a well-respected region who, although allied to French this year, still squabble bitterly with France frequently and declare their love for England every bit as regularly.

Just as Brittany does, he thinks with another roll in the belly.

In any case Buckingham (as do other nobles) makes money from wool exports to Burgundy even when Burgundy are more aligned with France, never mind when they're more aligned with England. So he's glad they didn't show. He can imagine King Richard's wrath in having to explain to his nephew how he went to France, to assist in Brittany's difference, and ended up starting a war with an amicable Burgundian state who have always shown much willingness to pour silver into England's exchequer.

But while Burgundy is simply not interested in battle with England at this time, neither is the French establishment. As to why, Buckingham is at a loss. It's something Buckingham never considered before, but it takes two armies to have a battle. When there isn't an army to fight, a battle becomes merely 5,000 men standing in a field. What is pre-occupying the French so that they do not engage with their most feared enemy?

His once-presumed expedition glory is becoming naught but a worryingly expensive march through a rainy French summer.

And there goes another rolling in the belly.

So yet again he pitches camp. Here, because, why not.

Now Duke John is chittering about how they should head south and sweep round westwards below Paris, because the *encroyable* Maine countryside is apparently almost as beautiful as Brittany or Kent. Buckingham considers starting a war with Brittany just to enliven his own stagnating soul.

Only a shout from the ranks that a messenger from England is riding up stops his sobering thoughts.

The message, as indicated by its signet seal, is from his eldest brother, John of Gaunt, Duke of Lancaster.

Perhaps, thinks Buckingham, if at least this is good news about the Bohun inheritance then his spirits shall be lifted.

=====

-- KINGLY COGITATION --

31st July 1380.

All prayers done, the king prepares for his bed.

King Richard feels it is his duty to regularly contemplate the things he sees, and lately he considers one court event over all others.

He recently presided over a tricky matter, whereupon he approved a marriage that would benefit his eldest uncle, annoy his youngest uncle, was advised against by his middle uncle, and then accepted the original proposal in return for writing off a considerable debt.

And the fact that this still troubles him does suggest to him that perhaps some part of this process of royal wisdom is imperfect.

To owe such a debt to a man as noble as Lancaster may well be wrong, but as uncle Edmund, Earl of Cambridge, had indicated, the royal Exchequer, that department of anonymous clerks responsible for the accounting of the King's wealth, was not exactly full of silver or gold these days.

Then, to rule in favour of a new marriage was perfectly legally his prerogative to do. But to rule against poor Buckingham - and in his absence, too - seemed harsh, although still quite within the king's legal power to decide upon.

In principle, the thing that most irritates him on a nightly basis, is the greed of his uncles. Lancaster, for proposing the Mary/Henry alliance only when Buckingham was overseas. And Richard knows that when Buckingham returns, his greed and pride will no doubt cause him to fight with his brother - possibly even the King, too - at the loss of half of such a large inheritance. He has also since detected a grim quiet in his middle uncle, whereupon Richard has concluded that Edmund is now jealous of his other two brothers sharing in what he would see as significantly good fortune.

In the end, one thing had helped his own clarity. Bereft of any other stratagem to employ, he had tried to consider how he would have ruled if he was not so closely related to the three uncles who participated in this troubling episode.

And the more he contemplates what happened, the more he does suspect that in order to rule wisely under some such similar future circumstance, then perhaps he is best to altogether discourage his uncles from the participation in such decisions.

Perhaps he should entirely dismiss them from his council chambers, let them alone to run their own lands awhile, and in the meantime appoint trustworthy advisers who are not quite so closely tied by blood.

He should choose wisely.

Perhaps more vigorous men; men who understand what a court and a kingdom should really be. Men who would advise on how his own court might be as highly regarded as any other court in Christendom. Men whom Richard feels aren't constantly jostling to go to France and kill Christians in their desire for the accumulation of more money.

And anyway, apart from anything else, his uncles are so old, dull, and dreary.

Surely there must be some such way of ruling a kingdom, without leaving him with the misgivings that his traditional advisers are causing?

Lords closer to his own age, perhaps.

=====

-- ***CHATEAU DE BEAUTE, PRÈS DE PARIS*** --

Le 16 septembre 1380.

With white-gloved fingertips, they pinch an edge.

The cloth of gold is slowly drawn over the waxen face that lies in peace before them. Reverent placement complete, they return their hands to their sides, bow their heads, and retreat into the shadows of the warm room.

It is as it should be.

The boy to which the doctors, men, women, and servants now look to without actually looking at, is silent. He is sad, but he is in truth more scared than sad; a rising urge to panic is being quelled but it still takes all his restraint to maintain his own royal dignity.

The room seems inordinately full. And though he is surrounded by supporters and sycophants - he cares not which, for now - they stopped murmuring *vive le roi* some time ago. They await his own first wise majestic proclamation with respectful patience. For now, at least.

He takes this time to consider what he should do first as the new King of France. But the light-headedness that emerged when the old physician politely muttered that the time of his father is come, has not, as he had hoped, abated.

Instead something akin to a ferocious storm now roars silently inside his head, and his belly. These tempestuous internal displeasures are caused by the vague notion of too many responsibilities that do not conveniently align before him as might a group of soldiers awaiting their captain's order, but like intangible leaves in a great wind; each not remaining still enough to be given his royal consideration, but rushing off hither and thither among ten thousand others.

At last, one clear truth emerges from the tempest, and he meditates upon it in order to discern others that may steady and rally around this truth. His gaze has lately been attentioned on his father, but that distinctly wise man and undeniably successful king will not return from under his blanket.

This time is come.

Nothing is going to stop the crown from passing rightfully to this young approved head; a head strong with the passion and vitality of a young man who has for all his life been prepared to lead. A head that has been educated to be everything required to be a king. A head that seethes with rapidity, fills with invigoration, and mercifully finally begins to calm with a most agreeable clarity.

The lands across the north and down the west are still, after all these years, scattered with English lords who have come to regard their foreign soil as their own. But such comfort brings laxity. These lands are not of England, for England is an island. These lands are of France, and a strong king - even stronger than his stiffening father - is needed to unite those who would be French-born dukes of Burgundy and Brittany and Gascony and Normandy and wherever else into action and war.

His destiny is this.

He seeks the eye of the old king's - and now his - most senior adviser. He sucks air into the royal chest, and prays to God that when he speaks next his voice will resonate with all the depth and purpose required to cause confidence and obedience in the men he was born to lead.

His first words in his new guise will undoubtedly by reported across his country and beyond. So they must be meaningful and newsworthy such that all who listen will nod in approval and shine with pride.

"*Pour travailler, mes seigneurs, que nous puissions enfin débarrasser nos terres des Anglais,*" are fine first words, thinks **King Charles VI of France**.

To work, my lords, that we may finally rid our lands of Englishmen.

And the old men, the women, and the servants in that darkened room...

...they, all of them, bow their approval.

=====

-- BRITTANY'S REAPPRAISAL --

Le 24 septembre 1380.

To read in secrecy is challenging.

But now the rolled parchment has been read in private with success, **Duke John IV of Brittany** folds a crease into it and places it into his waxed leather saddlebag so that no others might read the words therein.

So. Old King Charles the Fifth is dead, and young King Charles the Sixth is now ascended to the French throne.

Two boys on two thrones; one in England, one in France. And both surrounded by some of the most vicious conniving barons in the civilised world.

This news means there is now a great argument for the reconsidering of this expedition with young Buckingham.

To continue this *chevauchée* with the naive and ineffective Lord Buckingham, and to continue upholding its sole objective - which let's face it has become after all these weeks to merely irritate the French court and nothing more - is alike to walking past a bear's cave while bashing a drum with a cudgel: it may yield more of nothing, or it may invite a swift and ignoble end that would in retrospect have surprised nobody.

Perhaps a more diplomatic approach towards France is in order. Perhaps an unsettled French court, with its new eleven-year old King Charles VI, may be more positively receptive to a friendly Breton approach as opposed to the continuation of irritations of this tedious campaign.

But such a delicate approach to France must be done in secrecy, and any bridges to be built will not be easy while Brittany plays host to a large English army.

So what, then, of Buckingham?

Pffff.

He is not responsible for all the fools in the world. Buckingham can go to hell or go to God.

=====

SCENE. RENNES, BRITANNY – DAY

Le 2 octobre 1380.

Thomas of Woodstock, the Earl of Buckingham, is concentrating on a crudely-drawn map.

Duke John IV of Brittany has his finger pressed on it very specifically.

THOMAS OF WOODSTOCK, EARL OF BUCKINGHAM

Nantes?

JOHN IV, DUKE OF BRITTANY

Mais oui.

THOMAS OF WOODSTOCK, EARL OF BUCKINGHAM

Isn't Nantes a Breton city?

JOHN IV, DUKE OF BRITTANY

Pffff.

The Montforts hold the city independently. They pay me no fealty, so now you pay them some attention, *non*?

Buckingham isn't sure.

JOHN IV, DUKE OF BRITTANY (cont'd)

My Lord of Buckingham, you know I am England's greatest ally!

Take your 5,000 men there and siege it! Camp outside the city walls and starve them until they give yield.

THOMAS OF WOODSTOCK, EARL OF BUCKINGHAM

You want me to besiege a Breton city?

<u>You're</u> a <u>Breton</u>!

JOHN IV, DUKE OF BRITTANY

In the name of accord. It would make Brittany a stronger ally to England.

And the Montforts are rich! They have much gold and silver with which to pay you a tribute so great that King Richard would revere your name.

You have five thousand men. More than enough!

Brittany nods his head eagerly, agreeing with himself.

THOMAS OF WOODSTOCK, EARL OF BUCKINGHAM

Over winter, though?

JOHN IV, DUKE OF BRITTANY

Pah! It is never so cold in France as it is in England.

THOMAS OF WOODSTOCK, EARL OF BUCKINGHAM

Nantes.

JOHN IV, DUKE OF BRITTANY

Glory!

THOMAS OF WOODSTOCK, EARL OF BUCKINGHAM

(smiles)

Glory.

The two men laugh. One less genuinely than the other.

JOHN IV, DUKE OF BRITTANY

You would return to King Richard a hero.

THOMAS OF WOODSTOCK, EARL OF BUCKINGHAM

I would.

JOHN IV, DUKE OF BRITTANY

Maybe make you a duke.

THOMAS OF WOODSTOCK, EARL OF BUCKINGHAM

Duke of Buckingham!

JOHN IV, DUKE OF BRITTANY

Sounds good, *non*? Even to a Breton ear!

THOMAS OF WOODSTOCK,
EARL OF BUCKINGHAM
No. I can't.

JOHN IV,
DUKE OF BRITTANY
Pourquoi?

THOMAS OF WOODSTOCK,
EARL OF BUCKINGHAM
Because I cannot afford to keep my army over winter.

JOHN IV,
DUKE OF BRITTANY
Aha! But you are King Richard's brave uncle *en chevauchée*!

Let us send our best messengers to the English court, and request more money!

=====

SCENE. PARLIAMENT, NORTHAMPTON – DAY

8th November 1380.

Simon Sudbury, Archbishop of Canterbury and Lord Chancellor of England, is addressing the gathered knights and gentlemen of the Commons.

SIMON SUDBURY,
ARCHBISHOP OF CANTERBURY
I speak, now, of an urgent matter regarding the King's exchequer.

Those in attendance murmur ominously.

SIR JOHN HONYBOURNE
He's spent the fifty thousand pounds of silver he taxed off us last year, has he?

Loud guffaws and howls from the gathering. Sudbury isn't fazed.

SIMON SUDBURY,
ARCHBISHOP OF CANTERBURY
(to the benches)
Sir John Honybourne speaks every bit as loosely as I would expect from a man who is lately better acquainted with his own blunt farm tools than the King's account rolls.

Whereas I recently noted some of the expenditures that His Royal Highness is expected to bear each and every year.

More ominous murmuring as the Archbishop Lord Chancellor unfurls a parchment roll to read from.

SIMON SUDBURY,
ARCHBISHOP OF CANTERBURY (cont'd)
The keeping of the peace in Ireland... £7,000 per annum.

The maintenance of the Scottish border... £4,000 per annum.

The ongoing occupation and upkeep of our garrisons at the barbican ports of Calais, Cherbourg and Brest... £35,000 per annum.

There's a great deal of muttering from the benches. Most men here aren't surprised at these numbers, but they are concerned as to why Sudbury is quoting them in parliament.

SIR JOHN HONYBOURNE
We all pay taxes to the King, and he takes levies on imports and exports.

The royal levy on wool exports alone is £40,000 per annum.

Where's <u>that</u> money?

SIMON SUDBURY,
ARCHBISHOP OF CANTERBURY
Sir, I petition this parliament for a reckoning not the cost of our King, but on the cost of our peace.

SIR JOHN HONYBOURNE

Aye, but I thought we paid our archers six pence a day, not six shillings.

Where's our return? Our silver is pouring away! I fancy there's a few fat fingers keeping the King's peace in this realm.

SIMON SUDBURY, ARCHBISHOP OF CANTERBURY

Sir JOHN! Only a fool would cast such treacherous aspersions in this honourable company.

SIR JOHN HONYBOURNE

Oh I meant no offence to this great assembly, I'm sure.

But, speakin' o' fools, you haven't read Buckingham off that sheet yet. I'm sure he's on there, awaiting a hearing.

SIMON SUDBURY, ARCHBISHOP OF CANTERBURY

Ah, well, indeed.

It would seem that our Lord Buckingham and his glorious expedition in Brittany will require a certain additional subsidy to keep them safe in the field over winter.

Howls from the benches.

SIMON SUDBURY, ARCHBISHOP OF CANTERBURY (cont'd)

Gentlemen, please!

My gracious lord, the Earl of Buckingham, does in the name of England's glory report an additional requirement of some £50,000.

Absolute pandemonium from the benches.

SIR JOHN HONYBOURNE

Saints' bones! Is Brittany charging him rent?

Guffaws from all but Sudbury, who maintains a sombre tone.

SIMON SUDBURY,
ARCHBISHOP OF CANTERBURY

It is, therefore, the King's command...

The benches go silent.

SIMON SUDBURY,
ARCHBISHOP OF CANTERBURY (cont'd)

That a personal tax...

Uproar from the benches.

SIMON SUDBURY,
ARCHBISHOP OF CANTERBURY (cont'd)

...of <u>twelve</u> pence per person-

SIR JOHN HONYBOURNE

Twelve pence!

Three groats, he says! A full shilling, he says! On top of all the other taxes we've paid recently!

SIMON SUDBURY,
ARCHBISHOP OF CANTERBURY

(insistent)

...be levied upon all subjects of England forthwith.

Those in parliament are outraged and their frustration and disorder is loud and passionate.

ANONYMOUS VOICE

(shouting over the uproar)

Let the Church pay a third of it, they own a third of England's land!

Parliament is a tumultuous commotion everyone is shouting, and the Archbishop of Canterbury is attempting to wave the noise into suppression.

Gradually, the noise diminishes to concerned muttered conversations all round. Honybourne is worried, and wants to speak.

SIR JOHN HONYBOURNE
My Lord Chancellor! Sir!

Parliament hushes with expectation as Sudbury concedes the floor to Honybourne.

SIR JOHN HONYBOURNE (cont'd)
This twelve pence tax. This three groats, if you will.

It shall be applied without prejudice to all men and women of England, great and humble?

I shall pay twelve pence, my blacksmith pays twelve pence, my seamstress pays twelve pence?

SIMON SUDBURY,
ARCHBISHOP OF CANTERBURY
Indeed. However we shall, with the greatest of charity, exempt those humblest among us who beg for their living.

SIR JOHN HONYBOURNE
(to the benches)
And thus, gentlemen, doth our King exempt himself!

Sudbury leaves the parliamentary chamber to jeers, guffaws, and riotous uproar.

=====

-- A WINTER'S TALE WITH LUSTRE LOST --

17th November 1380.

The first hard frost of the winter has come.

Thomas of Woodstock is an earl of Buckingham who yearns for things he doesn't have. His bed, his home, the smells of England, the sounds of England. English women. His wife.

One person he is not missing is Duke John of Brittany, that most irritating vole of a man whose submissive twerks and jerks, once considered elegant and birdlike, have now become to Buckingham with closer familiarity untrustworthy and rodentlike, and therefore quite repulsive, and it is something of a relief to

Buckingham that Brittany has had to leave the uneventful siege of Nantes for some reason of business.

What this unknown 'business' is for Brittany causes a dull ache in his own heart given that the respected old French king has died, and elevates a boy who, like Buckingham himself would, would wish to make some lasting mark of his own on this continent's history. Were Buckingham Brittany he too would want to at least meet the new king, though Buckingham has no evidence that this is the business that has caused Brittany to leave him in merciful peace awhile.

And so given what cannot be known is not worthy of the worry, Buckingham will continue to consider the walls of Nantes and it inhabitants. How to break the walls, and then what to do with the inhabitants, are both matters that he is still not altogether clear about.

The morning sun is presumably just over the horizon treetops - it is hard to tell through the thick grey clouds - and Buckingham stretches out of his tent and into the white world of Nantes' rural countryside, finds a fire to stand over, and beckons Sir Hugh Calveley closer on account of the fact that his most trusted knight and captain looks like he would burst open if he were not to relieve himself of this morning's camp news.

Words and numbers are muttered into the earl's young ear. The fire cracks and spits. Presently the earl nods in glum thanks, and he breathes in and deeply so the cold air hurts his nose before huffing the steam out towards the flames near his feet.

More men have deserted overnight, no doubt overwhelmed by the tedium of the autumn just gone, last night's frost, and the ferocity of winter to come. What was five thousand in the height of the summer is now less than four thousand, and this is long before the worst of the weather.

How odd it is, that men who go to war would rather face danger and death on the field than the safety and camaraderie of the wait.

=====

SCENE. THE KING'S CHAMBERS AT ELTHAM PALACE, KENT – DAY

2nd December 1380.

*The thirteen-year old **King Richard II** and his eldest uncle. **John of Gaunt**, the Duke of Lancaster are nearing the end of dinner, sitting in silence at a large heavy oak table.*

The young King bites into an apple with disinterest. Doesn't chew. Then tips back his head, aggressively spits the mouthful of fruit out on a high arc across the table in front of him, and insolently slams down the rest of the apple on the dark wood of the table.

Lancaster stops eating his spiced baked pear, regards the lump of apple flesh that came to rest on the table near him, and privately but visibly exercises patience before addressing the King.

JOHN OF GAUNT,
DUKE OF LANCASTER
Does the apple displease you, Sire?

Richard is troubled.

KING RICHARD II
If aught displeases us, it is not apples.

JOHN OF GAUNT,
DUKE OF LANCASTER
Then I will listen with interest, Your Highness, but pardon me if I continue to eat.

KING RICHARD II
When a lord truly offends a king, what is a king to do?

Gaunt stops eating and places his spoon down.

JOHN OF GAUNT,
DUKE OF LANCASTER
Have I offended you, Sir?

KING RICHARD II
Not you! Buckingham!

He left with great fanfare, promised stories of great victories none of which transpired...
...and he asks for more money to do more of the same nothing.

And old Sudbury took it to parliament.

In consideration that he has not fought any battles, won territories, or sent any tributes back to our court, I would

consider Buckingham to be negligent in
this matter, *non*?

**JOHN OF GAUNT,
DUKE OF LANCASTER**

Mmmm.

I'm not sure any promise of a return was actually made. Perhaps the raising of a tax, though, in this instance, is a little harsh.

Perhaps Buckingham should instead be urged to return?

KING RICHARD II

Perhaps. Are not our representatives already collecting, though?

**JOHN OF GAUNT,
DUKE OF LANCASTER**

You could recall them. This is the third or fourth such tax in only a few years, and such income raised has lately only been spent on the stabilising of England's defences against foreign invasion.

Many of your subjects see that as no return and thereby unacceptable!

KING RICHARD II

Perhaps.

Gaunt begins eating again, but Richard hasn't finished speaking. Gaunt's spoon almost reaches his mouth.

KING RICHARD II (cont'd)

What if Buckingham <u>had</u> committed some offence? What legal recourse would we have?

Gaunt concedes he will not eat his pear. Not warm, at least.

JOHN OF GAUNT,
DUKE OF LANCASTER

Would this undoubted suppositional offence be a grievous offence or a slight offence?

KING RICHARD II

Let's say a grievous offence. Perhaps treasonous.

JOHN OF GAUNT,
DUKE OF LANCASTER

Very well. In the case of a serious offence, a king might - in theory, mind you - petition parliament and serve upon the hapless lord of Buckingham an act of attainder.

KING RICHARD II

(commits word to memory)

Attainder.

JOHN OF GAUNT,
DUKE OF LANCASTER

It is a legal term, otherwise known as 'corruption of the blood'.

KING RICHARD II

(disgusted face)

What does <u>that</u> mean?

JOHN OF GAUNT,
DUKE OF LANCASTER

If a lord were so attainted, his blood is declared corrupted and he is deemed unfit to retain his noble status.

He might then, upon the King's command, be punished by the stripping of his title, his lands, and his property.

KING RICHARD II

Then what would a lord do?

JOHN OF GAUNT,
DUKE OF LANCASTER

Attainder is so terrible a punishment that it has yet to be used. But, I suppose he would rely on the charity of his family, or of believers in his name, if he is somehow fortunate enough to have not already shamed them into silence.

KING RICHARD II
Would you assist your brother financially if his blood was declared corrupt?

Gaunt ponders... then...

**JOHN OF GAUNT,
DUKE OF LANCASTER**
No.

KING RICHARD II
Then he would starve! A king might just as well command the execution of an errant lord.

**JOHN OF GAUNT,
DUKE OF LANCASTER**
Ha! We lords fear corruption of our blood more than we fear death.

KING RICHARD II
That makes no sense, uncle.

Gaunt considers how his lesson should continue.

**JOHN OF GAUNT,
DUKE OF LANCASTER**
An execution is merciful. The moment a lord's head is sliced off, God willing his soul goes to heaven and that is that.

And yes the axe gets rid of the man, of course. But declare their blood corrupt... that's one way a king gets real respect. Puts the fear of God into 'em, does that.

KING RICHARD II
I...

...do not understand.

**JOHN OF GAUNT,
DUKE OF LANCASTER**
These are complex legal matters, to be adjudged on an individual basis. But a king might declare an act of attainder to corrupt a nobleman's blood so badly that he is forbidden to pass on any of his titles, land, goods, or chattels.

KING RICHARD II
The sons cannot inherit from a lord so attainted?

**JOHN OF GAUNT,
DUKE OF LANCASTER**
Corrupted blood, you see.

In such a case, a baron's noble bloodline, cultivated since the beginning of history, would be ended.

This is a truly shocking thing for Richard to learn, and he takes a moment to understand fully.

KING RICHARD II
Although a merciful king may attaint a baron but still allow him to bequeath all he has to his sons, to continue his bloodline uncorrupted?

**JOHN OF GAUNT,
DUKE OF LANCASTER**
If the King wishes to show such mercy, yes.

KING RICHARD II
Perhaps, then, it is the threat of such corruption that keeps the barons subservient to their King?

**JOHN OF GAUNT,
DUKE OF LANCASTER**
In part, yes. Although a good king is strong, wise, just, and maintains the respect of the barons without the need for fear.

KING RICHARD II
Is there not, then, an implication that a nobleman's bloodline is worth more than his life?

JOHN OF GAUNT,
DUKE OF LANCASTER
Of course there is!

Any honourable nobleman would die for his sons if he knew with certainty that it would benefit his family and maintain or promote their noble bloodline.

This is too complex a concept for young Richard, and he is confused. So the Duke of Lancaster places his spoon on his pewter plate, and pushes his dessert away to give the King his full attention.

JOHN OF GAUNT,
DUKE OF LANCASTER (cont'd)
Consider this.

Why are you the king?

KING RICHARD II
Because we were crowned and anointed?

JOHN OF GAUNT,
DUKE OF LANCASTER
Hmmm. Put another way, then. Why did the barons make you king, but not me?

KING RICHARD II
We inherited the crown from our grandfather, albeit through our dear late father.

JOHN OF GAUNT,
DUKE OF LANCASTER
That is precisely what you did, young master.

The ability to bequeath and inherit from generation to generation is what makes a kingdom so glorious.

Now, the serfs, the farm workers, they haven't got much to bequeath nor inherit. No point in attainting a serf, nor troubling the axeman, for that matter. Just hang the commoners, if needs be.

But the nobility. They have land, and money, and property to leave to their children.

But more than that, they have their precious bloodline.

An act of attainder might not only do for the noble, it can do for their children an' all! And their children, and so forth, for eternity!

So if the King serves an act of attainder on a nobleman in full and without mercy, then that nobleman stands to lose his title, his possessions, and his income...

...and so do all his children.

KING RICHARD II

So being attainted, *in extremis*, disallows one from bequeathing all that one has lived and worked for, and all that one's ancestors have lived and worked for.

If we so attainted poor Buckingham, then we presume his land and possessions thereafter go to the crown?

JOHN OF GAUNT, DUKE OF LANCASTER

The King already owns England's land. You grant it to the lords who pay you rent and profits. A lord dies, his heirs inherit those lands... with the King's approval.

KING RICHARD II

But if a King attaints said lord, his heirs are not approved.

JOHN OF GAUNT, DUKE OF LANCASTER

Ha! Well said. In which case, the King decides who should benefit from poor Buckingham's attainder.

KING RICHARD II

But let us say that the King wants the estate for himself.

JOHN OF GAUNT, DUKE OF LANCASTER

Hmmm, tread with care, my lord. For why do you have an Earl of Buckingham in the first instance?

KING RICHARD II

To call upon when a war is required. An earl will call to arms his men from the land on which they work, and rally for his king.

JOHN OF GAUNT, DUKE OF LANCASTER

Indeed.

But you've mentioned two importances without rightly marking their greater meanings.

An earl does indeed manage men who in turn manage the land.

KING RICHARD II

(concentrating)

Men. And land.

Yes.

JOHN OF GAUNT, DUKE OF LANCASTER

A good earl knows his land well, and has in place several knights and sheriffs and mayors and lesser lords - these we call retainers - who are all well versed in making the most of the land in their counties, towns, manors, and villages.

Do you know where the Earl of Buckingham's land is?

KING RICHARD II

Ye-

-er...

...no.

JOHN OF GAUNT, DUKE OF LANCASTER

The Earl of Buckingham's land is, like all noblemen's, spread out in patches all over the kingdom.

You don't normally want any lord accumulating a huge single block of land, for that is how dangerous power is begun. Look at how much at odds the King of France is with Brittany and Burgundy and all them dukes. They all have large blocks of land.

KING RICHARD II

I know Buckingham's principal residence is at Pleshey in Essex.

JOHN OF GAUNT, DUKE OF LANCASTER

Very well. Do you know whether Essex is better suited to sheep and wool, or forestry, or growing crops?

KING RICHARD II

(frowns)

I do not.

JOHN OF GAUNT, DUKE OF LANCASTER

Nor I, for sure. But the Earl of Buckingham does.

The Earl of Buckingham knows what to do to make as much money off his land as possible.

And the more money he makes, the more money he gives you as a tribute to keep you happy enough to maybe grant him more land. Then the better off you are, and the better off the kingdom is, you see?

So if you attaint a lord, and prevent any sons inheriting the attainted lord, you'd be better for having the next capable man all right 'n ready to become the next Earl of Buckingham.

KING RICHARD II

But you do not explain why the king would not keep all attainted lands for himself.

JOHN OF GAUNT, DUKE OF LANCASTER

Well young master, you consider that too.

There are three very good reasons for not doing this.

In the first instance, inheritance is an ancient law, one of our oldest.

Your whole kingdom is built on land that is managed by men of noble birth, and the right to pass on that land to their heirs is what makes a family loyal to their king; their king being the sovereign lord who upholds the laws of the kingdom.

In the second instance, you must recall that the nobility is the nobility <u>because</u> of their noble <u>bloodlines</u>.

A nobleman may normally only marry a lady of quality, that is to say a lady with at least some blood connection to a noble or royal family. To marry a commoner would be to weaken the noble blood that we all hold so dear.

If every kingdom were to pursue that same policy, then at some point there would be no noble-blooded princesses for a king of England to marry. Eventually, the King's blood would become impure; no better than the commoners'.

And in the third instance, and this is perhaps most important of all, a king may not attaint a nobleman without just and legal cause. Not even a king may break the laws of a kingdom. For if he does, he risks causing anarchy in his kingdom from the very nobles who have sworn to protect and serve him.

KING RICHARD II

I thought a king might do whatever he so pleases.

JOHN OF GAUNT, DUKE OF LANCASTER

Did you.

A king rules his nobles. But only for as long as the nobles accept being ruled by their king.

KING RICHARD II

What if the nobles do not want a king?

JOHN OF GAUNT, DUKE OF LANCASTER

Oh we do. Because when we have a good strong king who rules fairly, the kingdom is secure, everyone is able to use their land fully for the provision of their products and services, and we all make lots of silver. It is the way of kingdoms. You'll see, with guidance.

KING RICHARD II

What makes a good strong king?

**JOHN OF GAUNT,
DUKE OF LANCASTER**
Knowing that is a lifetime apprenticeship, my Lord.

KING RICHARD II
Well, then, what if a king breaks the laws of the kingdom?

**JOHN OF GAUNT,
DUKE OF LANCASTER**
Any well-bred man might break a few minor laws, from time to time. We should not worry about this.

KING RICHARD II
What if a king breaks a great law?

**JOHN OF GAUNT,
DUKE OF LANCASTER**
Like serving an attainder on an earl, without just cause?

Richard is embarrassed that his true question has been read so easily, and looks down at the table. He briefly shrugs.

**JOHN OF GAUNT,
DUKE OF LANCASTER (cont'd)**
Such is tyranny, King Richard, and something none of us should ever have to consider.

They sit in silence awhile.

KING RICHARD II
I do not think I should serve an act of attainder on my uncle of Buckingham, after all.

**JOHN OF GAUNT,
DUKE OF LANCASTER**
Thought not.

=====

SCENE. THE FRENCH COURT AT THE HÔTEL SAINT-POL, PARIS – DAY

Le 17 decembre 1380.

***Philip, Duke of Burgundy**, and one-fourth of the French council of regency which has been appointed to conduct affairs of state on behalf of their eleven-year old **King Charles VI of France**, stands before the throne brandishing an intriguing crumpled parchment.*

KING CHARLES VI OF FRANCE
(leans forward)
Approche, mon oncle.

PHILIP,
DUKE OF BURGUNDY
A communication, Your Majesty, from the Duke of Brittany.

KING CHARLES VI OF FRANCE
(sits back)
Oh.

PHILIP,
DUKE OF BURGUNDY
He wishes to visit Paris and pay tribute to your Royal Majesty.

KING CHARLES VI OF FRANCE
Does this impertinent duke not still roam our lands causing havoc with Buckingham?

PHILIP,
DUKE OF BURGUNDY
Duke John insists herein that, as a mark of respect for the new King of France, he does bankrupt Buckingham's campaign with cunning and aforethought.

KING CHARLES VI OF FRANCE
Mon Dieu.

Outwitted by the Duke of Brittany.

Just how green must this Buckingham be?

=====

A.D. 1381

=====

-- A TALE OF INGLORIOUS TRUTHS --

13th January 1381.

He shivers with cold that will not leave him.

Thomas of Woodstock, Earl of Buckingham, does not want to see the Duke of Brittany ever again. Not unless he holds a sword at his neck, at least.

He has tired of watching Nantes' white walls, the dirty Loire river, and nothing else. He has tired of awaiting some kind of communication with Brittany. And he is weary at the news from London that in spite of the exchequer's request for taxed funds, the early signs are that tax collections in his homeland are not producing anything like the silver that previous poll taxes have done. It seems that an awful lot of commoners have recently apparently lost wives to the great pestilence, and yet when collectors enquire at the parish church there is no record of such an inordinate death rate. Treasonous rats, them all.

So that is that. He will run out of money to pay for this disastrous campaign within weeks.

And Duke John lied about the weather. It is every bit as cold here as it is in England. Apart from everything else, it is now snowing heavily.

The thoughts of returning to England with precisely nothing to show for a six-month expedition are not endearing. He must return and face the King, parliament, and worst of all his brother of Gaunt having won neither gain or glory. And furthermore, because of his absence and misplaced trust in his brother, if King Richard or his bloody serjeants-at-law ever release the Bohun Inheritance, he must share it with Gaunt's son Henry Bolingbroke.

Damn this expedition. Damn France. Damn Brittany. And damn Gaunt.

A raven caws without concern for his pitiful thoughts. He looks up as it looks down, sitting in a skeletal larch tree. Buckingham can see smoke from the raven's beak. It twitches its head in a way that reminds him of the errant Duke of Brittany.

Actually, damn himself for being so green.

Never again will he allow himself to be swayed by the promise of unseen treasures.

His own breath steams before him. It is pushed out from his lips, slows, then escapes towards the raven, quickly becoming nothing.

Upon his return there will be turmoil. It will cause discomfort for him, anger for some, and entertainment for others but, he supposes, then it will become nothing.

Everyone has one bad campaign, and many do not enjoy the luxury of returning upright, so that is something to build upon; a fine opportunity to become more learned in politics and ensure the employment of common sense to matters of court. As the youngest uncle to the King of England, he enjoys a level of privileges that almost no other man in England could even imagine, and this will not change after one bad campaign.

So he shall observe the goings on in the royal court. The way noblemen are. The way the King is. And he shall recognise the balance of court, and the balance of court when it tilts, one way or another. The court needs a man of balanced nature, to identify the imbalances caused by men who, like Lancaster and Brittany on this occasion, decide to tilt affairs in their favour like a scoundrel who plays with weighted dice. He shall be the balance for a tilting court.

He has embarrassed himself to those who have such understanding. But he shall thank God that he has an opportunity to redeem himself, and truly become the wise nobleman he presumed he was, but wasn't.

Perhaps these past few months have been God's way of making him wiser to the ways of some men in this world.

If so, then this damned expedition wasn't such a damned waste of his time, after all.

=====

-- A GLORIOUS PLANTAGENET WEDDING --

5th February 1381.

A bud yet to bloom has no less beauty.

Young Mary de Bohun is indeed a most virtuous heiress, and for **John of Gaunt**, it is a happy day. For his thirteen-year old son Henry of Bolingbroke, the Earl of Derby, it is a happy day. And for the twelve-year old Mary it is a happy day.

Not so happy is Eleanor, elder sister of Mary. For Eleanor, recently having become fourteen, is old enough to understand that she was the likely sole benefactor of her father's great inheritance; which was surely to have been released at some point to her own brave husband, Thomas of Woodstock and Earl of Buckingham, for them to live in great comfort until their time came to pass such great estate on to whatever issue they could raise.

But he is in France, and they are here in Essex at Rochford.

Gaunt's happy gaze meets another. The widow Lady Joan and mother of Eleanor and Mary, is also no doubt emboldened this day that, quite unusually, her second daughter has married better than did her first daughter.

While young Eleanor is wedded to old King Edward's youngest remaining son, the younger Mary is today wedded to the heir of old King Edward's oldest remaining son. And in doing so she has availed herself of being forced to enter the convent that Buckingham was leading her to. And indeed would have led her to if he hadn't so recklessly sallied off to France to support Brittany.

John of Gaunt is not a part of the King's Council because it is widely thought that he would influence King Richard badly and manipulate matters to grab Richard's crown for himself. What nonsense. However, others' fears pay well for Gaunt, and while he doesn't sit at the council's table, his seniority as the King's eldest uncle does open its door. His recent suggestion for his own noble son to marry Lady Joan's noble daughter was ruminated upon and then welcomed by a committee with one eye on protecting young Richard's green and vulnerable rule, and another on the next generation of royal blood.

Gaunt has no doubts that King Richard himself will marry well and endure because that is Gaunt's next intention, once his own son Henry is today well married. Gaunt is always looking for a wife for Richard, but to date none have emerged as suitable in all respects. And this worthy stratagem will wait until today's well worthy celebrations are done.

After today, whenever the Bohun inheritance is subsequently settled, it must be settled between Gaunt's brother and Gaunt's son. If his brother rages upon this move, as he will, then he should have pressed their sovereign lord and nephew to settle the inheritance quicker and that is that.

After wedding off Henry, and finding King Richard a wife, the realm will have better foundations than it had before.

After that, as God in his heart does surely truly know, Gaunt may begin to action his claim for the Spanish crown of Castile.

=====

SCENE. WESTMINSTER PALACE - DAY

30th April 1381.

***Thomas of Woodstock**, Earl of Buckingham, spots a familiar figure across the courtyard. It is his elder brother, **John of Gaunt** the Duke of Lancaster.*

The younger races toward the elder's back, but Gaunt swivels to meet Buckingham holding a stabbing knife up towards his brother. This, naturally, causes Buckingham to skid to a halt.

Even so, Buckingham is bold enough to lean in close with menace.

JOHN OF GAUNT,
DUKE OF LANCASTER
Well met, sir. How was France?

THOMAS OF WOODSTOCK,
EARL OF BUCKINGHAM
You are a scoundrel and a cheat!

JOHN OF GAUNT,
DUKE OF LANCASTER
Careful, brother.

THOMAS OF WOODSTOCK,
EARL OF BUCKINGHAM
That inheritance was all mine!

JOHN OF GAUNT,
DUKE OF LANCASTER
There was a spare daughter, and I had a spare son.

And now they're married.

When the Bohun inheritance is finally released, now both of our bloodlines benefit.

It is good for our bloodline and therefore it is good Plantagenet business.

Buckingham strongly grabs the duke's richly decorated heavy woollen houppelande at his chest.

THOMAS OF WOODSTOCK,
EARL OF BUCKINGHAM
I should-

JOHN OF GAUNT,
DUKE OF LANCASTER
(speaks with great and calm menace)
-I said careful, Thomas!

You are not exactly the King's favourite after your campaign. And the court is not well humoured lately with all the tax evasion goings on in the provinces these days.

So unhand this duke, learn some lessons, and be on your way.

Buckingham is seething, he really wants to hurt Lancaster. But he knows that a violent assault on a senior member of court would be yet another mistake, and he has determined to be more mature.

So he backs off a couple of steps in submission.

JOHN OF GAUNT,
DUKE OF LANCASTER
Good boy. Oh, and, my Lord Buckingham.

THOMAS OF WOODSTOCK,
EARL OF BUCKINGHAM
What?

JOHN OF GAUNT,
DUKE OF LANCASTER
Your tax is still being collected, even though you are no longer in France. So as well as spending £60,000 of the exchequer's money on a pointless expedition with no return...

...do not forget that you now also owe King Richard your twelve pence.

Buckingham is left on his own to try and gather his dignity.

=====

3: The Great Revolt

=====

SCENE. MAYDAY CELEBRATIONS IN KENT - DAY

1st May 1381.

In the background, several villagers dancing to enthusiastic music, and groups of men and women gather. They wear well-worn dull rags because they are workers of the fields. They have all been drinking their own locally-brewed ale, which is more reliable on the stomach than most water supplies.

***Wat Tyler**, a wiry-featured man of the land, is a charismatic member of the village. **Jack Miller** is a burly young man known well for his preference for using his fists long before employing his reasoning.*

The two men are casually observing their partying neighbours on the village green, but with a fair amount of disinterest.

JACK MILLER
They're back.

Tyler wipes ale from his lips, and nods.

WAT TYLER
Aye.

JACK MILLER
There's one has made his home-from-home at an inn on Watling Street. Who knows when he'll come a-visiting.

Tyler spits, and nods again.

JACK MILLER (cont'd)
(*suddenly stressed*)
<u>Wat</u>! <u>Three</u> <u>GROATS</u>! It takes the likes of us more than a week to earn that much.

I ha'n't got three groats to give to another tax collector! In fact I ha'n't got two, nor one.

Tyler swigs his ale, and grunts.

JACK MILLER (cont'd)
Walter!

WAT TYLER
None of us have!

JACK MILLER
Why should we give silver to the King's collector so the barons can go and bash the Frenchies?

It's <u>our</u> silver. What <u>we</u> earned. With <u>these</u>!

Miller is staring at his dirty calloused palms.

JACK MILLER (cont'd)
Walter. We need to...

WAT TYLER
We need to <u>what</u>?

If our Lord Jesus Christ and all his disciples walked into this village and asked for your last penny, what would you do?

JACK MILLER
Why- they'd have it, and with grace.

WAT TYLER
So while this ain't Jesus Christ doing the asking, it <u>is</u> the King of England.

Therefore, same as makes no difference.

The two men stare sadly at their surroundings for a while.

JACK MILLER
Well I don't reckon Jesus Christ nor the King his self would touch us workers for silver in the first instance.

WAT TYLER
Our king touched me for a groat last year, and three groats this!

And if that don't take yer fancy then take it up with the devil when you go to hell for not obeying your king.

JACK MILLER

Aye, but what if it weren't my king that I weren't obeying?

Tyler groans as he swigs.

JACK MILLER (cont'd)

No, hear this. How old is King Richard?

WAT TYLER

Fourteen?

JACK MILLER

And a king since ten. What does a boy know of being king?

I fancy it's not the king that's asking for silver, I fancy it's John o' Gaunt and those lordly oafs that guide him.

WAT TYLER

There's much fancying going on, around here.

JACK MILLER

I saw a cousin o' mine last Sunday, from over the meadows.

He heard there's a general accord among many in Essex that believe the King don't even know he has collectors collecting tax in his own divine name.

And if so...

WAT TYLER

Oh, here we go.

JACK MILLER

Wat, I tell you this.

If young King Richard hisself rode into our village and bid us, "Good day and where's my silver?", then I'd happily fling my purse at him from bended knee.

WAT TYLER

Uh-huh.

JACK MILLER

But what if there's a tax collector in our neighbourhood, collecting under the King's name, and yet not really under the King's name but under Gaunt's or Sudbury's name.

WAT TYLER

Impossible.

JACK MILLER

Whenever has a king before touched the land workers for this much silver, Wat?

I've asked as many old uns as I can find.

(*whispered desperation*)
<u>It's never been done before</u>.

WAT TYLER

Our days are indeed extraordinary, Jack. Before the great pestilence, who would have imagined the likes of us might choose the villages in which we work?

JACK MILLER

The Pestilence saw many of us off. Still does.

WAT TYLER

And yet that is why we, the lowest of the low, might today command an extra penny a day here and there.

JACK MILLER

Aye, but still pennies a month!

Do you think our beloved boy-king is counting on old Jack Gong's extra three groats to go to war? I doubt King Richard - may God bless his divine anointed soul - is altogether fully conversant with the economics of shit shovelling.

I put it to you; his divine highness has always taxed the lords because it's the lords what have always made the silver.

But these days, we're making a little extra coin, more so than we ever did. But it's the lords that are having to pay us, not the King. And they're still payin' their dues to the King as well.

So now it's the lords taking it off us, not the King.

Mark these words; it's Gaunt, or Sudbury, who's sending the collectors out.

WAT TYLER

Or perhaps it is God's intent that we work the land, for food and nothing more.

JACK MILLER

That's a minority view, my old friend, given God's late generosity in granting us a world in which we can earn more than we ever earned before.

WAT TYLER

But it's not for me or you to presume God's will. I have my opinion, let every man in Kent oppose me and see if I care.

JACK MILLER

I say join the majority, Wat.

For there is now a substantial number of working men, that stands for our dear King, against the tyranny of the barons.

WAT TYLER

What benefit is there in me, Wat Tyler, one man, a land worker, sharing a majority view?

JACK MILLER

We need a leader.

WAT TYLER

Ha, a leader indeed. How will leading a popular opinion enable us to learn who the masters of the tax collectors really are?

JACK MILLER

Oh, we'll find that out soon enough.

WAT TYLER

How?

JACK MILLER

We're gonna string one of 'em up and see whose song he sings.

=====

-- A TALE OF BUSINESS WELL MADE --

2nd May 1381.

John of Gaunt, the Duke of Lancaster, silently toasts himself with the smallest of sips of *aqua vitae*. The little bottles of liquid - brown, like ale, but still, and fiery strong - were a gift from one Nicholas of Lynn, well-known to Gaunt as a friar of the Order of the Brothers of the Blessed Mary of Carmel in Oxford. The Lancasters had been generous patrons to the Carmelite community for many years and Gaunt had followed Nicholas's progress with interest. It is good to have one so close to God on one's side, but not even Gaunt expected his friendship to bear such intoxicating fruits in this life. Rather serendipitously, it seems that his acquaintance is evidently experimenting in the production of some medicinal catholicon in between his spiritual duties. And, while it tastes like horse shit and honey, the satisfying burn and potency, and its ready inclination to induce a fair night's sleep, has become a private pre-bedtime pleasure for the greatest of all English dukes.

He is deserving of it because he has just hosted one of his greatest dinner parties. There have been quite a few of those, and the Lord knows Savoy Palace, located by the Thames between the city of London and the village of Westminster, is a perfect venue for entertainment and impression. But tonight he has fulfilled a pledge he once made to God.

He enjoys the fear that comes from negotiating terms of *bysinesse.* The drawing up of contracts to combine resources for the making of profit where none previously was before, it's a privilege that the common man cannot even conceive of. And this deal, well, this is the greatest of all.

When it was first learned that Wenzel, the young King of Bohemia, had written to King Richard's court, many unkindly presumed it was to request money for his famously impecunious exchequer or, more unkindly, for some charitable repayment of his infamous gambling debts. "*If the King o' France pays half, I'll pay t'other half,*" as court wags gaily repeated in any number of amusing situations.

But, as it turned out, Wenzel was not begging. He was offering. Anne, Princess of Bohemia, his sister and of age, is an extremely suitable pairing for young King Richard.

Wenzel's kingdom is not a great one. His late father, with numerous legitimate heirs, had with poor judgement split his territories into smaller independent realms - Bohemia, Moravia, Silesia, Lusatia, there were several - in a misguided attempt to give all his beloved offspring somewhere to rule. Wenzel's Bohemia had, it transpired, been too small to be economically viable, which is why that king invited such a disrespectful response by those well-versed in foreign relations.

But Wenzel's family, as a whole, is traditionally rich, well-placed to the north-east of the Holy Roman Empire, and most impressive of all, classes His Holiness the Pope Urban VI as a great family friend.

One of the problems with being geographically located at the north-western edge of the civilised world, as England is, is that it becomes difficult to maintain a relationship with the Pope when one must circumvent the kingdom's greatest enemy France to do so.

But with a Bohemian princess as Queen of England, not even the French would dare to interrupt eastbound messengers in the name of Anne of Bohemia.

England has recently negotiated strong treaties with Portugal to the west of France, Gaunt is married to Constanza of Castile and has a claim to the crown of that proud region also to the west of France, and now Gaunt has the opportunity to negotiate a great alliance with the Holy Roman Empire to the east of France.

And even more importantly, this is the first step towards buttressing Richard's position as king by having a son and heir.

Only one thing spoiled the evening as far as Gaunt is concerned. When the subject of the dowry was introduced, the Bohemian representatives - the Duke of Teschen and his envoys Peter de Wartemburg and Conrad Creyer - all smoothly suggested they discuss the terms at some other occasion.

A royal bride ought to come with a huge dowry payment. Perhaps Gaunt should have pressed them to commit, but the diplomatic cost of mismanaging this deal would be most irritating. This transaction demands prudent caution rather than carefree handling. For more important than all other things, is that King Richard begins producing royal heirs.

England's noblemen will all make more money with a well-founded family on the throne than they can with a little stripling that God's wind might blow away.

=====

SCENE. A PRIVATE CHAMBER, WESTMINSTER PALACE – NIGHT

10th May 1381.

***King Richard II** and his cousin **Henry Bolingbroke** (John of Gaunt's son and Earl of Derby) sit together at a table. Their tutor, Sir Simon Burley, is talking through an open ground floor window to somebody who is outside. The boys cautiously stop writing and continue a whispered conversation.*

KING RICHARD II
What is it like?

HENRY BOLINGBROKE,
EARL OF DERBY
(*shrugs*)
It's alright.

KING RICHARD II
Do you have to kiss her?

HENRY BOLINGBROKE,
EARL OF DERBY
Don't <u>have</u> to.

KING RICHARD II
But, do you?

HENRY BOLINGBROKE,
EARL OF DERBY
Father says I ought wait til she's older.

KING RICHARD II
How will you know when...?

...to kiss her?

HENRY BOLINGBROKE,
EARL OF DERBY
(*shrugs*)
When my father says, I suppose.

KING RICHARD II
Don't you have to tell her what to do, though? She's your wife.

HENRY BOLINGBROKE,
EARL OF DERBY
I haven't really seen her since the wedding.

Burley looks round mid-conversation. The boys slickly pretend to be separately contemplating their own writings. Burley resumes his unknown conversation.

KING RICHARD II
Your father says I am to marry.

HENRY BOLINGBROKE,
EARL OF DERBY
A princess of Bohemia. He told me before he went to Scotland.

KING RICHARD II
Will I have to kiss her?

HENRY BOLINGBROKE,
EARL OF DERBY
Suppose so.

KING RICHARD II
I mightn't want to.

HENRY BOLINGBROKE,
EARL OF DERBY
You have to. Kings definitely have to.

KING RICHARD II
Earls have to as well!

HENRY BOLINGBROKE,
EARL OF DERBY
I think earls can wait a while.

It's kings who have to straight away.

Richard looks like he may cry. Or vomit.

KING RICHARD II

Do you think she likes chess?

=====

SCENE. ROYAL COUNCIL, WESTMINSTER PALACE – NIGHT

31st May 1381.

The ***Lord Treasurer to the King, Robert Hales****, and* ***Lord Chancellor the Archbishop of Canterbury Simon Sudbury*** *are discussing the economics of the day.*

King Richard II *sits on a wooden throne that dwarfs him. He looks baffled.*

KING RICHARD II

They're not allowed to refuse to pay! Are they?

SIMON SUDBURY
LORD CHANCELLOR, THE ARCHBISHOP OF CANTERBURY

Your Highness, as trusted adviser to my king, I fear the latest tax may have proved to test the economy to a point of imbalance.

KING RICHARD II

But I give them laws to obey. Do they not have a duty to obey the laws I give them?

SIMON SUDBURY
LORD CHANCELLOR, THE ARCHBISHOP OF CANTERBURY

It helps to think of the commoners as beasts of burden, Sire.

One man may legitimately only plough one acre in one day, so to ask for two acres is an unreasonableness that not even a king can command.

Likewise, we would love to tax everyone a pound of silver, but not many have the means to fulfil this demand.

KING RICHARD II

But it isn't a pound, it's three groats, sir! A shilling. Twelve pence!

SIMON SUDBURY
LORD CHANCELLOR, THE ARCHBISHOP OF CANTERBURY

Sire, it is indeed my belief that many of the shoeless ruffians in your realm simply do not have three groats with which to pay your tax collector.

KING RICHARD II

Then I'll see the oafs run through!

SIR ROBERT HALES
LORD TREASURER

You may well, Your Grace. They'll be upon the walls of London presently.

KING RICHARD II

H- here? At London?

SIR ROBERT HALES
LORD TREASURER

I regret that a short time after payment of outstanding taxes was recently demanded by our honourable servant Mr Bampton, local men in Essex and Kent put down their tools, grew their support, and in rebellion now march upon our city for a hearing with the King.

KING RICHARD II

A hearing? With the King? The King cannot treat with cattle, my Lord!

YOU! Stop them! I command it in my name! In <u>our</u> name!

SIMON SUDBURY
LORD CHANCELLOR, THE ARCHBISHOP OF CANTERBURY

We have posted men-at-arms, of course, Sire.

SIR ROBERT HALES
LORD TREASURER
But many of the realm's knights are presently in the far north with the Duke of Lancaster.

KING RICHARD II
Will these local men-at-arms suffice?

SIMON SUDBURY
LORD CHANCELLOR, THE ARCHBISHOP OF CANTERBURY
My Liege, it is my pained duty to share with you certain intelligence. The rebels number perhaps five thousand.

KING RICHARD II
And our men-at-arms?

SIMON SUDBURY
LORD CHANCELLOR, THE ARCHBISHOP OF CANTERBURY
Alas. Perhaps the same five, albeit in hundreds.

Richard looks to Henry Bolingbroke. The two boys both have wide eyes.

KING RICHARD II
Then... what? Ten to the one?

Canterbury! What do we do?

Send for Lancaster, he will know!

SIMON SUDBURY
LORD CHANCELLOR, THE ARCHBISHOP OF CANTERBURY
We bide our time, Sire.

I have sent word to even up our numbers. Your uncle of Lancaster, included.

The rebels won't be here for a few days, so may I suggest we repair to the Tower and wait.

Only as a precaution, of course. There is every possibility the rabble will be too drunk to march much further.

=====

-- WILLIAM THE BAKER'S TALE --

13th June 1381.

The sun is setting after quite a day.

Unlike every other year before it, **William the baker** has not enjoyed 1381's Corpus Christi celebrations as a baker might. As a man who loves the colours paraded by the city's guilds, and their usual willingness to break bread on one of Christianity's most joyous occasions, William on this Thursday does hold the ecstasy of Christ in his heart, but dread for the city he loves.

On this day he expected to see a great many folk on Bread Street, pressing silver into palms in return for the morning's wares. But by evening his purse is nowhere near as full as it might be. And the unsold bread he carts to church is more in volume than he has donated to the poor than he can ever remember.

Three times was today's festival interrupted. The first shout that rang out through the streets of London, the most shocking, declared *London Bridge is open.* The people, normally boisterous in their revelling, had quieted as many men considered the effects of this news. They would know within minutes, as strange noises began to be heard from, it seemed, the rooftops. Many in Bread Street stopped and looked upwards to discern the source of the odd whooping. Having once visited the Tower's menagerie, William's first conclusion was that perhaps hundreds of apes had escaped, but there weren't hundreds of apes at the Tower. So not apes. In fact thousands of Kentishmen crossed the bridge northwards that day and, as if collectively privy to their cause, all had entered London then swarmed west. Some ruffians, presumably lost and by general accord by far the minority, careened up Bread Street in their dirty rags terrorising the people as they went with surprising actions unbecoming of Londoners. But soon they were gone, to rejoin the howls of the other intruders that were disappearing off in the direction of the city's west wall.

All in attendance did check their pockets, their purses and their partners. And the bakers checked their stalls for damages and missing produce. But all agreed that they had, somewhat oddly in retrospect, been left surprisingly untainted by the filthy madmen who had lurched their way through the crowd with their unknown agendas.

Not half an hour later, with merrymakers having dwindled due to that unexpected unpleasantness, did another shout go up from unseen dependable voices echoing over the city's roof gables. This time, *Ludgate is open.* William along with many others in attendance had quickly surmised this nearby gate in the west wall was the pressing destination of the commoner yawpers who had made an appearance earlier. Why they would exit the city so soon after entering wasn't clear at first, but presently the black smoke that appeared, climbing the air from outside the city walls, was a disquieting sign to add to the speculation.

For on Fleet Street and the Strand, those fine thoroughfares that followed the bend of the Thames' north bank west of Ludgate, the most respected residences of the Bishops of Exeter, Bath, Coventry, Llandaff and Worcester are built. As is John of Gaunt's Savoy Palace. He'll be glad he's in Scotland right now, someone said.

And then, even as the dark of the smoke steadfastly established itself over London's blue sky, another call had gone out. This time, *Aldgate is open.* This meant the Essexmen had breached the north-eastern city wall at their own first approach, and sure enough not quarter of an hour later more now-familiar shrieks did ring through the streets. What few Londoners had remained in Bread Street swiftly made their way home just as the grubby eastern farmers did ignominiously dance among the folks as they made their way to the fires that could by now be heard crackling their destructions amid the panic this instigates.

Again, to the relief of William and all the other bakers, the scurrilous peasants ignored the stalls in exchange for swifter arrival at their desired goal.

Delighted (and horrified) calls of *Savoy burns!* clang through London, but William is not unduly alarmed until *Free the gaols!* becomes a popular chant from the unwelcome newcomers. Upon leaving the city by Ludgate, and even before crossing the Fleet, one encounters those miserable institutions Fleet Prison and Newgate Gaol; home to malcontents of all kinds. William thinks with speed that while the debtors among the incarcerated may relish their freedom in peace, there were undoubtedly many violent undesirables who held grudges against those whom had contributed to their imprisonments.

So that is when he decided to pack up his stall cart and wheel it away back to his home on Cressingham Lane in London's Vintry neighbourhood, just a couple of hundred paces away down Bread Street, across Old Fish Street and thereafter down Cordwainer Street towards the river.

He'd deposit his remaining bread just before getting home, at the St James Garlickhithe, and morosely (given the distasteful behaviours of today and the portents for tomorrow) he parks his cart outside the church. Not his usual point of call for charity, but the St James was known for its well-attended Flemish laity and after the hate exhibited by the rustic Englishmen, William feels his charity is better served to the funny-speaking foreigners who, in spite of all their *acchs* and *gracchs*, had always passed the time of day with William with good grace whenever the two peoples had crossed paths in the lanes.

Now William the baker has stopped, he is aware that several well-to-do people, dressed in fineries that identify them as Flemish, are scurrying into church. And now he is aware of that, he then notices the downbeat praying and wailing coming from the church interior; evidently there are many frightened people in there right now.

And from behind him what at first sounds like fast-flowing water, and at second becomes like dozens, *no!*, hundreds, *no!*, thousands of *men!* He turns, instantly breathless, with eyes seeking anything extraordinary.

In fact ghostly shrieks of men, and of men's victims, are getting louder as they flow through London's skinny streets ahead of the unseen crowds that cause them. And suddenly the dullness of the terrible sound becomes sharp with clarity just after the first of the raucous crowd appears to William on both Cordwainer Street and Thames Street; two fronts running at speed toward him from left and right, howling at nothing, bouncing off house frontages, the countless charred ruddy angry faces at the front changing places with others with swift regularity.

The bloodlust of the men is undeniable, and fear affixes William to the dusty floor. The men act as one entity, like a river that has burst its banks, and they are upon William. The noises of anger and the pungency of dirty sweat and smoke are at him, and William's head swoons amid the darkness that arrives with the peasants. His knees shake and he grips his cart handles, shutting his eyes while hunching over towards the familiar scent of his leftover loaves as he awaits the first blow upon his body from the madmen.

But they have run past him as if he wasn't there.

He dares to look among the shouting around him. Men have entered the church, armed, sweaty and dirty, and the hideous sounds of Christian men, women and children who have never been so scared swoop up into the rafters and then fall pitifully upon all those in this vicinity.

Disgusting mortal attacks are happening, and never before has William heard such astonishing yelpings and screamings and shoutings and injuries.

Innocent men are dragged back out into the street, all urging for mercy with strong accents. Several Englishmen grab the wrists and ankles of their captives to render them prone on the floor. And other Englishmen reveal hand-axes. One captive who is face up to see and understand what will happen next speaks fastly now in tongues, one continuous unintelligible outpouring of pleadings or defiance - William cannot tell which - as an axe falls, hitting the mark well at the neck to briefly cause a puffed cloud of darkred and, upon the raising of the instrument reveals a blowhole in the open neck wound that briefly twitches and produces wind in accordance with the unspoken words the well-dressed Flemish merchant is still trying to speak even as his light leaves him.

All around William on the street, dozens and dozens of Flemish men are culled in this way until after some unknown time, he begins to comprehend that the incensed men are diminishing in number, taking their smells and noise with them.

Eventually, he is alone and remains untouched. Strewn on the bloody floor are headless men and menless heads, and a few sobbing wretches emerge from the church door; most acknowledge the scenes of depravity and fall to their knees in pure heartbreak. The sounds of London's normality return to William, and the first thing he notices is his own speedy breathing. The next thing he notices is the rising bile, and it hurts as he twists and pukes; the vomit misses his cart but covers a Flemish face which most unnaturally does not react as the open mouth fills with another man's belly contents.

William groans and returns upright.

As silence settles, a soot-covered sweaty peasant stands at his cart, inspecting blood-spattered loaves one-by-one with great care, and arranging those freshly tainted in red to elsewhere on the cart. Finally he finds one unblemished. He smiles, then fumbles inside his shirt, opens the purse that hangs around his neck and pulls out a tiny coin, offering it to William.

William nods with open mouth, untightens his fingers from the cart handles, and takes the silver.

The peasant roughly takes a bite from his loaf, then, running after the mob towards the city's darkening skies and the White Tower, he whoops, kicks a dead body, and lifts his hands high, one still gripping his loaf, as if relishing a victory.

=====

-- A TALE OF PRIESTLY CUNNING --

13th June 1381.

A stout shadow creeps on the battlements.

Grim-faced, he leans a shoulder against one of the thick stone merlons that form a perimeter around the roof of the White Tower of London. He slowly tilts his head around it and in so doing looks out through an embrasure, grips his crucifix, and reviews with no cheer whatsoever the cityscape beyond the moat below. There are likely few if any active archers among a rabble made of smiths, rivermen and farmers, but now in his sixty-sixth year what **Simon Sudbury, Archbishop of Canterbury**, lacks in vigour he makes up for with over-cautious guile.

The Tower of London is all-but impregnable, but after several days of living behind its walls, and with no sign yet of the Duke of Lancaster, the views it offers of the wanton carnage are discouraging.

Late evening and the far western hills still glow from God's sun, but more ominously orange is the city itself. From this view the glistening river to his left sweeps towards the sunset before arcing away left beyond sight. The old twenty-foot high Roman walls of this ancient city stretch across from his right side like a giant protective arm embracing and enclosing the degeneration of the city within. Pops and crackles of flames stab through the air clearly even from up here and, as he has now surmised, where there are not flickering flames there is yet smoke aplenty from dozens of the roofs of London's homes, shops, inns and even churches. Through the billowing, almost a mile away, the highest spire in Christendom is visible, and Sudbury prays with much dread and without much confidence that the heathens do not violate his most favourite building of all, St Paul's Cathedral.

Over a mile up river, beyond London Bridge and on the far bank of the Thames bend, a silent explosion engulfs John of Gaunt's Savoy Palace in amber and crimson sparks, giving life to considerable flames at about the same time that God's disapproving roar of Gaunt's loss reaches Sudbury.

The peasants are becoming ever bolder.

The hot weather and southerly wind ensure the smells of the river waft nonchalantly past the Tower, and he regularly holds the backs of silk-gloved fingers to his nose and mouth by way of defence against the sharply tainted air of human waste.

Men, murder, violence, looting, and burning churches. Is God revealing what hell would be like?

Screams from women, shouts of men, and occasionally numerous individual shrieks followed by a tense silence followed by a group cheer; the latter already a gruesome recognisable mob tradition for when known supporters of the royal government are found, arrested, and then summarily hanged by the neck or beheaded altogether.

The King's men, led by Lancaster, should have been here by now, but Heaven knows where they are. Certainly no intelligence has entered these age-old premises since they barred the gates after the King and his council were safely concealed behind the fifteen-foot thick stone walls. Such absolute safety is both deafening and blinding; how galling that any great castle's absolute refuge should be an enfeebling weakness as well as its greatest strength.

"For the King!" they shout from the smoky streets.

What nonsense. These drunken clods do not raze villages on their way to London for the King.

"For the King!" the rally ripples out away through the city; an indication that the unknown rebels that populate the unseen streets are many.

Aye, shout away and be damned.

"For the King!"

Such uncouthness sorrows the Archbishop greatly. No respect for rank or royalty have these peasants. His sweat-soaked jowls shudder as his distaste becomes too much to withstand.

"For the King!" they yell, merry with destruction.

Aye, and what would you do with him, you reckless lawless lot?

"For the King!" they still maintain.

He sighs. He knows the Tower should guarantee his safety, but he is nonetheless perturbed in the extreme. For should the mob breach their present sanctuary, they are too few within these Tower walls to quash such disorder, then all is lost, he would die violently, and this precious royal Plantagenet bloodline of mighty England would pass to the boy king's uncle of Lancaster.

Ahhhhh...

...he recoils from the White Tower's battlements as if touched.

Such God-given clarity!

For the King, indeed!

He quickly plots, this old man of Sudbury. He swiftly tests a stratagem, counter-stratagems, and potential dangers, all based on his experience of men. On the roof of the White Tower, and close to God, his whispers are his own, and finally his thoughts illuminate.

He shall send young Richard out, to speak to the rabble! The young king would believe, if told, that his subjects simply want to parley. But of course their blood is up and has been for weeks; the carnage they have wreaked in London's twisting streets means these are men who may be too far reached into the darkness of destruction that they would surely tear the youthful embodiment of the source of their angst to pieces.

The sacrifice of the boy to a mob in the shorter term, while in expectation of the arrival of that right experienced and worldly Duke of Lancaster and his royalist army soon after, would inevitably place a man upon the throne instead of the boy.

The boy is small. Not especially weak nor ill-hammered, but slight. No leader of men to battle is this boy, and with Richard under the crown England's profitable warring with France is like to be still postponed for several long impecunious years yet.

Whereas John of Gaunt, Duke of Lancaster, is a fully blooded warrior of proven stock, who will surely grasp the opportunity for a legitimate inheritance of England's crown and who will surely quickly bring the realm together and, strong and violent, re-assume a war with France that with their own boy king are ill-equipped to defend.

Gaunt! The man to rule a kingdom which needs a man to rule. And a man with an heir in the young lord Bolingbroke, to boot.

A man with every bit as much royal Plantagenet blood in his body as the little flax-haired stripling who quivers in the chapel below.

A man who would slash and gash and restore this Great Revolt back to its previous peaceable balance; less a few hundred Essex and Kentish heads of course, and then take us to unfathomable great victories and riches in France.

For the King, they say!

Aye, for the King.

And the King they will receive.

=====

SCENE. THE CHAPEL OF ST JOHN AT THE TOWER OF LONDON – DAY

14th June 1381.

To the distant background noises of thousands of menacing men, a much agitated 14-year old king is pleading with his advisers as he paces in great anxiety.

KING RICHARD II

I cannot leave! You must protect me! Sir Robert!

SIMON SUDBURY
LORD CHANCELLOR,
THE ARCHBISHOP OF CANTERBURY

My Lord King, our intelligence is thus: the men cry for their king and no more. Keeping you locked away behind these fine walls is like wood for their fire.

KING RICHARD II
They'll kill me!

SIR ROBERT HALES
LORD TREASURER
My King, you must trust in the archbishop, and trust in God. You are anointed, and therefore untouchable by the common man.

KING RICHARD II
(shaking)
But I do not wish to leave this sanctuary of ours.

SIMON SUDBURY
LORD CHANCELLOR,
THE ARCHBISHOP OF CANTERBURY
King Richard.

All kings must stand strong in the face of war.

But you are well to contemplate now, that usually a king faces some foreign enemy and therefore no respecter of his crown.

However, the men outside are <u>your</u> men. Englishmen one and all! They are <u>not</u> your enemy!

KING RICHARD II
Do not make me face them.

<u>Please</u>.

Have I not been raised above you all? I thus command you to disperse these villeins!

SIR ROBERT HALES
LORD TREASURER
Sire. The men simply wish their king to hear their demands. You shall do so.

King Richard II is shaking, but something in him is steeling him for the inevitable.

SIMON SUDBURY
LORD CHANCELLOR,
THE ARCHBISHOP OF CANTERBURY

For now, grant them their wishes, My Lord.

Your uncle of Lancaster is moving south from Scotland with numbers enough to effect a suitable subsequent revenge at the royal convenience.

SIR ROBERT HALES
LORD TREASURER

And so now is the time for bravery, Sire.

KING RICHARD II

Sirs, do you not see that I look upon you with terror unbecoming of a king.

SIMON SUDBURY
LORD CHANCELLOR,
THE ARCHBISHOP OF CANTERBURY

Au contraire, King Richard. You look upon us all with the courage of your royal ancestors.

Richard, through tears, considers his own trembling hands. He makes them into fists.

KING RICHARD II

Is... is this the same as they felt?

In battle...?

SIMON SUDBURY
LORD CHANCELLOR,
THE ARCHBISHOP OF CANTERBURY

Without any doubt.

All men and kings feel fear. Courage is the measure of their Godly faith during that fear.

Richard looks to Henry Bolingbroke. He feels embarrassed at expressing such emotion in front of his cousin. Bolingbroke shares the feeling and runs away, out of the chapel. The king breathes so his chest grows, and tightens his jaw. He knows that he may not run away.

KING RICHARD II

And there is no other way?

The men in attendance are quiet. Sudbury shakes his head a subtle amount, before bowing it in respect.

KING RICHARD II (cont'd)

Oh Lord. Oh Mary, Mother of God, be with me. May God be with us all.

=====

-- THE COMMONER WHO SAW THE KING --

A hush. Can what the whispers said be true?

Is my God-given king even now behind this iron-studded oaken gate before me? Richard, a boy, anointed. A crownéd king. A man-to-be whose name is already beloved by God Himself!

I can scarce hold my hand-axe for, what, fear? Ecstasy? I cannot tell which! Am I somehow closer to God because my king rides out to see me, or enraptured by the devil for the ills I have done to enable my attendance at this ominous episode?

Deliberate shouts of men and uncertain wooden thumps behind the Tower gate would indicate that King Richard II is indeed almost upon us.

I dare not look, and yet compelled am I to stare and Oh Lord he is there! A beautiful yellow-haired boy! And gasps abound round me and my kind. It is he! Our King, so young! Our sovereign lord in all his glowing majesty!

He is astride a white stallion and sits upright staring straight ahead. His chin struck proud, he slowly walks the magnificent beast forwards for a yard or two before haltering before our filthy lot.

I cannot breathe. I hear nought but the crackling of local fires behind me, while the kingly horse doth snort and nod and tip taps to ensure its footing during his own uncertainty.

I cannot speak. For what was in my chest now fills my throat with its pounding, but if I could hail, "Oh, for King Richard!", with all my breath I would.

The King, in full control of his mount, clops onward to us for another couple of yards, then stops. As does everything around me. I now behold his retinue, for behind His Grace are the Mayor of London in his golden chains and fineries, and several armed guards on horseback.

"Wat Tyler!" his royal highness shouts both lightly and strongly across our heads.

*I, **Geoffrey of Burntwood**, am not a welcome hand on this particular stage. And so I move. Shuffling into the man and men behind me. And they shuffle and move, as do those around them. Only slowly do we part. Like the Lord parted the sea for Moses, so we part for King Richard.*

And only when our parting becomes reliable, does our gracious boy-king walk on and through us. Beyond us.

When air returns to me, the purpose of our great uprising is thus further clarified.

King Richard has left the Tower to seek our tainted leaders and, now young Dickon is passed, our attentions turn to the stone walls before us.

And their gates.

The reason that prevented us from trespassing into the Tower and thus violating the King's peace has been removed.

The king is a boy, and misadvised by evil men. The same evil men who continue to tax the subjects of the kingdom who can afford it the least. The same evil men who are now left behind in the Tower.

The same evil men who, if any sense of purpose is to be gained from these last few weeks, must now die.

And now King Richard has clopped out of sight, this great English army of enlivened working men are left with muscle and fire, and brute will and desire, to compel those at the Tower gates who are sympathetic to our cause to open up and let us rid the realm of those who deserve their brutal end.

=====

-- THE FINAL TALE OF SIMON SUDBURY --

The shouting and the screaming will not stop!

Simon Sudbury, Lord Chancellor of England and Archbishop of Canterbury, does shiver and shake and shake and shiver, even though the warmth in his head feels numb.

Commoners are tainting the Tower grounds, thousands of them, and one or more of them will presently punch a blade into his body or swipe a hammer across his face.

He thinks they would not kill an archbishop, and yet all the same knows they will, and all he can think is that he doesn't want to die.

The chapel offers sanctuary. Can a man step into God's house with intent to murder? With intent to murder an ordained representative? He wants to believe that he will be safe, and yet knows these men are at this moment no true respecters of his own faith. He prays to God, Jesus, and Thomas Becket.

Now his end is come, his tears do not console him, for it was he who with deadly misunderstanding recently sent the only living person that could save him out beyond the walls.

The last he will see of this earth is a scowl of hatred in some stranger's eyes, and the last he'll feel in his privileged life is of barbarous steel punching into his flesh.

Oh God! Dear Lord!

His knees weaken at lethal shouts that abound unseen within the stone building, and he uses the altar as the means to lower himself carefully to the tiled floor of the chapel.

Is this really how it ends? Is this really what his long life was for? To wait in fear at God's altar as some anonymous death growls louder as it nears him.

If only he could... *aha!*

A thought! A plan! *A resolution to this...*

But the chapel door bursts in, and dirty-faced bloody-toothed snarling white-eyed men rush forth; instantly recognising him.

No! Too soon, Lord Jesus!

Praying hands now part and plead for mercy as the boldest of the intruder heathens approaches.

This is not the time! I have one more part to play, please God!

The arm is raised, the weapon comes down, and church bells ring so loud that he discovers he cannot hear his own screaming. Clubbed into submission, he is dragged out onto Tower Hill with bloody knees where an axe is ready.

He pleads to the men for peace and mercy.

He is granted neither.

It takes the drunken axeman eight chops to hack off his twitching head from his gurgling neck.

=====

Darkness means life, while out there is deadly.

He cries freely in silence, but must not to sob, lest he be heard, revealed, and murdered.

For hiding is the game that shall confirm his life or his death on this hateful vengeful evening; being a fourteen-year old innocent will surely not save him tonight.

Henry Bolingbroke, eldest son of John of Gaunt the Duke of Lancaster, sits cramped in the dark on his hands and knees in a cupboard space recently emptied with urgency by a generous soldier of the Tower so he could be secreted therein.

It's dark, dusty, scary, and the next clear sound he hears will probably be the opening of the door he hides behind. After that, if the inquisitor is unfamiliar to him, he'll have moments to live.

Voices are everywhere but in this blackened cubby-hole. The angry shouts of men, urgent orders from accents familiar, but also increasingly from accents unfamiliar. Terrifying death screams too, that make this boy in the pitch black space shiver like someone has just boxed his ears. The peasants number in the thousands and will no doubt win the evening's battle; he is of the other side, the landed gentry, the hated minority.

More than a few times have persons unknown clattered the stoic oak door in their various violent struggles, causing the boy within to jump like a startled rabbit before regaining his wits and control of his arms which, without thought, would push that door that conceals him. To release him. So he can breathe warm but deadly London air again.

His battle, as for most soldiers, is with his own fear. He desires to push the door and flee, but he assumes with more fear that would prove his undoing. And so the fear of feeling a long blade slicing his blood out marginally overpowers the fear of some assailant ceasing their bloody activities amid the urgency of battle to instead look with curiosity inside a closed cupboard door.

In such private battle does he spend his time until, a shock in its own, he realises that the shouts and altercations have all but stopped.

And in that moment does his breath now pant louder than before, although in truth he has not changed the way he breathes. His breathing noise fills the tiny chamber, and even in his breathlessness he postpones the breathing out occasionally in order to hear better what's beyond the wooden portal.

There are tired shouts aplenty, but none in this vicinity. His eyes are wide; the Tower has fallen already!

He considers his two options. Be still and be found, thus affording a certain surprise to the discoverer that he may not recover from sufficiently to hold his sword tip from thrusting into the unexpected little lord. Or reveal himself openly as the innocent he is, and trust the aggressors have sated their bloodlust in the face of the enemy, and in addition trust that they're too relieved to have won the day to trouble themselves with a young un that would happily leave them be to drink to their fortune.

The longer he tarries, the more suspicious this subterfuge is. Even aged fourteen he knows that in this life you have to face fear and stab it, or stare it down and hope to stab it some other day. Or else, greet God in Heaven with honour and glory.

He pulls opens the door, and takes with him his hope out into the shadows.

Henry Bolingbroke, Earl of Derby and heir to the Lancaster fortune, learns that blood-covered wood flooring is both sticky and slippery to walk upon.

And at the very moment he prays that cousin Richard will fare better, a door opens. Into the corridor, from a dark antechamber steps a large ruffian with wide shoulders.

And he's covered in blood.

=====

-- A YOUNG LORD MEETS THE COMMONER --

Geoffrey of Burntwood is first startled at the wretch but as his faculties are acute this night, recovers to appraise the situation as quick as is required of him.

It is not a wretch, but a fine clothed master, looking as terrified as one should under the circumstances. Geoffrey thinks for a second it is Richard, but it cannot be since he saw the young king vacate the Tower some time ago. And in any case this stripling does not brandish such golden hair as Richard is famed for.

Fighting the urge to bow to his better in spite of tonight's atrocities, Geoffrey instead considers what he ought do next. He notes the lad's big bowl eyes are now fixed on his hand axe. It is sticky with blood and hair and it shames Geoffrey for such innocence to see the result of such sin.

Other rough sounds from unknown origins close in. The firelight of torches lick at the walls at the end of the corridor. The elder steps to one side, to reveal the doorway from whence he entered this scene. He nods inwards to the younger, and the younger (less frightened of the dark room than the lights around the corner) scampers past Geoffrey.

Just in time. The torchlight men reach Geoffrey, words are swapped, and the men go on their way.

Geoffrey takes a last look into the room. The boy is unseen. And, upon thanking God for the opportunity to do some good in the midst of this anarchy, he continues looking for more of King Richard's councillors.

=====

SCENE. SMITHFIELD, A FIELD OUTSIDE LONDON'S WALL – DAY

15th June 1381.

The day after the looting of the Tower of London.

All here are on horseback.

***King Richard II** faces the leader of the uprising,* **Wat Tyler**. *Behind each of these men are several of their bodyguards. One of King Richard's advisers is the Mayor of London,* **William Wallworth**.

Richard is shaking within his armour, but he is determined not to show it. When he speaks, he speaks unsurely but carefully.

KING RICHARD II

You decapitated our Archbishop of Canterbury, nailed his mitre to his skull, and placed the head on a spike.

WAT TYLER

(frowns, then smiles)

Aye, brother Richard. But we leaned him back, so at least he can see heaven from 'is pole.

WILLIAM WALLWORTH,
MAYOR OF LONDON

Keep that tongue civil when you speak to your king, you unsavoury dog!

King Richard II raises his right hand to request peace from his mayor.

KING RICHARD II

Tyler.

Why are you still here at London's gates? Have we not already agreed to your charters, acceding your rights to better paid work?

WAT TYLER
Ha! We reckoned on enjoying town life a little.

Your ale tastes like piss, but the wine is sweet and London has the most beautiful women I ever saw. I'm not minded to return just yet, if you can appreciate that what I'm not saying.

WILLIAM WALLWORTH, MAYOR OF LONDON
Damn you, Tyler.

When your King requests that you take your leave-

WAT TYLER
-Aye, this here charter.

We thought of a few more things we'd like our virgin king to put his name to.

WILLIAM WALLWORTH, MAYOR OF LONDON
<u>Tyler</u>!

WAT TYLER
Tis thirsty work, my Lords. Got any of that Bordeaux stuff what I've heard you kings sup?

King Richard indicates to an esquire, to throw Tyler a small leather bag of wine.

KING RICHARD II
Mr Tyler, is there ought else we might serve you with?

WAT TYLER
Oh aye.

You see, the likes of me don't have much dealing wi' kings. Thus I'm minded to make the most o' such unprecedented access, like.

WILLIAM WALLWORTH,
MAYOR OF LONDON

I swear, you'll rot...

WAT TYLER

Our lives aren't worth a sad goat's fart, Your Royal Highness.

You wring us for a shilling so you and your lot can clank over to France for a few extra acres and share out a pot full o' French gold among yoursel's.

But us. We haven't got the shilling in the first instance. And we don't see a thing for it, except maybe our own blood an' that's often the last thing we see.

Do you know what it's like to have six pennies left in your pocket, and then have some snippersnapper in a cape come from London and demand off you all what you got as well as another six pennies what you ha'n't got?

KING RICHARD II

We accept that the tax was harsh, Sir.

WAT TYLER

HA! Harsh, he says!

I've known mothers who starved themselves to exhaustion so their children could eat what pitiful swill they share with pigs.

I've seen men cry with their women cus their sons have left home to find food in other counties. They never return.

I've heard babes crying in mangers cos they're hungry for even a scrap of food. Do you know how it feels when you finally realise you can't hear the babe anymore?

You failed us, King Richard, but king you are and king you shall remain.

KING RICHARD II

And so, Sir, how might a king serve a gentleman?

WAT TYLER

No more serfs.

KING RICHARD II

What?

WAT TYLER

No more serfs, tied to someone else's land.

No more barons. No more lords and masters. No more taxes for poor people. And a share of our own land, with no penny to pay for rent.

And better justice, and fairness for us commoners.

I propose a commonwealth, Sir, and all headed by a right royal King, in London, to make it all so.

KING RICHARD II

I cannot command a change to God's own plans for us all!

WAT TYLER

(indicates back to his army)

Then this lot...

(indicates towards London's wall)

...raze that lot...

...and afterwards we meet again to discuss terms once more.

Except next time you'll ought be wearing filthier rags than us!

Wallworth has had enough and rouses his horse to beyond King Richard.

WILLIAM WALLWORTH,
MAYOR OF LONDON
TYLER!

Foul and treasonous wretch!

Tyler, laughing, throws his wine away as Wallworth sidles up. Tyler pulls out his dagger and expertly plunges it into Wallworth's midriff, but with an unexpectedly unyielding soft thud. Time stops. The two men look at one another as Tyler pulls his knife away from the Mayor of London's hidden armour.

It's the last mortal decision he makes.

=====

-- AN ESSEXMAN AT SMITHFIELD --

He gasps along with the gasps of a thousand sweating men, and then silence sends pain, fear and anger across the field.

Wat Tyler, a fool to the end, has drunkenly reached out at London's Mayor, and the gentleman of the pair has produced a blade unseen from all his cloak and fineries and slipped it into Tyler's chest.

He falls!

An age passes as the mass of common folk will their leader to get up. Or even to move.

Tyler had fallen into a dusty old heap on his back, and some in the crowd with younger eyes now whisper *he breathes*, but that the cough spews up darkred is seen plainly across yellow sun-scorched meadow and over grey-brown weather-beaten old Wat.

At this, his own face heats up, and those with bow and arrows around him click otherwise silently into attack stances. He, **Geoffrey of Burntwood**, grips his hand-axe tightly, then loosely, then tightly again to check his own readiness.

He looks at his knuckles, all dirty, white and flecked with red, and despairs at the shaking in his arm. It's a quivering he's suffered since, as part of this mob, he has kicked, punched and chopped several odious men, richies and foreigners, into the dirt.

Odious they may have been, Christian they certainly were, and now on this field he faces not richies and foreigners but the King and his men and thus the killing of them would be treasonous. A hundred snakes slither and coil in his belly, as he readies to defend himself from whatever men King Richard sends over now.

The King!

He feels the hard dry ground drumming under his feet, and when he lifts his gaze his terror turns his legs and arms to twigs; once strong and reliable, they are now useless, for what he sees is not possible.

The ground is rumbling harder, the magnificent white courser is charging closer, and the dazzling rider shines like God, like Jesus Christ, like King Richard!

King Richard has ridden over and does address them himself, on his own!

This golden-haired king has a radiance and a presence that slows the royal beast, rears it upon its hindquarters, and then down again as it paces it to the left and to the right, each time he moves another sun from his armour blinds them all. In terror, and not knowing what else to do, they all of them fall to a knee before their king.

At first he dare not look anywhere but his foot and the ground. But seeing an axe in his fist, in the presence of the King, as the King continues to address him and all who kneel with him, feels treacherous and grim.

And so he must lift his face to see the anointed one. He can't breathe when he sees that King Richard the Second sits astride his tall gracious horse all but as close as his master would be in the fields back home.

And then, that right royal face looks down at him alone! The royal exalted eyes seek and keep his, and such dread does flood him that he is sure it would keep him on his knees for a lifetime. For in those sunlit eyes, is God. And in that clean-washed cherub face is Jesus Christ.

And in this moment, he knows that this boy, who through godly enchantment, has on this would-be battlefield instead commanded a rabble ten thousand strong into impotence, and does therefore sit in judgement upon them all.

Geoffrey joined this mob for the company of men, the enlivenment from dreary normality, and the deadly larks to be found by roaming the country with dirty lads all uplifted by their disobedience towards masters they left behind.

It was a worthy cause. At first. But a cause that quick became a murderous monster, even more unworthy than the monster they sought to repel.

And so by his own actions during these early long hot summer days, he has, before King and God both, for the sake of some sport, surely damned himself to hell.

Can anyone now save the worthless common souls on this field?

Perhaps only King Richard.

=====

SCENE. SMITHFIELD, A FIELD OUTSIDE LONDON'S WALL – DAY

***King Richard II**, resplendent in his silversteel armour on an impatient white horse, addresses the gathering.*

He shouts, which continually troubles his steed, but Richard's horsemanship is excellent, and the stallion is always pulled to obeisance.

KING RICHARD II

See me-!

Richard's voice falters, but only at the surprise realisation that all before him bend their knee to him and are completely silent. The realisation is enlivening, and he pulls his horse steady and begins again with the ecstasy of God in his blood.

His young voice now booms out with an utterly convincing regality.

KING RICHARD II (cont'd)

See me, and bend the knee, for I am Richard, King of England; your captain and your leader!

See this crown and bow if you, like me, believe in God, and rejoice that my anointing was, and is, His Divine Will!

See this boy before you, and readily yield to him if you do accept his place as your king in God's majestic realm!

For he is born of the Prince of Wales, who himself was born of King Edward the Third and anointed King of England long ago!

If you would stand against me and spill my royal blood, then I weep for your hellbound fates.

So instead disperse, and return to your own, this day, that I may greet each and all of you again in Heaven for our glorious eternity together!

=====

They went! And with them all their rage and bile!

They dispersed quickly, away to Kent or Essex or wherever their mud cottages stand.

His lords aplenty smiled and frothed with pride, and some with tears did state their everlasting troth for their own undoubted redoubtable boy who on this day became the greatest king who ever lived.

This boy.

This man.

This God-approved king.

"Hussah!" had they all sang to him, for the King, and for God, and for the realm, and for the fate of them and their sons. The Bishop of London had even taken him to one side, to question his most high-standing royal person in enquiry as to whether Lord Jesus or God had entered him while at Smithfield. His bemused answer had been, "*Perhaps,*" and the Bishop had wept in ecstasy.

The nobles are enlivened, for today their king stood strong, looked thousands of unruly subjects direct in the eye, and ruled them hard.

And the mob, they had relented. Why, he does not know. What makes a man march to London in rage, and face death from a lord's lance, and then quake when a boy on a horse shakes a sword?

The logic is clear, at the least. Common men really do quiver in the company of a King. Commoners, like cattle, are indeed bred to ultimately do the bidding of their betters. Even if a bull escapes a market in anger, it is quickly caught for lack of any stratagem other than that of its angry escape.

Today he has seen, for himself, that commoners are just as his advisers have said they are: oafish, ignorant, and drifting without the leadership of a superior. Lambs to the slaughter, whether that slaughter is on a battlefield or a farmfield. They are his inferiors, he is their superior. Cattle, sheep, oxen, peasants, gentlemen, lords; no difference.

King Richard considers his bravery in the saddle was perhaps in the moment encouraged by that part of his father's and grandfather's spirits he carries in his own Plantagenet blood.

So, why...?

So why does the King shake so now that he is back at the Tower alone? Why does he puke so often and temporarily relieve himself of terrors that subside with the ejection, but then return within the hour? A privy chamber thus has by royal command become a chamber of solitude, for Richard does not want anyone to see this weakness.

Tonight the lords have celebrated God's chosen vassal, as their hero. Will he, they have said, be known to the chroniclers of some forthcoming age as Richard The Great, as is Alexander known to them? What nonsense men spout when they drink wine after facing down anger, while the king they celebrate kneels in a dark chamber spitting sputum down a shit-hole.

He despises the cattle that walked all the way to London, caused his royal person to piss in his armour, and then made him suffer whatever palsy this puking sickness is.

If cattle strayed from the field, then the farmer would whip them back.

But these cattle caused murder and mayhem without and within London's walls.

King Richard II somehow found his ancestors' courage enough to encourage the rabble's dispersion at Smithfield, and the cowardly herds eagerly accepted the opportunity to return to their homes.

Their weakness shall be the judge of them.

You villeins, all, do not stand against your king, for if you stand and then disperse for home, a king is powerful and rich enough to burn your home before you return.

How dare they march to London. How dare they seek an audience with their king. How dare they speak to me like I was of the commons. They are beasts of burden that must be taught a lesson. Some difficult painful learning shall he prescribe.

He spits again.

He has loyal men who would manage a cull. And so, as many of the rebels as his retainers can find shall be executed for standing against their king.

The King's peace will be kept, and those identified as guilty shall be sent to hell, leaving behind men too frightened to break free of their paddocks ever again. And thus, will Richard's herd be tamed.

Villeins they are. And villeins they shall remain.

It is for the weal of the kingdom.

=====

SCENE. THE TOWER OF LONDON – NIGHT

20th June 1381.

A personal chamber, lit by candlelight, but still dark. ***King Richard II*** *and* ***William Wallworth the Mayor of London*** *sit in solemn silence.*

There's a KNOCK on the door, and the new ***Chief Justice of the King's Bench Robert Tresilian*** *enters, closes the door behind him, stands still and bows his head.*

KING RICHARD II

Tresilian. Our rebel subjects have caused lawless mayhem of late, and both London and our kingdom require retribution.

We are to Essex, presently. Come with us and rid us of some troublesome men.

Robert Tresilian, nods obediently.

ROBERT TRESILIAN

Do you have any names?

KING RICHARD II

Not yet.

Ask a few questions locally, whomever is named, they shall be executed.

ROBERT TRESILIAN

Visible punishments? In public?

KING RICHARD II

(nods)

We wish for our local insurgents a thoroughly restless and deadly period.

At this, Wallworth laughs and takes a sip of wine. Richard clearly revels in the favourable response.

KING RICHARD II (cont'd)

Together let us slaughter some of England's most odious cattle.

Robert Tresilian smiles.

=====

-- WILLIAM, AN ESSEX FIELDSMAN --

The laughing that flies across this Essex field, this furthest from the village centre of the three our village maintains, is all the break in concentration that I need to stop the swishing of my scythe on this hot summer afternoon.

But once I stop, I cannot see anyone in this field laughing, just people who are all now staring away to the verdant emerald line of hawthorn that obscures our view of our humble homesteads. Indeed none of the folk in the fields are laughing, and indeed some of those closer to our enclosure boundary are looking back in fear at me. Only when I see some of them drop their doings and run to the noise do I understand that those unseen are not laughing in our peaceful little village, they're screaming in it.

Our women are well-wrought by hard work, and it is normal that I presume a scream to be a laugh. But when the scream becomes a name, ***William****, I feel the devil punch my heart.*

With hell's bells in my head, I run to the cacophony, slowly at first across the wheat field and then faster past the patchwork of leek and pea plots while others run slower and I come to realise that their names are not still shouted.

But mine is, again and again. Along with Geoffrey! Geoffrey! Geoffrey! And there are no other Williams or Geoffreys in Burntwood but for me and my son.

My son!

My son, who was among a group who had not long gone with our field's latest bales to the granary barn!

Through the open field gate, I see a gathering of our people among our modest dwellings, as well as armed men, some on horses. My chest is burning from the air and my legs are burning from the running, and everyone who sees me changes their look from anger to fear.

As I close, and see King Richard's banner held by a horseman, then I know with another thump to my head why fear is visiting our community.

A young man is tied up, and roped behind a horse. My only son, dear Geoffrey.

I prayed and wailed when he ran away with the mob those few weeks ago, and I rejoiced and drank ale with him when he returned unharmed.

I hear nothing from the scene I am now a part of, although all around me is raucous. I see my boy shaking in fear, knowing as we all do what his fate is now, and I shake in fear too.

Our King has today come for him, and my foolish boy must pay his price.

Now on my knees, he is taken away. I pray and wail once more. And I know from this day onwards that I shall never rejoice again.

=====

To the Ryght Reverend William of Kereby,
Abbote of Leycestre Abbey,
firste day of August 1381

My Lord Abbote I wryte with gretest urgensie.

I wryte from thys sheymefulle county oppressed as it is by its owne sinnes! I beseeche yewe, cheynje youre plannes and do notte visit here thys sommer. For a devylle named Tresilian stalks our vyllagges in the name of oure sovereyn lorde Kyng Richard, assembling bloody assizes in grim payment for the part certayne foolishe men of englonde played in the Greate Revolte.

Nineteen hath he drawn and quartered yet in nearby Essex, and a further twelve has he hanged, many in the gloriouse presense of younge Kyng Richard so that seyd younge kynge can bear witnesse to our sheyme for hymself.

Trust in thys trewth, my dear friende, we do so hang our heads in greyte sorrowe which is thatte of oure owne makyng. We have synned ageynst oure Kyng, and we must bear the punishement.

I shall wryte ageyne, when oure greyte Kyng has deemed we have paid for oure unforgiveable belligerence ageynst the sovereyn Lord whom we love moste.

Pray, pray, pray for us.

May Godde in hys mercye bless and seyve us alle.

Youres respectfullye in Christe,
John of Ashby, Abbote, Croyland

=====

-- THE TALE OF THE PIOUS CONSTANZA --

5th August 1381.

Only once or twice each year is England warm like Spain.

The heat, which irritates the locals whether it is hot or whether it is not, today enlivens her not least because it reminds her of her childhood and such happy thoughts it seems bring her closer to the Lord.

Constanza the Duchess of Lancaster, kneels on the solid wood of her bedchamber floor and praises God above via the book of prayers before her on her bed.

Constanza knows she is well regarded by all for her devoted Faith. A keeper of all prayer times, she will not travel past a worthy shrine or church without stopping to pay her respects, and then never leaves without depositing at least a golden Noble coin with the senior clergy. She always hopes they'd spend the equivalent of a third of a pound of silver on the local villeins, but she'd never in her life (in Spain, France or England) encountered a parish in which the land workers have full bellies and the local church have no gold.

God will judge us all on our deeds.

After praying for King Richard, she prays for all good Christians in all God's lands, as she usually does. She prays that she and the Duke of Lancaster will together someday inherit the Castile crown that rightfully belongs to her. As she always does.

And then, as she always does, she prays in God's good name for the death of Katherine Swynford her husband's lover. And for the death of their bastard issue John Beaufort, Henry Beaufort and Thomas Beaufort. The ecstasy ripples inside her. May God damn Katherine Swynford and the Beaufort bastards to eternal hell. And may God damn the Spanish family who killed her father and stole the crown that belongs to her. May God send angels, saints and prophets to this world, to stand over those disgusting animals and righteously rip at their guts so their innards slop out and fall to the ground as surely as their souls would fall to Hell.

Her eyes, tightly shut, do now open to their limits and she gasps to find the air to reach inside her breast to bring her fully back to this world.

And as she always does she prays again, and this time for herself. She prays for the Lord to forgive her ghastly fantasies. She has immoveable faith that God will answer her prayers, and she is every bit as sure that God will forgive her and bless her soul for eternity.

There is a sharp, efficient, knock at her door.

She rises, crosses herself, and smoothes down her long dark hair.

Come in.

It is her husband's chamberlain. And when she smiles in recognition of him, he notes to himself, and not for the first time, that she is the most handsome pious woman he has ever seen.

=====

SCENE. BOHEMIAN PALACE, PRAGUE – DAY

12th August 1381.

***King Wenzel IV, King of Bohemia**, sits in a throne room with high-ceilinged walls that are decorated in a manner that is gaudy to English eyes.*

*A very capable finely-dressed **interpreter** who holds himself impeccably well stands on the floor at the foot of the throne's raised dais.*

*The Interpreter knows fine well he has just delivered devastating words to the English noblemen: **Simon Burley** and **Walter Skirlaw**.*

SIMON BURLEY

Please, sir. With all respect, what does His Majesty King Wenzel mean when he says, *ah*, "what dowry"?

The interpreter turns his chin to his shoulder and speaks German. King Wenzel speaks German in return. Then...

TRANSLATOR TO KING WENZEL IV

His Majesty does remind his guests that no dowry was promised.

Burley blinks a couple of times, then turns to Skirlaw. Neither speaks to the other. Burley addresses the throne again.

SIMON BURLEY

No dowry?

TRANSLATOR TO KING WENZEL IV

No dowry was negotiated, sirs.

King Wenzel barks something at the men, which is relayed by the translator.

TRANSLATOR TO KING WENZEL IV (cont'd)

A dowry is not mentioned in the contract.

So...

...no dowry is payable.

A very nervous Skirlaw leans towards Burley's ear and whispers. Burley nods eagerly.

SIMON BURLEY

Please kindly and respectfully inform His Majesty that in England it is the custom for a royal bride to make some payment of tribute to her new husband.

KING WENZEL IV

Ja, but in Bohemia, is custom to include dowry in contract.

=====

-- A DISENCHANTED KING --

10th October 1381.

The lord's mouth moves, but only for bleating.

He may just as well put a robe on a sheep, and let it *meh meh meh.*

And though this would undoubtedly prove more entertaining, **King Richard** accepts it as an impossibility. Heavy-hearted on his great and mighty chair and exclusively comfortable silk cushions, he looks around court and regards his great and mighty nobles who are not so great and mighty. The great and mighty nobles who do tell him every day that he needs a council to rule in his name, and yet who, on that terrifying day last June, jostled amongst themselves to hide behind him in the face of his frothing enemies.

Every long day do they *meh* at him from dawn until nightfall, and even thereafter. Court has become an eternity of tedium, so thank God for God and the solitude he can claim during his prayers to the Almighty.

He is tired of these decrepit old dodderers telling him what to do, and how to do it, and how when he is older he will, with the wise counsel they offered, be the greatest king who ever lived.

If they pay their service with their swords as they do with their lips then how did they ever succeed in battle, as they say they did?

Why would such brave men of battle who in court declare their solemn glorious chivalric ambitions to stand in battle by their warrior king, then tremble behind a boy on a field full of pitchforked commoners?

Not one of them rode to assist him as he presumed they would, when he rode to face his enemy. Not one of them shared his own faith in God or his trust in his courage at the moment he kicked his stallion in the ribs and silently called for the help of his Saviour. In that moment, his agitation presumed that his lords would ride with him. Not one of them joined him.

He hadn't considered it at the time, nor for some time afterwards. It is a kind of understanding that one only comprehends when one is reassessing the events in one's imagination some time later.

After puking and shaking that evening, Richard had awoken next day with an ecstasy of the victory, and thereafter similarly enlivened by the praise his closest tongues had spread onto him like honey. But when the humdrum business of the kingdom was returned to, Richard, bored, does so often now find himself pondering on the events of that hot and sunny day outside London's city wall.

Not one of these bleating imbeciles had ridden by his side.

This may not have been a full-force battle. They were negotiations marred by ale and temper. But even so when Tyler fell to the Mayor of London's eager *baselard*, all whom Richard had spoken to in the days and weeks since the occurrence had agreed that a grievous battle was shaping then and there.

And furthermore, one might well have presumed that those ten thousand unfriendly folk would have prevailed against the few dozen in the King's party.

Without Richard's courageous acts in the face of ruin, there would not now be a kingdom of England. His bravery had faced down a vicious unruly threat and saved them all.

Of course, no-one knows that their king still regularly awakes in the sweaty thudding dark, terrified by untrue dreams in which he is not victorious and in which he is instead cut and crushed and bashed to pieces by vicious men he will never know.

And just as he would tell no-one this truth, so he presumes no other man in court would similarly admit to their own night terrors. As his archbishop had said; courage is a measure of a man's faith. Well he has proven his faith, and he has concluded that the dedication of his life to God does hold a much fairer prospect than does a life of battle.

Aged fourteen, Richard has now seen hate on men's faces, and he was victorious over that hate with faithful dignity. But he had to succeed on his own. He decides in secrecy that he would not like to experience this feeling of lonely terror, ever again.

His old nobles would no doubt wail if they knew he isn't drawn to the battlefield with any delight, and so while he is bound by a committee who insist on telling him what to sign and when to say yes and no, he will keep his silence on the matter. And if he must replace the present old fools and surround himself with fresh faces who understand his desire to live long in peace rather than briefly in war...

...then this is precisely what this young king will do.

Perhaps if they'd shown their warrior teeth to the rebels at Smithfield, then their king would have more faith in their intent to fight with him in some faraway French affray.

No. He has felt his calling, and his calling is not, he perceives, soaked in foreign blood. He will instead reign over Christendom's most brilliant and greatest peaceful kingdom. And finally he laughs at the joy of such a stratagem...

...but mainly he laughs at the knowing of how difficult his senior noblemen will find adapting to peace with France.

=====

SCENE. KETTLETHORPE MANOR, LINCOLNSHIRE - DAY

14th November 1381.

John of Gaunt the Duke of Lancaster *speaks to Katherine Swynford, the mother of four of his illegitimate children: John, Henry, Thomas and the infant Joan. The children have all been given the family name Beaufort.*

Gaunt stands resolute facing a roaring fire in a large shabby room. Katherine sits on a simple wooden chair. She has tears flowing down her cheeks.

KATHERINE SWYNFORD

Because of Constanza?

JOHN OF GAUNT,
DUKE OF LANCASTER

No, my love.

KATHERINE SWYNFORD

Then, why?

JOHN OF GAUNT,
DUKE OF LANCASTER

The uprising caused me to think about myself. And us.

KATHERINE SWYNFORD

I shame you?

JOHN OF GAUNT,
DUKE OF LANCASTER

It's the commoners. They burned down Savoy. My greatest palace. And they called for my neck. If I'd have been there, I'd have been executed on the street. If you'd been there... with the children...

My young Henry barely escaped with his life, and he was in the White Tower.

KATHERINE SWYNFORD

That day was an extraordinary happening, My Lord. One that is not likely to occur again.

JOHN OF GAUNT, DUKE OF LANCASTER

And yet what happened proved to me two things.

One. The King is truly the only untouchable among us.

And two, I am not held in high regard.

KATHERINE SWYNFORD

Well God bless King Richard, but why must you cast me aside, so?

JOHN OF GAUNT, DUKE OF LANCASTER

I will provide. Money for you, and our children.

KATHERINE SWYNFORD

You are a man of great honour, sir. But this is my heart you cast aside and it was never for sale.

Gaunt walks to a window. It provides him no more solace and no less discomfort.

JOHN OF GAUNT, DUKE OF LANCASTER

I am to pursue my Spanish claim.

KATHERINE SWYNFORD

Very well. And so Constanza-

**JOHN OF GAUNT,
DUKE OF LANCASTER**
-is my lawful wife.

And Spain has always been my prize for marrying such convenience.

KATHERINE SWYNFORD
Everything you want is in here!

**JOHN OF GAUNT,
DUKE OF LANCASTER**
England has nothing more for me.

KATHERINE SWYNFORD
Me!

**JOHN OF GAUNT,
DUKE OF LANCASTER**
Katherine! If I continue this, us, I place you in mortal danger!

Richard's revenge on Tyler and his associates has created a disposition of great social morality among the people of the kingdom.

We must cease our couplings.

And so it is that I will use the opportunity to begin planning for that claim which I have always intended.

KATHERINE SWYNFORD
And what of Master John Beaufort? And what of Henry Beaufort? Thomas? Joan?

**JOHN OF GAUNT,
DUKE OF LANCASTER**
None of you will want. My attorneys have been instructed accordingly.

KATHERINE SWYNFORD
Even when you are King of Spain?

JOHN OF GAUNT,
DUKE OF LANCASTER
Even when I am King of Spain.

Katherine stares into the fireplace.

KATHERINE SWYNFORD
And so she becomes queen. And I become nobody.

Surely never before has any mistress fallen quite so far.

=====

4: England's Insolvency

=====

-- THE STORM THAT HERALDS A QUEEN --

18th December 1381.

The rain is so strong it all but turns afternoon to night.

John of Gaunt the Duke of Lancaster is glad of having such high a rank that he is offered shelter from the strong wind and icy rain that is pummelling Dover. The customs house is (like most others he's ever seen) a large long functional barn-like building that one must step up into through wide double doors at the most distant ends, and a series of open windows running along the heights of the long walls underneath the well-wrought well-overhung eaves.

Not used to having such a senior lord visit in person, this particular customs house is a thrive of activity, but Gaunt ignores the running around and the over-eager shouting of information knowing that these are undoubtedly usually lazy administrators all wishing to put on a worthy show of industry in the presence of the king's uncle.

Officious young men, *tide-waiters*, scurry onto ships to catalogue imports in order to bring the resulting parchment scrolls back to the customs house so that their superiors, *tide-surveyors* might approve their findings so that their import duty be calculated by a *comptroller* so that taxes can be paid so the goods can be unloaded and formally be passed into England.

The ships in the harbour wharves are six in number. Five cogs, their simple single mast construction with open deck and sheltered cabin at the stern are an average of 20 yards in length. Barely adequate for fine weather transportation, they are here still all fully-laden with cargo that is strapped tightly onto their low flat decks from Portugal, Galecia, Bordeaux, Calais, and Flanders.

The sixth ship, and first to berth, the first to be tallied, and the first to disembark is a twin-masted hulk of about 40 yards long which carries today's most precious cargo.

Anne of Bohemia, younger sister to King Wenzel and as yet unseen from her quarters in the hulk's sheltered poop, is arrived to become England's queen and Gaunt's niece-in-law. And now there are a small number of well-dressed women negotiating the gangway to the solidness of Dover dock stone, Gaunt feels fear in his gut.

This is not because of the way the large vessels are rising and falling with the angry swell to heights above most houses, or else he would have been feeling fear as the ships approached harbour in the diminishing sunlight of this filthy wintry afternoon. It's because this meeting - that he is to have in such short time now - is key to the success of King Richard's reign. The boy will still be a boy after today, and indeed so will he be after his marriage, but this alignment that has taken almost a year to arrange is necessary to eventually produce a son. That glorious day is far off, but even just for Anne's safe arrival will the kingdom settle just a little bit more.

The aggressive creaking of the oak behemoths are loud sounds over even the heavy winds. Such noises should not come from a ship and they terrify Gaunt, and God knows what they do to sailors in the middle of a tumultuous sea storm.

He decides to concentrate his attention instead on the dozen or so well-dressed men and women that are being herded respectfully away from their ship and towards the customs house, and even as Gaunt does so, the body shapes of the foreign visitors change, alerting Gaunt to a danger that he is not yet aware of. They flick looks of dread at the front ship, and in spite of their erstwhile demure ladylike demeanours begin to scream and shriek and run towards him, but from what? The wind and the rain?

Saints' bones!

Gaunt flinches a step backwards at the thunderous ungodly groan that passes like a wind of itself, too unworldly and inharmonious to be explained, and more terrifying for the mystery. *Thunder?*, but it continues and crescendos and is too near and too big to be thunder and, as it endures, other *spacks!* and *cricks!* rend through the air and breaking wood and men's screams are enveloped by a giant ghostly whale's deep roar that complements the unnatural yaw of the first great ship in the harbour. It leans as it shouldn't, as if an impossibly giant elephant or deer has been stuck and is being slowly felled by poison. Distinct and indistinct yells fly through the wind and away with the wind, and ugly crashing and breaking sounds signal the final seconds of a harbour disaster. As the thick timbers of Anne of Bohemia's vessel crack and sink, a bedraggled party reaches Gaunt, who ensures above all else that the soon-to-be Queen of England is safe.

All are weary, wet, cold, scared, but safe. Too shocked and shivery to speak, Anne herself seems eager to meet Gaunt with accord and assure him of her well-being. She is beautiful, with a cherubic face and clear blue eyes. Gaunt could gaze upon her for long, but must escort her out of here.

One last glance at the harbour. What's left of her ship - masts, timber, planks, sails - lean to and fro, battered and buffeted, in bits that thrust irregularly with the powerful waves. It is without doubt a portentous sign, sent to commemorate the arrival of England's next queen.

But a sign sent, Gaunt wonders, by God or by the devil?

=====

A.D. 1382

=====

SCENE. WESTMINSTER HALL – DAY

18th January 1382.

To great fanfare, King Richard II presents Anne of Bohemia to parliament and he guides her through the crowd towards their raised thrones at the end of the room. All in attendance strain to get a clear view of this truly beautiful young woman.

Two senior lords, ***John of Gaunt the Duke of Lancaster*** *and* ***Richard FitzAlan the Earl of Arundel*** *are part of the admiring throng and chat discreetly.*

RICHARD FITZALAN,
EARL OF ARUNDEL
Such a tiny scrap, is she!

Gaunt nods approvingly.

RICHARD FITZALAN,
EARL OF ARUNDEL (cont'd)
I was a guest at Warwick once, when a dog found its way into a pantry overnight. It ate about two pounds of liver mortrews.

JOHN OF GAUNT,
DUKE OF LANCASTER
(smiles)
A hound with a rich tongue.

RICHARD FITZALAN,
EARL OF ARUNDEL
We found it next morning, among all its shit and vomit. Wagging its tail while shaking like a fool.

I note the same demeanour for our king.

JOHN OF GAUNT,
DUKE OF LANCASTER
(slight shake of head)
Unfortunately her accounts aren't quite so pleasing to regard as she is.

Arundel raises his eyebrows and looks to Lancaster for more information.

**RICHARD FITZALAN,
EARL OF ARUNDEL**
What was the dowry?

**JOHN OF GAUNT,
DUKE OF LANCASTER**
What dowry?

**RICHARD FITZALAN,
EARL OF ARUNDEL**
God's nails.

**JOHN OF GAUNT,
DUKE OF LANCASTER**
That's not the half of it.

England's newest great acquaintance, King Wenzel of Bohemia, sent her over with a polite request for a £12,000 loan.

**RICHARD FITZALAN,
EARL OF ARUNDEL**
TWELVE...?

...what do we do?

**JOHN OF GAUNT,
DUKE OF LANCASTER**
If we don't lend, it would appear as if we can't afford it.

**RICHARD FITZALAN,
EARL OF ARUNDEL**
Can we afford it?

**JOHN OF GAUNT,
DUKE OF LANCASTER**
No.

**RICHARD FITZALAN,
EARL OF ARUNDEL**
(resigned)
So we must lend it.

**JOHN OF GAUNT,
DUKE OF LANCASTER**
(*nodding*)
I'll be alerting the richies for funds. You may have an audience with Anne in return for a gold purse.

**RICHARD FITZALAN,
EARL OF ARUNDEL**
Good lord. Well, be sure to ask Brembre.

**JOHN OF GAUNT,
DUKE OF LANCASTER**
(*chuckles*)
He suggested you.

The crowd in Westminster Hall cheers as Richard and Anne reach their thrones, turn to the masses, and acknowledge the goodwill of all with regal waves.

**RICHARD FITZALAN,
EARL OF ARUNDEL**
What does Richard know?

**JOHN OF GAUNT,
DUKE OF LANCASTER**
Nothing, until I appraise him next week, well after the marriage.

I don't want him worrying about debt on his wedding night.

Richard and Anne keep sharing what appear to be genuinely happy looks. Richard in particular looks like he already idolises her.

**RICHARD FITZALAN,
EARL OF ARUNDEL**
I would venture that there's no chance of that.

=====

-- A KING DAYDREAMS --

21st April 1382.

Oh sirs, you bore us, so.

We must laugh and dance and pray and rejoice for all to see, but the private thoughts of a king are so much more complex than one who hasn't been anointed might behold. For all the rank and privileges, a young king is trapped in more dark-panelled palace rooms like this one here and now than any other young man.

This council of ours, made of men, lords and priests, is constructed by wisdom and well-meaning, no doubt, but what is the efficacy of a council who must by England's own laws render itself silent upon one word from the boy at the end of the table? For how many... two? or five hours? or more might they truly deliberate with great intensity on some constitutional fox, only for us to sigh loud, whereby the tabled discussion would cease for the fear of some lord that he would cease living by the blade of an axe if he does not cease talking.

Some days do I try, and God knows that I do. But some days the sun shines and the blossom smells sweet, and lads arching arrows into straw are heard which are most alluring sounds to a boy instead hearing money and laws and such things that we think of the arrows and tire of this room and these men. How we tire of these scrolls and these laws of the realm. How we yearn to associate more with those fashionable court peacocks who are well versed in silks, furs and velvets. The dullards in here are so much less enlightening to a young man with money and attentive friends who share an appreciation of beautiful things above this ink on a roll.

To hell with our uncles who have forgotten how to be young and full of life, although, not hell, for as dull as they are they are at least no traitors to the crown. We mischievously wailed of late, "Is there somewhere God might send them that is not quite so severe as Hell or Purgatory," "France?" *said de Vere, and we had laughed until we cried and hurt from the laughter.*

A smile, now, at the recalling.

Perhaps we might commission a private story by old Chaucer in which John of Gaunt suffers from some irritable malady with farts and pains and which concludes with the devil clambering from out of his arse, desperate to leave, being no longer able to live in such an rotten abominable old grot-hole. Oh, the imagining of it!

Our unexpected laughing is enough to - Oh Lord, no, not again - render the King's Council into obedient attentive expectant silent submission.

From whatever it was they were talking about.

=====

-- THE IMPECUNIOUS KINGDOM --

1st October 1382.

The boy king has his council, but it is interesting to **John of Gaunt** that, whenever something serious is afoot, Robert Braybrooke is always sure to call on him even if he is far from London and spending time at his favoured residence at Kenilworth.

Gaunt is excluded from the inner council in favour of men deemed to have a more objective interest in King Richard's wellbeing. And a man such as Braybrooke, Bishop of London and Lord Chancellor of the realm, is better placed than any other in England to have an opinion on the accounts of the kingdom. Unfortunately Braybrooke's opinion is grim.

It is well known among those highest in court that there are several challenges to England.

The first is, the Queen Anne is still not yet with child after nine months of marriage. Braybrooke asks Gaunt if he knows of any concerning impediment that might scupper a royal pregnancy but Gaunt, understanding the real question, is almost certain that while Richard is easily flattered, he does not share his bed with his male friends; not at least to the exclusion of his young wife.

The second challenge to England is that the alliance with Bohemia after the wedding has not progressed as hoped. King Wenzel has a well-established family, and together if not solely there is a great family fortune and the means to gather allies. It was thought that Wenzel might assist England in matters of political geography. Calais, England's great and strategically-advantageous port, is located at the north-east of mainland France, and further east of Calais lies the friendly region of Flanders. Well over a hundred leagues south of Flanders is the often-friendly landlocked region of Burgundy. However Burgundy is ruled by Duke Philip the Bold - how the Burgundians love their epithets - who is the uncle of King Charles the Sixth of France and one of the four regent dukes who together rule France on behalf of their own boy king. This France-Burgundy closeness is a worrying state of affairs, and it was hoped that King Wenzel of Bohemia, from his location another hundred leagues east of Burgundy might provide the resources to gather friendly armies to at least trouble Burgundy against aligning too closely with France. However, as both Gaunt and Braybrooke are aware, Wenzel, irritating in his inactivity, is proving to have not the slightest inclination to travel anywhere beyond his tiny realm, and nor has he indicated he would rally any kind of Bohemian army to stand on behalf of England. Although neither the kingdom of France nor the Duchy of Burgundy is presently overtly unfriendly, it is worrying that the senior Burgundy is one of the regent rulers of France. All wise men cautiously accept that being so close to a crown can cause greed and wrath in a man, and such dangerous unpredictability is unsettling to England's barons.

The third challenge to England is that recently the Flemish towns of Bruges, Ghent and Ypres had quarrelled among themselves over certain domestic administrative decisions that began with, of all things, the building of a trade-advantageous canal connecting the river Lys with Ghent. The other large trade towns of that region had protested, and something of a local war had emerged. This esteemed region still imported many tons of England's particularly high quality wool and so English sheep farming and Flemish weaving industries were in rude health, but according to sources the French - and in particular Duke Philip of Burgundy were showing a greater keenness in stepping in to restore peace on the behalf of the great Flemish cities' elders who were led by a certain Count Louis of Mâle and who was, it was thought, a wealthy recipient of French funding and who had incidentally agreed to build that damned canal in the first instance.

Braybrooke asks Gaunt if he considers French-Burgundian interest in the occupation of Flanders to be of concern. Gaunt responds that yes, this activity is of great concern, because should a French-Burgundian alliance control Flanders then the huge wool imports could no longer be relied upon. The risk to England's economy is astonishingly large, for with any such trade restriction England's continued fortunes would diminish alarmingly quickly.

This is where a strong, wealthy and numerous ally beyond all this nonsense would be advantageous to England. That is, Bohemia, who might have provided an army of the east with the muscle to gather east of that region to discourage any future French movement into Flanders.

So. Braybrooke urgently summarises his conversation with Gaunt.

Item 1. There is no sign of an heir to strengthen Richard's crown and England's good standing in the known civilised world.

Item 2. There is civil disorder and much uncertainty from one of England's major importers; that great economic ally, Flanders.

Item 3. There is a potential France-Burgundy alliance that looks increasingly interested in invading Flanders.

And item 4. There is a total failure of King Wenzel to provide men in numbers in support of England to discourage a France and Burgundy alliance.

Gaunt scratches his head. Each item in isolation is enough of a threat to perturb a great duke. Together, they are as like the heat of the midday sun on a gunpowder barrel.

There is only one traditional proven and necessary response, and Gaunt offers it to his friend now...

=====

SCENE. KENILWORTH CASTLE – DAY

1st October 1382.

*At Kenilworth Castle, **John of Gaunt** continues his illuminating discussion with **Robert Braybrooke, the Bishop of London and Lord Chancellor of England**.*

JOHN OF GAUNT,
DUKE OF LANCASTER
So we muster, and go to war. To Flanders, to stand against French invasion.

BISHOP ROBERT BRAYBROOKE,
LORD CHANCELLOR OF ENGLAND
No! That's what I'm here to tell you. We can't afford to send even a thousand men.

England has no money left!

King Richard spends money as if he has a silver mine that will never run dry, and gives land away to impress his young friends, who are then not experienced or skilled enough to make as much taxable money for the exchequer from their good fortune as they ought.

JOHN OF GAUNT,
DUKE OF LANCASTER
What is the purpose of this council of yours, if not to guide Richard away from such extravagances?

BISHOP ROBERT BRAYBROOKE,
LORD CHANCELLOR OF ENGLAND
Sir, Richard often uses his personal signet seal to make purchases the council would not ratify.

JOHN OF GAUNT,
DUKE OF LANCASTER
You toothless old fools!

Do you know how much we make from our wool exports...? We must arm, and go to support Flanders!

BISHOP ROBERT BRAYBROOKE,
LORD CHANCELLOR OF ENGLAND

How, my Lord?

JOHN OF GAUNT,
DUKE OF LANCASTER

If there is no money in the royal exchequer, then we must petition parliament for a tax to fund th-

And finally, John of Gaunt understands the peril that England faces.

BISHOP ROBERT BRAYBROOKE,
LORD CHANCELLOR OF ENGLAND

You see?

Do you really think we can send the tax collectors out to the King's subjects again, after what happened last year?

=====

A.D. 1383

=====

SCENE. WESTMINSTER – NIGHT

18th June 1383

A world-weary ***Thomas de Beauchamp, the Earl of Warwick****, is sitting on a bench located against a tapestry-covered wall in a corridor at Westminster Palace. He looks overheated, troubled, and tired.*

Thomas of Woodstock, the Earl of Buckingham*, was on an errand but stops to see if the old earl is well.*

THOMAS OF WOODSTOCK,
EARL OF BUCKINGHAM
My Lord Warwick, are you well?

Warwick looks up, recognises the young man with respect, shakes his head, and offers up the scrolled parchment he holds in his left hand.

THOMAS DE BEAUCHAMP,
EARL OF WARWICK
Oh, it may be nothing. Or it may be something.

Buckingham opens the parchment as he sits down next to Warwick.

THOMAS OF WOODSTOCK,
EARL OF BUCKINGHAM
Would you summarise?

THOMAS DE BEAUCHAMP,
EARL OF WARWICK
A much-respected contact suggests that our king will, shortly, demote our esteemed Lord Chancellor.

THOMAS OF WOODSTOCK,
EARL OF BUCKINGHAM
Braybrooke, out? Is he still nagging at Richard about going to Flanders?

THOMAS DE BEAUCHAMP,
EARL OF WARWICK
Constantly. But Richard won't go.

THOMAS OF WOODSTOCK,
EARL OF BUCKINGHAM
If Wenzel would march with his family...

...the whole of Bohemia on one side, England on the other!

THOMAS DE BEAUCHAMP,
EARL OF WARWICK
Wenzel won't. And England cannot afford to war. And more worrying, that is a conclusion that France will be fast approaching.

THOMAS OF WOODSTOCK,
EARL OF BUCKINGHAM
Oh why doesn't Richard call a tax and let us go to war in God's glory?

THOMAS DE BEAUCHAMP,
EARL OF WARWICK
<u>Another</u> tax?

(pause)

If you want to war, then you'll have to finance it yourself.

Buckingham contemplates the floor.

THOMAS DE BEAUCHAMP,
EARL OF WARWICK (cont'd)
It's not just that. They also disagree about the inability of Richard to live of his own.

THOMAS OF WOODSTOCK,
EARL OF BUCKINGHAM
(pulls a face)
Richard doesn't seem to understand the concept of spending less than one's income. Can't the Royal Council curtail his expenditure?

THOMAS DE BEAUCHAMP,
EARL OF WARWICK

Richard has all but dissolved his council.

Our young sovereign lord is becoming a young man. He insists he can spend as he wants and, of course, the honourable Braybrooke, in his wisdom, doesn't.

It seems that's enough for Richard to rid himself of his advisers, these days.

THOMAS OF WOODSTOCK,
EARL OF BUCKINGHAM

So who replaces Braybrooke?

THOMAS DE BEAUCHAMP,
EARL OF WARWICK

I can scarce believe it, but...

...Michael de la Pole.

Buckingham knows the name but can't place it.

THOMAS DE BEAUCHAMP,
EARL OF WARWICK (cont'd)

Of the Yorkshire wool merchant de la Poles.

THOMAS OF WOODSTOCK,
EARL OF BUCKINGHAM

(nods, puzzled)

Not a spiritual lord, then?

THOMAS DE BEAUCHAMP,
EARL OF WARWICK

He is but a knight banneret.

THOMAS OF WOODSTOCK,
EARL OF BUCKINGHAM

A low estate Lord Chancellor, indeed. Odd times.

THOMAS DE BEAUCHAMP,
EARL OF WARWICK

But that is still not yet all.

I worry that our dear King is lately taken with Robert de Vere, and with old Suffolk's demise last year, I hear it spoken that Richard wants to elevate, if not de la Pole, then de Vere to Earl of Suffolk.

THOMAS OF WOODSTOCK, EARL OF BUCKINGHAM

With all grants of land?

Warwick pulls a face to indicate that this is as he understands the matter.

THOMAS OF WOODSTOCK, EARL OF BUCKINGHAM (cont'd)

Are you sure? Neither is worth such favour. And I miss out again.

THOMAS DE BEAUCHAMP, EARL OF WARWICK

I fear that Richard does grant many unworthy royal favours in return for whispered sweet nothings.

THOMAS OF WOODSTOCK, EARL OF BUCKINGHAM

Damn it. How many times must I say this: Richard needs his uncles close to him, so we can guide him more intimately and more wisely.

THOMAS DE BEAUCHAMP, EARL OF WARWICK

Our sovereign Lord has already petitioned several nobles privately regarding de Vere and others, claiming old Edward the Third favoured men on occasion and so therefore would he.

THOMAS OF WOODSTOCK, EARL OF BUCKINGHAM

Indeed. But old Edward favoured those who earned his favour first.

THOMAS DE BEAUCHAMP,
EARL OF WARWICK
And king's favourites are usually far better born than either Pole or Vere.

Oh, it has come to naught for now. But keep an eye on those court peacocks, young Buckingham. I fancy there's trouble there.

I would not be surprised to learn that Richard is making subtle plans for our kingdom.

=====

SCENE. THE FRENCH COURT AT THE HÔTEL SAINT-POL, PARIS – DAY

Le 25 juin 1383.

*The fourteen-year old **King Charles VI of France** receives **Philip, the Duke of Burgundy**, to the royal presence. Burgundy represents one of the adult members of the French council of regency which has been appointed to advise their young king during his minority.*

KING CHARLES VI
OF FRANCE
We have noted that England are yet to rise in force against us in support of the Flanders affair.

PHILIP,
DUKE OF BURGUNDY
I must concede, I expected more. Something.

KING CHARLES VI
OF FRANCE
Why would England not come to the aid of Flanders? The trade between the two is considerable.

PHILIP,
DUKE OF BURGUNDY
Your Majesty it is thought perhaps that King Richard and his council would rather fund an expedition to Castile for Gaunt.

KING CHARLES VI
OF FRANCE
A chess move to flank our own great realm.

PHILIP,
DUKE OF BURGUNDY
Others contend that England's exchequer is being mismanaged by Richard's councillors. England is almost bankrupt, so some say.

KING CHARLES VI
OF FRANCE
Ah that is more pleasing! When this Flanders affair is done, perhaps we can invade England?

PHILIP,
DUKE OF BURGUNDY
Mon Dieu, non!

KING CHARLES VI
OF FRANCE
Why not?

PHILIP,
DUKE OF BURGUNDY
To invade...

...the cost is prohibitive, Sire.

KING CHARLES VI
OF FRANCE
And the cost of keeping order in Ghent, Bruges and Ypres?

PHILIP,
DUKE OF BURGUNDY
High. But once the rebellions are quelled we might tax those great cities for ourselves. You can profit from England's exports as they come into Flanders.

KING CHARLES VI
OF FRANCE
They will export somewhere else, *non*?

PHILIP,
DUKE OF BURGUNDY
They could. But nowhere as cheaply as from Dover through Calais and into Flanders. Even with the additional taxes you might impose.

KING CHARLES VI
OF FRANCE
So when may we invade England?

PHILIP,
DUKE OF BURGUNDY
My lord. It may be many years before-

KING CHARLES VI
OF FRANCE
YEARS?

NON!

PHILIP,
DUKE OF BURGUNDY
Your Majesty, much has already been spent on the Flanders campaign.

KING CHARLES VI
OF FRANCE
We spend much on suppressing a skirmish that is not even in France! Are we imbeciles?

PHILIP,
DUKE OF BURGUNDY
No...!

KING CHARLES VI
OF FRANCE
Ah. Of course.

My beloved uncle of Burgundy. How is your wife?

PHILIP,
DUKE OF BURGUNDY
She... is well, thank you.

KING CHARLES VI
OF FRANCE
And how is her father, the Count of Flanders?

PHILIP,
DUKE OF BURGUNDY
Ailing, in truth.

KING CHARLES VI
OF FRANCE
Isn't it opportune that you have a nephew on the throne of France, whom you have persuaded to send an army of Frenchmen and appease the land of your birthright...

...just before you inherit?

=====

-- ENGLAND'S FUTURE IS DISCLOSED --

6th October 1383, Sheen Palace.

The Royal Council has dismissed early.

The hallowed twelve begin to emerge with great industry to discuss and confirm with their clerks what their most pressing priorities shall be subsequent to their latest audience with the King of England.

Thomas of Woodstock, Earl of Buckingham, is one of the young men of court who is not a member of the council, and who therefore stands strategically in the vicinity, the better to catch an eye of some regular acquaintance for a quick appraisal of the most recent goings on. There are rumours that England is destitute, and the French are massing for an invasion to England after Flanders. And there are still concerns that several young noblemen are to be elevated to earls upon Richard's arbitrary insistence. The great families of England are quite vexed by all the uncertainty, have questions pertinent to their own needs, and quite frankly wish to be assured that these rumours are being attended to, planned for, and managed well.

Most barons are unswerving in that they want what barons have always wanted. They want war, even if it means taxing the commoners to fund it. They want a show of strength in Flanders to deter the French-Burgundian aggression towards those great trading cities Bruges, Ghent, and Ypres - whatever England's own civil difficulties. Or a show of strength in France, perhaps to swathe across from Calais to Brittany and recapture some old Normandy glories, before fleeing back across the sea with chests full of silver and gold.

Whichever of these two options are chosen, the barons are united in their desire to see their king head this expedition. Many can recall how there is nothing so enlivening as heading to war with one's king! However Buckingham is closer in blood to the King than most, and is not certain that Richard has the stomach for war. It is worrying that he does seem utterly disinclined towards aggression, but time will reveal that supposition to be true or false.

The barons have collectively put as much pressure as they dare onto King Richard to go to war, so this particular meeting of the Continual Council is today expected to illuminate England's forthcoming foreign strategies above the many rumours that have gathered around the young king's young court.

But while the sprats of Richard's circle bring a vibrancy to our surroundings, not one of them is well-versed in making money. Or managing men. Or killing them.

Along with everyone else who all disperse accordingly, Michael de la Pole the recently appointed Lord Chancellor emerges swiftly with his clerk, and Buckingham reasons that the uncle of the King should speak with a man who is still a commoner but who has the ear of the King.

De la Pole is off like a rabbit, across the Great Hall, and up a spiral staircase, along a colourfully decorated corridor, and into a chamber room. Buckingham is discreet but insistent, and although while charging up the stairway he misses the instant that his quarry disappears, he calculates the door from the rattle and bang it made when it closed.

He wants to speak to the Lord Chancellor, and he is of the royal family, so there is no need to knock.

So. Open, and in, and, *what*?

It is de la Pole with the Duke of Lancaster, in a small room. De la Pole's clerk, upon realising an earl has entered almost breaks his neck to nod his head in subservience to the unexpected entrance of his better.

De la Pole appears anxious but similarly respectful at Buckingham's surprising appearance. Lancaster, after an initial surprise, regains his faculties with speed, and invites his younger brother in with a beckoning hand.

"*Tell him,*" says the duke to the Lord Chancellor. "*Tell him what our king bids England do.*"

De la Pole takes a deep breath, and Buckingham learns, as his elder brother already knew, that King Richard does determinedly obstruct all suggestions for action towards Flanders or in France.

But worse than that (for most of his barons, at the least), he does just as determinedly rule that England should heretofore live in peace.

And no amount of coaxing, persuasion or even flattery has dented this resolution.

=====

A.D. 1384

=====

-- A DUKE PONDERS PEACE --

Who am I?

For I do not recognise this once-fearsome phantom any more than I would recognise the Countess of Sutherland's chambermaid.

The name John of Gaunt would terrorise most men of note in the western lands. I fancy even the Scotties would check for devils on their shoulders if they heard the Duke of Lancaster was aloose. Perhaps this is why this distasteful diplomatic task was requested of me.

Either way, here I am, upon the sea and landward, considering the white cliffs as they near, and bearing news that had to be negotiated with those I dislike the most. And now it is I who must bend the knee to King Richard and tell him and his court that we are now in accord.

And so, by my diplomacy, in King Richard's good name and by King Richard's request, there is peace with France.

My Lord Chancellor Michael de la Pole had been most insistent that this was King Richard's dearest wish all those weeks ago, which of course means that this is Pole's dearest wish, for how else might a commoner feather his own nest as Lord Chancellor but during a long period of peacetime. Later Richard confirmed his desires for peace, no doubt well instructed by Pole. It was shattering news, though not nearly as shattering to be told that his king wished his 'dearest uncle' to negotiate the truce with France in person.

The negotiations were a strange accord for while much was said there was more unsaid. Particularly unsaid, although well presumed, is that England is destitute. The kingdom has at its head an anointed monarch who would spend a thousand marks on a fashionable tapestry to impress his young friends, when he doesn't have enough money to properly fortify the strategic five ports of England's south coast. And France too, it is now known, have their own financial difficulties having recently overstretched into northeast into Flanders when they really didn't need to.

These two great old kingdoms have, one supposes, been banging at each other like two exhausted bleeding stags, meaningful victory long since lost, and all on account of some largely forgotten honour.

It has taken great effort for this mighty lord to be the diplomat.

But I have done so, and in doing so I have given my beloved country some time to rectify certain overspending, to bolster shore defences, and school an immature king in the ways of the running of a realm until one day we will be ready to fight and prosper again.

So peace, for now, be it. And Pole would have his period of concord for England.

And fortunes which I myself may yet win on foreign fields beyond England and beyond France will have to wait.

=====

-- A TALE OF UNWISE CENSURE --

The Salisbury parliament, 11th May 1384.

The shock is sudden, private and baffling.

John of Gaunt appraises the uproar around him, and so surmises that perhaps he was on some level enjoying a small snooze while Arundel was speaking, only to be alerted to a full awoken state by the bawdy reaction of the lords around him. All heads are turned to Arundel. Now what has the fool said?

Only a fortnight in, this parliament - held at the Bishop's Palace in Salisbury due to an inconvenient outbreak of plague in London - has been entertaining in the extreme in that Gaunt himself has already been accused of plotting to kill King Richard. In quite the tiresome episode, some friar had declared Gaunt's treasonous intentions to murder his king and assume the throne. And yet before the fool could be impeached, some unknown and still anonymous assailant had stuck some sharp steel into him and the incident was over as quickly as it had begun. If some said that Gaunt had finished the scoundrel to silence him, Gaunt at least knows that it certainly wasn't anything to do with him. Who would want to rule this rabble?

That excitement was a week ago. Now, today, the Speaker of this session, Sir James Pickering, has requested Richard FitzAlan the Earl of Arundel to repeat his statement for the benefit of the clear recording of such, and so Arundel does while this time Gaunt pays his full attention.

"The Great Revolt in the fourth year of the reign of King Richard was in great part due to the exorbitant and negligent expenditure of the King's court."

More howls from these benches, but Arundel, that old rascal, is insistent for silence during his curiously bold opinion.

"And furthermore, King Richard's extravagances do continue unchecked, to cause a state of financial affairs that, if continued unchecked, will bankrupt the

kingdom, cause further civil disorder, and invite invasion from France. Therefore we must invade France before France invades England!"

Gaunt stretches his eyes at Arundel's words. The two men are similarly aged, and have fought abroad together on occasion so, while Arundel's courage is undoubted, Gaunt is surprised that Arundel is using this unpredictable forum to air such seditious considerations. For his part, King Richard sits silently and stares with unblinking eyes at Arundel, as if cruelly watching a rabbit struggle in a net and thereby assuring itself of its own slow grim destiny. Arundel, no doubt somewhat chastened by the riotous commotion he has caused, sits down and no doubt discusses the lords' reaction in this chamber with the Earl of Buckingham.

Gaunt sighs at the sight of his youngest brother's involvement. Buckingham is still young enough to have lofty principles, and presumably conspires with Arundel (who should know better) to petition the king to straighten his finances in order to better plan a foreign campaign.

However. For all the *haw-hawing* and *pooh-poohing* being made by the greatest men of England, one thing is being lost in the noise... the fact that Arundel is undoubtedly absolutely correct in his assertions. Richard is over-spending. He turns to his barons to request loans (that will not be repaid, for who would demand repayment from their king) or tribute payments (which many barons pay in the belief that their standing in court will improve). But this money must originate from somewhere. Many of England's lords are charging their commoners more in local rents and other charges to attend to the shortfall in silver that they experience when they give money to their king and thus ultimately tax the living out of those most humble in the realm in order that Richard can maintain his carefree lifestyle. And though it is quite natural for a young man to enjoy wealth and privilege, he should not do so without the having of a strong council to discipline him when he asserts himself in ways detrimental to the realm.

Looking around, there aren't many men who would stand against the king in parliament, even though they may indeed desire profitable war campaigns, and indeed may even acknowledge (though only to themselves) that they are in principle in alignment with poor Arundel.

This lord of Lancaster might once have stood in parliament to publicly align with Arundel in the name of common sense, but after his own recent accusations of treason finds he does not have the appetite on this occasion to defend his acquaintance's stance.

This Salisbury parliament continues. The whooping of its infantile commotion continues. Arundel and Buckingham look abashed at being the target of such ridiculed response. England is facing ruin in the absence of a strong king with strong councillors.

And the Duke of Lancaster once more considers that perhaps his fortunes do indeed lay elsewhere.

=====

SCENE. SALISBURY – NIGHT

11th May 1384.

***Thomas of Woodstock, the Earl of Buckingham**, and **Richard FitzAlan, the Earl of Arundel** are accepted past guards by recognised acknowledgment, and into **King Richard**'s private chamber. In there, **Robert de Vere**, seated on a* chaise longue *is clapping and laughing, as King Richard is pretending to sword fight some invisible opponent.*

The King stops as soon as he sees Arundel and paces to him brandishing his right fist.

Arundel desperately drops to his knee.

KING RICHARD II
You should give thanks to God <u>NOW</u> that there is no real sword in our hand.

THOMAS OF WOODSTOCK, EARL OF BUCKINGHAM
Sire, our lord of Arundel is truly penitent.

RICHARD FITZALAN, EARL OF ARUNDEL
Your Highness, I spoke with a passion due only to my love for your glorious realm.

KING RICHARD II
Misgovernment, you say? In <u>our</u> kingdom?

You lie through your teeth on your way to the Devil! Get him away from here, Buckingham.

THOMAS OF WOODSTOCK, EARL OF BUCKINGHAM
Richard. We bring a solution, not a problem.

King Richard is angry, but intrigued. He glances at them both and then barely nods his head upwards.

THOMAS OF WOODSTOCK,
EARL OF BUCKINGHAM (cont'd)

The French invade Flanders and have taken control of the great cities. Bruges and Antwerp have already fallen.

But Ghent stands fast, and looks to England for aid. Thus, we go the way of Flanders.

KING RICHARD II

AH!

This parliament is concluding, and you come before us to request an army. And a tax that will demand the arrangement of another parliament!

Against a kingdom we have only this year agreed peace with!

THOMAS OF WOODSTOCK,
EARL OF BUCKINGHAM

Perhaps that is so, Richard. But more than that, we have the glorious opportunity we have awaited so long.

Break the peace treaty!

Call a tax and an army to pour through Calais and into Flanders, then meet the French on the field to protect our economic allies and assist our exports and fill our coffers, once more.

Consider it, Sire! An English army! Led by our King!

Richard is so shocked he takes a step back.

KING RICHARD II

...Me?

=====

SCENE. SALISBURY – MORNING

12th May 1384.

***Thomas of Woodstock, the Earl of Buckingham**, is dressing in his private chamber. There's a sharp rap at the door. Buckingham is puzzled, and answers the door cautiously.*

*He didn't need to be cautious. It is **Michael de la Pole**, the Lord Chancellor of all England, and now one of King Richard's closest advisors.*

De la Pole is gentle, but the visit is extraordinary, nonetheless.

MICHAEL DE LA POLE,
LORD CHANCELLOR
I come in peace, my Lord.

THOMAS OF WOODSTOCK,
EARL OF BUCKINGHAM
Then peace we have.

Buckingham steps back and sits on his four-poster bed. Although de la Pole has a demeanour that suggests great superiority, and while he enters humbly and closes the door behind him, one feels like every action is smooth and deliberate and all the more dangerous for it.

MICHAEL DE LA POLE,
LORD CHANCELLOR
Your visit last night was unwise.

THOMAS OF WOODSTOCK,
EARL OF BUCKINGHAM
I spoke to the King with true heart, as might any esteemed baron of this kingdom.

MICHAEL DE LA POLE,
LORD CHANCELLOR
Indeed, sir.

But...

...you would truly wish your king to lead a war against France?

THOMAS OF WOODSTOCK,
EARL OF BUCKINGHAM
It has been too long since a king of England led his army. Now it is time.

MICHAEL DE LA POLE,
LORD CHANCELLOR

England recently agreed peaceable terms with France.

THOMAS OF WOODSTOCK,
EARL OF BUCKINGHAM

And no kingdom ever broke a peace treaty before?

De la Pole is like a serpent, regarding its quarry without unnecessary movement. He would not physically strike, but Buckingham understands that there is political venom in this man.

MICHAEL DE LA POLE,
LORD CHANCELLOR

Richard is not ready to lead an army. Have you considered the consequences to England if our young king lost in battle?

Without an heir of his own?

Buckingham wonders why the Lord Chancellor is speaking in this way. Discussing the future of the King is considered treason.

THOMAS OF WOODSTOCK,
EARL OF BUCKINGHAM

I trust that you do not accuse me of foretelling King Richard's death.

MICHAEL DE LA POLE,
LORD CHANCELLOR

(laughs)

Oh, you are not a traitor.

I believe you to be honourable, sir. But naive, sir.

It is unpleasant to hear such analysis of one's character. Buckingham elects to stay silent, but raises his eyebrows and opens his hands as if to request an explanation.

MICHAEL DE LA POLE,
LORD CHANCELLOR (cont'd)

Our sovereign Lord is still too young to earn his spurs.

THOMAS OF WOODSTOCK,
EARL OF BUCKINGHAM

Richard has seventeen years.

His father earned his spurs at Crecy aged, what, sixteen?

MICHAEL DE LA POLE, LORD CHANCELLOR
(nodding vaguely)
How should I say this? Richard is more his mother's son than his father's.

THOMAS OF WOODSTOCK, EARL OF BUCKINGHAM
All I see is a king, sir. And a king should lead his kingdom in battle.

MICHAEL DE LA POLE, LORD CHANCELLOR
True. Ordinarily.

I fought with Richard's father, you know. Oh, what a king that prince would have made!

But Richard is not built for war, Buckingham. To push him to war here and now is a risk to the realm. Or is that the intent?

THOMAS OF WOODSTOCK, EARL OF BUCKINGHAM
Intent?

MICHAEL DE LA POLE, LORD CHANCELLOR
If some mishap were to...

...well...

...who wouldst the crown seek, afterwards?

THOMAS OF WOODSTOCK, EARL OF BUCKINGHAM
Sir!

MICHAEL DE LA POLE, LORD CHANCELLOR
John of Gaunt is a very ambitious lord.

THOMAS OF WOODSTOCK,
EARL OF BUCKINGHAM
And?

MICHAEL DE LA POLE,
LORD CHANCELLOR
And there are many who might wonder if that great magnate's younger brother is promoting a stratagem to prematurely push Richard into war, and thereafter put the elder uncle on the throne...

THOMAS OF WOODSTOCK,
EARL OF BUCKINGHAM
How dare you!

MICHAEL DE LA POLE,
LORD CHANCELLOR
Oh hush, sir! As I said, you are no traitor. I merely wish to lead you away from a naive faith that may well see your eldest brother on the throne.

Has it gone unnoticed to you where John of Gaunt is in all this?

Buckingham's eyes narrow. Is there something to what de La Pole is saying? Surely the Duke of Lancaster is not pulling such treasonous puppet strings in the King's court?

THOMAS OF WOODSTOCK,
EARL OF BUCKINGHAM
And if the king's Lord Chancellor leads me away from such unlikely path, what path wouldst he lead me towards?

MICHAEL DE LA POLE,
LORD CHANCELLOR
Defence before war.

THOMAS OF WOODSTOCK,
EARL OF BUCKINGHAM
God's Blood!

We are barons! We seek war, and silver, and respect through hard-won foreign land!

MICHAEL DE LA POLE,
LORD CHANCELLOR

And how much of all that did you win four years ago?

It is as if Buckingham has been punched in the belly.

MICHAEL DE LA POLE,
LORD CHANCELLOR (cont'd)

I am also acquainted with the cost of your Brittany excursion.

THOMAS OF WOODSTOCK,
EARL OF BUCKINGHAM

So?

MICHAEL DE LA POLE,
LORD CHANCELLOR

Over sixty thousand pounds, my Lord, and that was with five thousand men.

A king's army would have to be twice the size, and more than twice as expensive. And with no guarantee of winning.

And also at the risk of losing our young sovereign in battle.

THOMAS OF WOODSTOCK,
EARL OF BUCKINGHAM

If that were true-

MICHAEL DE LA POLE,
LORD CHANCELLOR

-It is all true. My Lord, England cannot afford to go to war. You may want to, and you may want to for all the right reasons. But, sir, entrust in me...

...you cannot afford to. None of us can.

THOMAS OF WOODSTOCK,
EARL OF BUCKINGHAM

So what is Richard's governing policy for these war-less days to come?

MICHAEL DE LA POLE,
LORD CHANCELLOR

He wishes to build a spectacular, wondrous, colourful, vigorous and peaceful court that will rival any other seen in Christendom.

Buckingham can't believe this.

THOMAS OF WOODSTOCK,
EARL OF BUCKINGHAM

What is this, the romantic words of a group of adolescent chamber knights?

MICHAEL DE LA POLE,
LORD CHANCELLOR

They are the words of our king, Sir.

THOMAS OF WOODSTOCK,
EARL OF BUCKINGHAM

Our kingdom slowly rots from within and without, and you have the ear of the king, and still you dance to this tune?

MICHAEL DE LA POLE,
LORD CHANCELLOR

I submit to my king, Buckingham.

As do we all.

=====

SCENE. KING RICHARD'S COURT AT ELTHAM PALACE, KENT – DAY

21st July 1384.

*This is a court chamber full of noblemen and noblewomen, with a focus on **King Richard** and **Queen Anne** sitting together on thrones.*

*The King leans to his right, away from the Queen, and is examining extravagant flared cuffs as worn by **Robert de Vere, Earl of Oxford**.*

*Meanwhile, **William Courtenay, Archbishop of Canterbury** stands before King Richard patiently. In each of his hands he holds a parchment; from the parchment in his left hand hangs a large wax seal about the size of a lady's palm, and in his right is a parchment on which is pressed a small flat wax seal about the size of a man's thumbnail.*

Courtenay looks embarrassed at being ignored, and glances sideways to the King's uncle, ***Thomas Woodstock, Earl of Buckingham****.*

Buckingham acknowledges the Archbishop's discomfort and steps forward. As the King's uncle, Buckingham can dare to be a bit more familiar.

**THOMAS OF WOODSTOCK,
EARL OF BUCKINGHAM**
Your Highness!

My Lord Archbishop makes a relevant point regarding your own administration that is most worthy of the King's attention.

King Richard sighs heavily and reluctantly returns his attention to the Archbishop, then Buckingham, then back to the Archbishop.

KING RICHARD II
Yes, yes, our kingdom. It is still in here and out there, we trust?

Richard's immature friends snigger in approval of their king's wanton disrespect, and Richard himself can't help but smirk at how funny he is in front of such older boring men.

**WILLIAM COURTENAY
ARCHBISHOP OF CANTERBURY**
Sire, I implore...

This is...

I, I mean, I must...

KING RICHARD II
Oh goodness me, SPIT and have done, sir.

Here!

Richard hocks up and then launches a large glob of sputum that lands on the archbishop's vestments. There is hysterical laughter from Richard's young friends, which Richard eagerly acknowledges.

KING RICHARD II (cont'd)
(laughing to his friends)
And then later he shall forgive me!

Buckingham, shocked to his core at such godlessness, needs to act.

THOMAS OF WOODSTOCK,
EARL OF BUCKINGHAM
Nephew! You are lately making some eccentric decisions, sir.

KING RICHARD II
(instantly deadly serious)
How so, my suddenly brave Uncle?

WILLIAM COURTENAY
ARCHBISHOP OF CANTERBURY
Sire...

With no warning, like a viper King Richard LEAPS UP toward his archbishop with a previously unseen DAGGER and THRUSTS it at the archbishop's neck with a HAHH cry, and yet the tip of the blade stops short. The poor archbishop shrieks and his knees fail him, falls to the ground, his hands shielding his face.

The King's eyes are manic, and he stands tall, steps closer to the most holy spiritual lord in England and lightly PRESSES the deadly sharpness to Canterbury's wrinkled fleshy neck. It however does not pierce the sobbing cleric. Richard maintains his deadly presence, for a time mesmerised by the way the old man's skin yields to the point as it is pressed in by quarter of an inch, and then recovers itself as the point is withdrawn by quarter of an inch.

When Richard speaks, it is quietly and almost to himself, so distracted is he.

KING RICHARD II
The word of God is not requested, Canterbury, for mine uncle of Buckingham would speak.

Buckingham can't believe what he sees. Out of learned habit in the face of aggression, his right arm is across his belly, his hand already on his sword grip and it takes great effort to overcome his instinct to unsheathe the weapon. He must gather his wits and distract Richard to save the clergyman's life.

He holds his empty hands openly outwards in a conciliatory gesture to his king.

THOMAS OF WOODSTOCK,
EARL OF BUCKINGHAM
My sovereign Lord.

See how Canterbury has two documents. One with the King's Great Seal, the other with a smaller signet seal.

Richard glares at Buckingham with menace, but his uncle's boldness is admirable. Everyone ignores the archbishop's sobs.

KING RICHARD II
A document, and a document. What of them?

THOMAS OF WOODSTOCK,
EARL OF BUCKINGHAM
As His Grace the archbishop was explaining, the two documents are grants of land.

However the older document has the Great Seal and was therefore approved by the King's exchequer, whereas the younger document has only a smaller signet seal.

This tells us that the King has personally approved the younger document without the approval of his accountants.

Richard, distracted, has forgotten the cowering archbishop even though he still has him at the point of his dagger.

KING RICHARD II
Indeed.

Richard is glaring into Buckingham's eyes. The King is almost imperceptibly swaying to a rhythm that would be more becoming of a venomous snake.

THOMAS OF WOODSTOCK,
EARL OF BUCKINGHAM
This suggests that our king is undertaking administrative duties in ways that have proved surprising for his councillors to learn.

Richard speaks so slowly that many in court would later claim that perhaps they dreamed these events on this morning.

KING RICHARD II
The King is wearied by all the many sweaty ruddy-faced men who require this or that, in the name of that or this.

THOMAS OF WOODSTOCK,
EARL OF BUCKINGHAM
I see. But our court has several well-meaning and experienced noblemen who

would advise the King personally and with great efficacy.

The Great Seal would in this way be legitimately added to much documentation as approved by the Privy Council. And King Richard would be well regarded an even greater and more glorious ruler in the eyes of his subjects.

KING RICHARD II

The king welcomes all opinions in this court with openness, My Lord.

But we will take advice from whomsoever we wish.

Buckingham looks over Richard's shoulder to observe Robert de Vere, who is standing by Richard's throne. De Vere is smiling with a very threatening curled lip.

THOMAS OF WOODSTOCK,
EARL OF BUCKINGHAM

King Richard.

You are neglecting your duties.

And you are spending too much money.

Finally Richard takes the knife away from Canterbury's neck and points it at Buckingham.

KING RICHARD II

Careful, uncle.

Buckingham bends his knee and bows his head.

THOMAS OF WOODSTOCK,
EARL OF BUCKINGHAM

Sire, I am your most loyal servant.

Without any acknowledgment, Richard's manner becomes light and friendly.

KING RICHARD II

Uncle, we have been considering our royal styling.

THOMAS OF WOODSTOCK,
EARL OF BUCKINGHAM

I...

...beg your pardon?

KING RICHARD II

We do already like "Your Highness" and "Your Grace", of course.

Buckingham dares to look up at Richard, but Richard is slowly striding around the court, deep in his own thoughts.

KING RICHARD II (cont'd)

However we are beginning to yearn for "Most serene Prince and Lord".

(pauses)

Richard is physically close to some courtiers, who bow and curtsey with well-practised respect.

KING RICHARD II (cont'd)

(to Buckingham)

Or...

..."Your Majesty."

Richard catches a lady's attention and leans towards her.

KING RICHARD II (cont'd)

(whispers mischievously to the lady)

It is 'French' in style. It will annoy them SO much!

The lady is desperate to laugh out loud, but suppresses herself.

THOMAS OF WOODSTOCK,
EARL OF BUCKINGHAM

Very well, Your... Majesty.

Richard raises his eyebrows to the lady and shares the moment, to her delight.

KING RICHARD II (cont'd)

(mischievously)

Yes, Buckingham?

THOMAS OF WOODSTOCK,
EARL OF BUCKINGHAM

I implore His Majesty to avail himself of my services, and indeed the services of my great and honourable peers, if our kingdom is to be great and prosperous once more.

Richard seems to be considering these words and nothing is said for a short while.

Then de Vere clears his throat, and Richard twitches at the sound, then smiles with charm to Buckingham.

KING RICHARD II

Mmmm. And so. While we thank you for this advice, uncle, we must sadly depart court for more interesting appointments.

Buckingham screws up his face in frustration, as Richard, Queen Anne, and Robert de Vere gather themselves to leave.

Then, as he is leaving the throne room, a thought occurs to Richard, and he shouts back.

KING RICHARD II (cont'd)

Canterbury!

Methinks Buckingham saved you a slice across the throat, today. Grant him some of your land, by way of your thanks. And bring the deeds to us...

Richard holds up his signet ring finger.

KING RICHARD II (cont'd)

...and we shall SEAL them!

Richard and his friends hoot with laughter on their way out, although Queen Anne glances back at the archbishop, clearly unnerved by the scene she has witnessed.

Buckingham, still kneeling after Richard has left, lets out a brief roar of frustration and punches the floor with the flesh of his fist. He looks up and across to Canterbury. William Courtenay is as pale as watery milk, sweating, and shivering, though manages a nod of appreciation to his redeemer.

=====

-- A QUEEN'S CURIOSITY --

Westminster Palace, 30th July 1384.

Three ladies walk, for none would walk alone.

Queen Anne and two attendants glide like swans with a beauteous outward calm, acknowledging with deference all others who walk the constitutional corridors of Westminster Palace freely and who therefore bow or curtsey despite their own hastily-controlled surprised recognition as they go about their own businesses. Businesses that are as unknown as one another's, which is a state of affairs that on this occasion does suit the Queen, indeed.

Her chaste companions swim closely in Anne's wake with unquestioning sober decorum, and they slow as one and stop outside a thick dark wood black-studded chamber door.

All is well, and the propriety of the trinity is kept. Anne reaches out a delicate royal knuckle, gives three swift raps, turns the handle for herself, and enters with sombre import and purpose.

Inside, anyone close enough would hear some thick chair legs scraped back across a tiled floor, together with a surprised "*Your Highness!*" exclamation offered with the choked urgency of a tubby old incumbent trying both to stand and bow at the same time in the most unexpected presence of his queen.

=====

-- A KING'S PROMISE --

Sleep on, dearest Anne, that the smile at the corners of your lips remains a declaration of innocence against the sins of this mortal world. A smile on a face that is private only for me.

What dice fell into place that we lay here and now? For so long had my old advisers insisted that a king must marry and marry for duty, and therefore for so long had I dreaded this. So long had I dreaded the day I would meet the princess who would become a queen. A lifetime with a fish head for a companion, for duty? Yes, if that was my duty.

But when I saw you, Anne, I knew once more that God has blessed my reign. Old uncle of Gaunt knew naught of your beauty, only of your suitability. And here we now are and it so happens that, to me, your beauty is your beauty while your perfection is your purity. Such purity that would delight the Blessed Virgin Mary whom, as God knows, I love above all.

I am a boy blessed by God who is a king blessed by God with a queen blessed by God. Then let my court be God's court, for me and for you. We are indeed a beautiful pair, the like of which is rare seen atop any realm, so it's right and proper that we show our true and loyal subjects that we are worthy of their adoration of us.

We stand above all others in England, and no doubt above all others anywhere in Christendom.

And so it is my kingly duty that I lay out before you a glamorous court full of silk and gold and beautiful youthful noblemen and noblewomen to surround us with love and esteem.

As do I, you delight in well-told tales and fantastic stories of virtue, honour, cunning, wisdom, and of deeds of worship, where knights abound and keep the chivalric standards we hold in our hearts. Our court does and will continue to patronise minstrels, tale-tellers, writers and artists from afar, and we shall be honoured to welcome those best versed in their chosen arts.

And such art and wonder and chivalry shall ever infuse through our court! Where we laugh, clap, cheer and jeer, and where only the noblest of knights and the prettiest damsels with the purest of hearts shall be the favourites who earn our affections.

I shall give you everything for you and for us, dearest Anne, but for now, sleep on.

For even as you smile, God smiles upon you as He smiles upon me.

And together, with our most virtuous grace, we shall truly be immortal.

=====

SCENE. WINDSOR PALACE – EVENING

3rd August 1384.

***King Richard** and **Queen Anne** sit at a small dining table in a personal chamber. They sit at either side of a corner of the table, so they can tenderly touch one another. They genuinely adore each other's company.*

The meal has ended, and a few candied fruits are left untouched.

KING RICHARD II

(playful, intrepid)

Ask me a question.

QUEEN ANNE

Oh, My Lord! What questions do bold queens ask of their kings?

KING RICHARD II

Why, none! Unless their kings give them leave to do so.

QUEEN ANNE

(laughing)

Then I must not waste such an auspicious constitutional opportunity.

KING RICHARD II

Come! Ask anything.

QUEEN ANNE

Very well. Have you ever seen a real Welsh dragon?

KING RICHARD II

Of course! We have one in the kitchens! What do you think lit the ovens this morning?

QUEEN ANNE

Richard!

KING RICHARD II

Seriously, though.

You have a private audience with King Richard the Second, and to a degree more than any nobleman in England can dream of.

If you were the... Duke of Salop, what would you ask me?

QUEEN ANNE

(giggling)

Salop? There is no such dukedom!

KING RICHARD II

For tonight there is!

Ask anything of your king!

Anne places her hand on his.

QUEEN ANNE
Anything?

Richard playfully slaps her hand with his fingertips.

KING RICHARD II
(smiling)
Anything a duke would ask.

QUEEN ANNE
(laughs)
Very well, I, the Duke of Salop, have a private audience with King Richard the Second, and I hereby request the asking of a question of constitution.

KING RICHARD II
The King doth grant your request, Your Grace.

QUEEN ANNE
(giggling, then quite serious)
Does his high and mighty majesty King Richard, consider that his realm's expenditure is greater than its income?

KING RICHARD II
(suddenly hurt/enraged)
What?

QUEEN ANNE
Ah. Well. It's just that I do worry about certain royal expenses, and the lords-

KING RICHARD II
-Such IMPERTINENCE, and from a lady!

How dare you!

And what do the lords say?

QUEEN ANNE
My Prince, I meant no-

KING RICHARD II
WHAT do the lords say?

QUEEN ANNE
My noble lord, if I have offended-

KING RICHARD II
You tell me what the lords say or, My God, I shall-

Anne is crying.

QUEEN ANNE
Richard-

KING RICHARD II
TELL ME.

QUEEN ANNE
(composes herself)
After the incident with Canterbury and Buckingham...

...it was Buckingham who said in court that you are spending too much.

She doesn't want to continue.

KING RICHARD II
Continue.

QUEEN ANNE
I have always found your Uncle Edmund of Langley to be kindly and learned.

I requested his audience - while you were out hunting with Robert - and I asked him if the royal court is living well off its own.

And he told me that such things are not to trouble a queen.

And that is all.

KING RICHARD II
And that is all.

QUEEN ANNE
And that is how I know we spend too much.

Richard, we do spend so much!

KING RICHARD II
I spend it for you! To create a court worthy of a beautiful Bohemian queen!

QUEEN ANNE
Spend it for your realm, not me, my love.

It's true that I do not understand the ins and outs of the exchequer. But I was close enough to my brother to understand that just as income is limited, expenditure must be also thus.

Richard is shaking with rage. Sweating.

KING RICHARD II
I forbid you to speak to ANYONE without my permission EVER again.

QUEEN ANNE
That's not a practical demand, my love.

Richard roars with rage as he stands violently, his chair is hurled backwards, he slams his fist and then his palm onto the table many times as he screams at the pain it causes.

Anne is petrified, doesn't move. Richard stops. Sobbing. Dribbling. Sweating.

KING RICHARD II
(weakly)
You are my foundation.

QUEEN ANNE
I am!

KING RICHARD II
(distant)
With you by my side, we rule all Christendom.

QUEEN ANNE
Of course!

KING RICHARD II

Please, Anne...

QUEEN ANNE

Yes, Richard?

KING RICHARD II

Please, just obey me.

=====

-- DILEMMAS OF A CHRISTIAN KING --

As sovereign lord, I rule how I will.

Often do I dream of Wat Tyler and the way is eyes bulged as he fell from his horse so unnaturally.

And when I awake, I contemplate the ride across the meadow to that spiky malevolent crowd. And how, as I reached them, their knees became unable to support them in The Presence, and how the tops of all their heads lowered toward me.

Has any king of England come closer to his common subjects, than I?

This smelly, dirty peasantry. Unremarkable Englishmen sent across a field to provide a deadly living wall between a king and his enemy until one side has bled more than the other. Anonymous masses, though in truth fellow Christians, placed on earth by God to provide a labourer class from which a kingdom might earn and deserve its own glory through honest hard work. And it is also truth that each and every man be devoted to his king or if not devoted then fearing of his lords if he were not to make his sacrifice as his lords intend him to.

Those lordly purses do chink of silver and they do slap each other on the back and laugh at their good fortune. But do they ever think of the man they left on the field with his skull crushed into the dirt, or of the uneasy women and children who tend to the home while their men stand gripping their billhook, ready to march into some bloody destiny or some bloody glory?

This savage tradition. Surely this cannot be the only stratagem for success in our great God-given world.

And, so.

I renounce blood. And I am therefore determined to earn my place in England's great chronicles as a king with the worthy ability to recapture our kingdom's great name not in the name of war but in the name of peace. An economy that lives off its own, that does not overtax those who cannot afford to pay, that shall provide processes that do reward loyalty and labour, and do encourage its subjects to find ever more practical and ingenious ways of earning more money that will thus cause the distribution of more money to be distributed more fairly.

Not that our great lords would agree with the emergence of such a middling class. But, given time, their sons will accept such a spread of silver as being usual and therefore unworthy of lament or rebellion.

And of course, a king must resemble a king.

So what is needed to enact my wishes, is a budget.

Therefore, a tax, yes. But a tax to war, no. A tax to consolidate the defences of our great island to shield us from our great enemies, and while within such an indurate shield our fruits shall flourish, grow and rejoice. A tax that shall be based upon affordability!

I will defend my realm against all enemies with a ceaseless ferocity, happy that God will judge in my favour as He did when I defended my kingdom from Tyler's misplaced passion. And I will punish with unmerciful vigour anyone who does threaten my peace.

But I will not seek Christian blood to fill my exchequer with silver. On that matter I am content to remain steadfast.

And so to sleep again. And when I awake to the cock-crow, I will send my honourable Lord Chancellor to deliver the King's considerations upon England's great future.

=====

-- A SPEECH THE NOBLEMEN DID NOT WISH TO HEAR --

Westminster Hall, 14th November 1384.

To speak loud before lords demands courage.

As Lord Chancellor, **Michael de la Pole** may stand at any gathering and expect a respectful silence, even when he stands in a Great Hall at Westminster that is filled by the most famous and powerful names in England who have been blessed with the privilege of gentle birth.

And well might the hush come. For the Lord Chancellor always speaks for the King, and the King is not here today, which means when Pole should begin to speak, it is as like King Richard's voice should bark their commands.

But this afternoon he knows the reverence shown to him will not last. A hall full of bloodthirsty barons with ambitions built on foreign silver and gold do not wish to hear the message that de la Pole is about to impart.

As France continues her aggression in Flanders, as a consequence the Flemish demand for English wool diminishes. England's exports have never been lower. The flow of money into the kingdom thus diminishes. A tax is demanded by many loud noblemen such as the Earl of Buckingham, so that King Richard and his great and mighty English army might cross the sea and bash the French to reconquer old inheritances and begin the restoration of an economic policy that will revive the fortunes of the Exchequer. But such demands are what caused that great revolt, and who has the belly for all that?

And so, yes, the king does demand a tax. But not a poll tax taxed to all and sundry, a tax taxed only to landowners with land and income worth greater than £100. And the tax shall not finance war, but instead the necessary reparations to England's own law, order, and defences, and never mind what strategies the French might pursue.

De la Pole readies himself to request fealty from those among the highest in the realm. A long breath, then a reminder to himself, silent, that he serves the realm, the King, and God, and humility is well-pitched.

The barons are too high-born to actually rebel, but today will not go well for King Richard's attorneys. For everybody comprehends that, just like when King Richard spends over £1,000 on Sicilian silk as he did recently, there will be no return on a tax for England's defence.

Only expense.

Their expense.

Their silver.

=====

-- THE ANXIETY OF AN EARL --

*An **earl of Buckingham** ought be able to enjoy better wine than this vinegar piss. Or perhaps it is the palate that is spoiled as opposed to the berry. It is still being well drunk, even as it assaults the neck, in that it dulls the troubling taste of that recent ill-tempered gathering in Westminster.*

A Lord Chancellor who proposes a tax, only for the landowners, and not for aggression, but for defence!

What news!

And what nerve from the old fool, De La Fool, and what fury aimed at him from the benches!

Never mind where the payment of this tax is coming from in this lord's case, from an estate that yields barely enough to pay for its running each year. An estate small enough that while I might look and behave like an earl well enough, the thought of some unexpected expense - like a tax on landowners - is alarming.

However, while today's rabble quite rightly aimed its ire at de la Pole, one cannot help but ponder on a central truth; de la Pole speaks for the King. And while a big-mouthed wool merchant's son is worthy of the flinging of a few insults in parliament, a king who sits in silence in resistance to the leading of his kingdom into war is well worthy of much more consideration.

Richard is young, some may say. Well, yes, and yet at the same time he is old enough to comprehend that he pays more for Sicilian silk than French silk. When one sees a boy often, one forgets that he is becoming a man.

Richard's minority has been like a tap holding ale in the barrel, however he is now surely old enough to understand that his behaviour has consequences that might flood the whole realm, and beyond.

So why really is he so reluctant to go to war? Does Richard drape himself in expensive silks to cover his own cowardice?

Just like I cloak my own anxiety with this wine?

=====

A.D. 1385

=====

-- A ROYAL HUNT, SPOILED --

5th February 1385.

The hunting is always good at Waltham.

The Abbey is well kept, the town's subjects are affable, and the venison sublime. The highly-regarded red deer provide such tasty lean meat because of the quality of the local forest grasses and sedges, so the forest masters say, and **King Richard II** is not as well versed in such matters as they to question it.

Having been out at dawn, Richard's group caught sight of a beautiful mature hart with glorious antlers, though it wasn't to be caught this day and the small party were back by midday. Richard was looking forward in great expectation to some afternoon hours of prayer in the Abbey and having long satisfying discussions about God and Jesus with the abbot and senior monks but, given the latest news, he isn't doing that and his disgruntlement is evident to all.

Instead he awaits his three uncles. Upon returning from his forest hunt, Richard accepted a messenger who bore a note upon which his three uncles respectfully though urgently requested an audience. An event unusual enough of itself, made even more unusual by the fact that he knows his eldest uncle and his youngest uncle have lately fallen out over the Bohun inheritance affair, which Richard has elected to not release until their bickering is spent, on the advice of his middle uncle.

There is no reason why the king would refuse such an audience with his three most senior noblemen, and so here he is, in the *hospitium* (a simple mid-sized room, but otherwise not unlike most of the great Great Halls he has governed within) on a great chair, under a great canopy (that indicates he is now on constitutionally active duty), and respectfully admired by a smattering of lords on his Royal Council who were already here to discuss some darkly uninteresting local business.

A hustle and bustle outside. Horses approach, clatter on the cobbles, slow, and cease. No-nonsense men bark commands or welcomes. The council's attendees begin to bubble with murmured speculation. Now, more curt voices, this time from nearer, just beyond the closed doors opposite Richard. Metallic scrapes from sword-bearing guards, a brief conversation, and heavy iron door latches chunk and echo even as the doors open.

Three well-dressed men spout steam trails as they stride with purpose to their royal nephew. They stop the respectful distance before The Presence, and bow low before standing tall.

To the right, the prime maturity of Thomas, Earl of Buckingham. To the left, the rotund innocent Edmund, Earl of Cambridge. In the middle, a weather-beaten John of Gaunt, Duke of Lancaster.

Their king nods a polite welcome to them, then looks to Michael de la Pole, his Lord Chancellor, who twitches a nod towards his king.

And so de la Pole is ready for whatever the brothers bring, whereas Richard wants to pray in the Abbey rather than sit here and now.

For whatever the reason these brothers are here, they do not bring good news.

=====

SCENE. WALTHAM ABBEY – DAY

5th February 1385.

***King Richard II** sits before his uncles; **Thomas, Earl of Buckingham**, **Edmund, Earl of Cambridge** and **John of Gaunt, Duke of Lancaster**.*

KING RICHARD II
Speak, Sirs.

John of Gaunt is of course the most senior brother, and so speaks first. Gravely.

JOHN OF GAUNT,
DUKE OF LANCASTER
Your Majesty, Flanders is lost.

The court murmurs, gasps, a wail or two.

KING RICHARD II
How so?

JOHN OF GAUNT,
DUKE OF LANCASTER
The King of France and the Duke of Burgundy, have together finally overcome Ghent, which was of course the final great city to fall.

KING RICHARD II

Very well.

**JOHN OF GAUNT,
DUKE OF LANCASTER**

Sire. We have all lately received many letters from the *Ghentois* and those allied to them, pleading for our assistance in their stance against our great enemy.

But we in England did not rally...

...to, I believe, our great dishonour.

The court murmurs.

**MICHAEL DE LA POLE,
LORD CHANCELLOR**

My Lord, I pray you not to implicate the king in any discussion of dishonour.

**THOMAS OF WOODSTOCK,
EARL OF BUCKINGHAM**

(to Pole)

Sir!

The French hold Flanders, with Burgundy's assistance. Our stronghold of Calais is now entirely surrounded by enemy, and the route taken thereafter by our kingdom's considerable wool exports is now blocked!

There are many in England who rely on their wool income to see them through winters.

KING RICHARD II

We presume you speak for yourself on that matter, uncle?

Sniggering from the court.

**JOHN OF GAUNT,
DUKE OF LANCASTER**

(bellowing)

A HUMOROUS comment?

KING RICHARD II
Uncle...

JOHN OF GAUNT,
DUKE OF LANCASTER
My noble brother apprises my king and his court of the most grievous news I have heard in many long years, and my king finds humour in such calamity?

Richard is sullen, but not drawn into discussion.

JOHN OF GAUNT,
DUKE OF LANCASTER (cont'd)
Does my king, or his great councillors, have an alternative plan to turn wool into silver?

MICHAEL DE LA POLE,
LORD CHANCELLOR
Actually, sir, we have, by way of insurance against the loss of Flanders, initiated discussions with the trading men of the Hanseatic League in respect of our wool.

Gaunt almost runs up to de la Pole to stand directly before him. De la Pole is visibly threatened by the wrath of England's greatest nobleman.

JOHN OF GAUNT,
DUKE OF LANCASTER
And does it cost us more, or less, to send our wool to lands beyond Calais and Flanders?

De la Pole is trying very hard to maintain his dignity, but is clearly too scared to speak.

KING RICHARD II
The point is, Lancaster, there is a workable and peaceful plan. Flanders would still have fallen had we sent ten thousand men.

JOHN OF GAUNT,
DUKE OF LANCASTER
Aha! My royal nephew does foretell what only God would know!

KING RICHARD II

(fuming, but still not drawn)

Suffice to say that we are well apprised of goings-on in Flanders, and beyond.

JOHN OF GAUNT, DUKE OF LANCASTER

Then in which case, might King Richard tell us all, with his great surety, where the aggressive kingdom of France will now turn their attention, while England accumulates fleeces instead of silver?

=====

SCENE. THE FRENCH COURT AT THE HÔTEL SAINT-POL, PARIS – DAY

Le 19 mars 1385.

From his elaborate dark wood throne, the sixteen-year old ***King Charles VI of France*** *beckons* ***Philip, the Duke of Burgundy****, to the royal presence.*

KING CHARLES VI OF FRANCE

You will have news for us, today.

PHILIP, DUKE OF BURGUNDY

My news is, uh, inconclusive, Your Majesty.

King Charles VI observes the Duke Philip of Burgundy, while waiting for more information in complete silence and without any movement on his behalf in spite of the increasing awkwardness of the silence. Eventually...

KING CHARLES VI OF FRANCE

So it would seem...

Burgundy is sweating as he struggles to find the words.

PHILIP, DUKE OF BURGUNDY

All indications suggest that if we wait one year-

The King wails loudly to the startlement of all in court.

KING CHARLES VI OF FRANCE

Ohhhhhhhhh BURGUNDY!

Do our agents not report that England is all but bankrupt?

PHILIP, DUKE OF BURGUNDY

They do, but there are certain inconsistencies in the intelligence. King Richard recently spent almost 2,000 marks on silk from Sicily!

KING CHARLES VI OF FRANCE

(shouting)

And I would have it, on which to spit!

PHILIP, DUKE OF BURGUNDY

If Richard spends over a thousand pounds of silver on silk, then we cannot be certain that England is as impecunious as our agents suggest.

What if our agents have instead revealed themselves to King Richard, or the Duke of Lancaster, and are taking even more money off them to tell us untruths that we then act unwisely upon?

KING CHARLES VI OF FRANCE

I believe our agents to be trustworthy.

PHILIP, DUKE OF BURGUNDY

I advise caution, until we can be certain.

KING CHARLES VI OF FRANCE

So, what do we know for certain?

PHILIP,
DUKE OF BURGUNDY
We understand that Richard is still reluctant to cross the water to engage in battle, in spite of the insistence of his barons.

Why he would not come and at least defend Calais in numbers, we cannot tell.

PHILIP,
DUKE OF BURGUNDY
He cannot afford to!

PHILIP,
DUKE OF BURGUNDY
We cannot tell. Yet.

In a year, we shall know how they have reacted to the collapse of their wool exports.

KING CHARLES VI
OF FRANCE
We are still building ships, *non*?

PHILIP,
DUKE OF BURGUNDY
We are.

KING CHARLES VI
OF FRANCE
Then continue. At least this peace of ours does give us time to build a fleet and army to rival Flanders, England and Spain combined.

PHILIP,
DUKE OF BURGUNDY
Of course, Sire.

KING CHARLES VI
OF FRANCE
But still I wish to test England's defences.

Who is our greatest military commander?

PHILIP,
DUKE OF BURGUNDY
I would say, *Jean de Vienne.*

KING CHARLES VI
OF FRANCE
Send his garrison to Scotland. King David will welcome our strength.

The English will not. And we will observe their reaction.

Burgundy is impressed with his young king's stratagem, but still cautious.

PHILIP,
DUKE OF BURGUNDY
They are likely to go north to quell a French garrison.

KING CHARLES VI
OF FRANCE
Oui.

I predict that Richard will take the opportunity to earn his spurs without having to cross the sea.

And if he gathers a great baronial army to travel north to Scotland, it will leave the south of England more unprotected than ever before.

PHILIP,
DUKE OF BURGUNDY
Your Majesty, if we wait one year for a more aggressive stance against England, then we can understand what profits or otherwise we have made from our continued Flemish campaigns, and commit more readily to an invasion of England.

KING CHARLES VI
OF FRANCE
We do this now. I wish to learn more about Richard.

Charles is clearly enlivened by this new distraction.

PHILIP,
DUKE OF BURGUNDY
Jean de Vienne to Scotland, then.

KING CHARLES VI
OF FRANCE
Good.

=====

SCENE. ELTHAM PALACE, KENT – DAY

17th May 1385.

***King Richard II** is demonstrating his archery skills for his friends, including Robert de Vere, the Earl of Oxford.*

***Michael de la Pole, the Lord Chancellor of England**, approaches but waits a respectful distance away. Richard likes his most senior adviser, and notices that the elder holds a scroll. The younger ascertains from de la Pole's demeanour that this is news of considerable import.*

Richard bids de Vere to continue, and approaches de la Pole.

KING RICHARD II
Yes?

MICHAEL DE LA POLE,
LORD CHANCELLOR
Intelligence from Northumberland, Sire.

KING RICHARD II
A first for Northumberland, *non*?

MICHAEL DE LA POLE,
LORD CHANCELLOR
(concern)
I would beg His Majesty's solemnity on this occasion.

Richard was ready to go back to his archery, but now faces his most trusted parliamentary advisor fully.

KING RICHARD II
Hmmm. Speak, then.

MICHAEL DE LA POLE,
LORD CHANCELLOR
It is learned that Scotland's King David hosts a garrison from France.

KING RICHARD II
An invasion?

MICHAEL DE LA POLE,
LORD CHANCELLOR
Barely two thousand soldiers, sir, so, no not an invasion. But a gathering worthy of the royal attention.

KING RICHARD II
The French. On our island!

What is their intention?

MICHAEL DE LA POLE,
LORD CHANCELLOR
No-one knows. Though I understand that the French presence is likely to be not temporary.

KING RICHARD II
So, in residence, then!

This is terrible!

MICHAEL DE LA POLE,
LORD CHANCELLOR
On the contrary, sire. I rather feel that these events might prove particularly fortuitous for you.

=====

SCENE. WESTMINSTER PALACE – NIGHT

18th May 1385.

***Michael de la Pole, the Lord Chancellor of England**, drinks and appreciates the delicious - and most expensive - Bordeaux wine that **John of Gaunt the Duke of Lancaster** has given him.*

The two do not like one another, but they are both loyal servants of the crown, in their own ways.

**JOHN OF GAUNT,
DUKE OF LANCASTER**

What are they doing in Scotland?

**MICHAEL DE LA POLE,
LORD CHANCELLOR**

One suspects their intention is simply to make us wonder what they are doing in Scotland.

Gaunt grunts his agreement.

**JOHN OF GAUNT,
DUKE OF LANCASTER**

And you've advised Richard to travel north and meet them in battle?

**MICHAEL DE LA POLE,
LORD CHANCELLOR**

I have.

First, he thus earns his spurs, and that is an end to that court uncertainty.

Second, he is seen, by all in Christendom, to finally lead an army.

Third, it costs us little to achieve the first and the second.

**JOHN OF GAUNT,
DUKE OF LANCASTER**

But we'd need to raise another tax.

**MICHAEL DE LA POLE,
LORD CHANCELLOR**

(shakes his head)

You're a man of letters. Do you recall "scutage"?

**JOHN OF GAUNT,
DUKE OF LANCASTER**

Good Lord. Barely.

MICHAEL DE LA POLE,
LORD CHANCELLOR

My own findings suggest it has never been revoked, and therefore still a legal principle.

JOHN OF GAUNT,
DUKE OF LANCASTER

A feudal summons, though? It belongs in the past.

MICHAEL DE LA POLE,
LORD CHANCELLOR

We have been invaded, Lancaster. A distasteful act against God's will, that demands we react in whichever legal manner we can find.

We draw up military ordinances, send writs to all of England's barons and knights, and then declare all bound by ancient feudal law to defend the realm by joining our king at their own expense or pay the scutage due.

JOHN OF GAUNT,
DUKE OF LANCASTER

Fight or be fined.

MICHAEL DE LA POLE,
LORD CHANCELLOR

I predict that some barons will rally for the fight. Other barons will fund it.

JOHN OF GAUNT,
DUKE OF LANCASTER

But if this is the way that Richard gets a taste of what we all want him to taste, then why can't we enforce this for further away?

MICHAEL DE LA POLE,
LORD CHANCELLOR

A feudal obligation only lasts forty days, and it would take half that to get an army over the sea and in through Calais.

So this is not a stratagem we can apply to go to France. But, then, neither can King Charles afford to come to England.

JOHN OF GAUNT,
DUKE OF LANCASTER
How do you know?

MICHAEL DE LA POLE,
LORD CHANCELLOR
Because if he could, he'd have sent that garrison, and more, to Kent or Cornwall rather than Scotland.

=====

SCENE. A PRIVATE CHAMBER IN WESTMINSTER PALACE – DAY

19th May 1385.

***John of Gaunt**, Duke of Lancaster, awaits his younger brother **Thomas of Woodstock, the Earl of Buckingham**.*

The two haven't been close allies since Lancaster married his son Henry Bolingbroke to the sister of Buckingham's wife, thus claiming half of the two daughters' family inheritance; the whole of which is still held by the crown.

Enter Buckingham.

THOMAS OF WOODSTOCK,
EARL OF BUCKINGHAM
Be quick.

JOHN OF GAUNT,
DUKE OF LANCASTER
Very well. Get ready for war.

Lancaster turns and leaves.

Buckingham puts a hand on Lancaster's chest to stop him.

THOMAS OF WOODSTOCK,
EARL OF BUCKINGHAM
Why? I don't have any more sisters-in-law for you to kidnap.

JOHN OF GAUNT,
DUKE OF LANCASTER
Thomas. Writs for war are being issued, now. Pole has advised Richard to travel to Scotland, to shoo the French and rattle the Scots.

THOMAS OF WOODSTOCK,
EARL OF BUCKINGHAM
Richard? Leading an army?

JOHN OF GAUNT,
DUKE OF LANCASTER
He still avoids going to France or Flanders, but it is progress.

THOMAS OF WOODSTOCK,
EARL OF BUCKINGHAM
And it's a damned sight easier earning one's spurs when you're facing a bunch of knock-kneed Scots than King Charles's army.

JOHN OF GAUNT,
DUKE OF LANCASTER
And so, you have it. Use this news to your advantage, and make your arrangements quickly, to be close to the King. He will still very much need family among his personal guard.

Do not wait to be asked.

THOMAS OF WOODSTOCK,
EARL OF BUCKINGHAM
Does de Vere know?

JOHN OF GAUNT,
DUKE OF LANCASTER
By now, probably.

Buckingham looks very worried about something.

JOHN OF GAUNT,
DUKE OF LANCASTER (cont'd)
Thomas.

The inheritance-

THOMAS OF WOODSTOCK,
EARL OF BUCKINGHAM
-I'd have had it by now!

JOHN OF GAUNT,
DUKE OF LANCASTER
The law moves to its own unsympathetic beat.

THOMAS OF WOODSTOCK,
EARL OF BUCKINGHAM
So does my income. You should try being a youngest brother, managing lands with pennies to spare.

JOHN OF GAUNT,
DUKE OF LANCASTER
I've arranged for four chests of silver to be delivered to Pleshey. If you need any more to get you next to me, I will provide surety against any other expenditure you need.

Lancaster pushes past towards the door.

THOMAS OF WOODSTOCK,
EARL OF BUCKINGHAM
Brother?

Lancaster freezes as he pulls the door handle.

THOMAS OF WOODSTOCK,
EARL OF BUCKINGHAM (cont'd)
Thank you.

Lancaster grunts, then leaves.

=====

-- NEWCASTLE, 29TH JULY 1385 --

Oh so many, and all for ***King Richard****!*

Men and weapons, horses, tents, and colours and noise, and all for me!

My throne is raised, my crown is adored, and barons bow, and all the while I never comprehended that my many palaces are in fact my many prisons.

Occasionally have I wondered at the various absences of my lords, and just as often have those closest to me indicated their respected whereabouts without any further curiosity on my part. But had I known the sky was so big, and the sun so warm, and my subjects so obeisant, well, perhaps, like my lords, I would leave the well-dressed stone temples of my magnificence more often.

I suspect I might learn more from my elders, in that while naturally everyone I meet knows well who I am and greets me as they ought, I find myself wanting in regard of who is addressing me, and more often than not my beloved Duke of Lancaster or the Earl of Buckingham would discreetly - or indiscreetly - indicate with whom I am required to converse. I am indeed proud that my uncles are well met and well thought of by all who encounter them.

And then I see the wonder of my own regal grace reflected back at me by de Vere, and my heart leaps to see such true devotion in one such best friend. How must it feel for him to know the most important man in all the realm! And what tragedy that I shall never know that particular stirring, for I am that man of greatness!

All these men - great, gentle, and small - on campaign for a common good: to rid our realm of foreign evil.

Look upon me, oh Lord, and note from your throne in Heaven, that while your exalted son had twelve disciples, this Plantagenet king, anointed especially for you, and marching in your name, has fourteen thousand!

=====

SCENE. NEWCASTLE – DAY

30th July 1385.

***King Richard II**, **John of Gaunt**, Duke of Lancaster, **Edmund of Langley**, the Earl of Cambridge, **Thomas of Woodstock**, the Earl of Buckingham, **Michael de la Pole** the Lord Chancellor, and **Robert de Vere** the Earl of Oxford are seated around a large table top during their early evening meal.*

KING RICHARD II

And so!

The heads of the army of fourteen thousand sit together at last!

Buckingham sneaks a look at Lancaster, who smirks and gives an almost imperceptible shake of the head.

KING RICHARD II (cont'd)

As leader of our exalted campaign, we have hereby decided to make our return to London in celebration.

THOMAS OF WOODSTOCK, EARL OF BUCKINGHAM

My Lord, should we not consider the enemy ahead in the first instance?

KING RICHARD II

Aha, consider this first, my beloved uncle. Your king travels with but one duke.

Richard nods regally at Gaunt, who reciprocates carefully.

KING RICHARD II (cont'd)

And I wish to war with a crown adorned with a great many more precious gems and stones!

THOMAS OF WOODSTOCK, EARL OF BUCKINGHAM

Well said, Sire. But surely a battle helm will for now suffice?

Richard and de Vere look at each and laugh, to the incredulity of everyone else. Presently they become more serious.

KING RICHARD II

My Lord, I speak in poetic metaphor.

ROBERT DE VERE, MARQUIS OF DUBLIN

They don't read Chaucer, Sire!

They two share another laugh. Gaunt narrows his eyes. He has patronised Geoffrey Chaucer for many years.

KING RICHARD II

And so. The jewels of which I speak are gathered here, tonight!

Our uncle of Cambridge. We wish to elevate you to a dukedom. You will henceforth be known as Edmund, Duke of York!

Edmund of Langley, still Earl of Cambridge but now also known by the higher ranking of Duke of York, clasps his hands together and silently prays thanks to Richard. Lancaster looks genuinely happy for his younger brother and taps the table top approvingly.

But Richard is not yet finished.

KING RICHARD II (cont'd)

My Lord of Buckingham. You are also a king's uncle, and we wish you also to be elevated to duke, of Gloucester.

Thomas of Woodstock, still Earl of Buckingham but now also Duke of Gloucester, is delighted. Lancaster's facial expression is neutral but he forces a half-smile and nods. He observes the new Duke of Gloucester, but also de la Pole and de Vere.

KING RICHARD II (cont'd)

Michael de la Pole, our esteemed Lord Chancellor.

We wish you to be elevated to Earl of Suffolk.

From Michael de la Pole, the new Earl of Suffolk's eyes, emerge tears. The new Duke of Gloucester is surprised at the dizzying elevations happening around the table. Lancaster observes King Richard, who is now looking at de Vere with great reverence.

KING RICHARD II (cont'd)

And finally, our dearest Robert.

Never had a king such a great and true friend.

We wish to dignify you with a new title, thus: Marquis of Dublin.

The words might have been jabbed into Thomas of Woodstock, the new Duke of Gloucester, who cannot help but let a small cry from his open mouth as he looks at King Richard in disbelief. Gloucester looks to Lancaster, who silently and discreetly uses staring eyes to urge his newly-elevated younger brother to control himself.

ROBERT DE VERE,
MARQUIS OF DUBLIN

Oh, My Lord!

Richard turns to his eldest uncle for approval.

KING RICHARD II

Uncle of Lancaster, do you see our glory herein?

Edmund of Langley, Duke of York.

Thomas of Woodstock, Duke of Gloucester.

Michael de la Pole, Earl of Suffolk.

Robert de Vere, Marquis of Dublin.

What say you? Is not our realm strengthened by these glorious appointments? Do you not agree, that we bestow honours onto wise and honourable men?

JOHN OF GAUNT, DUKE OF LANCASTER

Well. It is certainly difficult to speak against a king's such glorious appointments.

I am so gladdened, in fact, that I may volunteer to escort young de Vere to Ireland myself!

=====

-- THE TALE OF THE DISAPPEARING SCOTS --

11th August 1385.

Do they know the word 'summer' in the north?

He cannot help but imagine that if he were today in Essex, he might be napping on soft dry grass under bushy green leaved trees, where the only anxiety is the wonder of where the next apple may fall. As opposed to this wet hell.

Instead, **Thomas of Woodstock, the Duke of Gloucester** considers the constancy of the tapping of hard rain upon his surcoat, steel plates and padded jupon beneath, and the insistence of that cold water to invade through those outer layers, and also the chain hauberk beneath that covers his torso and head, and then bind the wetted linen undergarments he wears to his person. Quilted linen jupons weigh uncommonly heavy when they are wet, and furthermore every movement of himself or his horse does encourage the plates to mash the damp undergarments as the clothing shifts about him, where the resultant never-ending squeezed-out dribble does eagerly ease down his skin to encourage an ever-deepening melancholy.

His misery is all the worse for the recollection of how it feels to cold undress at the end of another uneventful day. And the worse still at the recollection of how it feels to dress it all again at the beginning of the next undoubtedly uneventful sodden day.

Richard's glorious expedition has become more malodorous the further north from Newcastle they've travelled. While many set out from Richard's London, Newcastle is where the total fourteen thousand gathered from all over the realm, and the new duke of Gloucester had privately rejoiced in being a worthy part of such a great number. With great fanfare did they make a trail up through the vastness of Northumberland and its uncertain clime, and ever-closer to the perceived Scottish border, whereupon as the plod to danger continued the blood began to rise and the weather deteriorated as cloud enjoined with land.

And then of course, to the surprise of none of the senior lords, upon the first emergence of this well-appointed royal English army, the Scots had fled into the mist-covered nooks and crannies of their own hinterlands. And even though they made their savage sounds and noises through the swirling clouds, no scouts were able to find any gathering, fair or foul, for which to commit arms to.

When the rain came, even the Scots fell silent. They could be anywhere. They could have all gone to their huts and caves and be enjoying their fires and their women, while we sit and soak in due misery and for the want of a fair fight that instead laughs upon us from unknown places. As for the French, they could be back in Paris for all anyone is aware.

King Richard, though as saturated as anyone else, at least has a steady number of middle-ranking well-wishers all taking advantage of an opportunity to bow and kneel in front of their actual king as opposed to their manorial lord.

If they ask after his daring deeds of the Great Revolt, as some courageous fellows do, then they are entreated to a tale that Gloucester has heard embellished so much that by now he expects to hear how a fourteen-year old King Richard did smite Welsh dragons and sea serpents as well as every villein present.

And in other cases, where Richard, doubtless delighting in the love shown to him, does not have the opportunity to tell of his youthful magnificence, then he at least insists on ensuring they are all acquainted with the cognizance that they are part of fourteen thousand in their noble quest to intimidate England's dread enemies back across the water whence they came.

Although, as Gloucester wonders, should this rain ever cease and these mists ever raise, and the count be made again, he should not be at all surprised if only half the fourteen thousand would yet remain.

Indeed, more than once had he himself considered returning home.

=====

SCENE. THE FRENCH COURT AT ROUEN, NORTHERN NORMANDY – DAY

Le 12 août 1385.

*Sixteen-year old **King Charles VI of France** is staring at **Philip, the Duke of Burgundy** in fury.*

The King suddenly literally SHRIEKS in rage and fury to the face of his uncle.

**PHILIP,
DUKE OF BURGUNDY**
Your Majesty, we cannot be certain.

**KING CHARLES VI
OF FRANCE**
JE SUIS CERTAIN!

**PHILIP,
DUKE OF BURGUNDY**
We are not! I am sorry, but we are not.

**KING CHARLES VI
OF FRANCE**
Fourteen thousand Englishmen went north, Burgundy.

**PHILIP,
DUKE OF BURGUNDY**
And then fourteen thousand were lost in the weather.

The Scots, of course, did not stay to fight but instead scattered hither and thither. Many, emboldened by their unprecedented gathered numbers, went west and then south across the border lands to settle local scores a hundred miles away.

**KING CHARLES VI
OF FRANCE**
HEATHENS!

PHILIP,
DUKE OF BURGUNDY
All of which means, while we cannot count English numbers in the fog, and while we are not engaging them in battle, we cannot be certain of the precise whereabouts and strength of Richard's army.

KING CHARLES VI
OF FRANCE
We might presume with strong conviction.

PHILIP,
DUKE OF BURGUNDY
What if Richard has in fact sent half his army back south without our knowledge?

We already know that our invasion is barely financeable as it is. Vienne describes Scotland as containing nothing of worth, just wild beasts, forests and mountains.

I believe him. Scotland is not a reliable ally for a stratagem against England. They hate them more than we do.

KING CHARLES VI
OF FRANCE
I propose we now invade southern England.

PHILIP,
DUKE OF BURGUNDY
Your Majesty...

Burgundy looks meaningfully into the youthful face.

And in that moment Charles understands that his role as a boy king is one of merely a figurehead, the King indeed but king in name only and, at least until he is twenty-one – in three years' time – he is bound by the decisions that the regency make. Burgundy really does have the right to refuse a king's order if he truly believes it is to the detriment of the kingdom.

France will not today be invading southern England. They almost did, but they will not.
King Charles VI, SCREAMS with as much fury and malice as his young character can muster until he is red, and then purple, in the face.

Philip, Duke of Burgundy, elects on this occasion to allow the young king to release his frustrations.

=====

SCENE. THE JOURNEY SOUTH THROUGH NORTHUMBERLAND – DAY

17th August 1385.

***John of Gaunt, Duke of Lancaster**, and his younger brother **Thomas of Woodstock, the Duke of Gloucester**, are on horseback among a greater entourage behind King Richard's.*

The weather is cloudy and drizzly, and all the men have their heads bowed in natural defence against the wet weather.

The whole company is tired and hungry, except it seems for King Richard who, five horse lengths ahead of his uncles, is talking incessantly to Robert de Vere about matters of which the two uncles have no interest.

**THOMAS OF WOODSTOCK,
DUKE OF GLOUCESTER**

Does he know the Scots were ransacking Cumberland while we waited for them in the fog at Edinburgh?

**JOHN OF GAUNT,
DUKE OF LANCASTER**

Well I haven't told him. I'm not telling him about his mother's death either, until we approach London.

(pause)

He told me last night that he has thoroughly enjoyed this war.

**THOMAS OF WOODSTOCK,
DUKE OF GLOUCESTER**

He thinks <u>this</u> was a war?

They share a humorous moment.

**JOHN OF GAUNT,
DUKE OF LANCASTER**

I think Richard, as with many things, enjoys the spectacle as opposed to the practical.

Gloucester peers forward and squints through the rain towards King Richard and Robert de Vere who are riding side by side.

The King is chatting with an animation that suggests he is not inconvenienced at all by the wet weather.

THOMAS OF WOODSTOCK,
DUKE OF GLOUCESTER
I almost pity de Vere. Richard is probably describing the design of his next tapestry.

Lancaster smiles. He is happy to be close to his younger brother again.

JOHN OF GAUNT,
DUKE OF LANCASTER
Thomas, I think you may have to accept that you have an artist and a poet for a king rather than a warrior.

Something about that comment seemed odd, and Gloucester frowns.

THOMAS OF WOODSTOCK,
DUKE OF GLOUCESTER
He is your king, too.

Lancaster doesn't say anything for a short while.

JOHN OF GAUNT,
DUKE OF LANCASTER
I have other priorities. Priorities that will take me away from England for some time.

THOMAS OF WOODSTOCK,
DUKE OF GLOUCESTER
Since when?

JOHN OF GAUNT,
DUKE OF LANCASTER
Since two days ago. Along with news of the Lady Joan's demise, the messenger brought certain information.
My wife's beloved Castile was defeated by King Joao of Portugal some days ago.

THOMAS OF WOODSTOCK,
DUKE OF GLOUCESTER
So?

JOHN OF GAUNT,
DUKE OF LANCASTER
Portugal have finally won their independence. And Castile is in disarray... King Juan is despised by all around him.

THOMAS OF WOODSTOCK,
DUKE OF GLOUCESTER
His father was the rascal who murdered your wife's father to take her Castilian crown?

JOHN OF GAUNT,
DUKE OF LANCASTER
The same.

So now I shall take my household abroad, win support of the beleaguered Spanish lords, and claim my right, through my wife, as King of Castile.

THOMAS OF WOODSTOCK,
DUKE OF GLOUCESTER
And how would the presumably battle-strong Portugal feel about that?

JOHN OF GAUNT,
DUKE OF LANCASTER
King Joao of Portugal will support my claim.

THOMAS OF WOODSTOCK,
DUKE OF GLOUCESTER
Why would he do that?

JOHN OF GAUNT,
DUKE OF LANCASTER
(smiling)
Because I sent to Portugal two hundred of my finest longbowmen to assist him in his disagreement against Castile. It seems they were the difference in the end.

**THOMAS OF WOODSTOCK,
DUKE OF GLOUCESTER**

You sent two hundred men to the King of Portugal, while your own king drew battle orders for Scotland?

**JOHN OF GAUNT,
DUKE OF LANCASTER**

He mustered fourteen thousand for this folly, and he's delighted. I do not think Richard missed my bowmen, do you?

**THOMAS OF WOODSTOCK,
DUKE OF GLOUCESTER**

He'll miss your counsel if you go.

**JOHN OF GAUNT,
DUKE OF LANCASTER**

You must guide Richard wisely in my absence.

**THOMAS OF WOODSTOCK,
DUKE OF GLOUCESTER**

You'll be back, though?

**JOHN OF GAUNT,
DUKE OF LANCASTER**

Not if I'm King of Castile, I won't.

**THOMAS OF WOODSTOCK,
DUKE OF GLOUCESTER**

You have no consideration for the rest of us?

**JOHN OF GAUNT,
DUKE OF LANCASTER**

Pfff. Much of England has been seeking to rid itself of John of Gaunt for many years, now.

It is time I fulfilled those expectations.

=====

SCENE. A PRIVATE CHAMBER IN NOTTINGHAM CASTLE – NIGHT

25th August 1385.

***John of Gaunt**, Duke of Lancaster enters the private chambers of **Michael de la Pole**, the newly-elevated Earl of Suffolk.*

The latter is lying on his bed, trying to relax after weeks in the saddle, and he is surprised by the intrusion but not overly alarmed.

**JOHN OF GAUNT,
DUKE OF LANCASTER**
A word.

**MICHAEL DE LA POLE,
EARL OF SUFFOLK**
Of course.

**JOHN OF GAUNT,
DUKE OF LANCASTER**
The King elevates several of his court. Including some whom some others may deem unworthy.

**MICHAEL DE LA POLE,
EARL OF SUFFOLK**
The King feels that the commoners are stronger than ever before. And as such the kingdom would benefit from having more titled lords with which to administer them.

**JOHN OF GAUNT,
DUKE OF LANCASTER**
You, an earl? De Vere a marquis!

**MICHAEL DE LA POLE,
EARL OF SUFFOLK**
We are both humbled and honoured by our king.

Gaunt studies de la Pole. The new Earl of Suffolk does not pass Gaunt's analysis.

**JOHN OF GAUNT,
DUKE OF LANCASTER**
My Lord, I am certain that the King's business proves far more exciting and

profitable than your late father's Yorkshire wool concerns.

But let me assure you, that the games some men play in this court are very dangerous.

MICHAEL DE LA POLE,
EARL OF SUFFOLK
I'm holding my own, Lancaster.

JOHN OF GAUNT,
DUKE OF LANCASTER
HA! Thus speaks new money.

Make no mistake, Michael. You may have your title, but you do not have noble blood. You have commoners' blood.

That you have to hold your own is a weakness to conceal, not a strength to boast about.

=====

To the Ryght Reverend William de Kereby,
Abbote of Leycestre Abbey,
ist day of Septembre 1385

To the most reverent fader in Godde and full gracious Lord Abbote.

I wryte in examinacion of a yonge man, lately favoured by our souvereyne Lorde the Kinge Richard.

Item, Robert de Vere. Saide lorde, who hath but xxii yeres himselfe, may be well known to yewe, sir, as the ixth *earle of Oxford, having been graunted such honour by way of inheritaunce upon the dyth of hisse fader some yeres hence. However meyght I call attencion upon saide lorde of Oxfords recent unprecedented elevation as it plaeses his higheness, to Marquess of Dublin along wyth apropriate graunt of lands.*

Oure greyte reaulme doth ryghtly dypende on greyte men of nobel qualities, howevre yonge Oxford is yet unproven in the enryching, welfare and diligence of his lands inasmuche that receipt of addicionale titles by saide lorde is undoubted by alle but oure kinge to be premature.

De Vere and otheres similar in attendaunce do command suche attencion from and give counsel to oure kinge, albeit saide chambere knyghts, and their long sleeves thatte sweepeth the floor, are by alle accounts sureley more valiante in bedde than in battel.

Upon such observacions I pray thatte alle in the royale householde who attend oure welbeloved lorde kinge see that naught hangith bitwene kinge and hys greyte and nobel lordes inasmuch as all othir subjectes wolde kepe respectfulle distaunce from the kinges person.

May Godde in hys mercye bless and seyve us alle.

Youres respectfullye in Christe,
John of Ashby, Abbote, Croyland

=====

-- THE KING'S REVELATION --

Sheen Palace, 10th September 1385.

Leafy brown, gold and crimson surroundings.

King Richard loves God's tapestries of nature at this time of year, but like all men he cannot help but fear the coldness and the darkness to come.

It has been a fair summer, though it was tainted by the passing of his beloved mother who was called to heaven during his campaign to Scotland, and tainted more by those nobles closest to him who saw fit to not tell him about this news until they were approaching London upon their return.

She would have loved to see the trees today. He often forgets that she's gone, each remembrance a pinch at the heart.

He thinks about Scotland often. Though he did not earn his spurs, for he now understands that he never met his enemy on the field even if he showed willingness to do so, he was surprised at how intoxicating it was to see for himself how so many men-at-arms did gather around him.

It would take a great army indeed to violate the King's person, with so many men standing for him and before him.

Even greater was the feeling of joy to be returning south. Such a journey had its dangers, for there are outlaws everywhere, but he'd travelled around England before and never felt particularly at risk. But he now understood that the ecstasy of returning from battle (even if it wasn't a battle) causes a joyous camaraderie for those returning, and these are feelings that he never had the cause to know before. Perhaps his uncles had not disclosed his mother's death so that he could more fully enjoy his return, even though they later expressed their underwhelm at the battle that wasn't really a battle.

Whatever their reasons, he had not liked feeling not told. That skittery unrest caused by not being fully informed of matters closely pertaining to himself. His uncles should be there to keep him fully informed. They did not, and so there is one more good reason for him to develop a more trusted inner council of his choosing that separates him from those untrustworthy wrinkled farts.

And yet, there is more to this. For if such an inner council included men of arms, then no doubt Richard would be able to enjoy a feeling of greater security in court than he now feels. Thus, an inner grouping of retained knights, to stand between their sovereign lord and his untrusted lords, to defend their king and enforce his most intimate requests. This seems so glorious an undertaking that he wonders why no king has done it before.

Gaunt, Gloucester, York, and all the rest, they have all since said the Scottish expedition was a waste of time and resources, with poor de la Pole the object of their anxieties in his role as instigator for the campaign.

Well, to blame their king would be treasonous, after all.

But if he learned anything from the Scottish affair, it is that he discovered new and enjoyable feelings, those of 'safety' and 'security'. Such safety and security that comes from having numbers around him, like he had during the Scotland trip, though of course it would not be practical to employ quite so many as fourteen thousand in his court. So, no, not fourteen thousand, but such numbers still that he can truly trust and rely upon, for as long as he lives, to stand for him if his uncles or parliament insists upon forcing him to do anything he would not wish to do.

What a king wants, a king shall have.

He does not want his spurs. He wants peace. And with peace will come the respect and prosperity of heading the greatest kingdom in Christendom. And the way to ensure that is to retain a private army to keep him feeling as secure as he was with his fourteen thousand.

A private army that is, if not larger, then so many times more intimidating than any that is retained by his noblemen.

=====

5: The King's Manoeuvres

A.D. 1386

=====

-- WARWICK'S LOSS --

17th March 1386.

A private chamber, lit well by glass panes.

Thomas de Beauchamp is comfortable at his home, for Warwick Castle is a most impressive citadel that is both conspicuously menacing and impregnable from the south and east, and yet all but hidden from northern and western approaches until a welcome visitor, ill-fated prisoner, or unwary army is upon it.

He is the 12th such earl of Warwick in a long proud and unbroken line of earls of Warwick that reaches back to those dark and unknowable early Norman days of 1088. It is an impeccable earldom unmatched in England with, as he compresses the wrist of his sword and quill hand to alleviate the gripe within, all the weight of import to accompany such a well admired title.

There is quite a sheaf, it seems, of tired scrivened ink thus reporting on this and that which despite the employ of stewards, chamberlains and sheriffs, all evidently this day needs the highest of noble attention.

The latest scroll he has read, from one such sheriff does describe how at Wedgnock Park, a worthy expanse of meadow and woodland some miles to the north and east of the castle, is causing this day's aching bonce.

A well-known local ne'er-do-well, Matthew Cooper, was lately apprehended as the sole recidivist in the criminal felling of a young hart; an act which, in these impecunious days represents a crime the like of which could be compared with sending at arrow at the king himself. The venison thus butchered would feed many starving families and, if truth be known, Thomas de Beauchamp – having sickened himself of executions and killings on more foreign battlefields than he cares to recall – is, privately at least, willing to stand the occasional such loss.

But, once a sheriff has made his arrest, forest law and the King's justice must be upheld.

A local matter, then, but for young Cooper's admirable insistence on avoiding the rope. Escaped his trial and punishment, he did, and, according to the last letter Warwick read, is presumed concealed in the nearby village of Leek Wootton.

And so the earl determines to show the scallywag outlaw what it feels to be hunted, by contacting and employing his greatest, best known, and most feared knight in that locale. Sir John Russell, retained by the Earl of Warwick for a most generous salary of £28 per annum, resides in Whitenasshe Manor conveniently in the vicinity and, being presumably presently idle, may well appreciate the opportunity to run through a local outlaw and thereby no doubt add to his considerable fearsome reputation.

Warwick scratches a note to himself on the original scroll to call in his great knight, places the item in a box indicating '*nondum resolutis*' so he knows he must return his attention to this matter later, and opens the wax seal on the next scrolled parchment, adjusting his eyes to the spattered inked missive therein.

Within twenty heartbeats he is shrieking and hastening with purpose towards his wardrobe room, hustling and bustling the rest of his household into a brisk activity which at first is only heard from the creaking and clomping around him. As attendants and valets appear to him, he demands with animated splutters that those in his closest retinue do ready themselves for an urgent visit to a very senior duke.

=====

SCENE. THE GREAT HALL AT KENILWORTH CASTLE – EVENING

17th March 1386.

A giant hall with a giant fireplace and a vigorous log fire. ***Thomas Beauchamp, Earl of Warwick****, is warming himself but is agitated and paces in front of the heat.*

A great oaken door opens, and ***John of Gaunt****, Duke of Lancaster, enters and approaches his old friend. The visit is extraordinary, and Lancaster knows Warwick well, and so has already presumed that this involves news of great import.*

THOMAS BEAUCHAMP,
EARL OF WARWICK
(extremely agitated)
He's procured Russell!

JOHN OF GAUNT,
DUKE OF LANCASTER
Who has?

THOMAS BEAUCHAMP,
EARL OF WARWICK
Richard!

JOHN OF GAUNT,
DUKE OF LANCASTER
(nods calmly)
Very well. The King has procured Russell.

Who's Russell?

THOMAS BEAUCHAMP,
EARL OF WARWICK
Sir John Russell!

Ah yes. Sir John Russell is a well-known and most respected knight in this area.

JOHN OF GAUNT,
DUKE OF LANCASTER
(nods)
And Russell has been... kidnapped?

Warwick is extremely agitated, and snaps at his old friend.

THOMAS BEAUCHAMP,
EARL OF WARWICK
No! Bought! Richard has taken him from me, and now employs him as his own retained knight!

JOHN OF GAUNT,
DUKE OF LANCASTER
That's odd. And without informing you?

THOMAS BEAUCHAMP,
EARL OF WARWICK
There was a letter from a lawyer.

JOHN OF GAUNT,
DUKE OF LANCASTER
Giving notice?

THOMAS BEAUCHAMP,
EARL OF WARWICK
Yes.

**JOHN OF GAUNT,
DUKE OF LANCASTER**
Why would he do that?

**THOMAS BEAUCHAMP,
EARL OF WARWICK**
I was hoping you would know, he's your nephew.

**JOHN OF GAUNT,
DUKE OF LANCASTER**
Sir, I'm planning for Spain. I haven't even seen Richard in weeks.

In fact, he promised me £13,000 for this campaign but it hasn't shown yet.

Warwick is exasperated. He was hoping for answers.

Gaunt is saddened at Warwick's demeanour, and more than a little intrigued by King Richard's aggressive acquisition of a knight from the employ of England's oldest earldom.

**JOHN OF GAUNT,
DUKE OF LANCASTER (cont'd)**
Do you want me to ask Henry to keep an eye on Richard, while I'm away?

**THOMAS BEAUCHAMP,
EARL OF WARWICK**
He's not going with you?

**JOHN OF GAUNT,
DUKE OF LANCASTER**
He'll manage my estate in my absence.

**THOMAS BEAUCHAMP,
EARL OF WARWICK**
He is so young to speak to the king. So perhaps not a son, but...

...a brother, recently elevated to Gloucester?

Gaunt smiles with a genuine warmth.

JOHN OF GAUNT,
DUKE OF LANCASTER

```
Thomas, then.  Perhaps it is right that
we keep a discreet eye upon Richard and
his conduct.
```

Warwick knows that this is the best resolution he will get, under these circumstances.

=====

-- THE ACCOUNTS OF ARUNDEL --

8th April 1386.

The air, and no doubt much rain, sit heavy.

Dark dismal clouds have fixed their positions for the kind of day that makes you wonder if God Himself has melancholy.

As the pittering of the raindrops splash the leaves of the trees on the edge of the field before the grounds near to the great castle of Arundel, it is the sign for all who were out to find shelter, and **Richard FitzAlan** the earl of that great Sussex town elects to return to his private chamber to do something he has been delaying for some weeks in truth.

Like all senior noblemen, he employs a receiver, a trusted man of accounts, to report on his affairs, and to advise on how much and when to pay tributes requested by King Richard's exchequer. FitzAlan finds them a terrifying group of men who only ever ask you a question if they already know they can prove the answer.

Administration not being a skill close to Arundel's greatest desires, he searches for the latest roll, and inspects it with reluctance. Records, written in perfect inky handwriting, list a daily record of moneys received and dispersed by the FitzAlan household, followed by a right-aligned notation of the value of the transaction. He must admit that it is all quite ingeniously laid out so one can quickly see the description and the value of the transaction.

He can see that the total annual rental income as paid by all his tenant farmers was equal to £1,125, and because the farms and manors were of different productions, the yearly payments ranged in value from £6 up to £34. This was managed by his bailiff, for whom he paid a total of 120 shillings per annum for that management.

He can also see that he owned just fewer than one thousand sheep at the time of the accounts last year, all of which had been sheared for the sale of their wool, and many of which would be sold prior to the forthcoming yearly Martinmas slaughter, with that income earmarked for the purchase this spring of new lambing stock.

Other income from sales of livestock and harvested stock amount to almost £100, although he spent as much on purchasing new livestock. Another £100 was given to clothes, where several drapers were patronised, almost all of whom were based in London, with satin, velvet and damask being the most expensive cloths purchased by this earl.

His household staff salaries totalled a significant £42 per annum. And as did all senior barons, the Earl of Arundel additionally made a payment to personally-chosen knights; this annual payment retained their services and was anything from a few pounds to £20 per annum per knight, although it was understood that each knight might also make request on occasion for extra payments; officially to keep them well-equipped or, more likely, for private payments by the concupiscent curs to keep the peace of certain jealous husbands or fathers.

Repairs to property costs are alarming. Over £160 for materials, plus wages for masons, carpenters, plumbers, smiths and labourers: for improvements and renovations to various buildings, chambers and towers. Arundel Castle is already ancient, it is well kept and so the present earl would like to regard these as investments rather than expenses. But he cannot help but feel that his income would not have been reduced if these improvements had not been made. And furthermore he can recall a similar large figure being the expense for last year's improvements, and he suspects that next year will demand a similar figure too. Although thanks be to God that the construction on that damn chapel, built in accordance with instructions from his father's will, was finally finished.

Household expenses - over £200 per annum - are always so high a figure because they include running costs of managing land, and all the foodstuffs required to keep a household running. The cost of appearing rich to other people, and so be it.

And of course legal expenses for being able to prove the integrity of his accounts to any who would challenge them. As well as these fees, Arundel notes, the receiver this year also relieved the household of a flagon of ale. So be it.

When all is taken into account, Richard FitzAlan's household has a surplus of over £250.

£250!

This is an incredible amount, for in the past his annual surplus has typically been between £100 and £150. How on earth has he made such an improved surplus? He runs his eyes over the descriptions and the figures once again. And then he sees the discrepancy, and his eyes widen. And his skin turns cold. And then hot, so very hot. And bile rises quickly and it spews out of his mouth, the taste of his last meal of fish causing all the more to spew as it spews. He must recover. He must recover his belly and also his wits.

And he must now ride to London as fast as he can.

=====

SCENE. THE EXCHEQUER AT WESTMINSTER HALL – DAY

14th April 1386.

Richard FitzAlan, the Earl of Arundel*, seeks his receiver,* ***John Lincoln****.*

RICHARD FITZALAN,
EARL OF ARUNDEL
Lincoln! My men-at-arms! What happened?

JOHN LINCOLN,
RECEIVER
What do you mean?

RICHARD FITZALAN,
EARL OF ARUNDEL
My retainers! A dozen knights, four dozen esquires, and five-score archers.

Why are they not listed on my accounts?

JOHN LINCOLN,
RECEIVER
You don't know?

RICHARD FITZALAN,
EARL OF ARUNDEL
Why would I know?

Lincoln is embarrassed for Arundel, and bids him to come to a quiet corner of the room.

JOHN LINCOLN,
RECEIVER
The King has them.

I thought you knew?

Arundel blinks with disbelief.

**RICHARD FITZALAN,
EARL OF ARUNDEL**
What in God's name is King Richard doing with my retainers?

**JOHN LINCOLN,
RECEIVER**
They're the King's retainers since he requisitioned them.

You didn't know this?

**RICHARD FITZALAN,
EARL OF ARUNDEL**
Why would I-?

-Since when?

**JOHN LINCOLN,
RECEIVER**
As I understand this, he has been pursuing a stratagem of offering the kingdom's freelancers a little more money than they are currently earning to retain them for himself.

**RICHARD FITZALAN,
EARL OF ARUNDEL**
From other barons too?

**JOHN LINCOLN,
RECEIVER**
It's not just you.

(whispers)
Receivers talk, and sometimes indiscreetly. I'm sorry.

**RICHARD FITZALAN,
EARL OF ARUNDEL**
<u>You're</u> sorry!

Richard is gathering a private army, I'm a hundred and sixty men light, and I now have a surplus that awaits the King to tax as he wishes.

JOHN LINCOLN,
RECEIVER
Hmmm. One supposes the King will need the extra tax if there really is a French invasion.

RICHARD FITZALAN,
EARL OF ARUNDEL
(renewed panic)
What invasion?

=====

-- THE STREETS OF DOVER, 30TH APRIL 1386 --

Bells ring, and screaming people rush blindly.

Dark fast shapes, they are, and woe betide they come too close and push you bash you knock you to the floor.

I stopped helping people up when the helping in the gloom of the cobbles invited all the more men and women to better kick us over or fall beside us in this animal wrath. Now if you lose your feet in this madness then, rather than assisting, I pray for your life with what breath I can spare.

The castle stands black and large and safe. But just how safe is our castle once the French have berthed and riddled through our streets, into our houses, and across our pastures? What then?

As thousands of us stampede, this rabble, the strongest become stronger and the weakest become weaker, but strong or weak if God has chosen you then rest assured a stone or some such awaits the unwary foot to signal that you will be first to die when invaders crunch up the streets behind us.

They tell you; when you hear the dread clanging then you run to the castle and claim your security, and that is that. But they do not tell you how you are not alone in your pursuit of life, and in that pursuit you compete for space with every man, woman and child of Dover. They do not tell you of the screaming of the fear and the wailing of the broken legs and the crying of the children who are lost to their parents and the crying of the parents who have lost their children and do not know whether to now save themselves or risk their lives in an almost hopeless deadly search.

They do not tell you that your fellow people, those you hail well every morning, become thrashing vicious devils in need of a nest safe from the melee and the foreign death that swift stalks us all in this night. Mild men have already readily bashed me during my dash to the castle, and I feel certain that I too have blood on my fists that is not mine own, and whose it is man woman or child I do not care.

The thickening of our crowd before the gateway happens quickly, and even as I notice this I run into a fleshy wailing wall of backs that does not travel any further in spite of how I push. In fact many others later to this blocked dam than I are now pushing me from behind, and the imagination that these are Frenchmen catching me causes me to turn and there elbow what turns out to be a slight young mistress in the nose so that her dainty nub pops and crunches easily upon my connection.

I turn for'ard once again, for nothing will stop me from grinding through these castle gates.

However hundreds of others are pushing through also, and despite every ounce of strength I have we do not now move at all, but for our gasping and wailing.

The French are surely culling and reaping through Dover's streets behind us.

My erstwhile courteous neighbours do now thrash at me, as I do them.

And so, this is how we die.

=====

SCENE. THE PRINCE'S CHAMBER, WESTMINSTER PALACE – DAY

1st May 1386

***King Richard II** is laughing heartily at the news **Robert de Vere, the Marquis of Dublin**, has just imparted.*

KING RICHARD II

And yet there were no Frenchies in Dover at all?

**ROBERT DE VERE,
MARQUIS OF DUBLIN**

Fifty dead, and it was a false alarm! The origins of which, no-one can say.

KING RICHARD II

Ahhh, well, that is just so.

Now.

I have an errand for my Marquis of Dublin. We recently received a tribute payment from Brittany, and my old men advisers insist that we employ this windfall to requisition five hundred men-at-arms and a thousand archers to fortify our holdings in Ireland.

I am minded to cede to them on this occasion.

Requisition the men and take them to Ireland. We shall share any spoils you and they may pass upon.

ROBERT DE VERE,
MARQUIS OF DUBLIN
I would be honoured.

Speaking of Dover, those good people might assist me insofar as they are still alive.

Dover, and the other four ports, they pay you no taxes in return for certain concessions, including the building of ships to defend the south coast against this non-existent enemy.

Might I commission a couple of captains of this idle fleet of ours to use on my Ireland expedition?

KING RICHARD II
Indeed! What fun!

ROBERT DE VERE,
MARQUIS OF DUBLIN
(bowing)
Your Majesty.

=====

-- SIX DREAD LETTERS --

17th May 1386.

The six are flat, and arranged together.

Half a dozen short letters did **John of Gaunt** write, and half a dozen more lengthy replies has he received. And half a dozen dimensions of illumination into recent Westminster court activity has Gaunt now experienced, all the more worrying now they are all laid out side to side on the dark wood table of his most private of chambers.

The six informants are minor noblemen of the middling class each to whom Gaunt pays what, a pound per annum each, in return for intelligence when requested. The middling classes value their connection with the upper classes, especially in return for money. In Gaunt's considerable and experienced opinion, the middling classes have this the wrong way round. Perhaps they are only middling, because they value those above them more than those below them.

Men like Gaunt have traditional arrangements with armed retainers to call upon when kings declare a war, and such retainers include men-at-arms, archers and knights who do indeed always answer the call in settlement of the moneys they have happily received in order to be retained thus. The number of a nobleman's retainers does almost always indicate the wealth of that honourable gentleman, so while an impecunious Earl of Stafford may have a few score, a great duke like himself might call upon around five thousand.

But kings?

Kings do not usually have many retainers at all.

Kings have noblemen, and noblemen have retainers. In essence, the king has his kingdom's noblemen for retainers except that retainers are paid by noblemen and noblemen pay their king.

Of course retainers, while not necessarily in proximity to their paying lord, serve another purpose. Noblemen have all sworn fealty to their king, but not necessarily to one another. And disagreements are common among those who jostle for position in relation to the King and each other. Lords will be lords, and disagreements will happen, but would a lord toss a rock at a beehive if there were four thousand bees to reply in anger? And wouldn't a lord be tempted to take too much honey from a hive if there were no bees to protect it?

A king may have his favourite men-at-arms, of course, and gladly make some payment to them for naught much more than a show of wealth. And similarly a king's court will have chamber knights a-sprinkled throughout the public halls; a practice that embellishes a court's reputation as well as providing unspoken security against some wicked visitor who might find himself touched by the devil and thereby overcome with evil malice when in proximity to the sovereign lord.

Gaunt has several other anonymous trusted spies, at home as well as abroad, who tell stories of French garrisons massing and training in Normandy. The French can do what they like where they like, and although some contacts are more concerned about foreign invasions than others, Gaunt surmises that this French activity does not smell strong enough to be a prelude to an invasion (something that they've never managed before since William the Bastard if one discounts the curious Scottish episode). He still plans to travel to Spain and claim the Castilian crown, at least.

But notwithstanding the mildly threatening behaviour from France, there is an undeniable stratagem laid out before Gaunt as transcribed by his six independent court contacts, on their six independent reports.

And it is in truth more worrying to Gaunt than any French activity, for this is uncommon activity by his own king. At least the French have always been untrustworthy and can be relied upon for that, but this new intelligence is unfamiliar and worth attention for that reason.

The letters cause unnatural dread in Gaunt, the more he considers their contents. Why indeed would King Richard II be engaging in the accumulation of retained knights? And knights who, furthermore, were otherwise retained by his own noblemen?

The evidence is compelling. King Richard appears to be secretly retaining knights at the expense and liability of his own loyal noblemen.

But if Richard is collecting knights from noblemen all over the kingdom, this creates an imbalance that leaves the kingdom's peace and security at risk to ne'er-do-wells. French, or otherwise.

While this is heartrending, part of Gaunt is glad he is leaving for Castile, soon. And perhaps this foreign adventure is good insurance against the possibility of losing everything in England.

=====

SCENE. THE BLUE SHIP INN, DOVER – MORNING

9th July 1386.

***John of Gaunt, Duke of Lancaster** is saying goodbye to his son and heir **Henry Bolingbroke, Earl of Derby**.*

They are in his private quarters. There is much hustle and bustle, with porters carrying luggage out, but nobody pays any attention to the conversation.

JOHN OF GAUNT,
DUKE OF LANCASTER
There is one other matter. It seems Richard is employing subtlety to accumulate knights from his earls.

I do not know why.

HENRY BOLINGBROKE,
EARL OF DERBY
One presumes he wishes to dress them up to look nice in his court?

JOHN OF GAUNT,
DUKE OF LANCASTER
(smiles briefly)
You have found humour where I could not. If I were remaining in England, I would discreetly learn more of his intentions.

HENRY BOLINGBROKE,
EARL OF DERBY
But you're not.

JOHN OF GAUNT,
DUKE OF LANCASTER
And you are.

HENRY BOLINGBROKE,
EARL OF DERBY
What should I do?

JOHN OF GAUNT,
DUKE OF LANCASTER
Richard's activities are odd when all his barons already pledge their fealty to him. So I am curious.

While several have confirmed this state of affairs, it was Warwick who first alerted me to them, and he is still most aggrieved by them, so observe him with discretion.

It is the kind of activity that is like to draw my brother of Gloucester into politics at a level that may be beyond him. Therefore if you discover any kind of clandestine collaboration, learn about it.

HENRY BOLINGBROKE,
EARL OF DERBY
I will try.

JOHN OF GAUNT,
DUKE OF LANCASTER
Use your wits, Henry. Warwick is a whiner, and for some men it is enough to have other men listen to them whine, so just observe if you can.

But tread carefully if he plots anything.

HENRY BOLINGBROKE,
EARL OF DERBY
Of course.

JOHN OF GAUNT,
DUKE OF LANCASTER
I mean this, Henry.

Though I leave my estate with you as its lieutenant, I wish to be apprised of Richard's activities. And of Warwick's, if he makes any.

I do not wish to hear the heir to Lancaster is executed for treason and my beloved House of Lancaster served with attainder.

=====

-- KING RICHARD AND HIS COURT PEACOCKS --

10th July 1386.

His nephew wears the crown, much good it does.

For Richard holds the greatest headwear in Christendom poorly. Not with the solemnity deserving of such weighty responsibility but with all the care of a rich full-bellied old man throwing nutshells onto his fire.

Through heavy-lidded eyes does **Thomas of Woodstock, Duke of Gloucester**, regard his cockerel nephew and his coterie of fluffing peacocks.

This king before me has nineteen years to him, but confiscate the gold regalia and ermine and he has no more presence than a parish old maid.

The duke has but a dozen years on the boy, but he feels much older than he ought in a court full of clamouring yammerers that simper language at each other that the elders struggle to comprehend, and enter into uncouth intimate informalities that on occasion, like the sharing of each other's rings and shoes, seem just plain odd.

France, wars, and sieges long since fought, all seem forgotten in Richard's protected and protective, decorated and decorative, sanctum. Aye, forgotten and but still worse; lately irrelevant. Did this faithful duke sail to France and occasionally slice across Frenchmen with his steel; all for, what, this royal fool and his popinjays to shriek like women as they compare the rings on their fingers?

Does King Richard care that Thomas, Duke of Gloucester, still sometimes scrubs his finger ends silently in the night to rid his nails of French blood and soil even more than five years after the last scream was heard? The killing of men is easy to say, and easy enough to do as it turns out, but not so easy to forget even when you thought you'd forgotten. It is the mark of a real man to live and prosper after having killed in God's name to do so.

And yet all the while a dangerous court of innocence and innocents does here in Westminster legislate a waning kingdom that may yet bankrupt itself. He watches the lads' eyes as once again a small but eager audience gathers for King Richard to retell the tale of how Wat Tyler met his end, and how immediately thereafter a boy became a man. And yet with the recounting of every detail in every re-telling of that tiresome tale, the young man who tells it becomes more boy.

One lad, above all others, holds rapt his king's gaze although Gloucester can bear witness that this young man has heard about the greatness of his best friend and king times that number at least several score. Robert de Vere, long-time Earl of Oxford and for unknown services rendered to his king, lately Marquis of Ireland, is a fellow whom King Richard no doubt holds almost as dear as his queen. It's a relationship that bears an uncomfortable closeness. No man alive can recall the blasphemous recklessness of the unfortunate King Edward II and *his* favourite courtier who no doubt favoured each other in ways for which God would damn them both to Hell.

What King Richard does with de Vere in night-time chambers, if indeed anything, is of little concern to the Duke of Gloucester.

He just wishes Richard would at least respect his court and his kingdom enough to place a princely heir in his queen before turning his head towards the pretty marquis.

=====

SCENE. WESTMINSTER PALACE – NIGHT

14th July 1386.

***Thomas of Woodstock, the Duke of Gloucester**, sits by the fireside, in firelight, in a chamber full of scrolls. It looks like he does a lot of administration in here.*

*There's a tap at his door, which is opened by a tired and old-looking but respectful **Thomas de Beauchamp, the Earl of Warwick**, who enters nervously.*

Gloucester likes Warwick, and the elder is invited to sit opposite the younger, also by the fire.

THOMAS DE BEAUCHAMP,
EARL OF WARWICK
Thank you for seeing me, young Thomas.

THOMAS,
DUKE OF GLOUCESTER
I saw urgency in your note.

THOMAS DE BEAUCHAMP,
EARL OF WARWICK
I do indeed have a pressing matter, sir.

THOMAS,
DUKE OF GLOUCESTER
Then speak, my old friend.

Warwick ponders the crackling fire before speaking.

THOMAS DE BEAUCHAMP,
EARL OF WARWICK
I have a question: one of constitution.

THOMAS,
DUKE OF GLOUCESTER
Indeed.

**THOMAS DE BEAUCHAMP,
EARL OF WARWICK**

It concerns conversations I have lately held with an acquaintance...

Conversations regarding a certain philosophy.

A... well. A delicate one, in truth.

**THOMAS,
DUKE OF GLOUCESTER**

The pursuit of true wisdom is rarely without obstacle. What is the nature of such angst?

**THOMAS DE BEAUCHAMP,
EARL OF WARWICK**

Sir, I beg of thee... what is it that would make Richard a better king?

The Duke of Gloucester's expression instantly changes from friendly to severe.

**THOMAS,
DUKE OF GLOUCESTER**

Careful, Warwick, lest my hearing - which hath failed me in these moments - should return and comprehend such words that might lead an old lord up a scaffold.

**THOMAS DE BEAUCHAMP,
EARL OF WARWICK**

(holding his palms up submissively)

My Lord! I do not slander our great and glorious King Richard.

We are men of means. And experience. And wisdom, in matters of constitutional accordance.

I well recall the worthy deeds of our right and proper sovereign lord's grandfather King Edward the Third, and his most noble Plantagenet blood is undoubted in Richard.

Gloucester placates Warwick with a calming hand.

There is a pause.

Gloucester knows that Warwick still needs to say something more. Eventually...

THOMAS DE BEAUCHAMP,
EARL OF WARWICK (cont'd)

Perhaps, though...

...it is time the elders of his court provide an account of how our greatest royal prince may reach the greatness of his predecessor.

And in so doing, thereby direct our King's fancy to the weal of our great kingdom.

Gloucester is inwardly afraid of the potential treasonous subject of this conversation. But he knows Warwick well, and regards him as a trustworthy honourable man and unlikely to be given to traitorous urges.

THOMAS,
DUKE OF GLOUCESTER

You say you have had conversations with an acquaintance. Who is the third person in our furtive triumvirate, Warwick?

THOMAS DE BEAUCHAMP,
EARL OF WARWICK

I pray with all I have that we have the weal of the kingdom and of the King in our hearts.

THOMAS,
DUKE OF GLOUCESTER

I believe you. Tell me.

THOMAS DE BEAUCHAMP,
EARL OF WARWICK

My compatriot in this matter is one Richard FitzAlan, known well to us both as the Earl of Arundel.

THOMAS,
DUKE OF GLOUCESTER

An exemplary noble, of most ancient stock. What is it that caused such conversation about King Richard?

THOMAS DE BEAUCHAMP,
EARL OF WARWICK
Ah. Arundel and I have lately suffered, along with many others, at Richard's hand.

Warwick has stopped talking as if this were explanation enough. It isn't. Gloucester opens his hands to ask for more information.

THOMAS DE BEAUCHAMP,
EARL OF WARWICK (cont'd)
Is it not well known?

THOMAS,
DUKE OF GLOUCESTER
Not to me.

THOMAS DE BEAUCHAMP,
EARL OF WARWICK
My Lord...

...Richard is acquiring retained knights from his noblemen, all over the realm.

THOMAS,
DUKE OF GLOUCESTER
Why?

THOMAS DE BEAUCHAMP,
EARL OF WARWICK
You do not know? This is not a family policy?

THOMAS,
DUKE OF GLOUCESTER
King Richard is acquiring retained knights from his barons? He doesn't need to. We're <u>his</u> retainers, except we pay him to be so!

It doesn't make any sense, man.

THOMAS DE BEAUCHAMP,
EARL OF WARWICK
Indeed. And yet it is so.

THOMAS,
DUKE OF GLOUCESTER
Did your previous conversations with Arundel suggest a reason for this alleged behaviour?

THOMAS DE BEAUCHAMP,
EARL OF WARWICK
We believe the King is being diverted from his solemn royal duties by his favourite chamber knights.

Gloucester twitches into full focus.

THOMAS,
DUKE OF GLOUCESTER
De Vere.

THOMAS DE BEAUCHAMP,
EARL OF WARWICK
For one. Richard is a young man, and keen to be a fellow of great interest, particularly to other young men of about his age.

Gloucester is unnerved at the thinking of Richard's behaviour.

THOMAS,
DUKE OF GLOUCESTER
But sir, how does this explain his acquisition of knights?

THOMAS DE BEAUCHAMP,
EARL OF WARWICK
We believe he wants more retainers than his friends have.

Gloucester blinks.

THOMAS DE BEAUCHAMP,
EARL OF WARWICK (cont'd)
The crown can afford them.

And he is young enough for such things as 'size' to matter to him.

THOMAS,
DUKE OF GLOUCESTER

Richard should be spending more effort on matters further afield, and more threatening in nature.

THOMAS DE BEAUCHAMP,
EARL OF WARWICK

My honourable lord of Arundel wonders if Richard is attempting to recreate the glorious colourful court his late father held in Aquitaine.

THOMAS,
DUKE OF GLOUCESTER

(sighs)

All this does seem a little 'French'.

THOMAS DE BEAUCHAMP,
EARL OF WARWICK

There is more, sir.

THOMAS,
DUKE OF GLOUCESTER

Go on.

THOMAS DE BEAUCHAMP,
EARL OF WARWICK

Although de Vere is a fop, Arundel and I believe that a more grievous character in this tragedy is that senior statesman Lord Chancellor who, through grave negligence of duty, does protect our king from the full knowledge required to make wise policies regarding France and further.

THOMAS,
DUKE OF GLOUCESTER

Well, yes. Richard would be better served by someone better born.

THOMAS DE BEAUCHAMP,
EARL OF WARWICK

That is why I- we, think the efficacy of our undoubted King to rule his kingdom may be assured by the removal of the de

Vere boy, and Michael de la Pole, and perhaps others.

Thereafter, the King shall be free to concentrate on more kingly matters.

THOMAS,
DUKE OF GLOUCESTER

The removal of a Lord Chancellor? How-?

THOMAS DE BEAUCHAMP,
EARL OF WARWICK

Impeachment. On the grounds of negligence.

THOMAS,
DUKE OF GLOUCESTER

But no man of office has ever...

THOMAS DE BEAUCHAMP,
EARL OF WARWICK

I... know.

Gloucester is incredulous at the conversation he is having. It is terrifying, and yet enlivening all at the same time. He weighs the risk against the reward.

Presently, he begins nodding to himself.

THOMAS,
DUKE OF GLOUCESTER

Let us attempt to ease out de Vere with subtlety. At least in the first instance.

THOMAS DE BEAUCHAMP,
EARL OF WARWICK

We ought. Ought we not?

THOMAS,
DUKE OF GLOUCESTER

(nods slowly)

While Richard heaps land and titles upon one so green, he prevents us old guards from growing our deserved fortune.

THOMAS DE BEAUCHAMP,
EARL OF WARWICK

I do not speak for me. You do not speak for you. But we do speak for our great kingdom!

THOMAS,
DUKE OF GLOUCESTER

As for de la Pole. I don't know. To oust one of the Great Officers of State... ...no. Let us watch and wait for an opportunity to act against him with more confidence.

-- DISTURBED HENS --

20th August 1386.

If they cluck once more, then he'll rise to piss.

The dark is always menacing, so if **Roger of Hythe** ever wakes with the urge he is usually able to ignore it. But the hens have fluttered and cluckled times enough to reason that the taking of a piss would at least scare off the latest bold fox to come a-calling.

And there they go again.

To shout would wake the family at about, what looks like judging by the glow, about an hour before this summer dawn, so he and his linen undergarments emerge. He picks up his cudgel just in case there is something out there to bash, and shuffles out.

A soft wind comes from the south and so the sea air is fulfilling as he draws it into his nostrils and chest and then out through the mouth, stretching arms to behind his hips as he does so. He feels better for it. The scratching and pulling at the hairy old bodkins is equally satisfying.

The stars above are silver bright, and the glow to the north-east is a peaceful orange, and he quickly prays for a good day. A good day with all his hens intact.

He steps gingerly across the small grassy courtyard. Gingerly because when he was a young man making barefoot night-time mischief with his friends, he once had the misfortune to encounter an unseen and wholly innocent itinerant hedgehog; an experience so alarming that he can still recall not only every single spine quill that greeted the underside of his foot, but also the crunch of the poor young animal's bones that occurred due to the weight of the boy. When old Mother Harkness found the fly-ridden corpse next day, he had proposed that maybe a Frenchie had stood on him, to the belief of nobody.

The hen coop is a wooden construction secured to stop foxes from getting in by night surrounded by woven wicker fencing panels around the pen to discourage the hens getting out by day. They could easily fly over the yard-high panels but if they are well fed then they normally show no ambition other than scratting around in the dirt to dig up worms for a little extra juice. Although he'd once, with great amusement, witnessed the otherwise ambivalent clucking birds tearing a stray rat to pieces in the kind of bloodlust frenzy he'd only seen previously in the dog pits. And once or twice in France, when he'd been commissioned.

Ho, ladies. What ye sen? And why the roiling?

There are no breaches in the coop, as far as he can feel, and he fancies that the fox, if that's what it was has been scared right away. He stands up and stretches again, this time the east is a little lighter. Perhaps the cockerel got the ladies up a little earlier this morning, he thinks with a smile as he scratches his head.

The orchard is a few steps away. Somehow it is more satisfying to piss up against something solid like a tree rather than into something yielding like a bush, and once positioned accordingly he lets go easily and with rising pleasure at the full flow.

The *SNAP* behind him ceases his water with the sobering clarity of dread, for a dry stick would break thus with man-sized pressure and he spins around to locate the offence.

In the half-light stands not quite a silhouette. A daemon, with sturdy proportions and an ill will. The hair is black, long, and straggly, the skin glistens in the starlight shadows as if it is oiled, the shoulders are wide and the arms are thick, with leather wrist straps and several rings on the fingers. Horns atop his head, and cloven hooves stand him up on the ground. Or... not. Either way, nobody in Hythe or Rye or Dover looks like this, and the acknowledgement is a petrifying understanding.

The scene has been surveyed, and already both men have ascertained the foreigner has the upper hand over a barefoot farmer with his old boy in his hand.

Several swift strides forward, and a smooth heavy cudgel punches into just below the farmer's left ear. A whump, a crack, ringing, enough for a knockdown onto the fragrant grass.

Sheep and cattle, when their necks are sliced, do mostly meet their deaths at the time of their deaths with an uneasy calm acceptance.

And so does he.

Just before the thick wood finally whooshes toward his prostrate defenceless head for a second fatal time, Roger of Hythe hears the last sound that he hears.

It is whispered ridicule from his murderer.

"Bonjour."

=====

-- THE ROAD TO DOVER --

10th September 1386.

It is a fine autumn morning, indeed.

Richard FitzAlan the Earl of Arundel and half a dozen trusted men leave the tavern, leave Canterbury, and continue with purpose along the jarring rutted rural clay of southbound Watling Street.

Six horses, plus the two that pull the rectangular wooden iron-clad wagon, have been shoed, and the earl knows this should see them amble up through the downs, descend into Dover, pick up that which is being stored in one of Dover's customs houses, and then get back to Sussex again.

Canterbury Cathedral was a worthy diversion and the tavern was a fair hostelry, and now Dover lies ahead towards the mid-afternoon of a day's travelling.

But this morning's mood is sombre, for the plumes of grey-black smoke that hang like a gathered curtain from beyond the bronzing tree leaf-canopied horizon may well hang over their destination.

Their tavern landlord had taken being patronised by an earl the opportunity to bemoan the recent local lawlessness. Hens and sheep had been purloined locally, villages burned, womenfolk desecrated, and menfolk bashed or chopped.

Kent, for all its beauty and fair weather, was always susceptible to a steady trickle of English soldier deserters who, having found their way from military duties France, inevitably surreptitiously through one of the Cinque Ports at the south coast near Dover, and thereafter into England's hinterlands whereupon, without any clear belonging of anywhere, almost invariably took upon themselves the pursuits of common outlaws and pilferers. Though sometimes some would gang together and attempt more daring heinous raids upon the traffic and pilgrims travelling to or from Canterbury and beyond, most eventually would float back to wherever they called home. But even as some fugitives left, some more would arrive to maintain Kent's unknown number of unwelcome ruffians.

Arundel wasn't surprised to hear a tavern owner chirruping of the threats to his business to an earl of King Richard's court, but he was rather concerned that their host claimed that the perpetrators of these malicious crimes were not Kentish transients but men of France. Arundel remained largely disinterested in the innkeeper's prattle, but queried his hypothesis to find that other locals and travellers soon confirmed that it was true. Kent it seemed, particularly at the south coast, was regularly being visited by Frenchmen, who with great impertinence were alighting in small groups and causing great localised malice to good English folk.

If such thoughts of Frenchies desecrating these parts weren't discomfiting enough, then awaking to a chimney of idle well-established smoke to the south initiates alarming reactions all round.

The earl of Arundel had long ago decided to personally lead this particular expedition, because he was expecting a significant shipment of Venetian silk. He'd spent many months in written communications with a series of traders and agreed on an exquisite design as originally painted by the late Jacopo Bellini (still regarded as having among the best silk design portfolios in the world) and Arundel's communication that first hopscotched its parchmented way across the continent, squeezed in between French territories and all the way to Amalfi, and the well-remarked guild therein.

Highest quality woven silk. And not just silk but a full twenty yards of premium Asian Tatar silk. A small fortune, but an investment. For the silk is a gift, fit for a king. King Richard was still young enough to be impressed by such shiny nonsense. So, an expensive investment, then. And one that wouldn't fare well under battle, especially not with chancing vagabond Frenchies grabbing easy value during their raids.

The miles ramble by, and the smell of fired wood now cannot be ignored, and tales from the mucky northbound folk travelling in the opposite direction begin to chill the earl. Though some fair witnesses would cheerily report that Dover Castle stands as resolute as ever, all bear tales that ships and docks and import houses were invaded, emptied, and burned by pirates, or the French, who knows, who cares.

Only the earl's dread carries him into Dover, and upon arrival pays his own witness to a charred spectacle. His expected shipment is nowhere; either burned to nothing, stolen to France, or looted into Kent.

To accept the loss is somehow less agitating than the wondering of its whereabouts.

A devastated town, and a devastated earl. Why was Dover not defended as it should be by the Cinque Ports navy - the fleet paid for by the southern towns instead of paying the King taxes and thus charged with the defending of those vulnerable south coast ports from France and pirates?

He enquires of Dover's illustrious mayor where their defensive fleet was adjourned to.

And who by.

The answers he is given are enough to enrage.

=====

SCENE. WESTMINSTER PALACE – NIGHT

14th September 1386.

*Three men. The **Duke of Gloucester**, and the **Earls of Warwick** and of **Arundel**. The duke; uncle to the King. The earls; senior court officials. Not a secret meeting, exactly, but not a public one either. The mood is dark.*

THOMAS OF WOODSTOCK,
DUKE OF GLOUCESTER
All of it, gone?

Richard FitzAlan the Earl of Arundel nods grimly.

THOMAS BEAUCHAMP,
EARL OF WARWICK
Frenchmen? In Kent!

RICHARD FITZALAN,
EARL OF ARUNDEL
And increasingly often, too, by all accounts.

THOMAS BEAUCHAMP,
EARL OF WARWICK
In Kent, though! Damn them all.

THOMAS OF WOODSTOCK,
DUKE OF GLOUCESTER
Never mind damn the French. Damn the mayor and constables of Dover!

And damn the fleet that guards the port.

RICHARD FITZALAN,
EARL OF ARUNDEL
There was no fleet.

THOMAS OF WOODSTOCK,
DUKE OF GLOUCESTER
Of course there's a fleet.

THOMAS BEAUCHAMP,
EARL OF WARWICK
Indeed. Our Five Ports are relieved of the burden of tax in return for the provision-

RICHARD FITZALAN,
EARL OF ARUNDEL
-The fleet was not there in its entirety.

THOMAS OF WOODSTOCK,
DUKE OF GLOUCESTER
Then where was it?

RICHARD FITZALAN,
EARL OF ARUNDEL
Much of the Cinque Ports Navy, paid for by our southern towns to guard the docks of southern England was *en route* to Ireland...

...commanded on an errand of king's business by our friend, Robert de Vere, Marquis of Dublin.

The Duke of Gloucester carefully seats himself into a large wooden armchair. There's a very heavy silence in the room.

THOMAS OF WOODSTOCK,
DUKE OF GLOUCESTER
Leaving Dover unguarded?

THOMAS BEAUCHAMP,
EARL OF WARWICK
De Vere just left? Without safeguarding-?

THOMAS OF WOODSTOCK,
DUKE OF GLOUCESTER
(interrupts)
-How much did you lose?

RICHARD FITZALAN,
EARL OF ARUNDEL
Much.

THOMAS OF WOODSTOCK,
DUKE OF GLOUCESTER
Might you sue? For negligence, or some such?

RICHARD FITZALAN,
EARL OF ARUNDEL
I? An appellant to the King? Petitioning against the King's favourite?
My dear Gloucester, you have yet to conceive for me a swifter way to the block.

THOMAS OF WOODSTOCK,
DUKE OF GLOUCESTER
French pirates, though. A precedent that may one day end in our ruin.

THOMAS BEAUCHAMP,
EARL OF WARWICK
So what do you do?

RICHARD FITZALAN,
EARL OF ARUNDEL
What we have always done. Parliament convenes in October.

We have a fortnight in which to gather allies among England's noblemen and together make the firmest of demands of our King to go to France in war, and take more of what is ours.

=====

-- THE COURT OF KING CHARLES VI --

Le 15 septembre 1386.

The faces smile, but, no, the eyes are grave.

King Charles VI observes his advisers Philip *duc de Burgundy*, Louis *duc de Bourbon* and Jean *duc de Berry* - all of them his uncles - as they tread towards his throne, in and out of the bright sunbeams that shine in from high on his left to low at his right.

The faces lit, then darkened, lit, then darkened, lit, then darkened. By the third darkening he is always able to tell if the news is good for him or bad for him, regardless of the face that approaches, and thus he today readies himself for irritating news.

He is right to expect the irritation. As the older men relate their combined tales, their king's disposition darkens.

It seems that, in accordance with the recent dependable intelligence gained by spies who are always slapping back and forth across the sea, the Duke of Lancaster has taken his wife Constanza, a princess of Castile, along with a significant retinue, and has recently rounded Brittany, then sailed past the Bay of Biscay and beyond, to land in Spain's north-west corner at a small region known as Galicia, which is precisely to the west of northern Castile and to the north of Portugal.

The present royal incumbents of Castile are grossly unpopular after their previous aggressive usurpation, and so the returning Constanza, daughter and heiress of the rightful king who was stabbed several times in the face by his thereafter victorious brother, is being welcomed by many of the established Castilian families. As is her husband, John of Gaunt, a royal duke of the great house of Lancaster.

It is no surprise that the old blood of Castile is at this time rallying around England's richest nobleman - let the hens fluff around their colourful proud new cockerel - however the surprise to King Charles's French court is that the King of Portugal has also rallied to Lancaster's cause. Charles makes tight fists and clenches everything on his face hard to ease a private burden of intense hostility that rushes behind his eyes and above his teeth. His advisers want to tell him more but, recognising the expression on their sovereign lord as one that should not be troubled further, they elect to stand before their king with a silent respect.

A short while passes. Charles has ceased the clinching but breathes as if he has run around his palace. Only when the breathing slows do they then tell their king more about what he has already contemplated.

King Charles VI of France has before today enjoyed being apprised of his kingdom's activities in the training and building of an armed presence that would terrorise England at its heart. His is an army that has proved itself with antagonistic manoeuvres in Flanders, although in truth this cost more money than he expected for less return than he had hoped for. But, as his learned advisers are now imparting, Charles must consider now a world-to-be in which the Duchess of

Lancaster might claim her birthright; an act that would place England's greatest duke on the throne of Castile which would essentially make him King of Spain.

A well-ruled Spain, with an Englishman king at its head, is a most disturbing concept. And an unusually hushed England from beyond his northern coastline must also be relied upon to be mysterious enough to cause suspicion. And all the while, thanks to his eagerness to enter Flanders, he is losing money to his east.

King Charles VI meets the eye of his most trusted adviser Philip *duc de Burgundy* and knows that they agree.

An English king to his northern border, and an English king to his south-eastern border, is not a threat that Charles is going to tolerate. He must ensure that at least one of the Englishmen fails.

As Gaunt is so active, France will now lean to the west.

=====

-- MASTER HENRY OF MONMOUTH --

16th September 1386.

The babe is a chunker, and well for it.

He mewls triumphantly in life at the success of his first deadly adventure, and undoubtedly has the strength to go on and crawl to the stables and ride to Westminster and present himself to King Richard if he wasn't now swaddled and suckling at his mother. Mary's milk is undoubtedly more appealing.

Henry Bolingbroke is enjoying the warmth in the head that comes from becoming a father while retaining his wife. Many men do not share such great fortune and God be praised for his.

As he himself was born in the Lincolnshire castle town of Bolingbroke and is known as Henry of Bolingbroke so his newborn, birthed at Monmouth Castle, will therefore be known as Henry of Monmouth.

Henry of Monmouth. A noble sounding name indeed, and chosen at the very last instead of that which was planned. The babe, if a boy like he indubitably is, was to be named John, after Henry's own great father John of Gaunt the Duke of Lancaster. But, only once born, did the parents realise that "John of Monmouth" has a peculiar sounding rhyming couplet to it, and that was as much of an omen as they needed to instead honour Gaunt's father-in-law Henry of Grosmont, from whom Gaunt inherited the title Duke of Lancaster, and from whom in time the Henrys Bolingbroke and Monmouth will thereafter, God willing, do likewise.

After saying prayers for dear Mary and young Henry, in which he also poured unrestrained praise on the dutiful ladies-in-waiting who all mercifully performed their duties with great diligence and admiration, Henry dismisses himself from the clucking coven of the gatehouse tower and returns his thoughts and his person to the letter he received from his father, earlier that day.

Henry knows from previous letters that the duke, having enjoyed free passage and escort by a Portuguese fleet numbering around twenty fine ships from his great ally at the edge of the world the King of Portugal, has already berthed at La Coruna in Galicia - a north-western port in Spain's most north-western region - and is there receiving and successfully courting local Spanish allies having declared his intention to bring together the territories of Galicia, Leon and Castile into a more coherent united kingdom. Those local dukes of here and there, whom by all accounts are all weary of the disharmony caused by having a distasteful mistrusted usurper on the Castilian throne, have pledged their allegiance to the English duke who is after all married to the woman many of those over there consider to be the rightful heiress to Castile.

But this morning's communication, its contents arrived rightfully and faithfully conserved by the wax embossed by his father's seal, has greatly disturbed Henry of Bolingbroke, even on the occasion of the birth of his first son and heir.

If Henry had been troubled by the prospect of his father's absence prior to his departure, then such discomfort was now multiplied greatly due to the intelligence Henry has lately read by his father's own hand as it, incredibly, spoke to him gravely from a land far beyond the sea about secrets within England.

There are warnings in the letter, and the reason is quite explicit.

Henry you must protect our positions as heirs to this kingdom.

Well-known names and sinister doings are outlined within the parchment. Names well known in court. Names well known to Henry.

For two of those predictably named, Gaunt requests of Henry to make close but clandestine observations on Michael de la Pole - the Lord Chancellor and Richard's most senior official - and Robert de Vere - the Marquis of Dublin and Richard's effete confidant.

How his father is appraised of the realm's high-level goings on should not be a surprise to Henry, but it displays considerable political skill to be such an active part in court mysteries while so far away. Not for the first time is the younger reminded of how much more he has to learn from the elder if he is to someday be as great a lord as John of Gaunt.

Also documented in the letter is lordly activity John of Gaunt highlights as being most unbecoming. Three names he writes, each on their own enough to make Henry Bolingbroke's heart beat fiercely.

Henry shivers to think of the messenger forgetting how to be as loyal as this family of Lancaster would demand, and its unsettling and terrifying contents being instead delivered into the possession of one of those so named. Or even not one of those so named. Or, God save us, the King!

And what if John of Gaunt is wrong? Mistaken? Too far from court to hear true whispers? The distance between Gaunt and court is significant, and does a truth become into a lie with its vast stretching over miles?

No.

John of Gaunt would not have risked the letter merely on account of blab. This intelligence must be significant and weighty.

Given his new perspective as a new father, Henry's sudden greatest fear is some imbalance in the kingdom that might in times ahead affect his family. And if, as his father suggests, there is any group of senior lords who are surreptitiously gathering to appraise their king's shortfall in wisdom and behaviours, Henry of Bolingbroke decides he must be a part of it.

Emboldened and inspired by the success of his wife and son, Henry will gather his wits and seek clarity from the most shocking name so revealed in his father's letter.

For that most significant name is Henry's youngest uncle and John of Gaunt's own younger brother; Thomas of Woodstock, Duke of Gloucester.

=====

SCENE. ELTHAM PALACE – DAY

20th September 1386.

***King Richard II** and **Michael de la Pole**, Lord Chancellor and the Earl of Suffolk, speak together in a private chamber.*

The King is seated at a large desk with many papers on it. Suffolk stands politely.

MICHAEL DE LA POLE,
LORD CHANCELLOR AND
EARL OF SUFFOLK

I do not understand it, but I fear it. The French armies have moved south from Normandy.

KING RICHARD II
To where?

MICHAEL DE LA POLE,
LORD CHANCELLOR AND
EARL OF SUFFOLK
(shakes head solemnly)
We cannot at this time see quite so deeply into France.

There are still raids on Kent, though, so I continue to presume they are gathering information about our defences.

Richard is deep in thought. He does not speak for some time.

Eventually...

KING RICHARD II
And so no doubt the next messenger we receive is from some uncle or other, urging us to sail to France and press our claim to our ancestors' lands.

MICHAEL DE LA POLE,
LORD CHANCELLOR AND
EARL OF SUFFOLK
Possibly, Sire.

KING RICHARD II
What is this desire everyone has, Michael? To make war against other Christian men.

Suffolk frowns sympathetically.

MICHAEL DE LA POLE,
LORD CHANCELLOR AND
EARL OF SUFFOLK
They are French, at least?

Richard is still deep in thought. He cannot admit to anyone that he is terrified of actually being on a battlefield.

Eventually...

KING RICHARD II
I have eschewed aggression toward France.

(pause)

Now it comes to it, the King would declare to you alone, Michael, that he does not seek war against <u>our</u> own kind.

Suffolk looks uncomfortable.

KING RICHARD II (cont'd)
My dearest Suffolk.

If invaded, we would dutifully defend our realm like madmen, and in the knowledge that God shall be with us justly.
But our Lord Jesus preached a righteous path that is peaceful, and so it thus shall be.

We would rather a reign much admired throughout the world not for its war but for its good Christian standing.

MICHAEL DE LA POLE, LORD CHANCELLOR AND EARL OF SUFFOLK
My Lord.

I have to say, this extraordinary royal stance would see your elder barons unanimously against you.

Richard is troubled for some time.

Eventually...

KING RICHARD II
Does not a flock of sheep bleat lamentably upon a shepherd's direction, until they realise that the next field he takes them to is greener?

Suffolk nods, but isn't in a rush to say anything.

Eventually...

**MICHAEL DE LA POLE,
LORD CHANCELLOR AND
EARL OF SUFFOLK**

In support of my king, I would happily state that we truly still cannot really afford to go to war.

It is the truth.

KING RICHARD II

We <u>must</u> tread the way of peace.

Suffolk frowns once again, as if formulating an idea and testing the logic of it in silence.

Eventually...

**MICHAEL DE LA POLE,
LORD CHANCELLOR AND
EARL OF SUFFOLK**

By your command, I have a stratagem.

During the forthcoming parliament, I would declare your expressed devotion to respond to known French activities... by leading your army across to France.

KING RICHARD II

(edgy)

Hmmm. A policy well-conceived, had I not just expressed the <u>PRECISE</u> <u>OPPOSITE</u>.

**MICHAEL DE LA POLE,
LORD CHANCELLOR AND
EARL OF SUFFOLK**

Ah, but then having declared your <u>so-called</u> intent, it would be quite normal for you to petition parliament for sufficient aid, and then for your Lord Chancellor to declare the cost of such a venture.

KING RICHARD II

(scared)

And what would this tax be?

De la Pole smiles.

MICHAEL DE LA POLE, LORD CHANCELLOR AND EARL OF SUFFOLK

Entirely prohibitive.

=====

-- THE AFTERMATH OF A PARLIAMENT FULL OF WONDER --

1st October 1386.

Men run in all directions, all at once.

Thomas of Woodstock the Duke of Gloucester, eyes wide, uses his big arms to fend off other wailing lords flapping around him in outraged despair.

He is both attempting to locate Arundel or Warwick across a parliament hall of men full-vexed with great agitation, all the while desperately trying to calculate if the furore is about to cause him to be arrested, and then executed.

The Great Hall at Westminster is a most suitable venue for a parliament, which is itself usually a reasonably efficacious, if occasionally ponderous, method of communicating with the King. But today the King has taken flight in fury; flanked and followed by his young coterie of intimates. Today, a majority of barons caused a rage in their supreme leader that they might presume only to have seen on the battlefield in the face of an enemy.

And Gloucester, still buffeted by velvet-wrapped bodies, is now desperately seeking some, even untempered, assurance from his cohorts. For with any dread sense of panic comes a need to connect with others who share the same secrets, even though one may accept that there is little practical consolation for doing so.

Shouts and cries from surrounding rabbling barons are rap-a-tapping at his head through his ears.

The first day of parliament had begun as one would expect, with several good lords making the usual declarations of fair nature to their sovereign lord. And the King, on his throne, a few steps higher than all others just as God intended, seemed well-humoured.

But Gloucester, and Arundel, and Warwick had petitioned to declare in parliament to His Most Royal of Highnesses the news of the regular foreign desecrations in the south and their request for England to declare war on France. To the surprise of everyone, the King had responded by declaring his intent to lead a large English army through Calais and into Normandy and onto Paris. The parliament cheers would have been heard in Kent! However even before the cheers had diminished to nothing, the king's Lord Chancellor, Michael de la Pole the Earl of

Suffolk had with respect to the King's wishes beseeched his parliament for the advancement of taxed monies totalling £155,000 in silver and gold to in order plan and mount such an invasion.

Uproar. Such a sum, indeed!

Alas, the men that populate the parliamentary benches suffered this news loudly and King Richard, though gracing the darkening congregation with his attention for a short while, did presently begin to look evermore blackened of mood. Suffolk continued relaying his request on behalf of his king with earnest duty until, his part having been played out, he began to fear for his own welfare.

The sudden howl of pain that did issue from King Richard was astonishing. Witnessing England's liege lord lamenting so caused gasps and a cry or two from the benches, and several barons - no doubt fearful that the King had encountered some most unexpected malaise and happened upon a sudden death on his throne - dropped to their knees in case God would choose them next.

"*Outrage! Outrage!*" then shouted their young lord and master, as he most unbefittingly led an unkinglike exodus followed by the scampering of his tutting young cohorts. King Richard's disappearance left a baronial consternation that multiplied quickly into the bellowing violent despair that Gloucester is but a droplet of now.

He shares the fear of his peers. For if the young man who is above them all adjudges that his utter displeasure has been directly caused by any particular lords, then those particular lords are like to have their necks sliced through before the week is done.

=====

-- A CURIOUS DUKE --

3rd October 1386, Eltham Palace, Kent.

A beetle stutters across long-cracked oak.

It is traversing up a steadfast door, its destination unknown; or at least uncertain if its lack of purpose is anything to judge it by.

Thomas of Woodstock the Duke of Gloucester, buttresses the flesh of his first finger with the tip of his thumb, and presses his first finger's nail upon the hapless bug. It cracks unseen, except when he pulls his hand away to inspect the glop; little legs flickering, a little juice already congealing. He wipes its total earthly remains idly on his burgundy tabard.

His partners in the lonely chamber, weaponed guards, prevent an unauthorised entry to the King's chamber and attend to their own thoughts just privately as he attends his. For an audience with King Richard is at hand. A king who most haven't seen since parliament two days ago. A king who left his lords and his parliament, outraged. A king who has since been consoled only by his simpering sympathetic young friends. A king who has until now refused to consult or even see his elder councillors. A king who still behaves as a boy. A boy who holds the lives of everyone in his kingdom in his young royal hand.

Gloucester must concentrate and the frown reveals his effort. He does not know what humour holds his king. King Richard had wailed at the response poured out by his own parliament upon Suffolk's outrageous parliamentary request for funds for a French campaign. His Royal Highness had flung his hands high and fled, leaving the chamber to its countenance of despair.

Gloucester could guess at why his King would demand such a sum, and the prospect of having a coward king leaves a coldness in his belly. Though why the King had departed Westminster for Eltham Palace, no-one could say for sure except to presume with great sadness that Richard had merely behaved as a weak young man might. For Gloucester's part, he wishes to learn more about the King's humour, and if unconvinced of Richard's responses as to why he has demanded a King's fortune in tax, or why he abandoned parliament to itself, he will pressure his nephew to return, and if resistance is found thereupon, then Gloucester is minded to have a very short conversation about how and why such things as leaving the Kentish coastline undefended is acceptable to nobody. English subjects had been killed, English farms had been looted, imports and exports had been stolen; and all because there wasn't a fleet defensive enough to rely upon. Men misplaced in authority have been executed for less, imprisoned for far less, and Gloucester is just about senior enough to arrest de Vere for at least failure to do one's duty.

And then there was the tax. £155,000. It is so high a demand as to appear suspicious, and if King Richard is not taking his role as sovereign lord seriously, or if he is being encouraged by others to not take his royal duties seriously, then it is Gloucester's right and duty to inform His Highness of his close friends' dangerous actions.

But for now, Gloucester concentrates on his initial plan. He shall keep calm, inform the King of the urgent need to reconsider his demands for so much money, remind him of his duty to return to his parliament, and perhaps politely offer himself as a responsible guardian of the Cinque Ports fleet so he might reliably restore the south coast defences.

And, all the while, hope the King is not disposed to crush him like a beetle.

=====

SCENE. ELTHAM PALACE – DAY

3rd October 1386.

*The **Duke of Gloucester** bows to **King Richard II**, who sits on a throne while surrounded by four youthful male friends including **Robert de Vere, Marquis of Dublin**.*

THOMAS OF WOODSTOCK,
DUKE OF GLOUCESTER
I pray His Royal Highness is kept well these past days?

KING RICHARD II
The King is humbled by his uncle's concern, and thus reports favourably upon our wellness.

THOMAS OF WOODSTOCK,
DUKE OF GLOUCESTER
I should like the privilege of a private audience with mine own revered nephew, the King Richard.

KING RICHARD II
We acknowledge your dislike for my advisers, Gloucester. But they remain, at the King's expressed wish.

THOMAS OF WOODSTOCK,
DUKE OF GLOUCESTER
Of course. I merely request a duke might speak with a king without the audience of a marquis.

The younger men chuckle, then laugh, then guffaw. King Richard tries to remain impassive but can eventually not control his delight at some unknown witticism. Gloucester is, of course, already growing weary.

THOMAS OF WOODSTOCK,
DUKE OF GLOUCESTER (cont'd)
SIRE!

There are matters of concern that the kingdom demands...

The younger men laugh raucously and King Richard attempts to compose himself, and then uses slow open hand gestures to placate his friends.

THOMAS OF WOODSTOCK,
DUKE OF GLOUCESTER (cont'd)

Richard!

King Richard's head snaps round to face Gloucester, the young man's eyes glaring at his uncle's impropriety.

THOMAS OF WOODSTOCK,
DUKE OF GLOUCESTER (cont'd)

I'm sorry, Sire, I just plead an audience without the undue cackling of the Marquis of Dublin and these others.

There are faint sniggers from beyond the King, and Richard himself now looks mischievous rather than murderous.

ROBERT DE VERE

The Marquis of Dublin?

More sniggers from beyond the King.

KING RICHARD II

Oh, my dear uncle of Gloucester, there is no Marquis of Dublin, here.

The youngsters are laughing, and Gloucester glances at de Vere, and then wearily at his nephew.

THOMAS OF WOODSTOCK,
DUKE OF GLOUCESTER

(sighs)

What have you done?

A crescendo of laughing.

KING RICHARD II

Our beloved Duke of Gloucester...

The idiots are actually crying with laughter.

KING RICHARD II (cont'd)

...we present to thee...

...our esteemed friend and counsellor...

...our erstwhile Marquis of Dublin...

...now newly-elevated Duke of Ireland!

THOMAS OF WOODSTOCK,
DUKE OF GLOUCESTER
A duke?

But...

...he is not of the royal family!

KING RICHARD II
I know! It is quite unprecedented, isn't it!

The King and his friends all embrace with such joyous ecstasy, that not one of them notices Gloucester excuse himself, back away, and leave the room.

=====

-- THE RAGE OF HENRY BOLINGBROKE --

Dear God, what loathsome fools we tolerate.

Robert de Vere. The thinking of his face is quite sufficient for me to consider that the drinking of week-old milk wouldst be a much pleasanter consideration.

And the thinking of his manner does further make me consider that the corrupted cream would be all the better with the adding of a dog's warm turd.

Robert de Vere, oh Lord. The same crusty pig's arse who as if dishonouring his wife and my own cousin with his open adultery was not scandalous enough, hath lately blithely given her notice that they are to be divorced.

This odious brute whom Richard loves but whom is more deserving of a barrel of heated pitch, for whom one wishes some baited bear would tear itself loose and swipe some clawed fury across his eyes, for whom one would gladly spike a blade into his neck... that odious brute who does somehow find glory in his own dung-heap.

For here and now I learn that Richard has favoured him, elevated him, for us all to receive him as not only Earl of Oxford his undoubted birthright and not also Marquis of Dublin – his reward for kissing Richard's every spoken word. But this rat's prick is now elevated to such height a rat would not comprehend. Duke of Ireland.

Duke of Ireland, *oh Lord!*

Or, as I shall consider him, the most elevated rat's prick in all of Christendom.

It is time to join the men whom I am sure do plot against the chamber knights of the King.

=====

SCENE. WESTMINSTER PALACE – DAY

10th October 1386.

***Thomas of Woodstock the Duke of Gloucester** is walking down a corridor at Westminster Palace. He sees **Henry Bolingbroke the Earl of Derby** approaching him.*

As Gloucester is about to hail his nephew, to his great surprise Bolingbroke firmly places a palm on Gloucester's elegant smooth woollen russet houppelande at the chest and prevents the elder from proceeding.

When Bolingbroke speaks, it is with an enraged whisper.

HENRY BOLINGBROKE,
EARL OF DERBY
Add me to your triumvirate, Uncle!

THOMAS OF WOODSTOCK,
DUKE OF GLOUCESTER
My what?

HENRY BOLINGBROKE,
EARL OF DERBY
You, Warwick, and Arundel meet with subtlety, and I would wish an invite.

THOMAS OF WOODSTOCK,
DUKE OF GLOUCESTER
Henry, I don't know...

HENRY BOLINGBROKE,
EARL OF DERBY
I swear to you now that you shall include me, or I shall begin to speak this <u>conversation</u> <u>LOUDLY</u>.

Gloucester, clearly ruffled, looks beyond Henry. He spots an open chamber door and nods to it.

The pair enter, check it's empty, then close the door.

Henry Bolingbroke is edgy, and Gloucester needs to calm him down.

THOMAS OF WOODSTOCK,
DUKE OF GLOUCESTER

Have care, Henry. For though all we see are walls, there may yet be ears among them.

HENRY BOLINGBROKE,
EARL OF DERBY

You, Warwick and Arundel.

Are you enemies of the King?

THOMAS OF WOODSTOCK,
DUKE OF GLOUCESTER

HOLD FAST! The King is the King, and we are for the King.

But as your blood is up, and as we are family, and as we are alone, I confess that there are indeed three lords who have grave concerns for the weal of our kingdom.

And that is all.

HENRY BOLINGBROKE,
EARL OF DERBY

Aye. Good. Of course.

But tell me, dear uncle, if you care for the weal of the kingdom, logic suggests that you care not for the weal of our young lord Robert de Vere.

Gloucester relaxes a little, but is still tense.

THOMAS OF WOODSTOCK,
DUKE OF GLOUCESTER

Any good lord may well believe de Vere is a liability to our king's court.

But even so, King Richard and de Vere are yet so close that to acknowledge such a possibility leaves me unclear of what may be treasonous and what may not.

HENRY BOLINGBROKE,
EARL OF DERBY
Then fear not, Uncle. I love my king. But I do not love de Vere. In this, I presume that we are in accordance.

Long pause from Gloucester, tense expectation from Bolingbroke.

THOMAS OF WOODSTOCK,
DUKE OF GLOUCESTER
We are. But how has de Vere incurred such wrath in your person?

HENRY BOLINGBROKE,
EARL OF DERBY
You haven't heard? He shames both our families, sir.

Not only does he wilfully commit adultery against our cousin Philippa, he has petitioned to divorce her, to the ruination of her otherwise undoubted honour, and in favour of one of the Queen's ladies.

THOMAS OF WOODSTOCK,
DUKE OF GLOUCESTER
Oh, no.

HENRY BOLINGBROKE,
EARL OF DERBY
Are you speaking to Richard, soon?

THOMAS OF WOODSTOCK,
DUKE OF GLOUCESTER
(nods)
Parliament still awaits him. I am to try and entice him back from Eltham presently.

HENRY BOLINGBROKE,
EARL OF DERBY
I shall accompany you. I wish to cause fright to that pompous chamber knight who taints our king.

**THOMAS OF WOODSTOCK,
DUKE OF GLOUCESTER**

And I wish to avoid our kingdom's ruin before beginning another crisis.

Go to Hertford. I shall communicate with you presently.

Bolingbroke is somewhat placated.

**HENRY BOLINGBROKE,
EARL OF DERBY**

And so, dear uncle, I hereby join you, in whatever undertakings and adventures against de Vere that you may conceive.

Gloucester smiles.

**THOMAS OF WOODSTOCK,
DUKE OF GLOUCESTER**

I am sure I do not know what you speak of, young Henry.

Henry Bolingbroke is puzzled and frustrated.

**THOMAS OF WOODSTOCK,
DUKE OF GLOUCESTER (cont'd)**

But if 'the three' you speak of agree upon a next private conference, they shall expect 'a fourth'.

Henry Bolingbroke nods, understanding the continued need for secrecy on this matter.

=====

-- A SECRET MEETING AT HERTFORD CASTLE --

16th October 1386.

The three are now four, and safe in this room.

Gloucester, Warwick and Arundel - three who are greatly experienced in courtly matters - are now hosted by one court junior Henry Bolingbroke.

The most senior in rank. **Thomas of Woodstock**, Duke of Gloucester, who does carefully nurture intense dislikes about the unfairness of unworthy folk being favoured over him.

Then, two elders. First; Thomas Beauchamp, 12th Earl of Warwick, he who sits heavy with the troubles he harbours for the dislike of a king he is legally bound to obey. And second; Richard FitzAlan, 11th Earl of Arundel, he who would seemingly prefer to speak first then consider the words he hears rather than the other way around.

The junior. Henry Bolingbroke, Earl of Derby, he who is hot-blooded and sword-strong but thus far able to suppress murderous urges towards certain of the king's favourites that might indeed see him sometime ordered up a scaffold.

It is Bolingbroke who is imploring the other three about what ought to be done, and what ought to be done is in truth a conception they have all entertained and which gnaws at their souls. They feel the hunger that is duty, and a hunger to be fed, but it is a hunger which if not well satisfied may end their lives for their trouble.

Between them all and all their conversations, they each have gripes with their kingdom's court that irks them badly.

Bolingbroke is a young man who, without quite so much wisdom might otherwise be a part of King Richard's henhouse. Arundel, an earl in his ageing prime, stands earnestly while agreeing with Bolingbroke that the only duke of this party - Gloucester - ought to do what needs to be done.

Only old Warwick sits silently. Grim. Troubled. But it is he that Gloucester keeps looking to. Presently both Gloucester and Warwick realise, that the younger duke is all the while awaiting the elder earl's concurrence.

But concurrence for what? King Richard is acting to his own unknowable rules, rather than upholding and protecting the kingdom's laws that have been approved and accumulated by parliaments full of all the great men of England's past.

They first discuss that which needs to be discussed in order for it to be discounted: how might one bring to justice the anointed man who has been raised to king in order to rule over those who break the laws, if he is both defendant and judge? A king is a king! Once crowned, he is king until he dies and that is incontestable. So all here understand the riddle: ridding a kingdom of a king must be done without the death of the king... but that means he is still the king and therefore cannot be got rid of. Legally a king might abdicate, although that implies he has some desire to do so, and in this case Richard, that absolute ruler, is not minded to renounce his ultimate pleasures and responsibilities. Could one force abdication and thereby depose the king? It is unthinkable and yet two kings of England ago, not sixty years gone, exactly this was enacted by bold subjects desperate to improve England's fortunes. Poor King Edward the Second, ended before his time, presumed murdered most foul in Berkeley Castle by long-dead conspirators who now without a doubt burn in hell.

All concur that a king is untouchable and this is an inviolable law that would be judged and punished by men and God alike. And so the purpose in the first instance of this clandestine collective is agreed: to persuade King Richard to return to parliament. Gloucester tries cease his shaking, for even in trusted company should one always endeavour to not display the fear that stalks the belly or the weakness in the knees. If one can hide fear in these deadly days, one does.

But the fear is well-earned, for Arundel and Bolingbroke both continue to implore Gloucester that Gloucester, in his capacity as uncle to King Richard, must be the one to coerce his royal superior to return to parliament or face... what?

What authority is a king accounted by if he ceases to rule in the way that his barons desire to be so ruled? What legalities are broken when the King is behaving with negligence to the kingdom he has been born, raised, and anointed to rule? A kingdom requires a king. A king must rule. And a king must be obeyed. But essential to this agreed balance of power between a king and his barons is one uncomfortable factor that is implied within this relationship; a king might only rule when his barons agree to be ruled.

For the most part, this relationship is agreeable. A king has royal blood and is anointed, and thereby most suitably equipped to wear a kingdom's crown. A baron might not always agree with his king, but parliament is well established to discuss such disagreements even if a baron might have to bend his neck in obeisance and swear his acceptance even if all the while praying to God for the strength to smile while doing so.

But these days are more dreadful than those days.

It is Warwick who speaks next. With carefully-chosen words.

> *I am not gladdened by any path we may take, but then nor do I favour inaction. How much must our beloved kingdom weaken before we lords take terrible actions? We are naturally agreed that we must not act directly against our beloved king. And so it is clear to me, that the blessed King Richard is ill-advised by those closest to him, and it is this grave imbalance we must address. We have spoken about this before, Gloucester. Now is the time. Let us free our king from that negligent counsellor most close to him who by his poor guidance would shame our king and ourselves alike. And after so doing then return Richard to our parliament. Let us impeach our Lord Chancellor – and let*

us do it in the King's name – and thereafter let us shrewdly guide our sovereign lord to greatness without that obstruction.

Wise Warwick! For he has masterfully found a way of redefining the problem. If Richard is untouchable then, yes, let no man touch him and instead touch those who lead him awry. And yet the plan is not without its mortal danger for, as all know, Richard loves de la Pole as much as all his chamber knights, and will doubtless rage with fury at any attempt to impeach he who is closest to him. And so as all in this room understand, any attempt to rid the realm of the Lord Chancellor, that greatest of all Great Offices of State, must not be an unsuccessful attempt. A man, should he decide to, gets but one chance to grasp a snake.

Bolingbroke and Arundel allow their grave silence to agree with Warwick's plan, and those three now respect the Duke of Gloucester's heavy countenance. The latter cannot find an argument against this scandalous proposition, and he feels his fate in his belly. Gloucester must challenge the King, though he fears to. He must assail the character of England's Lord Chancellor, though he may not be able to. And he might well arrest those who lead Richard away from the weighty matters of the kingdom with fripperies and distractions. And if he goes that far then he must do away with them.

Three giant steps to a more profitable reign for everyone, as perhaps only then will Richard acquiesce. But falter at any of those steps and he will himself be declared a traitor. Richard is unlikely to offer mercy or clemency, and this it must be presumed would lead to his blood corruption. The next few days, for Gloucester, may be the ruin of him and the ruin of his family forevermore.

But the head dizzies at the considering of future possibilities that may not occur. For now, the matter is ostensibly quite simple. He must entice Richard back to parliament.

But he will insist that these three accomplices in this room swear to stand by him when he does.

=====

SCENE. ELTHAM PALACE – DAY

17th October 1386.

***Thomas of Woodstock the Duke of Gloucester**, and **Richard FitzAlan the Earl of Arundel** all bow to **King Richard II**, who sits on a throne while accompanied by **Robert de Vere, newly-elevated Duke of Ireland**.*

The older visitors do not acknowledge de Vere's presence in any way.

**THOMAS OF WOODSTOCK,
DUKE OF GLOUCESTER**

Your most gracious Highness, I bring word from Westminster.

KING RICHARD II

(to his friend)

De Vere, behold! The most illustrious messenger in all our kingdom!

Predictably, de Vere laughs with youthful arrogance. Gloucester isn't in such light a mood.

**THOMAS OF WOODSTOCK,
DUKE OF GLOUCESTER**

I bring with me a petition from your parliament, my gracious lord.

The King winces, perhaps over-dramatically.

KING RICHARD II

Tis a bold parliament that demands of its king.

**THOMAS OF WOODSTOCK,
DUKE OF GLOUCESTER**

I might propose that it is so emboldened only by your absence.

KING RICHARD II

By its ignorance, more like.

In any case, what is this obscenity?

**THOMAS OF WOODSTOCK,
DUKE OF GLOUCESTER**

In light of recent negligences, I speak for certain lords who would request a token gesture of their sovereign lord.

Our Earl of Suffolk lately shamed himself at Westminster with an undoubted untrue demand for taxes on behalf of the King.

This, we all absolutely understand, is surely an abhorrence on the part of Suffolk rather than the King's own will.

Therefore your humble parliament demands the immediate disbarment from senior office of that errant earl.

KING RICHARD II

Ha!

No.

THOMAS OF WOODSTOCK, DUKE OF GLOUCESTER

I beg a little more consideration, Sire.

KING RICHARD II

Ah! A messenger that bears first a demand to a king, then follows it with earnest advice for an errant nephew.

THOMAS OF WOODSTOCK, DUKE OF GLOUCESTER

Advice for an errant nephew, you say?

As an adviser to an errant nephew I might suggest His Royal Grace attaches himself to persons better regarded than these, for if he should, greater honour from his more worthy subjects would he earn.

Whereas if he does not disassociate with undesirables, there are many great dangers in this world that pretty young trinkets like these, collected and paraded around the crown, wouldst not protect you from.

KING RICHARD II

And from whom would you, in this glorious advisory capacity, protect our royal self?

THOMAS OF WOODSTOCK, DUKE OF GLOUCESTER

In this moment? I wish to protect the royal self from himself.

KING RICHARD II

Aha. A stern opinion with menace aplenty, all the while fluffed up in silks and fine linen.

So we rid ourselves of Suffolk, and the realm thereafter prospers?

THOMAS OF WOODSTOCK, DUKE OF GLOUCESTER

No, Sire. The state of the kingdom is more grievous than the ridding of an Earl of Suffolk alone would solve.

KING RICHARD II

Indeed. So a message this way, and now a message that way.

Tell our beloved parliament, Sir Messenger, that we would not dismiss so much as a scullion boy from our employ to appease that outrageous mob.

THOMAS OF WOODSTOCK, DUKE OF GLOUCESTER

And this is the King's decree?

KING RICHARD II

The King shall do as he chooses.

THOMAS OF WOODSTOCK, DUKE OF GLOUCESTER

I once knew a boy who understood that a King might well do as he so chooses, but only with the assent of his nobles.

KING RICHARD II

Hmmm.

You are one of our mightiest oaks, Gloucester. If we blew our orders, would you not happily bend to them?

THOMAS OF WOODSTOCK,
DUKE OF GLOUCESTER

I bow now to your softest whisper, Sire. But after today, His Grace would have to blow hard to reach Westminster.

KING RICHARD II

Why Westminster, when we are here at Eltham?

THOMAS OF WOODSTOCK,
DUKE OF GLOUCESTER

As of tomorrow, I, and all your other faithful lords, will remain awhile in Westminster awaiting His Highness's gracious person.

Over-confident, King Richard II is showing off to de Vere, and shares a smirk with him before responding to his uncle.

KING RICHARD II

Ah, but we choose Eltham.

The two young men are stifling giggles.

ROBERT DE VERE,
DUKE OF IRELAND

Eltham! Here! Bye-bye!

The Duke of Gloucester's hand is forced.

THOMAS OF WOODSTOCK,
DUKE OF GLOUCESTER

I beg to remind His Grace of his constitutional duty to attend parliament.

For, as I'm sure His Most Royal Majesty is aware, if The King leaves parliament and does not return within forty days, a parliament may dissolve itself...

...<u>independently</u> of the King. Thereafter, all manner of royal guidances would be undefined.

King Richard II searches his knowledge for confirmation of this dreadful scenario.

THOMAS OF WOODSTOCK,
DUKE OF GLOUCESTER (cont'd)

Wouldst thou be the king who scattered his own lords back across his realm to their own ungoverned mischiefs?

Wouldst thou be the king not kingly enough to command his own parliament?

And if so, for how long wouldst thou then remain King?

ROBERT DE VERE,
DUKE OF IRELAND

Have a care, Gloucester, the King is the King wherever he resides!

KING RICHARD II

Hush, Sir.

King Richard II is assessing the gravity of the situation he now finds himself facing. But he's absolutely furious.

KING RICHARD II (cont'd)

Perhaps we <u>shall</u> attend our parliament... ...but Suffolk is innocent of your charge.

And in parliament we shall declare thus that the Earl of Suffolk is absolved of any impropriety the lords of England may have ascribed to him.

The Duke of Gloucester must draw upon his courage, now.

THOMAS OF WOODSTOCK,
DUKE OF GLOUCESTER

I am afraid that His Grace is under the misunderstanding that his parliament would accept this absolution.

KING RICHARD II

(snaps)

A-<u>HA</u>!

I take my leave at Eltham, while Westminster takes to governance by traitors!

Long have I known there are such writhing serpents in my court, uncle! And long have I despised all who bow and smile and say 'Sire' to me, for long have I known they say <u>this</u> but mean <u>that</u>. Snakes, the lot!

Have you forgot France, uncle? And her king! My cousin, in fact, who has an army of his own...

So, yes! I come to Westminster! I come to Westminster, indeed!

But only when I have petitioned my dear king cousin over the sea for support on this matter! And if the King of France demands payment for this assistance, I shall pay him with this!

King Richard stands forward, grasps his crown and brandishes it towards the Duke of Gloucester, who is horrified.

KING RICHARD II (cont'd)

Would my nobles dare to take this crown? To hell with them, I say, for there is greater honour in yielding one's crown to an enemy, than to one's own dishonourable subjects!

The Duke of Gloucester stands his ground with terrified pride, silently praying that a short temporal madness has taken the King.

For now, Richard has exhausted himself, and he seeks his throne breathless like an old man. He sits, but remains distant to the matters at hand.

KING RICHARD II (cont'd)

(to himself)

My golden weight pulls heavy.

Do you know that on occasion I weep for my bed so I may rid myself of this cumbersome millstone for a few dark hours.

And all the while my cousin over the water does carry his own with such elegance and dignity.

THOMAS OF WOODSTOCK, DUKE OF GLOUCESTER

France represents our darkest enemy, Sire.

KING RICHARD II

(distracted, weary)

Am I really worthy, after all?

THOMAS OF WOODSTOCK, DUKE OF GLOUCESTER

Sire, let us not speak of France now.

KING RICHARD II

Oh, I wish to end this all.

De Vere! A scrivener, to scratch my wishes on over the sea. A royal declaration; God has revealed to me that I have failed my kingdom.

I yield England and all therein, to my good cousin in Fr...

THOMAS OF WOODSTOCK, DUKE OF GLOUCESTER

(to de Vere)

Hold fast, boy, or die.

(to King Richard)

Richard. KING Richard! I remind you there is only one final act that would cause the relinquishing of your crown.

Just a flicker of a response from Richard.

THOMAS OF WOODSTOCK, DUKE OF GLOUCESTER (cont'd)

Understand, that no king should rightly live to see the next.

If you truly relinquish your crown and all your God-given burdens and responsibilities, the precedent is alarming...

...that kingly ancestor of ours, not three generations ago, met an undignified end indeed at the hands of others.

KING RICHARD II

Ah. A precedent, and a violent precedent at that.
By all accounts King Edward the Second was unfit to bear his crown. Perhaps, uncle, some royal Plantagenet curse runs unseen in my blood.

Gloucester remains silent, but his respectful manner implores Richard to do his duty.

KING RICHARD II (cont'd)

Hmmm. And so, is this my choice.

My crown of gold and residence at parliament, or an unfriendly glowing iron administered in some dungeon or other?

THOMAS OF WOODSTOCK,
DUKE OF GLOUCESTER

I beg you. Choose the gold, Sire.

=====

SCENE. OUTSIDE ELTHAM PALACE – DAY

Thomas of Woodstock the Duke of Gloucester *is on his horse quickly and clops out across the wooden bridge over the impressive moat. King Richard's screaming and raging, and the crashing of furniture against walls, vases against great iron chandeliers and whatever else, can be heard across the immediate countryside.*

Richard FitzAlan the Earl of Arundel *rides beside him.*

RICHARD FITZALAN,
EARL OF ARUNDEL

You threatened King Richard with anarchy! And then death!

THOMAS OF WOODSTOCK,
DUKE OF GLOUCESTER
I had to say something.

Arundel looks aghast.

RICHARD FITZALAN,
EARL OF ARUNDEL
You play politics for higher stakes than I would.

THOMAS OF WOODSTOCK,
DUKE OF GLOUCESTER
We had to get our king back in parliament.

Richard's temper can still be heard, to Arundel's discomfort.

RICHARD FITZALAN,
EARL OF ARUNDEL
Richard's wrath, though.

THOMAS OF WOODSTOCK,
DUKE OF GLOUCESTER
He'll forget it when he gets to Westminster.

RICHARD FITZALAN,
EARL OF ARUNDEL
How can you be so sure?

THOMAS OF WOODSTOCK,
DUKE OF GLOUCESTER
Because by now my men should have arrested de la Pole for dereliction of duty.

=====

SCENE. SECURE LODGINGS AT THE TOWER OF LONDON – DAY

18th October 1386.

A jailer opens the thick oak door for ***Thomas of Woodstock*** *the Duke of Gloucester.* ***Michael de la Pole*** *– the Earl of Suffolk and deposed Lord Chancellor – pauses his writing of a letter at a modest desk by the window.*

MICHAEL DE LA POLE,
EARL OF SUFFOLK
Ah, you're still alive! Then Richard doesn't know I'm here, yet.

THOMAS OF WOODSTOCK,
DUKE OF GLOUCESTER
Even embezzlers with powerful friends should hold their tongues, my Lord.

MICHAEL DE LA POLE,
EARL OF SUFFOLK
Embezzlers?

THOMAS OF WOODSTOCK,
DUKE OF GLOUCESTER
Saint Anthony's Hospital. You have taken recent possession of a grant of revenues, have you not?

A grant that should have gone to the crown, before you intercepted it.

Should it not?

MICHAEL DE LA POLE,
EARL OF SUFFOLK
A favour from King Richard. And thus when all around us - including you - find subtle methods of diverting a shilling, you wish to hang me for a penny!

Gloucester smiles with understanding. It is true that all men in power use their position and authority to make money in ways that the common man cannot conceive.

THOMAS OF WOODSTOCK,
DUKE OF GLOUCESTER
Very well.

I admit, that your impeachment for embezzlement is a convenience designed to remove you from authority.

MICHAEL DE LA POLE,
EARL OF SUFFOLK
God can hear you, Gloucester.

THOMAS OF WOODSTOCK,
DUKE OF GLOUCESTER

And you, but no matter.

In truth, neither He nor I respect a man who cannot do his job.

And I have vowed to attend to this shortfall in ability.

MICHAEL DE LA POLE,
EARL OF SUFFOLK

How is the Duke of Brittany? Does he ever write to you?

THOMAS OF WOODSTOCK,
DUKE OF GLOUCESTER

(ignores the jab)

I do not like the influence you have on our young king.

MICHAEL DE LA POLE,
EARL OF SUFFOLK

Nor I the influence you have on certain others.

THOMAS OF WOODSTOCK,
DUKE OF GLOUCESTER

I beg your pardon?

MICHAEL DE LA POLE,
EARL OF SUFFOLK

My eyes are on you, Gloucester, even from in here, make no mistake.

I have not yet decided whether the cloak you wrap around King Richard is for the common good of the realm...

...or whether you wrap him with treason.

THOMAS OF WOODSTOCK,
DUKE OF GLOUCESTER

And yet you are sitting there and staying, while I am standing here and leaving.

**MICHAEL DE LA POLE,
EARL OF SUFFOLK**

Ha! The King will fine me, I shall humbly declare my intent to pay, and then be back by his side before Christmas none the poorer.

Will you have employed your stratagem to ruin us all by then?

**THOMAS OF WOODSTOCK,
DUKE OF GLOUCESTER**

I have no stratagem against my king, Sir.

But I certainly have one against a man not fit to perform the duties of a senior council member.

So enjoy your stay in this fine Tower, my Lord, for I promise you it is the last time you shall be safe from my deadly intentions.

**MICHAEL DE LA POLE,
EARL OF SUFFOLK**

Richard will re-instate me as Lord Chancellor, and then it is you who should tread through court with utmost care.

**THOMAS OF WOODSTOCK,
DUKE OF GLOUCESTER**

Sir! The last action you provided parliament with, was to request a tax three times higher than any man cares to recall.

If you think the King will have the authority to re-instate you, then you're as big a fool as everyone says you are.

**MICHAEL DE LA POLE,
EARL OF SUFFOLK**

I acted on behalf of our king, Gloucester. Remember that.

THOMAS OF WOODSTOCK,
DUKE OF GLOUCESTER

Indeed. But the law prevents me from prosecuting the King, whereas I have every right to impeach you.

=====

-- A TALE OF IMPEACHMENT --

Westminster Great Hall, 23rd October 1386.

The **Duke of Gloucester** breathes with heaviness.

His nephew has returned to Westminster and while it has taken courage to stand before the barons again, the King has an unfortunate manner that suggests arrogance is his motivation rather than bravery.

A bold king would jut out his chin and look at his lords and effuse a terrible grace in the distribution of wise decisions that would demand their obedience, while infusing confidence of great leadership.

But Richard's royal stance forces his chin to fall low so that when he looks out upon his subjects his overall demeanour is one of distrust and slyness. It does not engender confidence, and Gloucester is aware of many around him in the Great Hall are voicing whispers that dare to suggest they are not enamoured of the crowned boy.

The Earl of Suffolk has been brought to account for his unwise guidance of King Richard. Michael de la Pole, accused of negligence in his duties, and his unwise closeness to the king has caused concern for many who would rather benefit from advisors who would give the king wise counsel.

Richard looks unhappy as the barons state their cases against Suffolk. The request only three weeks ago of £155,000 in taxes was unwise, and although Suffolk requested this in the name of their king, the barons cannot impeach their king, and so they will impeach Suffolk.

To threaten one so close to the king, instead of the king, is as close to treason as Gloucester ever wishes to sail.

=====

-- A WISH FOR LOYALTY --

Oh Richard, save me in God's good name.

A boldness of stance, a royal wave of dismissal. A temper tantrum. Any such compassionate act would save this accused lord of Suffolk from rabble-raised notoriety. Close to God have I come when I stood by you, and I did never wither before my King on earth. All I did was do all I could for you.

Great Richard, young of year, mighty of kingdom, be wise and judge me on my loyalty to you and be steadfast before your lords who would surely serve themselves before their realm. Their precious families before their king. Perhaps even their silver before their integrity.
Oh king, you have the power to save me. Do you also have the desire? I served you fine well, and fine well enough for you now to serve me with your unbending loyalty to one who loves you.

=====

-- KING RICHARD LAMENTS --

Does he weep? Does he fear the axe more, or the disgrace more? Oh Michael. They attack him with words as they would rather with swords, and I am requested to preside over legal complaints that they serve to me.

And whenever they say This Disgraceful Suffolk it is like they say This Disgraceful King and I know it and they know it, except not even the boldest of them would speak to me so.

I am sure that if I arose and roared my angst about their behaviour then I would say Free Him Now and they would free him now.

But I would let them have their victory today and their pride will be sated. A hungry lion, if thrown a calf, would not pass up such easy meat for want of a bull, and so these barons of mine would rather have their victory in court and bask in Pole's disgrace if that appeases them.

We have been estranged these past weeks, my dear Suffolk, and in those weeks I have been courted by other young lords who would take thy place by their king, and I find this an alluring concept worthy of exploration.

To send Suffolk to prison would satisfy those in my court who wish to witness a weighty shock in my court today. So for now, goodbye Michael. To gaol with you. You are thus disgraced and my household is thus tainted and I cannot deny it. But to see you quiver in your desperate endearing of me enlivens me so, for I am now quite certain that you wouldst return to me within a heartbeat of my move to bring you back to me, and I shall then watch these cocksure lords writhe with their impotence as they realise they cannot force me to do what I do not want to do.

Be brave, Michael de la Pole my earl of Suffolk. And I swear that with every word against you, my lords do in fact prick themselves with daggers of my command.

Not today.

But someday.

=====

-- THE TALE OF AN AFFRONTED FRENCH COURT --

Le 12 novembre 1386.

So, England and Portugal have aligned.

France's enemies to the north, have joined forces with France's enemies to the far west.

The advisers of **King Charles VI of France** did contemplate this possibility of John of Gaunt processing his claim to Castile with the help of Portugal, and it is indeed a grave situation.

France is a kingdom comprising and surrounded by duchies who might contentedly proclaim both their fealty to France and their independence from France with the same single breath. It is a circumstance that is acceptable for most of the time, although such informal alignment sometimes makes the raising of taxes difficult; one must at least admire the English who, being the more united kingdom, do seem to be able to raise more money and be quicker about it, which is of course agreeable to them for reasons of both war and defence and also the reason why since 1066 only one such invasion has been attempted by France. And in any case, at the moment Charles would see the English out of Gascony and Calais before leading France into England.

This policy of not-peace-not-war - non-peace - has been barely acceptable. His youth has been a heavy yoke, no doubt. He knows his noblemen, like any noblemen, would wish for a warrior king to lead them around the realm, ridding all provinces of English in turn, and he has always accepted that this should happen. But, like his distant cousin Richard, he has not quite twenty years to him just yet and so Charles has always accepted that any aggression on his part would happen later rather than sooner.

But, as his trusted captains do nod their grim acceptance to their next steps, the King of France and all his lords are in agreement.

With the English/Portuguese alignment, any fantasies of taking war to England's shores must be disregarded for the time being. Instead he must turn to the south and west of his own kingdom and observe Lancaster's progress in Spain.

Without any provocation, and in truth there has been none directed to France so far, it is difficult to argue for aggression at this juncture, so King Charles VI of France must watch carefully and take time to be very clear about what he is to do if Constanza's claim for the crown of Spain is won.

France must rally, and call to arms. John of Gaunt, who travelled to Paris only a few years ago and declared that England would wish for peace, has behaved in the opposite to how he speaks. His uneasy alliance with Portugal is undoubted a design to usurp King Juan of Castile. And having identified himself readily as an aggressor against King Juan, a victory for him and backed by Portugal would place him in a powerful strategic position if he were to continue north-eastwards into France. Particularly if Gaunt's nephew King Richard would arm and invade from the north at the same time.

So while France must march against Lancaster in obvious opposition against his Spanish movements, King Charles of France would move in such ways that they shall incur as few losses as possible. For any stand against Lancaster is mere subterfuge.

The activities of those untrustworthy lions have confirmed a long-term desire in King Charles VI of France. Not this year, but some year...

...he will invade England.

Charles is content to wait and employ a policy of plotting obstacle upon obstacle in the way of John of Gaunt to discourage his Spanish ambitions. But John of Gaunt be damned sooner or later. Charles has already told his advisors that when the time comes, he would pull the innards of Richard, that popinjay prince, out for himself.

=====

SCENE. A PRIVATE CHAMBER, WESTMINSTER – DAY

19th November 1386.

***Thomas of Woodstock** the Duke of Gloucester accepts a visit from **Richard FitzAlan** the Earl of Arundel, who enters respectfully.*

RICHARD FITZALAN,
EARL OF ARUNDEL

Richard has released Suffolk.

THOMAS OF WOODSTOCK,
DUKE OF GLOUCESTER

Already?

It's a good thing we moved quick to elect your brother the good bishop as the replacement Lord Chancellor.

RICHARD FITZALAN,
EARL OF ARUNDEL
I wondered at the haste. Did you expect the release?

THOMAS OF WOODSTOCK,
DUKE OF GLOUCESTER
I reasoned Suffolk and Richard would write to one another.

RICHARD FITZALAN,
EARL OF ARUNDEL
"Do not fear, dear Michael, we shall secure your release forthwith," or such like.

THOMAS OF WOODSTOCK,
DUKE OF GLOUCESTER
So it would seem.

RICHARD FITZALAN,
EARL OF ARUNDEL
Richard is as like a carthorse in matters of war, but impeach one of his inner circle and he strikes quicker than a snake.

Are we in danger?

Gloucester sits back in his exquisite high-backed chair and ponders this. Arundel notices that the younger man does look worried about such an implication.

THOMAS OF WOODSTOCK,
DUKE OF GLOUCESTER
Our King is still not yet of age and we act for the good of the realm.

Together with the Archbishops of Canterbury and York, I am assembling a great and continual royal council with a mandate to rule this kingdom in the way it needs to be ruled if we are all to prosper.

We will overtly instruct Richard regarding how a king should behave, what he should say, and how much he can spend. Ours is a fine opportunity to discourage the puffery. We will urge accountants to slash at his expenses, and surveyors to assess the efficacy of his estates.

For the first time in his life we will show Richard how he might live of his own - and live well.

RICHARD FITZALAN,
EARL OF ARUNDEL

A fine stance, sir. And I shall stand with you.

God knows my south coast estates are riddled with Frenchmen on occasion, and our king's disinterest is a factor.

But Richard is twenty-one in less than two years, Thomas. After which he would surely elect to rule of his own.

THOMAS OF WOODSTOCK,
DUKE OF GLOUCESTER

Then we have less than two years in which to impress upon him the importance of the King's role.

RICHARD FITZALAN,
EARL OF ARUNDEL

A Royal Council to clip his wings?

He is not going to like that.

=====

SCENE. MARCOLF CHAMBER, WESTMINSTER – DAY

26th November 1386.

***King Richard II** enters Westminster Palace's Marcolf Chamber, followed by his uncle **Thomas of Woodstock the Duke of Gloucester**. Richard looks like he may be about to cry, or perhaps he has been crying, and Gloucester has helped him restore his public face.*

Standing around a large heavy table are several well-dressed lords and bishops including overt supporters of the king Alexander Neville the archbishop of York and Nicholas Morice the abbott of Waltham, as well as those at the table who regard Richard with caution including William Courtenay the archbishop of Canterbury. Other powerful men who sit on this council are the king's new Lord Chancellor Thomas Arundel the bishop of Ely, and his brother Richard FitzAlan the Earl of Arundel, as well as Richard's middle uncle, Edmund Duke of York.

All bow reverently as King Richard walks to the end of the table, pauses, and sits without acknowledging anyone.

The others then seat themselves with care.

Everyone waits for Richard to open the meeting.

He does not.

Nothing happens.

Some lords sneak discreet glances at one another.

Just as Gloucester opens his mouth, breathes in deeply, and is about to speak, Richard slams an open hand onto the table so that several lords jump at the noise, and stands violently. Richard slams both palms onto the table several times in rage.

KING RICHARD II

(outraged)

YOU LEAVE ME STRIPPED!

A KING IN NAME ALONE!

Most of the attendant lords slowly look down and stare at the table.

There is a terrible silence.

Then, the unrolling of a parliamentary roll. It is Gloucester, to business.

THOMAS OF WOODSTOCK,
DUKE OF GLOUCESTER

Your Majesty, might I bring your attention in the first instance, to a reduction in expenditure of the King's Wardrobe, from £17,000 per annum to £12,000...

Richard wails as he, slumps back into his high-backed chair and contemplates the table in front of him with great pain.

=====

-- REGAL FRAGILITY --

Le 20 decembre 1386.

The cold weighs wherever it caresses.

Thick snow blusters outside, and **King Charles VI of France** is not warmed even by the biggest fires he has ever seen in all his fireplaces. *What must this freezing weather be like for the peasants,* he wonders, before answering his own question with the obvious answer; *one supposes they are used to it.*

He has noted of late a kind of trinity. It is gloomy outside, it is gloomy inside, and it is gloomy in his belly. He is relieved that his kingdom cannot afford to invade England this year, for at this moment, and for some weeks now, he has not the care to do anything of note.

Perhaps it is Paris. The same city, the same court faces, the same problems, papers and piss to rule over. So Robespierre has fenced off some of Froissant's land, tell them to duel it out themselves because their King doesn't care. So John of Gaunt does conspire in Castile with Portugal, why should this spoil the King of France's breakfast?

Always usually interested with his household's accounts, he has lately found them uninspiring. But, then, the news from the ink on the parchment is uninspiring. His kingdom has not very much wealth. Plenty of money, but too many of it is moving about and without sitting safely in his exchequer.

As has been explained to him by his four senior advisers, he could not have afforded to win if he had pressed his kingdom's aggression over the sea in England, and had he pursued such aggressive foreign strategies then France would by now be administering bankruptcy, not that he'd still be alive to see that.

The men that form his advisory council are worthy, after all. And although while that should be noteworthy enough to celebrate, in truth, when does any eighteen year old man celebrate his elders proving to him that he was in fact wrong and they were right.

The truth is; Charles feels quite peculiar.

As if, while he slept, some wicked demon has poured spirits of heavy of lead coins into his belly and stuffed unspun wool into his head and, despite the impracticality of such supposition, such an explanation cannot easily be discounted so that the more one contemplates the hypothesis the more acceptable it becomes.

So while all he can do is worry about the very real possibility that he is suffering in silence from some kind of uncomfortable possession, the idiots still come at him with the issues of the day, of course. Foreign relations, internal relations, England, Spain, Flanders, the Holy Roman Empire; they can all just... go away.

And, then, his favourite subject of all... does he consider that, after over a year of marriage, he should have put an heir into Isabeau yet? He knows he ought to rejoice in the idea, but not even his queen's well-formed temptations are likely to rouse him into action in this humour. And what of *SACRE QUOI? QUOI? QUOI?*

Startled, then not startled, he heaves on his chest as his heart punches his bones gamely from within even as he notes that a large vase was there across this room dropped by the spotty black-haired cleaning girl. Her face is already as like as her spots, so that you would not tell where the one ends and the others begin.

The scene is amusing now that he has begun to manage his breathing again, but the discomfort of his internal humours does continue with more heaviness, damn them.

King Charles VI observes what used to be a large vase, about the size of a man's torso. While the half of it is pristine, that half has unnatural sharp edges where the rest of it collapsed away; a fine vase, and one he has known for many years as it served his court with continued silent efficacy from day to day. Until it dropped and thereafter shattered, thereby exposing its fragility to stress and the worthless emptiness within it, and proving that once a thing is truly broken into pieces it is useless, it is unfixable, and it is ended. Such realisations make the chamber turn about him and invisible bile pervades him.

Councillors, slow to realise, now increasingly alert themselves of the condition of their most beloved young lord, and spring into action until they realise that they do not know what to do next. For the King of France is weeping, and then sobbing with a bobbing head and lack of breath and much clear humour leaking out.

In truth, he doesn't even know why he is crying. At the broken vase, at this broken court, for his broken kingdom, for his broken self. But he finds it interesting to note that the sobbing does generate a warm relief.

Perhaps this relief will rub away at the blackness within him.

=====

SCENE. MARCOLF CHAMBER, WESTMINSTER – DAY

21st December 1386.

Another Royal Council meeting.

***King Richard II** sits miserably at the head of the table in Westminster Palace's Marcolf Chamber. Present are the usual notables including, going from Richard's right, his uncle*

***Thomas of Woodstock the Duke of Gloucester**, Alexander Neville the archbishop of York, Nicholas Morice the abbott of Waltham, William Courtenay the archbishop of Canterbury, the Lord Chancellor Thomas Arundel the bishop of Ely and his brother Richard FitzAlan the Earl of Arundel, and Richard's middle uncle, Edmund the Duke of York.*

Standing around the large heavy table are several well-dressed lords and bishops, clerks and scriveners; court attendants to assist in the running of the council.

Richard looks like he may explode with frustration. Having a council does not suit him.

A clerk gives Thomas of Woodstock the Duke of Gloucester an unfurled parchment roll. Gloucester apprises himself of the contents, and passes it to his right to Alexander Neville the archbishop of York and so on, so the document is passed round the table until it reaches Richard.

THOMAS OF WOODSTOCK,
DUKE OF GLOUCESTER

This next petition is from His Grace the Earl of Northumberland.

KING RICHARD II

Ah! Henry Percy himself.

THOMAS OF WOODSTOCK,
DUKE OF GLOUCESTER

(avoids eye contact obeisantly)

Indeed.

He petitions funds from His Majesty for a licence to crenellate, to fortify various of his estates along the Scottish Marches.

(pause)

Are we to approve such developments?

KING RICHARD II

(seriously, to the table)

Indeed, we approve. And happily.

Gloucester remains impassive, still avoiding eye contact.

King Richard notices the odd pause, and frowns a little. He looks around the table.

The barons are uncomfortable. One winces. Another puffs out his cheeks. Richard seeks his usually more amiable uncle, Edmund the Duke of York. Edmund smiles kindly, but then scrunches his face up and gives his nephew an almost imperceptible shake of the head.

Richard sighs loudly and throws himself back into his hard-backed chair.

Looks heavenward.

KING RICHARD II

OHHHHH, in God's name!

Why ask me, then?

=====

A.D. 1387

=====

-- KING RICHARD'S TEMPEST, 6TH JANUARY 1387 --

The water in the bowl reflects a face.

And nothing more. A face that I know and have come to accept as mine own. A face that today has now twenty years of wear on it. At times the face of a boy, at other times the face of a man. And the face of the king to others, even though it is not the face that makes a king but the blood that runs behind it.

And no-one can see that, like they see a face.

It is only in the minds of men and women that a boy or a man is recognised as a king, for it is they who call me king Richard, and I never emerged from my mother and declared my intent to rule this kingdom.

But now I am called a man when they want me to lead an army, yet I am treated as a boy when it comes to being a king. A man on some occasions, a boy on others. This is how a man's perception becomes the truth of a man's reality.

And then if all before this face do treat me with respect and obeisance, why do I then learn of dubious doings when certain men are not before me? Sir robert plessington, that chief baron of my exchequer, does have the gall to marry without my approval, in full knowledge that such illegal contrivance avoids the having to pay the exchequer for the required royal permission of his union.

And so four days ago, amid much baronial outrage at plessingtons slight, I ruled so according to the laws of the land and insisted on the dismissal and imprisonment of the errant knight. And I am king and so it was. But, by the time the sun arose today I had better considered my opinions. plessington did wrong me, no doubt. But he is otherwise a fair Christian and an otherwise obedient man, so I have sought his person, and when his person is brought to me I shall assess him for contrition and humility. And if he is contrite and remorseful, then I shall reinstate him.

Not one of my brave wise councillors stopped me from releasing suffolk from his gaol cell and I wish to observe which of them would dare to place plessington back under arrest.

I shall endeavour hereon to not worry about which face my lords see when they look at or think of me.

But I shall enjoy seeing their faces when I reinstate plessington.

=====

SCENE. WESTMINSTER HALL – DAY

10th January 1387.

***Thomas of Woodstock** the Duke of Gloucester is seated on one of the many stepped bench seats in Westminster Hall. **Richard FitzAlan** the Earl of Arundel, approaches, waits to be invited to sit down next to the duke, and then does.*

Arundel is perplexed.

**RICHARD FITZALAN,
EARL OF ARUNDEL**

I do not understand.

Plessington wronged Richard. Richard charged and dismissed Plessington. Yet now he re-instates Plessington.

**THOMAS OF WOODSTOCK,
DUKE OF GLOUCESTER**

Richard does what he can within the royal limits we give him.

As king he may charge Plessington. As king he may pardon Plessington.

**RICHARD FITZALAN,
EARL OF ARUNDEL**

The net result is nothing but grievous uncertainty for us all.

**THOMAS OF WOODSTOCK,
DUKE OF GLOUCESTER**

Grievous uncertainties to you and I are mere japes to a boy exercising a right to be king.

**RICHARD FITZALAN,
EARL OF ARUNDEL**

So he retracts the charges against Plessington, and re-instates him, to defy his council?

THOMAS OF WOODSTOCK,
DUKE OF GLOUCESTER
I think so.

RICHARD FITZALAN,
EARL OF ARUNDEL
Does Richard act illegally?

THOMAS OF WOODSTOCK,
DUKE OF GLOUCESTER
(shakes head)
I do not think so.

RICHARD FITZALAN,
EARL OF ARUNDEL
Have you sought learned advice on this?

THOMAS OF WOODSTOCK,
DUKE OF GLOUCESTER
I do not have the desire to question such a trifle. And especially not against my king.

Nor do you.

RICHARD FITZALAN,
EARL OF ARUNDEL
And thus, what Richard wants he gets. Why set up a council to guide him when it becomes deaf, mute and blind as soon as he breaks the rules set for him?

THOMAS OF WOODSTOCK,
DUKE OF GLOUCESTER
(extremely irritated)
What would you have me do, Arundel?

Arundel looks much older than his thirty-nine years.

RICHARD FITZALAN,
EARL OF ARUNDEL
I do not suppose there is anything that any of us dare to do. And, at the same time, I suppose that Richard knows this too.

=====

SCENE. PAINTED CHAMBER, WESTMINSTER – DAY

21st January 1387.

***King Richard II** and **Michael de la Pole**, Earl of Suffolk and though not now Lord Chancellor any more is still an adviser favoured by the king. They are discussing a matter that has become very important to Richard.*

MICHAEL DE LA POLE, EARL OF SUFFOLK

Sire... these Cheshire Archers...

KING RICHARD II

We are so enlivened by these appointments!

MICHAEL DE LA POLE, EARL OF SUFFOLK

My Liege, why would the king employ a private army?

KING RICHARD II

Because he does not have one, and he wants one.

MICHAEL DE LA POLE, EARL OF SUFFOLK

But, Your Majesty, you already have many faithful barons. And a yeoman guard for your safety in court. If you ever need an army, you call upon your senior noblemen and they-

KING RICHARD II

-call their armies!

Other men have private armies, how is it correct that a king does not have something that his barons do have?

MICHAEL DE LA POLE, EARL OF SUFFOLK

It is a waste of money, Sire. A king's barons are sworn to uphold the King's peace. They are already sworn to be the retained army you say you wish to pay extra for.

KING RICHARD II

And yet, did you see how easily our Uncle of Gloucester recently deposited you, the Lord Chancellor of all England, into the White Tower?

And me into a council of knaves.

The king's peace, you say. Do you think these acts of treason caused your king much peace, Michael?

MICHAEL DE LA POLE, EARL OF SUFFOLK

Treason? My imprisonment was excessive, illegal perhaps, but...

KING RICHARD II

(grunts dismissively)

We shall decide what is treason.

MICHAEL DE LA POLE, EARL OF SUFFOLK

Sire, the law of the land defines treason, not the K-

KING RICHARD II

-NOT one more word, sir.

MICHAEL DE LA POLE, EARL OF SUFFOLK

Your Majesty! A king must uphold the laws of the kingdom, by his exemplary royal behaviour.

KING RICHARD II

Very well. But imagine this.

How easy do you think Gloucester would have imprisoned you if he first had to negotiate a line of armed men, each paid for their dedication to the King's peace?

Michael de la Pole can see his king's point, but this is a principle that he does not feel comfortable with.

=====

-- THE TALE OF A DUKE'S ADVICE TO THE QUEEN --

10th February 1387.

To rid oneself of London's tedium.

It is a good thing that King Richard takes an interest in the kingdom beyond London's wall. **Thomas of Woodstock** Duke of Gloucester well knows that his king feels restricted and bound by his Council. A commission the young man finds irritating that forces him to justify expenses and decisions that all in attendance agree wouldn't be asked of an older sovereign. And so, upon one of those tedious outbreaks of pestilence in London, Richard has requested the dissolution of the council to take a break from the capital by undertaking a well-represented well-guarded gyration up and through the great towns and cities of his realm.

Apart from the Scotland debacle, Gloucester knows that Richard rarely sees beyond his capital's wall unless it is to repair to Windsor, Eltham or Sheen, or to seek the general anonymity of a hunting forest. And so, a tour of his kingdom. The travel will be good for Richard, and it is good for Richard's subjects.

He shall travel to Leicester for a week, then Nottingham for the best part of a month before stopping in Royston to meet with the northern bishops, and then looping down to Windsor. Then those friendly midland towns; Coventry, Lichfield and Stafford before staying awhile in Chester (a first visit by Richard to the region of the earldom he was elevated to in gratitude of his birth) in July. A second residence in Nottingham is scheduled for August.

Gloucester's primary concern is still regarding Richard's travelling companions. For he notes a worrying change in the King's behaviour when he is sharing his time with Robert de Vere the so-called Duke of Ireland and Michael de la Pole the recently-shamed Earl of Suffolk. No doubt their allegiance to a king of England is easily maintained when such proximity is guaranteed by sweet whispers that reassure the boy inside the man that he is great and mighty.

At least the time away from London will allow the King's Council to subtly inspect the crown's administrations and accounts and recommend ways of refashioning them in a more profitable manner. Without the in-person petulance of a boy who wears the crown, there is much that can be done to address and rebuild England's financial foundations.

And so Gloucester will try not to worry about the gilded tongues of his closest friends. The King will meet many mighty people throughout his visitings, so it is perhaps possible that such experience of other men will help him to re-assess and depreciate the value of those men he currently holds the closest.

At least he is also accompanied by Anne, and the beautiful calming influence she imparts on all who know her. After five years of marriage, for all Richard's other failings he is undoubtedly devoted to his queen, although there is some concern from even the most supportive of councillors regarding his nightly duties.

Just in case Queen Anne's role in this gyration of many months has not been made clear to her, before she left Gloucester discreetly requested an audience and ensured she was well briefed in her role for this expedition.

England, he told her, expects our beloved queen to return with a royal heir in her belly.

=====

-- THE TALE OF THE WHITE HART --

15th February 1387.

Beaumanoir: his residence for a week.

After the morning's trundle up out of Leicester's north gate, the roadway points through great rolling meadows of which **King Richard** approves upon the first sight. He has come to miss and therefore to appreciate good sleep in a bed knowing that he will be retiring back into the same comfortable structure on the following evening so he is looking forward to Beaumanoir.

He has learned several things. There are many forests and hills in England, and all his subjects are very happy to see him even if for the briefest of moments. It is good to see, although of course the travel is tiring and rattles the bones. They say Julius Caesar built the Fosse Way, but that was not long after our Lord and Saviour Jesus Christ lived, and he would wager that the roads had not been attended to since then. He has already, after several days of travelling, come to look forward to those regular occasions when the royal collective stops for mud or blockages in the road.

Except for today.

Today he prays for a speedy roll to Beaumanoir, in particular because his own personal excitement is higher than ever before now. For King Richard has just this morning taken a delivery in Leicester that was awaiting him after that delivery that had come down from Chester.

He holds the token in his right hand, which is clasped tightly so it sticks into his palm, his fingers, and the flesh of his thumb. It is heavy enough to feel its weight, and it is strong enough to withstand his excited grip.

Another look.

His fingertips open up like a flower, and the dark pink impression points in his skin from his fingernails remind him again that he grips this stunning trinket too hard in his pleasure of ownership.

A gleaming white ceramic badge, not half the size of his palm. The stag has been crafted as seated, with golden features, golden antlers, golden hooves, a golden crown around its neck and a golden chain fixed to the crown and laid across its body. It cannot speak but tells more than any book that has ever been written; for this beautiful little badge sings the song of King Richard the Second.

The white hart. The *fabled* white hart. A creature demanding of reverence, with the white of God's own purity, collared in gold by the crown of King Richard's authority and symbolic of every Christian man's quest to live without sin in the eyes of God. Originally this greatest of all heraldic symbols appeared on his mother's family crest, now adopted in full by her great sovereign lord and son in her honour.

His own livery. Paid for by himself. What's good for the barons is good for the King. Except the King has more money, power and authority than any baron; lord, earl or duke. And that means that a king's army would more effective and terrifying than all the barons' private armies put together.

Soon, all in England shall see the white hart symbol and cower in fear of it, for it shall stand as testament to King Richard's approaching power. A kingly authority forthcoming when he reaches the age of twenty-one in less than one year. For this is the new sign of the King of England and of France, and Lord of Ireland. And the first to bear it, someday if not soon, will be the private and secret army he has begun to assemble.

For now, over seven hundred footmen and archers await his arrival in Chester. And soon, he will rule as he wants, without interference from commissions and councils and meddling uncles who continue to shame him in front of his own parliament and kingdom.

Once he has his army, then he can rid his kingdom of everyone who opposes him.

Incompetents. Enemies. And, most especially, certain members of his malodorous family.

=====

SCENE. THE COURT OF EXCHEQUER, WESTMINSTER – DAY

8th April 1387.

***Thomas of Woodstock the Duke of Gloucester** visits **Sir Walter Barnham the Chancellor of the Exchequer**.*

It is a surprisingly large and busy room, adjoining Westminster Hall, with many well-dressed men attending to the many parchment rolls on several large tables.

Sir Walter Barnham was busy studying a roll, and startles at the appearance of the duke. Gloucester, however, waves Barnham's consternation away with a friendly hand gesture. The two men are of similar age, know one another, and respect one another.

**THOMAS OF WOODSTOCK,
DUKE OF GLOUCESTER**

I merely wished to call and impart my delight at all the fine accountancy herein.

England's royal council is very pleased with this administration's progress.

**SIR WALTER BARNHAM,
CHANCELLOR OF THE EXCHEQUER**

We have all but ceased our king's casual use of his personal signet seal.

Gloucester nods appreciatively.

**THOMAS OF WOODSTOCK,
DUKE OF GLOUCESTER**

Happy times, indeed.

**SIR WALTER BARNHAM,
CHANCELLOR OF THE EXCHEQUER**

I believe our sovereign lord does not return to London before November?

**THOMAS OF WOODSTOCK,
DUKE OF GLOUCESTER**

He left gladly when we agreed to cease council meetings for that time.

**SIR WALTER BARNHAM,
CHANCELLOR OF THE EXCHEQUER**

Well, hurrah for us all, then. I cannot imagine not seeing my own bed for months.

THOMAS OF WOODSTOCK,
DUKE OF GLOUCESTER
Speaking of which, I'm away home to Essex for the time being. Before I leave, what was the outcome of that Burley issue I requested clarity upon?

SIR WALTER BARNHAM,
CHANCELLOR OF THE EXCHEQUER
Hmmm.

It would appear that Sir Simon did recently take receipt of titles to certain manors that were listed in old King Edward's will.

THOMAS OF WOODSTOCK,
DUKE OF GLOUCESTER
They were the King's to give?

SIR WALTER BARNHAM,
CHANCELLOR OF THE EXCHEQUER
They were indeed.

THOMAS OF WOODSTOCK,
DUKE OF GLOUCESTER
Damn it. Again Richard gives away estate! And so, a slippery fish wriggles off the hook and that is that.

Keep up the good work, Barnham.

SIR WALTER BARNHAM,
CHANCELLOR OF THE EXCHEQUER
(deep breath)
Before you leave, my Lord. I have been lately inspecting this rather interesting - if anomalous - trifle.

Barnham indicates for Gloucester to read the roll on his table.

Gloucester frowns, and studies it for some time, trying to identify the intrigue.

THOMAS OF WOODSTOCK,
DUKE OF GLOUCESTER
Last year... a subsidy demanded by Richard... of two thousand pounds from

Cheshire. A goodly amount, but not uncommonly so.

SIR WALTER BARNHAM, CHANCELLOR OF THE EXCHEQUER

Oh, yes, as the Earl of Chester it is Richard's right to generate income, of course.

But it is also even The King's obligation to declare the income to his exchequer, and this princely sum remains unaccounted for.

One presumes the coin is held *localement*.

Gloucester looks at Barnham for an explanation.

THOMAS OF WOODSTOCK, DUKE OF GLOUCESTER

He's due there in July.

Why would Richard have two thousand unaccounted pounds of silver awaiting him in Chester?

Barnham has the satisfied look of someone in an unremarkable job who has just found something very remarkable.

=====

6: The Lords Appellant

-- THE OPENING TALE OF THE STANLEY FAMILY --

1st July 1387.

Not rags, not silks, but clean well-worn garments.

Sir John Stanley would dress, as all men do, in accordance with his status.

Having already put on his shirt and braie body linen, that two-part undergarment layer which separates the skin from the more grandiose but often itchy woollen overgarments, he inserts legs into his dark-dye hose and then wiggles into a mustard-coloured doublet; that long sleeved layer positioned over the top half that stitches up at the front and sides to fit the man and keep the hose from falling round his ankles.

Not an earl - and certainly not a marquis or a duke - he is a knight of the realm and a lord of the manor at Lathom in north-west England; the manor he owns and manages by right of his wife, the heiress Isabel Lathom whom he married but two years ago.

The recency of the marriage means that still now, every time Sir John Stanley notices some part of Lathom Manor, he encounters a breathlessness that he rather hopes will never stop occurring. As the second son of a modest landowner, the esteemed Master-Forester of the vast Forest of Wirral, the young John Stanley might have supposed that his fate lay in serving the military or the church given that he was unlikely to inherit anything of monetary value from his father so long as an older brother was alive at the time of the father's demise. As his brother had once chided; "*Perhaps tha'll get that which the cat leaves on the malt-heap.*"

He holds up a houppelande and checks the fabric for wear and tear. It's a magnificent heavy wool three-quarter length two-colour (brown and mustard) tunic that is fitted in at the waist and has great double sleeves that flare riotously at the wrists and are embellished with crenellations to mimic the great castles of England. And although Stanley is journeying to one of the great and yet least known of England's castles, a houppelande is far more suited to court than it is for a fifty-mile ride to a solitary Cheshire fortress in the middle of nowhere.

The constitutional secrecy entrusted in him by his king suits Stanley these days more than the blood and guts of the battlefield. He'd seen action in France, though he tries not to think about what happened over there, and what might have happened if God had not been favouring him on more than a few occasions. His willingness to slice Frenchies with a more than dutiful vigour had earned commendations from his superiors, when in truth all the time he'd harboured a secret from them.

-- A SHORT HISTORY OF SIR JOHN, THE FIRST LORD STANLEY --

Back in 1376 the young Master John Stanley had been an outlaw. After some nonsense up in Lancashire that had seen him charged with theft and murder, the young man had not fancied his chances against a sheriff in need of a quick resolution with less than certain evidence. The law was unremitting, he had no future, but he could at least orchestrate a worthy end. A noble death desire, he had called it privately to no-one but himself; a fine solution to escape a life that had promised much, given nothing, and taken all. He determined to travel a long way south, keep his own to his own, and lose his past in among the retained soldiers of 14th century England. But plans did not work out. Accepting of a fate of death in honour on the battlefield, he instead had the fortune to discover ownership of that greatest of all military skills: luck. Commendations followed commendations, and his stock rose greatly, until one drunken night he confessed his chequered past to his commander.

But what might have been a dishonourable end, turned out to be the making of the man. For Stanley's commander recognised great potential in a man who did fully repent the follies of his youth, and put in place the necessary administration to deliver a pardon to the soldier in lieu of his services to the old King Edward on the battlefield.

Upon returning, he attended King Richard II's royal court, and most inexplicably his story caught the ear of Sir Simon Burley, tutor to the boy king and senior chamberlain, who eagerly introduced the former outlaw to the young sovereign lord. The curious fall and rise, under distant circumstances that to Richard's cosseted court seemed so terrible and terrifying (and now glorious and chivalric) was enough to earn John Stanley a knighthood, and the King took great interest in him thereafter.

Seventeen years older than the Richard, Stanley was a generation ahead, and so wasn't ever part of the King's famous young and beautiful inner circle, but to have his own sovereign lord clearly thinking very well of him was a key to great expectations.

And so it was that Sir John Stanley returned to his homelands in northwest England, a relatively wealthy retained knight of the realm. And if his good name had been restored by a king's pardon, his financially security would follow presently, when Richard, always in need of a northern ally that he could trust, approved the marriage to Isabel of Lathom in spite of amazement and jealousy from Stanley's own family and to the annoyance of mighty establishment barons such as the Duke of Lancaster. Sir John Stanley now had the good name, the money, the land and the property for his family to endure.

And endure they would. He would endeavour to school his baby son, also named John Stanley, in the art of politics and to become a master of manoeuvring through court to get what you wanted from an establishment that for the most part didn't know what it was doing.

The Stanleys will succeed. He and his successors are not going to waste his good fortune. Several years ago he was an outlaw who was sentenced to hang, and yet he came back a knight and a hero and is now lord of his manor.

The *cottehardie* is well-fitted, with a linen inner lining, fashionable buttons up the front and up the sleeves to the elbow, and it also has a hood for the protection from the dust of the ride.

And it is indeed much more appropriate attire for a fifty-mile ride and, thereafter, a secret meeting with King Richard the Second of England.

=====

-- RICHARD RIDES --

Chester, 12th July 1387.

The ride, begun at dawn, is just ten miles.

Richard travels incognito and at speed, dressed down himself but with a dozen personally-chosen armoured guards, they speed away from Chester along the hollow-way once carved half-heartedly by the Romans before that ancient race declared their resources to be better used elsewhere.

Surrounding trees are thick and green, but even so the gaps between them reveal-conceal-reveal-conceal the strikingly mighty shadowed rocky assemblage that is near them in this part of the world. Wind races through the leaves about them, and occasionally spots of rain wet the royal face, but on they thud through those grassy lanes, and on indeed with great purpose.

Ever closer comes that sombre, almost mountainous, ridge, so violently struck at the start of time to now rest silent overlooking God's locality. A steep but navigable slope at the far side, and yet vicious rocky broken hill with sheer drops to the near, Beeston Castle is set 350 feet higher than the Cheshire plain that stretches on to the horizon on all sides; England to all eastern views, Chester to the north west, and then Wales to the west and south west, and the stone fortress in the sky is both admired and feared for many many miles.

Having steered around the edge of the ridge, they turn up the track to the castle with the early sun at their backs, the horses' rhythm changes for the hill, and more long-faced huffing and truffing signals new determination. Halfway up the slope the castle's small but strong stone outer gatehouse is a welcome sight, for none here are happy at the ever-present prospect of having a purposeful ride become a dangerous defence should any local brigands try their best to bash some silver out of whom they would presume was a local lord on business.

Into the vast outer ward of the castle, the enclosed bailey is more of a steep meadow, and filled with hundreds of archers and their tents. Many are sitting round fires, many are undoubtedly resting in their tents, and many are - encouragingly - practising their archery skills in the wide grass lanes that stretch from the outer stone wall. The first few dozen men fail to recognise their mounted visitors, but within a few moments whispers, murmurs, conversation and then shouts of the King do rattle out over the hubbub. Men who were in their tents poke their heads out in curiosity, men who were outside rest on a knee, and even the cooks and the smiths and the stewards step outside of their makeshift wooden buildings to join their brethren on the knee at the passing presence of their sovereign lord.

Richard squeezes his horse between his knees as he wends up the hill towards the castle, holding up a flat right palm in salute of his army.

Across the skinny stone causeway, trapping across the solid twelve-foot long timber drawbridge, and into the sparse inner ward with straight and deadly drops beyond its other three sides; these are the best castle views in all of England, and while Richard often relishes how it must feel to be a bird and look down upon God's world, he does not today go out of his way to admire them. Their retinue's horses are gathered in the courtyard, and England's sovereign lord offers a small prayer for his safe arrival.

The men in this castle are Richard's guarantee of safety here because they are all retained servants to the Earl of Chester who is also acknowledged as King of England and of France and Lord of Ireland. Or, that is to say, the men in this castle are all his and his alone; at the cost of £2,000 capital investment.

A hearty welcome by the constable of the castle Sir John Stanley, an acquaintance so trusted by Richard that he has recently appointed him Lord Lieutenant of Ireland and de Vere's deputy as Duke of Ireland, and this man - well-appointed of Richard's reason for this extremely short and secret visit - seats his sovereign lord in the modest south-west tower and presents the vital documentation.

The document is good and legal.

The men of Cheshire are raised by their fathers to be fighters. It is the way these people are because the Welsh have little regard for borders and do regularly send their most vicious representatives past Chester to terrorise the villages around. And so they train, and from a young age too. And their weapon of choice is the bow.

Seven hundred Cheshire Archers, bought and paid for, to be retained and ready until King Richard demands their attendance; trained men to be called upon whenever he needs their presence...

...their trusted assistance...

...their devoted violence.

=====

-- WESTMINSTER, REFURBISHED --

16th July 1387

Tapping, hammering, and men with purpose.

The Westminster Palace complex is alive with sounds and smells; of carpenters and their woods, mercers and their cloths, and, judging by the rich fabrics worn by some, the odd master mason here and there.

Thomas of Woodstock, Duke of Gloucester, is surprised to return to Westminster to find foremen, labourers and workmen of all kinds in spirited humour.

After a visit to the exchequer to discuss some trivial matter of accounting, with business completed he takes a leisurely stroll through the goings on. At the far end of the old Westminster Hall he exits left and then right along the short and narrow passageway that runs southwards along the west end of St Stephen's Chapel, into the comfortable space of the White Hall, and then once again at the far end, exits left and into the cosy familiarity of the Painted Chamber.

Although today not quite so familiar.

As with all the other parts of Westminster in which he has lately visited, scores of scratty men are working dutifully, some in silence, some with a whistle, some with a song and the rest with an incessant chattering and enthusiastic laughter at low level communications that Gloucester strains to understand.

The majority of the preparation work is complete, and Gloucester notes what has been done, for nary a familiar tapestry remains in the grand palace complex, and only a handful of workers' ladders still lean high against walls because almost all the older tapestries are rolled and ready to go, or gone.

To see the bare walls of a palace gives Gloucester a deep feeling of dread. It is not good to see the buildings that represent one's kingdom in such naked impoverished abashment, but he reasons that this state is temporary for there are many rolls of lustrous fabric lying on the stone floor to suggest that these are replacements for those removed.

Of course the bareness is temporary, for even as Gloucester shudders at the unexceptional harshness of a Painted Chamber that he loved for its splendour, so do more labourers - under the attention of their foreman - position a very large flag-type banner, folded at least a couple of times in on itself to better protect it as it is hoisted up. It is the wall the King would sit forward of, and the men work impressively as a team to attach the horizontal iron rod and its decorative end finials to the wall using the bracketed fittings left by the previous tapestry. The mercer himself, who bows low to Gloucester as he catches a duke of the realm in observation, is otherwise scrutinising the project to ensure that his precious cloth is not damaged by the ruffians. And if it is damaged, to ensure that he is there to personally blame one of them.

With no such ill happenings on this raising, the construction is complete, and the mercer and the foreman agree that all is well and squared. And so the mercer nods ceremoniously to the foreman, and the foreman nods ceremoniously to his men for the final flourish, and with purposeful shouts and commotion, the banner is unfurled. The dark splendour falls in full with a whoof, and reveals itself, flicking and wobbling itself to stillness against the otherwise white chamber wall.

Gloucester looks high to regard it from its top and gazes from up to down. Royal blue, it is, with many geometrically positioned motifs, created by intricate golden silken designs. At the centre, a beautiful seated white hart, with a golden chained crown around its neck.

Even as Gloucester understands it to be the motif of his royal nephew, so behind him do other shouts and commotion occur, and elsewhere in this chamber does another banner unfurl itself upon a wall; this second banner being a beautiful lustrous depiction of the Garden of Eden and featuring men, women and animals including a unicorn, a lion, dogs... and when Gloucester's eye is in, he espies a much smaller incidental representation of that which features so boldly on the first tapestry.

Richard is surrounding us all with his white hart.

But why?

And what does it cost to refurbish Westminster Palace with white hart tapestries? £50? £100? £200? A trifle to a king.

In which case what exactly was that £2,000 for?

=====

-- A DUKE'S DILEMMA --

25th July 1387.

Would his inaction damn him or save him?

Being both **Duke of Gloucester** and King Richard's much-respected uncle has allowed him a proximity to the crown that has, over the years, permitted him to understand its duality. It is blessed and yet accursed. It is a privilege and yet a burden. Jesus Christ Himself was made to suffer in order that man could be saved, well so it was with kings and the success of their realm.

Gloucester grips the parchment in his hand. A terrifying illuminating note written by a familiar trusted hand has concisely apprised him that the whispers he has heard are true.

That is King Richard is, as Gloucester suspected, colluding with several sneaking barons of this kingdom to raise in secret a private army. That Richard is not colluding with any of his own family is a distasteful indication that he will no doubt pay retainers once they swear deadly allegiances not to the realm but of Richard and his whims.

The implications are disturbing. While many barons employ a number of private freelancers to discourage overenthusiastic claims on their land and property, the King traditionally and openly relies upon the barons, and their working men, when he wishes to call arms.

It is intriguing how, as Richard attempts to show his power by buying his own army, he becomes less of a king and more like one of those he would wish to raise himself above.

A king must be glorious, revered, obeyed. Approved by God in Heaven. And this is how it has been forever. But how this wretched method of rule is flawed when the King is... not fit to hold his rank.

Rarely has this happened before.

The last deficient, King Edward the Second, was a royal Plantagenet with all the right credentials; pure legitimate Plantagenet blood and eldest son to old Longshanks himself; that mighty six and a half foot-tall Hammer of the Scots, King Edward the First. Though wed to the most beautiful woman of that age, Isabella of France, the younger Edward instead spent much of his time as a younger man with his close friend Piers Gaveston while the kingdom, struggling to function without a king who cared, slowly went to ruin.

Eventually, enraged by enemy victories, debts, and the second Edward's disinterest in anything but Gaveston, his nobles arrested that tousle-haired youth and lopped his head off in some Warwickshire woods.

Worse still, as a distraught Edward failed to recover his wits, he refused to ever again co-operate fully with those nobles he considered responsible for Gaveston's death. Even two decades later, the failure of that King Edward to quell increasingly ambitious uprisings and even invasions led to a group of nobles forcing their sovereign lord to abdicate, which he eventually did in return for assurances that his own son would succeed the throne and that his own life be spared.

But a new king should replace a dead one; that is the natural order of things.

And if a current king wasn't capable, and if God had presented an heir to replace that king, then was it possible that final riddance of the old king was thereby tacitly approved by the Almighty?

A distracting beacon to beleaguered supporters of the crown, poor Edward the Second was eventually executed in private. And to mitigate the abhorrence against God's once-approved vessel, he was killed in a way that did not leave any visible wounds. Any drunken fool in any fetid tavern would tell you in great detail of a glowing poker forcibly inserted into a void that would thus leave England's majesty untainted as it left the earth, although most would also boast that it was their grandfather who administered the deadly deed.

Gloucester drinks more wine, its sweetness somehow now too overpowering to be enjoyed. Any act against a king – whether with or without just cause – is an act directly against God, and the eternal fires of Hell would presumably await for such offenders. But King Richard insists on playing the part of antagonist in these particular politics. A private army may be the first brick in a tyrannical wall that has been unconstitutional since the days of King John and Magna Carta.

Then, what to do?

If a kingdom is rotting, does one let it rot because its king is untouchable? If a king's arm bleeds, how does one cauterise the wound if one cannot touch the arm? Does one cauterise it anyway, and save the king but then accept an eternity in Hell for the cauterising? Or does one accept the arm will bleed until the unfortunate injured king dies, so that one might go to Heaven?

Or, most terrifyingly of all, what if St Peter turned you from Heaven's gates for not having the courage to cauterise the wound and thereby save the king that you could have saved if your courage had held?

How must our ancestors look down upon us and wail from their golden thrones.

Gloucester carefully holds the parchment in the flames of his fire, letting it go once it has shown its eagerness to burn so its disgraceful words are black and unreadable.

And then, with a hellish roar, hurls his glazed goblet at the wall where it thumps his painted plaster so hard that a piece the size of his head clatters to his floor.

May God give him the courage to make his choices for the right reasons.

Whatever they may be.

=====

-- A SHERWOOD VILLAGE --

26th July 1387.

The dogs bark first, at shadows, she presumes.

Then magpies, gathered, clap their wings and take their flight to somewhere well beyond the tops of local trees; occurrences not unusual enough to stop the usual daily gabbing of the wives, the shrieking of the babes, nor the tinkering and the blowering of the smith.

Agnes of Calverton loves this time of year. Especially when the sun has shone well and any showers have rained with restrained respect for the growing of their harvest which this year is full and fruitful.

She tra-la-lahs a hymn she loves as she presses curds as tightly as she can manage with her smooth clean wooden contraption. While spring grass produces goats' milk that is creamy and more than willing to lend itself to butter, as summer lengthens and autumn dawns the thinner drier blades are loathe to yield such creaminess and so, then, cheese is easier obtained if one is diligent in cleaning hands and tools with salt, very hot water, and a vigorous scrubbing of everything of interest for the benefit of the cheese concerned.

Does she feel or hear the horses first, she is not certain. But it is clear in short time that horses in a heavy hurry are coming closer. Women gather their children to them as that urge within all mothers rings those uncanny clangs of danger, and the powerful drumming of violent fast-moving horses means they are expected at any time, though when they appear still makes the villagers gasp.

They canter from the hills and through the village, and finally this ordinary day is extraordinary, for it is perhaps twenty men in number; all equipped and dressed for war, and in no gentle mood.

They yelp and yelp and yelp indiscriminate roars, as their horses thrash down the gentle incline of the main lane. Then the ground tremors subside, and dust accounts for light brown blindness which when clears does leave the village just about as unremarkable as it was before.

And so she turns to return to her pressing of the curd, but as she turns a single distant bell begins to clang from several miles away, and more than enough to bring the villagers out onto the dusty lane that brings and takes travellers as they pass through. Such a church bell, when rung extraordinarily, is an ominous event that none relish.

Black smoke in the sky, there is. It plumes at the west, from whence the riders came, beyond the forested hills that overlook the village like a big black bouquet as if gathering for some thunderstorm on an otherwise beautiful day.

Bad news and bad smoke from a close by village; Linby or Papplewick perhaps. And twenty armed horsemen clad in low-to-middling armour. The sheriff and his representatives will no doubt come calling in search of witness testimony, and so she tries with a heaviness in her belly to recall any notable details with regard to the errant men.

Sadly, no such illumination comes to the recall, as all excitement was over just as soon as it had begun. They had the look of soldiers in mail and with hooded tunics of indeterminate dark colours, and some had saddlebags that now she recalled did rattle and sit heavy with guilt.

But that was that.

Later Agnes awakens well before the dawn with quite the start. How could she have forgotten and then now recall such specific remembrances is well beyond her ken. Perhaps God wished her to forget and then to remember, and who knows how and why God does His works.

She would later tell the sheriff, as in fact would many nearby folk, that all the men shouted not haphazard whoops and caterwauls, but words.

For Richard!, they had yawped aplenty.

King Richard?, wondered the sheriff, uncomfortably.

=====

SCENE. THE GREAT HALL AT KENILWORTH CASTLE – DAY

28th July 1387.

***Thomas Mowbray Earl of Nottingham** has ridden to visit **Henry Bolingbroke** at Kenilworth Castle.*

Nottingham enters the Great Hall eagerly to find a welcoming host. But Nottingham is extremely perturbed, and Bolingbroke sees it.

HENRY BOLINGBROKE,
EARL OF DERBY
My old friend! Are you well?

THOMAS MOWBRAY,
EARL OF NOTTINGHAM
Aye, for a fool.

HENRY BOLINGBROKE,
EARL OF DERBY
How so?

THOMAS MOWBRAY,
EARL OF NOTTINGHAM
Have you yourself had no reports of villainous knaves ransacking villages and churches of silver and gold?

Henry Bolingbroke thinks, then pulls a face as he shakes his head.

THOMAS MOWBRAY,
EARL OF NOTTINGHAM (cont'd)
They ride, a dozen or more at a time, and in full daylight do visit places of peace to pillage!

Full daylight!

HENRY BOLINGBROKE,
EARL OF DERBY
Who?

THOMAS MOWBRAY,
EARL OF NOTTINGHAM
Richard's Cheshiremen. They proudly shout his name as they plunder and desecrate!

HENRY BOLINGBROKE,
EARL OF DERBY
This is true?

THOMAS MOWBRAY,
EARL OF NOTTINGHAM
Definitely. The scoundrels need clipping, but...

...they're the King's own army.

HENRY BOLINGBROKE,
EARL OF DERBY
Hmmm. A complication, indeed.

THOMAS MOWBRAY,
EARL OF NOTTINGHAM
Henry. There are some who would hear my next words, and wonder if I was a treasonous lord. But you and I...

...you would not judge me harshly?

HENRY BOLINGBROKE,
EARL OF DERBY
I listen. Or I am deaf, depending on what you say.

THOMAS MOWBRAY,
EARL OF NOTTINGHAM
Our king...

...he does not control his men as a good lord should...

...other than the royal council, is there any way we might urge a king to enforce the law?

Bolingbroke considers his next words very carefully. Perhaps it is time to make the four lords, five lords.

=====

SCENE. HERTFORD CASTLE – DAY

31st July 1387.

***Thomas of Woodstock the Duke of Gloucester** and **Henry Bolingbroke the Earl of Derby**, walk through a walled garden.*

Though they are an uncle and nephew of great repute in England, they are mindful of who may hear them.

No-one can, but they are furtive and solemn, for Gloucester has discovered what Richard's £2,000 has bought.

HENRY BOLINGBROKE,
EARL OF DERBY
So my cousin is assembling an army, what of it?

Having them in court might have deterred whoever it was who thieved my hat.

THOMAS OF WOODSTOCK,
DUKE OF GLOUCESTER
That cheap wine you drink took your damned hat. What age have you, now, twenty?

HENRY BOLINGBROKE,
EARL OF DERBY
Almost.

THOMAS OF WOODSTOCK,
DUKE OF GLOUCESTER

You really must employ more care. You'll be Duke of Lancaster someday.

HENRY BOLINGBROKE,
EARL OF DERBY

Pfff. John of Gaunt would live forever.

THOMAS OF WOODSTOCK,
DUKE OF GLOUCESTER

Your father is a great lord and a great man. And Lancaster is the greatest duchy in England. It's about time you studied his ways a little more diligently.

HENRY BOLINGBROKE,
EARL OF DERBY

Perhaps.

I mean...

...I know.

THOMAS OF WOODSTOCK,
DUKE OF GLOUCESTER

This King's Army, for example. Why do you think I fear it, so?

HENRY BOLINGBROKE,
EARL OF DERBY

I really don't know! The King would do as he may. What care have we if he spends his money on an army only he commands?

THOMAS OF WOODSTOCK,
DUKE OF GLOUCESTER

Lord Jesu! Where do I begin?

HENRY BOLINGBROKE,
EARL OF DERBY

Well then, educate me, uncle, or hold your peace!

This jars Gloucester enough to stop walking, and it looks for a second as if he is angry with his nephew. But, as Henry Bolingbroke stops to see why Gloucester has stopped, there is no anger. The young man seems to really want to know more about politics, so they continue their walk together.

THOMAS OF WOODSTOCK,
DUKE OF GLOUCESTER

A king rules by being obeyed. Therefore it is those of us who obey, who assent to the King doing the ruling.

HENRY BOLINGBROKE,
EARL OF DERBY

I've never understood this. The King is the King, and that is that.

THOMAS OF WOODSTOCK,
DUKE OF GLOUCESTER

The King is the King for as long as he follows the laws of the land as agreed by those who assent to his ruling.

HENRY BOLINGBROKE,
EARL OF DERBY

And what if he doesn't? What if the King breaks the law?

Gloucester stops, screws up his face and pinches the bridge of his nose.

THOMAS OF WOODSTOCK,
DUKE OF GLOUCESTER

Then we all go to Heaven or Hell much sooner than planned.

HENRY BOLINGBROKE,
EARL OF DERBY

But the King has not broken the law by paying for these Cheshire Archers. So I don't understand why that should see us all to our graves.

Gloucester is trying to find the right words. Then a way of explanation occurs to him.

THOMAS OF WOODSTOCK,
DUKE OF GLOUCESTER

You play chess.

What is a chessboard if it is not the battlefield of two royal courts? Eight pawns, then towers, knights, clergy, and a queen all form a chess player's realm.

Two opponents; both manoeuvring against a king while defending their own. Do you ever win when you play?

HENRY BOLINGBROKE, EARL OF DERBY

Often, in truth.

THOMAS OF WOODSTOCK, DUKE OF GLOUCESTER

Then consider a chessboard in which your opponent has sixteen pieces which are fronted by an extra rank of eight Cheshire Archers, while you have none such.

Would you then fancy this game?

To the death?

And if you did, do you think you would win?

Henry Bolingbroke considers this with great seriousness.

=====

SCENE. SHREWSBURY ABBEY – DAY

1st August 1387.

***King Richard II** returns from riding with **Robert de Vere, Duke of Ireland**. The King and de Vere dismount, and adjust their appearance to walk to the business of the day. **Michael de la Pole, Earl of Suffolk**, awaits his king with an earnest look. Richard notices this as he walks past his senior adviser. De Vere follows, with a smirk. Then Richard stops, and turns to face Suffolk.*

KING RICHARD II

What.

MICHAEL DE LA POLE, EARL OF SUFFOLK

The Cheshiremen are known.

KING RICHARD II
How known?

MICHAEL DE LA POLE,
EARL OF SUFFOLK
Gloucester knows.

King Richard nods sombrely.

KING RICHARD II
Is there aught else?

MICHAEL DE LA POLE,
EARL OF SUFFOLK
There is a small group of noblemen who are taking a particularly clandestine interest.

KING RICHARD II
Gloucester and Arundel, I should imagine. Both have spun webs around the two of us this year.

MICHAEL DE LA POLE,
EARL OF SUFFOLK
(nodding)
And Warwick. And Nottingham. And...

Richard's eyes narrow.

MICHAEL DE LA POLE,
EARL OF SUFFOLK (cont'd)
...and His Grace, the Earl of Derby.

A low growl begins to emit from Richard, whose rage visibly increases. De Vere looks afraid and suddenly very young. Richard's growl becomes a wail, and as he turns to the wall to punch it, his wail becomes a 'B-'.

KING RICHARD II
-OLINGBROKE!

BOLINGROKE?

Richard begins to laugh with ferocity, just to let the fury out.

MICHAEL DE LA POLE,
EARL OF SUFFOLK
Sire-

Already breathless, Richard gathers himself.

KING RICHARD II
Oh, I tire of them all!

MICHAEL DE LA POLE,
EARL OF SUFFOLK
Sire-

KING RICHARD II
They plot! My uncle and my cousin plot.
And Warwick, and Arundel, and Nottingham,
they all plot.

MICHAEL DE LA POLE,
EARL OF SUFFOLK
They are afraid, Sire. Your Cheshiremen
would irritate any noble-

KING RICHARD II
-I'll tell you of irritation, SIR.

They have their council by which they run
MY kingdom. A COUNCIL comprising petty
men, content with power NOT condoned by
God and all the weaker for it.

For I remain anointed and do not hide
among a herd of councillors because in
truth no man in England would say no to
me.

And THIS is the advantage I shall now
play.

=====

-- NOTTINGHAM. AUGUST 1387. --

King Richard II glares at the confused decrepit dodderer, by now almost willing him to refuse the making of his mark.

He may spit in the old man's eyes, anyway. And if the shrivelled white goat frowns at the parchment in front of him any more times he might stab him in the spit with his own quill and pop his eye.

Nottingham is not London. It is not Lancaster. And it is not full of the Duke of Gloucester's spies. Though it is, he thinks with a sudden and surprising smile, full of armed ruffians who are paid to unquestioningly do as he bids.

Gloucester: that mouldy old duke of distaste, that intractable uncle. A mortal who opposes God's chosen before his own parliament without the respect for his betters that he was born with. And yet, according to the lawyers of the land, all the disrespectful insolence and arrogant impudence that this King has suffered from this simpleton - the impeachment of his Lord Chancellor, the construction of a committee to tell him what to do - does not constitute treason!

How can this be? It cannot! But how can this be? It cannot!

A fizzing firework in his belly that would never consume itself called for a stratagem, and so this stratagem is begun in Nottingham with twelve judges, presumed by Richard to be sympathetic to the King's cause on account of their selection by that old warhorse Sir Robert Tresilian; he who had proven so willing to hang countless peasants during that summer of revolt.

The twelve judges are gathered in secrecy to debate a simple premise.

Is an attempt to reform the realm or regulate the royal household, by any man other than The King, an act of treason?

The dozen, uncomfortably aware of the context of their latest commission, had at first twisted their tongues in forked legal knots so much that nobody could understand a word that was said. But Richard is not blessed with patience, and the introduction of swords wielded by big broken-faced men soon achieved an acceptable clarity for all concerned.

Before today, a man had to act or plot in violence against the King or wage war against the kingdom to be guilty of treason and then hanged, drawn and quartered as a traitor and that was that. But once Richard's documentation is completed, if a man disagrees with any of his king's prerogatives he would be punished as if he had committed treason. After all, a king rules for the benefit of his kingdom. So if a baron promotes some opposite advice to the desire of his king, in opposition to the weal of the kingdom, *ha*, what is the result if not to be punished as a traitor?

This is a statute much simpler to understand, and therefore much simpler to enforce.

Regrettably, not even he can apply this mighty improvement to English law retrospectively, but the barons have their own advisers who would in due course be able to apprise their masters of the modern implications of disagreeing with their king. Just, now, this; the final of the judges that must sign and approve the legislation. And making the king wait is a creature so old and bent that he no doubt smells his own rancid farts before anyone else.

Enough.

King Richard turns his head, meets the eyes of Tresilian, and nods at the haft at his waist. The gloved right hand strikes for it like a snake, and then whisks the dagger from his tunic belt so fast that, even as it glints ferociously in the candlelight as it flashes between the men, Richard is sure that the old man's blood is about to pour onto the table.

He is not pierced. Instead, Tresilian taps the point on the parchment and then rests the metal end on the elder's pathetic hunched back.

Never has a seventy-year old man skittered his nib across vellum so quickly.

=====

SCENE. HERTFORD CASTLE – DAY

14th October 1387.

***Thomas of Woodstock the Duke of Gloucester**, **Richard FitzAlan the Earl of Arundel**, **Thomas Beauchamp the Earl of Warwick**, **Henry Bolingbroke the Earl of Derby**, and **Thomas Mowbray the Earl of Nottingham** are gathered in a room. Five large pieces of parchment are either held or placed on tables.*

The meeting is secret, as evidenced by their surreptitious subdued nature.

FitzAlan, the Earl of Arundel scrunches his parchment in his fist. Bolingbroke, the Earl of Derby, throws his parchment to the floor.

HENRY BOLINGBROKE,
EARL OF DERBY
I can scarce believe it.

This is true and confirmed?

THOMAS OF WOODSTOCK,
DUKE OF GLOUCESTER
I believe it to be so.

HENRY BOLINGBROKE,
EARL OF DERBY
But, what does it really mean?

THOMAS OF WOODSTOCK,
DUKE OF GLOUCESTER
(glances at Warwick)
It makes a royal council difficult to administer. For it nigh on makes any of our opinions illegal if they differ from Richard's.

RICHARD FITZALAN,
EARL OF ARUNDEL
(shaking and sweating)
It makes us damned traitors, that's what it makes!

THOMAS BEAUCHAMP,
EARL OF WARWICK
Richard's legislation specifies any man obstructing the King's wishes to be punished <u>as traitors</u>.

Not even Richard could persuade his own lawyers to redefine treason.

RICHARD FITZALAN,
EARL OF ARUNDEL
(terrified)
Thank you, Warwick. I shall stop fretting now that I know I do not commit treason, but may still be drawn and quartered for disagreeing with my sovereign lord.

HENRY BOLINGBROKE,
EARL OF DERBY
(to his uncle)
Richard has not accused us of anything yet.

THOMAS OF WOODSTOCK,
DUKE OF GLOUCESTER
Yet.

However. If this new legislation were applied to many of my recent actions on the royal council, I would be punished as a traitor. I do not gain any comfort in that.

THOMAS MOWBRAY,
EARL OF NOTTINGHAM

But new legislation cannot be applied to old transgressions.

THOMAS OF WOODSTOCK,
DUKE OF GLOUCESTER

Nor can a King change laws to suit his whims, and yet he has.

HENRY BOLINGBROKE,
EARL OF DERBY

So how afraid should we be?

THOMAS OF WOODSTOCK,
DUKE OF GLOUCESTER

I have not wronged God, and I acted within the law of the time for the weal of the realm.

Am I afraid to meet God with my honour intact? No.

But in truth, I am afraid for how far Richard will progress this.

THOMAS MOWBRAY,
EARL OF NOTTINGHAM

So the question is; what will Richard do next?

HENRY BOLINGBROKE,
EARL OF DERBY

My question is; what will <u>we</u> do next?

RICHARD FITZALAN,
EARL OF ARUNDEL

What possible action is there?

This Nottingham legislation means that if Richard even considers that I advise against his own opinion then I would be punished as a traitor.

HENRY BOLINGBROKE,
EARL OF DERBY

We must find some advantage, somewhere!

**RICHARD FITZALAN,
EARL OF ARUNDEL**

Ha, advantage? We are all damned, and the King is untouchable.

Gloucester is frustrated at Arundel's declaration.

**THOMAS OF WOODSTOCK,
DUKE OF GLOUCESTER**

We already know this. The King is untouchable. His barons, not so.

But, Henry, you are right. If we ever act bold on behalf of our kingdom, to save our king from himself, we must do so now.

The other four barons are trying to ascertain Gloucester's meaning.

**HENRY BOLINGBROKE,
EARL OF DERBY**

De Vere?

**THOMAS OF WOODSTOCK,
DUKE OF GLOUCESTER**

De Vere. De la Pole. And any of Richard's favourites who are generally not held in high regard.

**RICHARD FITZALAN,
EARL OF ARUNDEL**

So... impeach Richard's circle but not Richard?

**THOMAS BEAUCHAMP,
EARL OF WARWICK**

Never Richard! Remember, we are not <u>actually</u> traitors.

**RICHARD FITZALAN,
EARL OF ARUNDEL**

Pah! Recall de la Pole not even one year ago. Richard would simply reverse the impeachments, re-instate them all, and execute we five having overtly stood against our king's wishes according to his new legislation.

He's almost certainly right. The group deflate. Until Gloucester...

THOMAS OF WOODSTOCK, DUKE OF GLOUCESTER
Then we do not simply charge them with malfeasance. We <u>sue them</u> for treason.

THOMAS BEAUCHAMP, EARL OF WARWICK
(nods)
We are entitled to bring an appeal of treason to trial. Common law. Not even Richard may deny us that.

THOMAS OF WOODSTOCK, DUKE OF GLOUCESTER
And furthermore, King Richard must preside over such a lofty trial.

HENRY BOLINGBROKE, EARL OF DERBY
Undoubtedly. So?

THOMAS OF WOODSTOCK, DUKE OF GLOUCESTER
Well, would the King want to perform this duty?

HENRY BOLINGBROKE, EARL OF DERBY
Of course not.

THOMAS OF WOODSTOCK, DUKE OF GLOUCESTER
Then what encouraging act are we achieving in this pursuit?

Bolingbroke does not know. He looks at the others. Do they?

THOMAS BEAUCHAMP, EARL OF WARWICK
We are forcing him, by common law, to perform a duty against his wishes.

THOMAS OF WOODSTOCK, DUKE OF GLOUCESTER
Aren't we just.

RICHARD FITZALAN,
EARL OF ARUNDEL

Oh, joy. The very behaviour for which he would punish us as traitors.

THOMAS OF WOODSTOCK,
DUKE OF GLOUCESTER

But, Arundel. It is our common law right to bring an appeal against an enemy of the kingdom, so accused.

Thus proving our wilful disobedience to be lawful. And thus proving Richard's recent Nottingham legislation to be unlawful.

HENRY BOLINGBROKE,
EARL OF DERBY

You would test our very lives on a point of law?

THOMAS BEAUCHAMP,
EARL OF WARWICK

Not even a thousand King Richards may break our ancient common laws.

All five attempt to consider all the implications.

HENRY BOLINGBROKE,
EARL OF DERBY

Mowbray? Arundel?

RICHARD FITZALAN,
EARL OF ARUNDEL

What if we lose in our appeal?

THOMAS MOWBRAY,
EARL OF NOTTINGHAM

(answering Arundel)

If we do nothing, then all Richard needs do is fashion some argument with any of us, then claim our demise.

HENRY BOLINGBROKE,
EARL OF DERBY

(to Gloucester and Warwick)

But we might lose. In court.

THOMAS OF WOODSTOCK,
DUKE OF GLOUCESTER

Many barons would be afraid of Richard's Nottingham legislation, for it applies to all noblemen. Not only we five.

So if, as appellants, we select our marks well, we would have much support.

RICHARD FITZALAN,
EARL OF ARUNDEL

Aye. Silent support though, from those without their necks in a noose.

THOMAS BEAUCHAMP,
EARL OF WARWICK

I believe that once we can make it clear that he stands against the majority opinion with regard to those accused, Richard would choose to maintain his fine style of life over the lives of his companions.

HENRY BOLINGBROKE,
EARL OF DERBY

And once de Vere et al are removed, Richard remains king with all God-approved benefits?

THOMAS BEAUCHAMP,
EARL OF WARWICK

Of course.

THOMAS MOWBRAY,
EARL OF NOTTINGHAM

This is not without great risk to us.

THOMAS OF WOODSTOCK,
DUKE OF GLOUCESTER

No. But as you say, Mowbray, if we do nothing then we may just as well wait for the summons to our deaths.

The group sit silently.

=====

-- A LORD'S REFLECTION --

20th November 1387.

Who knew that considering the fortune of a living king could be so terrifying?

Thomas of Woodstock, Duke of Gloucester, takes a private moment to sit down, lean forward, and hold his head in his hands. Predicting the future of the King is known to be the worst kind of treasonous witchcraft, but it is difficult to think about a time beyond these weeks ahead without wondering what King Richard's reaction will be once his advisers are dead.

Gloucester and his four associates are at present trapped by Richard's scheming. A king's court awaits in which one adversarial word may see any in attendance imprisoned and executed in the most unthinkable way of all. Consequently the five have no choice but to now appeal treason on several of the King's advisers for the good of the kingdom. But by challenging a boy-king who is fast proving himself unfit to rule, does Gloucester then play some damnation-worthy part in the undoing of God's anointed, thereby presuming for his soul an eternity in Hell?

And if not, then Richard is capricious enough to want his revenge on, as he would see it, his errant barons.

Damnation on the one hand, and death on the other, then? Two hands which hold the head that Richard would remove with great enthusiasm, given his chance.

His guts are steadfast; he would rather die by acting for the weal of the kingdom. But courage whines when one contemplates such importances in reality.

Well, so be it. To separate Richard from his Cheshiremen, Gloucester and the other four have committed to take possession of the King's person. Then in February's parliament, they will try all of Richard's bad influences before God and England's laws.

And whereupon those thus charged will surely all be found guilty of negligence of duty in their mis-advising of the king.

And whereupon they will all be executed in King Richard's name. Unless of course their closeness to the King gives them some unseen resource to wriggle off these charges. In which case, the Lord Appellants would become the Lord Appellees in a heartbeat.

And the worst of deaths by public execution will then await each of them.

=====

-- KING RICHARD TO LONDON --

27th November 1387.

The great carriage rumbles relentlessly.

He had felt happiness when he left Nottingham, but in truth now, the closer **King Richard**'s entourage ambles to London, the more anxious he feels.

Now, long past St Albans, London's city wall is growing larger all the while. The comforting familiarity of the White Tower, seen beyond the many roofs and spires, does gleam at the far east end of the city in the low afternoon sun.

However as he returns to the city through Newgate, today he senses some impropriety, concealed to him in the heavy city air and he dislikes this because, as king, nothing should be hidden to him.

Past St Paul's and onto West Cheap, that busy wide thoroughfare that would lead condemned and kings alike to the Tower. His melancholy grows. For one so close to the Lord Almighty, it is a curious state to cogitate upon. Puzzled, he observes his people; and his subjects behave incongruously. Rather than hussahing the royal wagon as it trundles past, the people stand and stare with a low enthusiasm that any would at best consider apathetic.

Oddly quiet are these Londoners. How can they work and earn when they stand and stare?

A large spider within his belly begins to scuttle uncomfortably. It is not long since the judges were finally persuaded to reconsider their views on matters of treason. Since this was not debated in parliament, any statute might by some be considered to be unlawful - although he is the king and this is his desire so that is that. But is it possible that news of his subterfuge has reached and been comprehended by the common man? And is their response to this news to act with this odd dull agitation?

London is most familiar to him, so it isn't long before his adjacent surroundings inform him that the White Tower looms large straight ahead. He loves to look out and regard his London fortress from the point of view of his subjects, and so with courage unbolts and opens the carriage door. What he sees enlivens the belly spider to even more discomfort.

Most disconcertingly, hundreds of armoured men await at the bottom of the hill by the castle gate at the riverbank, providing a lined avenue for Richard's carriage to process across the Tower's moat. Little wonder that the Londoners regarded him without their usual deference for this is quite the inauspicious day, then.

Out of habit, Richard seeks the banners as they flutter languidly. There are five, different. Those of an uncle, a cousin and three other lords.

Thomas of Woodstock, Duke of Gloucester, uncle, and in truth the man for whom he'd created his new treason legislation.

Henry Bolingbroke, the Earl of Derby, and cousin.

Thomas Beauchamp, the Earl of Warwick, and trusted nobleman.

Richard FitzAlan, the Earl of Arundel, and trusted nobleman.

Thomas Mowbray, the Earl of Nottingham, and trusted nobleman.

He surmises quickly, that intimate news of his Nottingham agenda has indeed reached the capital before even he has.

And already, several of his lords have combined.

=====

SCENE. TOWER OF LONDON INNER WARD – MID AFTERNOON

27th November 1387.

In the grounds of the Tower of London, the five lords' men-at-arms vastly outnumber King Richard's travelling guard.

***King Richard**, tired from his journey, emerges from his carriage without assistance. **Thomas of Woodstock, Duke of Gloucester**, meets his nephew with a suitable graveness.*

KING RICHARD II
Uncle.

**THOMAS OF WOODSTOCK,
DUKE OF GLOUCESTER**
My King.

KING RICHARD II
Am I a prisoner?

**THOMAS OF WOODSTOCK,
DUKE OF GLOUCESTER**
No, Sir!

KING RICHARD II
Then I may leave?

Gloucester says nothing. Looks at the sky. Dark clouds. Rain? Or snow?

Eventually...

THOMAS OF WOODSTOCK,
DUKE OF GLOUCESTER
No, Sir.

=====

-- THE KING HAILS FOR DE VERE --

To Sir Robert de Vere,
Duc of Ireland, Marquis of Dublin and Erle of Oxford,
29 day of Novembre 1387

My most humble liege lord, I pray apologie for this hastye wrytinge in secresie to your gracefulle personne.

Alas the kyng doth face mortalle dangour from five willfulle untrustey and unlawfulle senior lordes, to wit gloucestre, arundel, warwyk, nottingham and evn our oderwise beloved cousin henry bolingbroke erle of derby.

I wish that Godde take hede of your kyngs desyre for his myghty duc of Irland to gader men who bear the whyte hart livery, and retourn to london in spede to serve us fayithfulley and in honour in regarde to thisse grevious mater.

Hasten ye to cheshire, summone the archeres to london.

May Godde in hys eternalle mercye bless ye in this moste urgente preservacion of the common weal of oure grete kyngdom.

Youres respectfullye in Christe,
Richard, kyng

=====

SCENE. A PRIVATE CHAMBER IN THE TOWER OF LONDON – EVENING

12th December 1387.

The five lords, to be forever known as the Lords Appellant because of their forthcoming appeal to the King's Court sit or stand together in a comfortable chamber.

The strain of holding their king under house arrest is already extreme and visibly apparent. Thomas of Woodstock, Duke of Gloucester, has finished reading a letter and throws it on the fire.

HENRY BOLINGBROKE,
EARL OF DERBY
So I presume de Vere has hastened to Cheshire to gather Richard's men?

THOMAS OF WOODSTOCK,
DUKE OF GLOUCESTER
Undoubtedly.

HENRY BOLINGBROKE,
EARL OF DERBY
So, what do we do?

THOMAS OF WOODSTOCK,
DUKE OF GLOUCESTER
We must intercept him.

HENRY BOLINGBROKE,
EARL OF DERBY
Him and his army?

THOMAS BEAUCHAMP,
EARL OF WARWICK
He is no leader of men, and the Cheshire Archers are Richard's. This is not an army we should fear.

THOMAS OF WOODSTOCK,
DUKE OF GLOUCESTER
De Vere must be captured, killed, or run out of England once and for all.

Richard FitzAlan, Earl of Arundel, is not going to sleep well tonight.

RICHARD FITZALAN,
EARL OF ARUNDEL
What do we do with the King?

When Gloucester doesn't answer immediately, the other four each look to him as they feel their own discomfort.

Eventually...

THOMAS OF WOODSTOCK,
DUKE OF GLOUCESTER
That, my young friend, is an altogether different matter that demands much consideration.

Bolingbroke thinks long and hard.

HENRY BOLINGBROKE,
EARL OF DERBY
De Vere, then. I'll go.

=====

-- RADCOT BRIDGE, OXFORDSHIRE --

19th December 1387.

The cloth-swathed horses nod their impatience.

Henry Bolingbroke the Earl of Derby, a dozen mounted knights, and a few hundred men-at-arms await Robert de Vere. Constantly does Henry consider that he has taken up arms against an English duke, and this does not sit well with him. But while the common man sees Robert de Vere, Duke of Ireland, Henry himself would instead see a chamber knight; a man who might pamper himself in court, and papper himself in battle.

De Vere is coming because he has been called by King Richard, and he comes this way from gathering men from Cheshire and Wales because this is the most direct way to London. The directness is another indication to Henry that de Vere isn't comfortable with the prospect being ambushed, but his panic in the field is thus most readable to a man like Bolingbroke who trained hard in the arts of the warrior.

Henry's intelligence is as excellent as one might expect for the man who will one day inherit the duchy of Lancaster.

Having arrived here half a day ago, and being so confident of de Vere's planned route, Henry commanded his men to scupper one of the curious (if practicable) twin bridges and certainly found no resistance from the alarmed old men in the tollbooths.

He even has time to allow his archers a few practice shots through the mist at the old elm that overlooked the road at the mouth of the remaining bridge across the river to get their range, provided they retrieve their own arrows and do not injure any locals. More than a couple of arrows are lost to either the river or the woods, but the minor loss of ammunition is more than compensated by the good-natured mockery cast back and forth which causes plenty of smiles and laughs, and in the end it is good for men facing death or injury to laugh among themselves.

At the moment Henry's lookout scurries from the woods and across the bridge waving two arms at his master, his archers are in place and their range is well known.

Only de Vere's forward party is engaged; a few ragtag souls who quickly plead mercy and eventually dare to cross the bridge with their hands raised. Henry disarms them, then sends them off and away.

But the longer the main numbers of the enemy army spill out of the woods and into the range of Henry's archers, through the dangerous arrow-filled air, the more Henry begins to suspect that de Vere has indeed proven himself a chamber knight to the end, and elected not to meet in battle.

The enemy, such that it is, screams for mercy. Henry looks to his knights, rallies them, and charges across the bridge, scattering Welsh and Cheshire commoners who would sensibly not engage with a company of fast heavy deadly horses.

Henry would have as little blood shed as possible, except for that of one man. A man who shames himself with his fluffery. And he must be close by.

=====

-- OXFORDSHIRE. FLEE! --

19th December 1387.

Chests that seemed so large now seem so tiny.

He stuffs silver coins into large saddlebags as quickly as he can.

The money was for payments to the white harts, dribbled out in quantity just enough to keep them marching until they reach the lord and master, King Richard. But this is a strange day. He is no great leader but he can read men, and he knows the hardy northern souls ahead of him have silently grown more impatient with every step southwards. After all, they are paid to follow King Richard not his lackey. And now the distant screams and shrieks of mercy and surrender tell **Robert de Vere** which way the wind now blows for him.

A tempest rages in his chest, for that inauspicious day of feared expectation is here, in which the army he leads on behalf of the King has dispersed before him, and opposition horses are approaching to kill him.

All packed, and now to saddle. His horse is big, strong, and bad tempered. If only the beast understood the implication of staying here. Or perhaps he does, and wants to flee far quicker than he could with this lot on his flanks.

If only Richard was able to meet them in Northampton.

Need to hurry.

Although it impedes his efficacy, like a mouse he freezes often and darts his head round to some presumed noise. A hundred deadly horse hooves battering the track from a mile away. The snap of a twig as the Henry Bolingbroke stands on it from ten feet away. Or the short-lived swish of a deadly arrow as it whispers into his head.

All possibilities seem as real as any other, and amid giddiness he forces himself to breathe. Something he'd never considered doing ever before.

He can't rely on the Cheshiremen, so he'll have to rely on himself.

And he's off.

Across the Oxfordshire trails to London, Richard, and safety. Or more likely Exeter, then Brittany or France... and finally no doubt some improper destitution in some dirty foreign land.

=====

-- PORT SIDE AT KINGSTON UPON HULL --

23rd December 1387.

Christmas in England, or Christmas in France?

Or Christmas Eve drowned in that lot out there, thinks **Michael de la Pole, Earl of Suffolk**, as he reviews the ominous continuous dark swell.

He grew up here, and worked hard learning the wool trade from his father to avoid ever having to place two feet on the deck of one of these improbable things. Now his life depends on, or ends with, this journey to come. The people of Kingston Upon Hull, like all port citizens, are no strangers to shipwrecks and drownings and de la Pole knows well the power of the sea when it is angry. Even a slow sail to Lowestoft in the calm heat of June might turn into a deadly frenzy without warning.

Never mind setting off in the cold angry violence of midwinter.

Now the small heavy chests are all stored in his tiny cabin, the time has come. He would have preferred to sail to France from Dover, or from near to it, to make his time on the sea as short as possible. But when it came to it, he found he could trust nobody but faces familiar to him since he was a boy, and so a dangerous voyage from the East Riding of Yorkshire is the only way to guarantee the subterfuge necessary to escape from the long frightening fingers of those traitorous lords. Not that finding a captain to risk his ship or reputation was a cheap undertaking, despite longstanding familial connections de la Pole had hoped would begin his journey with a minimal effect on his worryingly finite collection of silver coin.

He could never previously have contemplated running to France, but when it came to it, the fear of death at the hands of the lords made his decision quite simple, if not desirable. Even then he knows nobody over the sea that might welcome him or protect him or even acknowledge him. He finally comprehends with the deep melancholy of understanding why the old money looks down upon the new. Their reliable connections run far further afield than just Kingston Upon Hull. All he knows is in England, and the establishment has forced him to leave that land.

There are no encouraging prospects ahead. He will be alone in a foreign land. He has no allies that he could trust. He will be stripped of his title and lands. And his coin will run out sometime.

Still, better than a traitor's death.

=====

-- THE LORDS APPELLANT MUSTER IN LONDON --

30th December 1387.

The five.

And 500 men.

Edmund, Duke of York, walks out to meet his younger brother the Duke of Gloucester. They meet well. They talk. They talk about the King in the Tower, and they talk about the King's friends exiled. And they talk of the days and weeks to come.

Presently the Duke of York nods. All is in accordance, all is legal.

The Duke of Gloucester orders the other four Lords Appellants and the five hundred men in through the Tower of London's outer gateway.

They enter, armed, but in peace.

And then, upon Gloucester's command, the Tower gates are closed. And then locked.

All is observed by a familiar flaxen-haired anointed man, staring with large eyes through a high tower window upon the unfriendly army that now resides in England's most invulnerable fortress.

=====

SCENE. TOWER OF LONDON, CHAPEL – DAY

30th December 1387.

***Thomas of Woodstock the Duke of Gloucester**, **Henry Bolingbroke the Earl of Derby**, **Thomas Beauchamp the Earl of Warwick**, **Richard FitzAlan the Earl of Arundel**, and **Thomas Mowbray the Earl of Nottingham** are all with **King Richard II** in a simple but comfortable chamber.*

King Richard has resented this room for a fortnight or so, as he by now understands this is his residence for the foreseeable future.

KING RICHARD II

See how treason stands before its king!

Everyone is extremely scared, but the five lords' courage is collective, at least.

HENRY BOLINGBROKE,
EARL OF DERBY

No, Sire!

What we do, we do for your kingdom as well as ours.

KING RICHARD II

And what you do, is imprison your king.

Treason!

HENRY BOLINGBROKE,
EARL OF DERBY

Damn it, Richard, I do not imprison you!

I - we - have contrived this private audience to implore you to be the king we want you to be!

KING RICHARD II

I am the king that God has declared I be.

**HENRY BOLINGBROKE,
EARL OF DERBY**

Richard, please! Let us speak as cousins, such as times before. Boy to boy, then. But man to man, now.

KING RICHARD II

No. King to earl, and that is that.

This is much tenser than the lords had even feared.

**HENRY BOLINGBROKE,
EARL OF DERBY**

Yes, you are my king! And I am your earl.

But we would speak with <u>you</u>, the man!

And for this, we manoeuvre you away from certain objectionable persons.

This animates Richard greatly.

KING RICHARD II

OHHHH! What have you done to him?

**THOMAS OF WOODSTOCK,
DUKE OF GLOUCESTER**

King Richard, I promise you this. You have much more to concern yourself than Robert de Vere.

KING RICHARD II

<u>WHAT HAVE YOU DONE TO HIM?</u>

The five lords are exasperated. They all look to Henry Bolingbroke, as Henry's and Richard's boyhood closeness is well known and he may play well as their best hand.

**HENRY BOLINGBROKE,
EARL OF DERBY**

Please talk to us calmly and soberly about the kingdom we love. And the king we want to love!

KING RICHARD II

(tearful)

I talk to no-one who imprisons me.

HENRY BOLINGBROKE,
EARL OF DERBY
You are not imprisoned!

KING RICHARD II
Then let me free.

HENRY BOLINGBROKE,
EARL OF DERBY
You...

...are not imprisoned.

KING RICHARD II
(sobbing)
Then LET ME FREE!

What have you done to de Vere?

Richard is so emotional that he bursts into tears, leans back against the wall, and sinks to the floor, his arse on his heels. He sobs into the crook of his elbow.

Henry Bolingbroke has no more argument, and turns to Gloucester.

THOMAS OF WOODSTOCK,
DUKE OF GLOUCESTER
Sire, we are here to appeal to you!

Five lords appellant! Five loyal lords appellant!

We are here to give our king all the assistance he needs to enjoy a glorious rule!

And that is all!

King Richard is now wailing openly.

THOMAS BEAUCHAMP,
EARL OF WARWICK
KING RICHARD, CEASE THIS WEAKNESS!

Richard is so shocked at the shouting at him, he stops crying and leans against the wall with wide eyes.

The Duke of Gloucester sees an opening.

**THOMAS OF WOODSTOCK,
DUKE OF GLOUCESTER**

Sire.

We here do solemnly declare our loyalty to our king and our kingdom. But mark this, if our king does not warrant our loyalty then our loyalty to the kingdom shall still remain.

**THOMAS BEAUCHAMP,
EARL OF WARWICK**

He's too bloody simple-minded to understand that we're trying to help him.

**HENRY BOLINGBROKE,
EARL OF DERBY**

No, he's not. Are you, Richard? You do understand that we desire to be ruled by our king! But we desire to be ruled wisely.

Ask us our advice and we would gladly give it!

All five lords are concentrating on their king with supreme patience.

He looks pained, but finally...

KING RICHARD II

Tell me...

He's exhausted. There's a long pause. Eventually...

**HENRY BOLINGBROKE,
EARL OF DERBY**

Yes! Tell you what, Sire?

KING RICHARD II

...what have you done with him?

=====

-- THE CROWN --

31st December 1387.

A table, unremarkable but for the crown placed upon it.

Thomas of Woodstock, Duke of Gloucester, is caught upon its simple beauty. The gold of course is alluring in itself, but fashion it with patterned crenelations, make a smooth ring of it large enough to fit the head, and prohibit all men but one from wearing it, and it becomes the most enthralling object in Christendom.

It is odd that he has never really looked at it before. He has been in its presence many times, always atop his nephew, but he has never considered the power of it while it is being worn by his sovereign lord. He supposes that he has always considered it part of the King, and he would normally no more covet the King's crown than he would the King's shoes.

But now it is placed on a cushion on a table in an antechamber connected to the room in which now sleeps King Richard II. And it sits, glinting alive in the candlelight, demanding attention.

It desires to be worn, he thinks.

What else would a crown want? It is silent, and yet it speaks. And what it speaks fills this duke with a passion that he has never felt before. His chest is hammering, his breathing loud and heavy, his neck shivers, his hands tremble...

=====

-- THE POWER --

I could take you.

I would have you.

=====

SCENE. AN ANTECHAMBER AT THE TOWER OF LONDON – NIGHT

31st December 1387.

***Thomas of Woodstock** the Duke of Gloucester, stares longingly at the King's crown.*

***Henry Bolingbroke** the Earl of Derby enters, halts as his uncle startles, and understands.*

HENRY BOLINGBROKE,
EARL OF DERBY
It's not yours.

To his credit, Gloucester does not deny his own thoughts. He doesn't speak for some time.

THOMAS OF WOODSTOCK,
DUKE OF GLOUCESTER
Our realm would rejoice if it were placed on me!

HENRY BOLINGBROKE,
EARL OF DERBY
Would it.

THOMAS OF WOODSTOCK,
DUKE OF GLOUCESTER
Oh, Richard, though! He proves himself unworthy.

HENRY BOLINGBROKE,
EARL OF DERBY
As do you in this moment.

Gloucester sighs and deflates.

THOMAS OF WOODSTOCK,
DUKE OF GLOUCESTER
I wish England to be great again.

HENRY BOLINGBROKE,
EARL OF DERBY
John of Gaunt is England's heir and I am his.

Do you think he would kneel before you? Do you think I would?

Gloucester looks extremely tired.

THOMAS OF WOODSTOCK,
DUKE OF GLOUCESTER
But has not God placed me here?

Here and now!

HENRY BOLINGBROKE,
EARL OF DERBY
He has.

But for Richard's sake, not yours.

Tears drop from Gloucester's chin.

THOMAS OF WOODSTOCK,
DUKE OF GLOUCESTER
I would rule fairly. And strongly.

HENRY BOLINGBROKE,
EARL OF DERBY
But this crown is Richard's. And if not Richard's, it is then the House of Lancaster's. Not the House of Gloucester.

THOMAS OF WOODSTOCK,
DUKE OF GLOUCESTER
Then take it now! For your father! And together let us help him make a rule truly worthy of England's history.

=====

A.D. 1388

=====

SCENE. A CHAMBER AT THE PALACE OF WESTMINSTER – DAY

1st January 1388.

***Thomas of Woodstock** the Duke of Gloucester, **Henry Bolingbroke** the Earl of Derby, **Thomas de Beauchamp** the Earl of Warwick, **Richard FitzAlan** the Earl of Arundel, and **Thomas Mowbray** the Earl of Nottingham are all with **King Richard II** in a simple but comfortable chamber.*

Richard, seated, is holding open a roll of parchment, and is reading from it.

This is not going to be easy.

KING RICHARD II
We are still your king?

THOMAS OF WOODSTOCK,
DUKE OF GLOUCESTER
You are our undoubted king.

KING RICHARD II
Then <u>what</u> IS <u>THIS</u>?

Richard throws the roll of parchment to the floor. He's gripping the arms of his great seat.

THOMAS OF WOODSTOCK,
DUKE OF GLOUCESTER
A mandate, Sire, for a respected committee to give you all the assistance you require to rule us.

Richard is silently apoplectic. Warwick has another parchment.

THOMAS BEAUCHAMP,
EARL OF WARWICK
Sir...

He gives it to Richard, who takes it after a considered pause and looks at the writing.

Gloucester speaks as he presumes Richard reads.

THOMAS OF WOODSTOCK, DUKE OF GLOUCESTER

Robert de Vere, Duke of Ireland.

Michael de la Pole, Earl of Suffolk.

Sir Robert Tresilian, Chief Justice.

Several others, named. We lords appellant duly charge them all with treason.

King Richard, sweating, trembling, glares at the Duke of Gloucester.

KING RICHARD II

I see.

HENRY BOLINGBROKE, EARL OF DERBY

Naturally the King will preside over the court in parliament.

KING RICHARD II

Naturally.

THOMAS OF WOODSTOCK, DUKE OF GLOUCESTER

Whereupon those charged will be tried, found guilty, and sentenced to traitors' deaths.

Richard's glaring at Gloucester intensifies to the point of being murderous.

KING RICHARD II

I see.

THOMAS OF WOODSTOCK, DUKE OF GLOUCESTER

After which, King Richard the Second will be surrounded by wise counsel, whereupon he shall flourish, bear sons, and continue the line of our glorious Plantagenet royal line.

From his seat, King Richard claps slowly and sarcastically for as long as it takes to realise that he isn't getting a reaction. Not that this troubles him greatly.

KING RICHARD II

I commend my gracious uncle on an exquisite plan well set so carefully, all so loyally in the King's name that the King need not even open his mouth to make the proclamation himself.

This is indeed a wondrous system of rule, I cannot conceive of why it has not been implemented before.

THOMAS OF WOODSTOCK, DUKE OF GLOUCESTER

As your loyal subjects, we accept that the King's conduct is without question.

And, given that, we understand that your royal judgment was maliciously misguided by persons unfit to advise on the complex matters of governing England.

The named are thereby accused of holding undue influence over the King and of abusing their power and taking advantage of the King's tender years for personal gain.

All contrary to the common laws of this great kingdom. And this we do to guarantee King Richard the Second's reign.

KING RICHARD II

I shall endure.

THOMAS OF WOODSTOCK, DUKE OF GLOUCESTER

Of course.

Richard is shaking his head. There's something Gloucester doesn't understand.

KING RICHARD II

I shall endure, and I shall regain my kingdom, if not this year then some other. And if not some other, then <u>some OTHER!</u>

Execute my friends. Go! I shall sit here. In my palace. On my throne. Under my crown. And while I do so, I shall wait for you all to die.

And if I should tire of waiting, as I may, I shall assemble every ounce of terrible authority that I can muster to assure each of your deaths at times that you would deem most unfavourable.

Your king has thus spoken, and will speak of it no more.

=====

-- A KING'S LAMENT --

17th January 1388.

The hole into which he looks is head-sized.

Grim thoughts have all men who place their face here instead of their arse.

Strings of juices hang long from his mouth and stretch into the dirty dark, and he sighs with such sorrow that he wonders if he could crawl into his grave and have it all done with, now. Heaven seems good from here.

King Richard spits, that the expelled food be gone proper. A scroll, that was unsealed before him, was then read to him. And so soon after his afternoon meal. Signed by five despicable barons, not least of which an uncle he respected and a cousin whom had been his only childhood friend. Five rebel lords with a legal request. Five lords, appealing. These lords appellant praying on behalf of King Richard that the success of the kingdom rests on the removal of certain other lords. His friends.

He recalls their familiar names, punching the latrine with the fleshy part of his fist with each one.

(*Punch*) Thomas of Woodstock, Duke of Gloucester. (*Punch*) His uncle!

(*Punch*) Henry Bolingbroke, Earl of Derby. (*Punch*) His cousin!

(*Punch*) Thomas Beauchamp, Earl of Warwick. (*Punch*) A trusted adviser to our royal family for many decades!

(*Punch*) Richard FitzAlan, Earl of Arundel.

(*Punch*) Thomas Mowbray, Earl of Nottingham.

Long silent wails become jerking sobs, and sobbing at least removes all the other emotions, causing him not to care that his royal wet cheek is resting on the smooth wood that lives to support the pudgy arses of shitting prisoners.

All alone in the world, he fiercely blinks out the tears to rid his body of his watery weakness.

This appeal to his majesty is a bold stratagem. Not for what it says, which is declared clearly enough apparently for the weal of the kingdom, but for its implications on his own stratagem. Young he may be, but he could read words that weren't scribed by his dangerously bold uncle and his lordly cohorts.

In most urgent lethal peril are de Vere and others.

He lifts his head, wipes his face dry, and blankly studies the smooth beige lines of the wood, almost careless of the insistent pong that rises. He tries to wonder how England's men think of him. A boy chosen by God to wield a golden crown. A young man tested by his subjects with the courage to face them on a battlefield (it was a field and there was certainly almost a battle which he averted with his courage and that makes it a battlefield). And a king with the courage to rule stiffly when required to whack his errant court when it misbehaves.

He wonders if God would approve of him, and his eyes flood again.

What was Smithfields and Wat Tyler, if it wasn't a test of his courage and strength as a king? And what was his continued life if not proof that God approved of his reign?

But now five lords appellant have declared their lack of confidence in his rule, due not to the King's own capabilities which are unquestionably all but sacred in the eyes of the Almighty, but of the apparent questionability of his close advisers.

His friends. His only friends, in truth.

The lords appellant cannot - dare not - question their king's competence, but they can - and have, clearly - blamed their own troubles on Richard's inner court. And if some tragedy should befall his friends, then the kingdom shall declare its horror upon such happenings for, what, a morning, and then, carry on as if no tragedy had occurred. And even then those lords who caused the tragedy would turn to their so-called beloved king to rule in glory, notwithstanding terrible past events.

King Richard II suddenly understands how lonely Jesus will surely feel upon his return. It is unacceptable that he cannot rally his own Cheshiremen, protect his friends, and oppose the lords appellant with steel instead of words.

So he has only one stratagem. The lords are weak in that they dare not harm their king, they would only harm those around their king whom they accuse of misgovernment and this means that whatever aggravation and discomfort might befall him over the next weeks and months, they will not be permanent and he can rely on the supposition that when the lords appellant have done what they would do then their king will still be living.

And given that, then he must wait, for years if need be. Wait. And rule. And wait. And rule. And then pour out his anger in deadly ways when those distasteful lords have long relaxed.

=====

-- THE "MERCILESS" PARLIAMENT, THE WHITE CHAMBER, WESTMINSTER --

Begun 3rd February, ends 31st May 1388.

They pleaded innocence, now they're all gone.

Having purged the kingdom of all who whispered poisonous words into his nephew's willing ears **Thomas of Woodstock, Duke of Gloucester**, uncle to King Richard II, feels... distaste.

Four of the five highest-ranking writs he oversaw (including of course de Vere) were tried and found guilty *in absentia.* Only Brembre attended his own trial; pleading innocent in the face of such ferocious prosecution that at one point he requested trial by combat; to no avail. Trial by battle, if it happened at all these days, was only a satisfactory legal option if the crime committed had no witnesses, and the lords appellant produced plenty of those. He was sentenced to death and executed within the hour.

After the five, several others were called for impeachments that ranged from 'taking advantage of the King's tender years' to treason, and executions and exiles were distributed accordingly. But so it had to be, in order to purge King Richard the Second's court of new money and ambitious men who cared more for their own short-term success than the success of the kingdom that clothed and fed them all.

There's nothing wrong with making money, but the balance of power and peace is precarious and, if the truth were known, it is a mercurial balance; nobody really knows how this works. It just does.

In the end, seventeen men were sentenced to death in almost as many weeks, although for eight their sentences were commuted to life exile to Ireland; two of those eight were men of the cloth and the other six were the otherwise highly regarded judges whose gravest error perhaps had been their recent misplaced over-eagerness to help a fraught king obfuscate the laws of treason in Nottingham.

The court's most senior name, Michael de la Pole, could not be found and is presumed away to France. If he ever returns, or is identified, he will die the traitor's death that was sentenced in his absence. Either way, his estates and titles have been forfeited to the crown.

De Vere evaded capture by Bolingbroke last December, and is also missing; and also presumed, if various accounts are believed, to be in France. It is not an auspicious fate, for while being welcomed by a foreign land and fighting in a foreign land are both states that encourage respect from the foreigners, one's presence in a place, enforced because you're not welcome in another place, gives one's presence a whole different perspective. Even if you're part of an invading army you have friends, and lords do not make good beggars, and especially when they've fallen from as high as from beside the King's throne.

When de Vere runs out of coin, which he will do quickly, he would try to sell his rings, first, and will refuse the first few offers for being much lower than he himself had calculated. Then, when he realises that gold values offered to beggars are not the same as gold values offered to lords, and when he later understands that all the local markets he encounters are in collusion to seek his gold at cut-price rates, he shall wail and gnash in anguish at his plight.

Who cares.

The Duke of Gloucester cracks his knuckles. He does wish that de Vere had been quartered to provide a certain end that particular story. For it is a worry to many that Richard does pine for a man that he knows is still alive. If de Vere were dead then that would be an end to him and an end to it.

He thought he'd feel better now the kingdom is a little purer. But every time he thinks about his nephew, he feels unease. Because the King's recent actions and reactions suggest to Gloucester that he is convinced of his own absolute rule. The deep belief that he is being guided by God and that however he behaves is by definition (by the fact that he is behaving that way) approved by God.

Thus, were Richard to slip a sword tip into the Archbishop of Canterbury and watch him bleed to death, then that must be God's will because it would be the King who did this deed. And if he were to point at the Earl of Northumberland, and say "Execute that man," and Northumberland was thus executed, then that would be divine on account that the words had come from the King's infallible mouth.

God's implied command, by the King's explicit command. Richard has often not behaved in a responsible manner, and such behaviour is not tenable for any length of time. A bad reign causes unrest. And unrest must be managed.

The Merciless Parliament, they're calling it. The parliament where five rebel lords, in obeisance to their king, used their combined seniority to lawfully compel that same king to execute his own negligent advisers.

This was all for the weal of the kingdom, but if Gloucester thought that times past were dangerous, then he knows the times to come are even more so. For the execution of negligent advisers was, when the dust has settled, a compromise. A flexing of baronial muscles in front of a king who is still the King.

And what happens next?

This particular tale has not yet run its course.

=====

-- THE FINAL ACT OF THE "MERCILESS" PARLIAMENT --

1st June, 1388.

The hellish damned creatures all rise as one.

To murmurings, and then an increasingly heavy silence, they come together in the middle of the hall, as there is presumably strength in their number, and **King Richard** learns with great enlightenment that the closer those five Lords Appellant approach, the more he wants to shiver with rage. But he must not, and with effort he does not.

Youthful thoughts of being revered by appreciative subjects have ebbed away long ago. And here he is, bearing witness to the cause of his kingly malaise. Ten traitorous serpentine eyes approach their destiny.

Slowly do his sombre puppeteers negotiate the hall. With dread and silence do the assembled people watch, and with sombreness do the lords appellant step nearer the king.

Once they reach the steps upon which their king is raised, they form a line before him, and the crowd of well-dressed guests stop breathing lest they interrupt some terrible spell. To be witness to this has an intoxicatingly joyous delirium, for close enough are they to absorb whatever happens next and thereby share in some success, yet far away enough are they to avoid damning themselves by association if this outcome proves ungodly. The next few dozen heartbeats may send them all to hell.

Thomas of Woodstock, my so-called uncle and Duke of Gloucester. Henry of Bolingbroke, my so-called cousin and Earl of Derby. Noble Warwick, noble Arundel, noble Mowbray. Filthy traitors, all.

His extreme disgust for the men that stand before him, he finds, does stem his rage. And this pleases him greatly. A strength, lifted by hate, warms his person. While his heart was previously furious, now his belly is pleasantly fiery as if connected with God or some angel.

You filth. Distasteful rats. Traitorous flea-ridden curs. Rotting fish-eyed peasants. I will feed you to bears when I can.

His uncle now dares to speak, but who knows what filthy breath seeps from that ulcerous mouth. The room's audience ripples, as if a hundred horses clopped at once nearby without anyone expecting them to. The faces of his gathered parliament are wide-eyed. *Why?* Is now the King indeed sentenced to die along with all the other noble casualties of the last four months?

Or...

Wait.

There is intrigue to be played out yet. But what? Must he listen to the despicable lords' malodorous words after all?

In fact, no!

Miraculously, pitifully, the five men... kneel before him.

They sat him on a throne and made him judge some of his most beloved Englishmen. And now their deadly wrath and lust is sated, they bend to their sovereign lord and declare their patronage, after all!

They are still his subjects. He is still their king.

Pathetic cowards, all five, and none deserving of the life they insist upon living.

He smiles at his own disgust for these soon-to-be or long-to-be dead men.

=====

-- FIVE LORDS A-TOASTING --

2nd June 1388.

They raise their beakers and give thanks to God.

Henry Bolingbroke, Earl of Derby, stares through a window and grimaces at nothing. The bordeaux is good but immediately overpowering. Perhaps the wine too eagerly strokes warmth at the inner chills he is sure the five all suffer, when he considers what they did.

The five. The Lords Appellant. The lords who sued their king's advisers and won and then, duty bound, bent their knees and gave away their win by offering to renew their fealty to their king.

How close did they come to deposing their king? And how close after that would they be to eternal damnation, for how does one depose he who has been declared untouchable? Only God may take Richard, and damned to hell forever is the man who dares to even think of ending the mortality of an anointed king.

In the end, they acted as barons should act; with decisive vicious courage in England's interests, ridding their kingdom of weak men. The weak men that circled around Richard like a hound circles around its bedding before flopping to rest. Men that were bad for Richard. Bad for their kingdom. Bad for the maintenance of the *status quo.*

Richard, of course has promptly demoted the lot of them from his newest council and none resisted. But their king, Bolingbroke is sure, has been stung and will surely refrain from pursuing the follies of surrounding himself with foppish chamber knights, re-focused as he now is on the running of his realm.

Although what use is his council, really, when our king matures so quickly?

Three times now has England appointed a Royal Council to reign by committee, and twice in recent years has Richard tested its authority by acting outside and beyond the council's wishes, and twice the toothless council has acceded to their king. Now Richard is old enough to understand such things, he understands that his lords might advise him, encourage him, coerce him even. But in the end there is no higher power on this earthly kingdom than our king. It means the king may well does as he wishes.

But at least His Majesty does now know there are those in his kingdom that would defend his kingdom from unworthies and negligent guidance.

To rebel directly against their king was too bold a step to take for any God-fearing man. And though none of the five might say as much, when they lowered themselves to their knees before Richard, they were also kneeling before God, and praying to both him and Him to be forgiven for their behaviour.

And so they continue as they were, although like covert adulterous lovers attending a formal gathering, both sides are quite unsure of how they should behave. An uncomfortable silence from both parties persists, neither wishing to fan flames that may be burn them all to death. While they rebelled against their king - they at least did so in his name - and because of that they are still alive.

And that is, as Bolingbroke contends with a heavy retrospective wonder, perhaps the only success the so-called Lords Appellant could ever have hoped for.

=====

-- A DUKE, NOW WELL ENDOWED --

4th June 1388.

With fond thoughts of Pleshey, he leaves London.

Soon **Thomas of Woodstock, Duke of Gloucester** and his riding party slow from a canter to a trot to a walk, and he gently pulls with care at his reigns occasionally to negotiate the traders, travellers and beggars that accumulate in the hamlet of Mile End.

He has a heaviness in his heart and his gut, despite his recent good fortune.

He, as senior lord of the five Lords Appellant did not have the courage (or the legal obligation, or the moral right) to depose Richard when or if he had the opportunity to do so. He failed to depose Richard because that prospect - of deposing his king - was too terrible to comprehend. And in failing to depose King Richard the Second, he has confirmed the most dangerous hypothesis that exists in the whole of their kingdom.

As a consequence of the Merciless Parliament Richard now knows, without question, that he's untouchable.

Would England be better off without Richard? None of them have said it, but Gloucester has thought it, and he is sure that all four others have thought it too. Either way, Gloucester's unwillingness (or inability) to remove Richard from office may yet be the ruination of the kingdom after all. Not to mention untimely deaths of the five. Perhaps not today, or tomorrow. But sometime.

For now, in lieu of the great services he and the other four lords had performed for King Richard's realm, parliament had agreed to set aside £10,000 for the five, to be paid by the King's exchequer and shared as they saw appropriate. He, the only duke of the five would expect at least half of that windfall. And furthermore, parliament decreed, land worth £2,000 income per annum was to be awarded to Gloucester. Of course his share of the Bohun estate - worth perhaps £15,000 - is still to be negotiated with Bolingbroke and still held by the crown. The wisdom of his gut suggests he should bide his time on that score, given the recent discordant events.

Even without Bohun, his estate is now enough that would be worthy of a senior earl, and is enough for a young duke to feel comfortable. It's all he ever wanted.

So why does this achieved ambition feel like such a particularly perilous victory? He is a duke of the realm, and blood relative to the king. Such status should guarantee his longevity. But Richard will not forget these weeks and months.

So perhaps he might henceforth play a more subtle role in Richard's court.

For now, at least.

=====

-- KING RICHARD'S RAGE --

Do they want their king to forgive?

Or, God be praised, forget?

They crown a king, anoint a king, then tell him to not rule. And then disperse from 'parliament' all hailing hollow victories.

Seventeen servants of the crown did they cull. Each trial conducted as if their king was complicit in a verdict of treason that was crafted even before the accusations were openly heard.

They watched impassive as my dearest Anne - no less, THE QUEEN OF ENGLAND - lowered herself to the floor on her knees to beg for the life of my beloved Burley, for much time once tutor to both me and Bolingbroke!

Yet still did they execute an old man with good in his heart. What blackened offal must they have behind their own breastbones.

A rule by committee is humiliation enough, but still they saw more ways of chastening their king these last weeks. Such low magic withers the royal opinion of those errant lords beyond disdain and into fury.

Am I not King of England, and therefore King of Gloucester? And King of Warwick and of Bolingbroke? Of Arundel and of Nottingham?

Oh nobles, no my body is not battle-beaten. My armour has not diverted any blade or arrow. Nor has my sword seen blood.

But my glory is already known to God, and I stand with God against them, which is why they are already damned. The battles I shall fight against them will be battles of the wit, and I renounce my armour for my finest silks and cloths in preparation for what must come to them all.

I shall look majestic while I laugh at their stupid faces as they die. For die they will, by my command when I recover my crown's full strength.

Die, Nottingham and Arundel. Die, Warwick and Gloucester. And die, my treacherous cousin Henry Bolingbroke of the House of Lancaster.

I, King Richard the Second, am the dread instrument of your destructions. I swear it.

=====

-- ÁLAVA, NORTH-EAST SPAIN --

5th June 1388.

Endless heat, dirt and shrubland is this hell.

Dust falls and settles upon the parched valley because exhausted soldiers tramp it up as they march to the north-east, and so it again falls and settles. They are determinedly heading for the French border, and thereafter into France; not a route usually considered with eagerness by English foot soldiers.

He's tired, thirsty, sweaty and dirty as he watches his men snake away to beyond the hills and mountains ahead. He will not march with them, he merely negotiated their safe conduct up through France to Calais with the French Duke of Berri and his right and honourable colleagues. He has released many hundreds of his men from their military contracts to save their lives, for the bloody flux that rushes through the insides of Englishmen abroad has carved hundreds from his numbers these last two years. He pulls at his own ever-moist beard and inspects the red mud on his fingers. Will he ever feel clean again?

Turning away from the disappearing soldiers, **John of Gaunt, Duke of Lancaster** returns to his large tent. The air in here is hotter than the outside. While the sun roasts you outside, at least the breeze caresses the sweat on your body. Not so in here; just the roasting.

The wax on the protective box is much softened, but the seal has held, so the contents remain private. He opens it and reads the letter inside. His eyes narrow as he sighs. The deep wrinkles so formed collect more red dirt while squeezing sweat out to run down his mucky face.

At his tent opening behind him, he hears the clicks and squeaks of armour. Envoys from Portugal, Spain and France respectfully await their invite to enter the tent of John of Gaunt.

They are beckoned in. Once he's negotiated his way through this next business, he thinks, perhaps a return to England, as the richest man in Christendom, is in order.

=====

END OF VOLUME ONE

=====

Illustrations

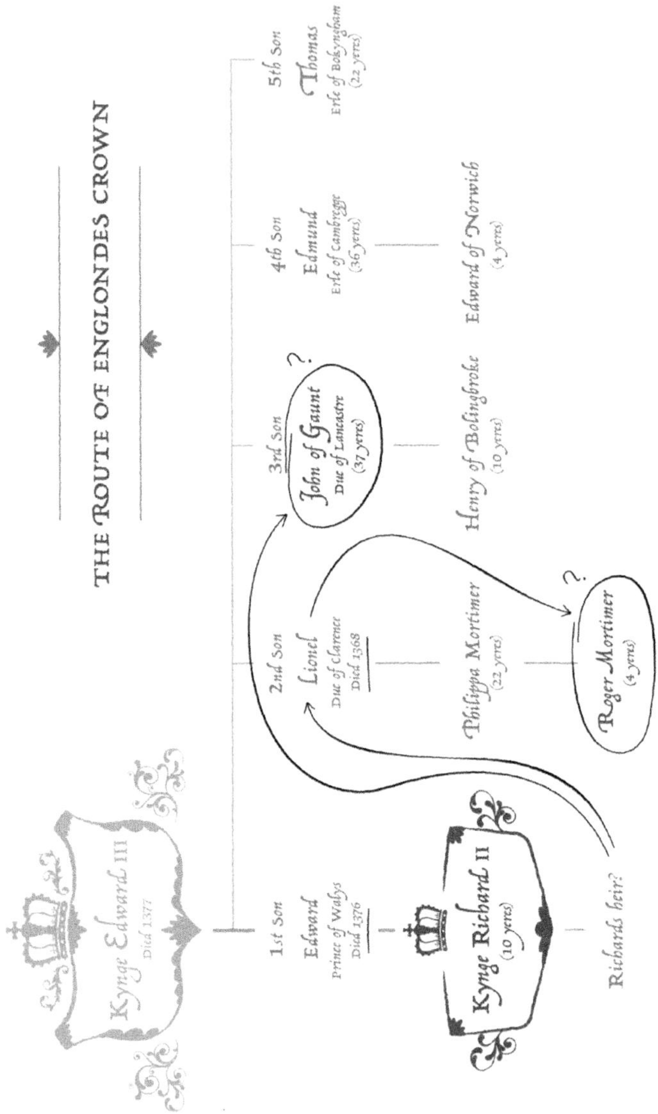

THE TALE OF THE FOUR FRENCH KINGS

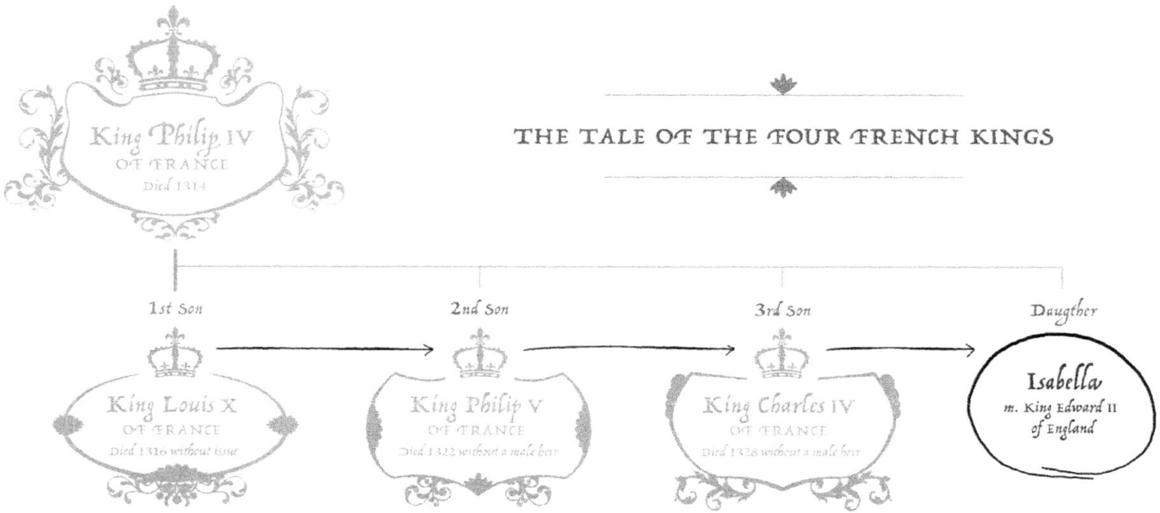

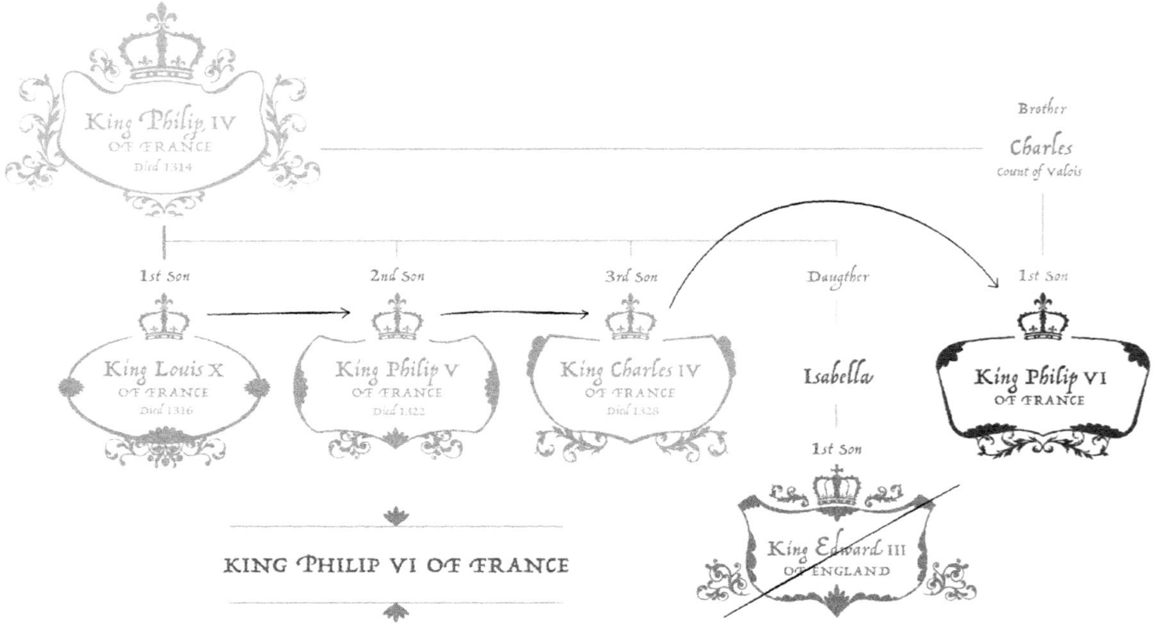

King Philip IV
OF FRANCE
Died 1314
Brother
Charles
Count of Valois
1st Son
King Louis X
OF FRANCE
Died 1316
2nd Son
King Philip V
OF FRANCE
Died 1322
3rd Son
King Charles IV
OF FRANCE
Died 1328
Daugther
Isabella
1st Son
King Edward III
OF ENGLAND
1st Son
King Philip VI
OF FRANCE
KING PHILIP VI OF FRANCE

Recommended Reading

Richard II, Nigel Saul, (Yale English Monarchs)

Richard II and the English Nobility, Anthony Tuck, (Arnold)

John of Gaunt: The Exercise of Princely Power in Fourteenth Century Europe, Anthony Goodman, (Longman)

The Receipt of the Exchequer 1377-1485, Antony Steel, (Cambridge)

The Estates of the Higher Nobility in Fourteenth-Century England, GA Holmes (Cambridge)

English Political Culture in the Fifteenth Century, Michael Hicks, (Routledge)

John of Guant(sic): King of Castile and Leon, Duke of Aquitaine and Lancaster, Earl of Derby Lincoln and Leicester Seneschal of England, Sydney Armitage-Smith, (Kessinger)

The Hollow Crown, Dan Jones, (Faber & Faber)

The Plantagenets: The Kings who Made England, Dan Jones, (William Collins)

Westminster Hall: Nine Hundred Years of History, Dorian Gerhold, (James & James)

The Palace of Westminster Official Guide, (Houses of Parliament)

The History of the House of Stanley, John Seacome, (J Gleave)

Summer of Blood, Dan Jones, (William Collins)

The House of Beaufort, Nathen Amin, Amberley

Red Roses: Blanche of Gaunt to Margaret Beaufort, Amy Licence, (History Press)

Lancaster and York, Alison Weir, (Vintage)

Life in the Middle Ages, Martyn Whittock, (Robinson)

COMING SOON...

PLANTAGENET TALES: VOLUME 2 (1389-1422)

King Richard II's vengeance and tyranny leads to rebellion, followed by the unthinkable... deposition. Thrust forward as usurper, King Henry IV struggles with ill health and crippling guilt during his relentless efforts to manage noblemen unaccustomed to such unsettling times. His successor, King Henry V, survives a shocking facial battle injury to become England's most vicious warlord and finally claims the French crown for the Plantagenet dynasty.

Other books by Mark Wilson
(all available from Amazon)

"If you enjoyed this book, please leave a review on Amazon, and take a look at my other books!"

HISTORICAL FICTION

Plantagenet Tales: Volume 1 (1377-1388)

MIND, BODY & SPIRIT

The Secret of How to be Happy
Meditation: How to transform your life

The Supercharge Your Subconscious ultra-focus book series:

1. Unleash Your Inner superstar
2. Self-Image Sizzle
3. Create Irresistible Habits (That Are Good For You)
4. Smashing (Your Own Self-Limiting) Boundaries
5. How To Manifest Your Deepest Desires

COLOURING BOOKS

The History in Colours colouring book series:

Illuminated Letters and Celtic Designs
Posh Portraits Through The Ages
Myths And Legends Through The Ages

CHILDREN'S BOOKS

Mish and Mash: Time Travel Treasure
Animal Friends: 18 Bedtime Stories For Young Children

The Have Fun With... series for early

readers:

1. Toby's Seaside Holiday
2. Maya's Zoo Adventure
3. Ravi's Circus Visit
4. Amara's Day At The Farm
5. Malik Explores A Museum
6. Zoe Bakes A Carrot Cake

FINANCIAL TRADING

Gap Trading for Beginners

Printed in Great Britain
by Amazon

49537002R00219